CLA$H

A Novel

by David R. Turgeon

Contact the author at www.clashthebook.com
Visit our website at www.stillwaterpress.com for more information.
First Stillwater River Publications Edition 2019.
Library of Congress Control Number:2019913578

ISBN-10: 1-950339-34-3
ISBN-13: 978-1-950339-34-1

1 2 3 4 5 6 7 8 9 10

Written by David R. Turgeon.

Published by Stillwater River Publications, Pawtucket, RI, USA.

Publisher's Cataloging-In-Publication Data
(Prepared by The Donohue Group, Inc.)

Names: Turgeon, David R., 1957- author.
Title: Clash : a novel / by David R. Turgeon.
Description: First Stillwater River Publications edition. | Pawtucket, RI, USA : Stillwater River Publications, 2019.
Identifiers: ISBN 9781950339341 | ISBN 1950339343
Subjects: LCSH: Capitalists and financiers--Fiction. | Political corruption--United States--Fiction. | Finance, Public--United States--Fiction. | Presidents--United States--Fiction. | LCGFT: Thrillers (Fiction)
Classification: LCC PS3620.U751 C53 2019 | DDC 813/.6--dc23

DEDICATION

To my family and for my country.

ACKNOWLEDGEMENTS

I'd like to express my deepest thanks to Dawn and Steven Porter of Stillwater Publications in Pawtucket, Rhode Island. As a first-time author, I needed a significant amount of assistance and direction. Without their help, the completion of this novel and getting it to market would not have been possible. I'd strongly recommend their use to any independent author.

A NOTE FROM THE AUTHOR

This book took me years to write. During that time, I was constantly disappointed by our elected officials and a Washington that's out of touch with the country. Each disappointment inspired me to return to work and complete the novel.

The book is also the result of hundreds of conversations with people from all over our country and political spectrum. Regardless of politics, many share the belief that we have problems with our country that need to be addressed sooner rather than later.

We created a web site, www.clashthebook.com, to share more information about the story and see if it's possible to start a movement of like-minded citizens. Like the book's characters, we believe change is needed, consensus around reasonable solutions is achievable using today's technology and it's our duty as Americans. I hope you'll join us.

1

Boston, Massachusetts

The temperature has dropped to 6 degrees Fahrenheit. The snow that fell all day has stopped. The sidewalks are narrow and slippery.

Teresa is walking alone and turning her head frequently to see if she's being followed. She's wearing a black cocktail dress and high heels. She's so cold that her hands and feet are becoming numb. She breathes onto her hands to warm them and then rubs her hands against her upper arms and shoulders. Her efforts do little to fight off the cold.

On the sidewalk ahead is a group of three young men. They're standing on the steps of a brownstone building, smoking cigarettes. They're eager to start up a conversation and quickly invite her inside. They explain that it's a fraternity house of the Massachusetts Institute of Technology (MIT) and they're having a party. While she wouldn't normally accept the invitation to come inside, she desperately needs to get out of the cold.

She enters the building and texts her mother to say she's on her way home. She sits in a large, comfortable chair in the foyer, thinking she'll get warm for a couple minutes and leave. She accepts a drink from a trustworthy looking young man after he says, "This will warm you right up." The drink is delicious and makes her feel better immediately. Three guys are vying for her attention.

Within minutes her head is spinning. Another fellow joins the conversation. The trustworthy fellow with the drink offers to take her upstairs so she can lie down. She's lightheaded. She blinks her eyes to clear her head. It doesn't help. Concern quickly turns to panic as she realizes something was in her drink. She feels scared and helpless.

2

New York, New York

Gene lies awake in bed with his eyes closed. He begins a ritual that he repeats throughout the day. He thinks about upcoming events and sees them unfold with the best possible outcome. He feels a deep sense of gratitude for what's going to happen. His visualization is so convincing that it's as if the event has already happened. He thanks God for his blessings and begins his day.

Waking up ahead of his 5:00 a.m. alarm is routine. At first, waking up early felt unnatural. Years ago, he decided who and what he was going to become. He committed to doing whatever was required to achieve his goals. People were counting on him.

His closet is larger than most apartments in the city. A suit has been laid out for him along with a shirt, tie, cufflinks, socks, shined shoes, and monogrammed handkerchief. A personal assistant handles the details. While he has no sense of fashion, he is keenly aware of his brand and the impressions made by nonverbal communication. He wants to convey the unmistakeable message that here is a man of intelligence, wealth, and exquisite taste.

He kisses his sleeping wife on his way out of the bedroom.

A chef has prepared his breakfast following a strict plan. The goal is to keep his weight and blood pressure within limits. Foods are mostly organic and flown in from a specific farm.

An elevator takes him to the first floor where a limousine awaits. He'd prefer to walk the short distance to his office, but a security team prefers the car as a precaution.

He arrives at his office before 6:00 a.m. There are pictures of him with family, friends, and world leaders on display around his office. One item stands out; it's a very large gold plaque with a man sitting on a stool. He's looking at a globe with a large grin. An inscription reads:

"Give me control of a nation's money and I care not who makes the laws."

~Mayer Amschel Rothschild, 1790

Gene looks out over the skyline. It's January and the sun's not yet up. He pauses and wonders how the rest of the world spends their Sunday mornings.

#

An executive assistant delivers coffee and a three-ring binder filled with phone messages. On the front of the binder is Gene's itinerary for the day. He scans down to 5 p.m. when his two sons will visit. He's looking forward to seeing them.

Gene has a unique way of managing calls. Callers are told there's no voicemail so assistants take messages. But all calls are recorded. Gene studies human nature and learns a lot by listening to messages. He pays attention to the tone, urgency, and treatment of his assistants. How people treat others is important to him.

There are eighty-four messages. Gene opens the binder in front of his computer. On the computer screen is a reference number to each call along with the caller's name and a brief description in the headline of the message. By double clicking the message, he can listen to the call's recording.

Gene O'Neil is a banker. When asked what a banker does, he answers, "A banker helps get money from point A, where it currently resides, to point B, where it can be put to its best use." Many are satisfied with that explanation. He might add, "A banker's role is critical to a well-functioning economy because he gets capital to where it can be used most efficiently."

The truth is Gene's job is nothing like that. Yes, he moves money from one place to another for a fee. The job of the world's leading bankers, however, is to develop relationships with the most powerful, wealthy, and influential people in the world. Along with his partners, Gene focuses on the ten thousand people who will determine the fate of the other seven billion inhabitants of our planet. The ten thousand who make up today's global elite.

He scans the list of messages. He'll forward almost all of them to Peter Hollingsworth with instructions. Peter is a close friend and his most trusted employee. Prior to that role, Peter was Gene's boss. Peter considered leaving the bank when Gene was promoted over him. While having the younger man climb the corporate ladder faster was a blow to his ego, Peter's position with the bank and Gene is too good to give up.

A message arrived Saturday evening from a chief executive officer (CEO) and important client. He's hoping to get help with his child's admission to Stanford University. Gene forwards it to Peter. There's always a connection to leverage. It may be an alum who donated generously to the school, the person managing the school's endowment, or someone on the university's board. Peter will find the connection that will guarantee admission. Gene will return the client's call and offer sincere congratulations. He'll leave the unmistakable impression that the client is slightly indebted to him.

There is a call from a young woman who's heir to an industrial fortune. She wants more cash now. She's twenty-seven years old and receives $2 million per month. It's not nearly enough to keep up with her lifestyle. She'll receive her full inheritance of over $4 billion at age thirty-five. Gene's bank manages her trust fund. He forwards the message to Peter and to the bank's counsel. Gene will get her whatever she wants, but prefers not to break the terms of the trust agreement. He has a team of lawyers who specialize in trusts. While it's important to respect the wishes of the deceased, the living choose which bankers to employ going forward. To guarantee the correct outcome in matters involving trusts, Gene has a relationship with several judges.

The messages and Gene's instructions go on for a couple hours. Some tasks are important. Others are not. The people, however, and Gene's relationships are all terribly important. The world is all about relationships.

#

For years, bankers provided little in the way of services. That changed in the 1980s and 90s as competition in "private banking" and "wealth management" exploded. Gene and his partners at Morgan Sachs created teams of people to support their clients' needs. The bank's services expanded right along with their clients' wealth. Now, there is literally nothing clients can't request from their banker. Banks operate like a twenty-four hour a day concierge service. Handle a college admission. Make a criminal investigation go away. Take care of a jealous mistress. Arrange a date with a supermodel. Every wish imaginable has been requested and granted. Extreme wealth allows people to live life by a very different set of rules.

Gene is tired and bored with such things. He'll now focus his efforts only on his most important clients and his two sons.

3

Boston, Massachusetts

Teresa's head is pounding as she opens her eyes. "Where am I?" she asks. She sees a young man sitting at a desk with his back to her. Memories of last night are coming back to her. She struggles with a headache. "Hey," she says to get his attention.

He turns and smiles. "Hey. You want aspirin or something?" he asks.

She was sleeping on his bed. While she has many questions, her immediate needs are aspirin and a giant bucket of ice water. "Yeah," she mutters and, "What did you do to me?"

"Nothing," he answers. He hands her two aspirin and a bottle of water. "You were sitting in our frat and pledges gave you a drink." He shakes his head. "I don't know what was in it but it must have been strong. One guy wanted to carry you off so I figured I better help. I brought you up here."

Wow, she thinks to herself. This guy looks so young. She doesn't recognize him as one of the guys she saw last night. That's comforting. "I don't remember you," she blurts out. "You didn't take advantage of me, did you?"

He shakes his head and answers, "No, never." He returns to the desk and what she assumes is schoolwork. Something about him makes her feel calm and out of danger.

"My purse. Shit, do you have my purse?" she asks.

"On the floor next to the bed." He points.

She grabs her phone and begins texting. “My mom is going to be so upset. Shit.” After sending a text, she lays back down. “More water,” she commands.

By the time he retrieves another water bottle she’s gone back to sleep.

An hour goes by and she opens her eyes again. He’s still at the desk. “Hey,” she mutters.

“Hey again,” he replies.

“Are you worried that I’m not going to leave?”

“No, I’m not worried,” he answers.

“Is this how you get women to your room? You do this a lot?”

He doesn’t respond.

“Bathroom?” she inquires.

“Over there.” He points.

She gets up and walks to the bathroom. She’s still wearing the very short, tight cocktail dress from the night before.

“Nice place,” she declares, and looks around. It’s a beautifully decorated one-bedroom apartment with a view overlooking the Charles River.

“Are you in college?” she asks from the bathroom. “This is a really nice place,” she says again. She looks around the bathroom. It’s clean and well organized.

She hears him answer, “Thanks, yes, in college.”

“Are all the rooms like this?” she asks. This doesn’t look anything like the college dorms she’s seen.

She cleans herself up and collects her purse and high heels. She walks over and stands next to the desk. He continues working. She leans against the wall next to the desk. “Did anything happen last night? I mean you didn’t do anything right?”

“No,” he answers. “Nothing. You just passed out. I put you on the bed.”

“Yeah, well someone put something in my drink and had some very bad ideas. Maybe I should call the cops or tell my dad.” After a pause she adds, “Thanks for helping me.”

“You’re welcome. Glad to,” he answers.

Above the desk is a shelf with oddly shaped pieces of paper. She picks one up and then another. “What are these?” she asks.

"It's origami," he answers. "They're models made from one sheet of paper. You fold the paper. One sheet, no cuts."

"Really? These are all folded from one sheet of paper?" She sees a donut, a flower, and a teapot in perfect shapes. "That's crazy. Are you lying?"

"No, really. One sheet and no cuts."

"What are these?" she asks of unrecognizable shapes.

"They're proteins," he answers. "Nature is the ultimate folder. Many shapes, even the proteins inside us, are made by folding, you know, like amino acids. I'm in a club. We have competitions. It probably sounds lame."

She picks up a couple of the models and stares at them.

"Are you hungry?" he asks.

"Ah, yes, I'm hungry," she answers. "But I'm not exactly dressed for breakfast. Maybe it's better if I hop on the T."

"Why do people in Boston call the subway the T?" Jack asks.

"I don't know. It's a short version of the Massachusetts Bay Transportation Authority or the MBTA, just became the T I guess."

He nods. "I understand if you need to get going."

She doesn't want to exit the room or this guy's life yet. She stands frozen for a few moments. "Do you have some clothes I could borrow?" she asks.

"Yeah, I mean if sweatpants are ok."

"Yeah," she answers.

He opens drawers and assembles an outfit. T-shirt, sweatshirt, sweatpants. She takes them into the bathroom. "I'll be just a minute." She closes the door. Next thing the shower is running.

So much for just a minute, he thinks, but it's nice to be talking with a female. Finally, he's got a girl in his room.

#

She exits the bathroom in his clothes. He's fixated on her long legs, narrow hips, perfect skin, and brown eyes. He doesn't want her to catch him staring.

He's been wearing a T-shirt, shorts, and sneakers. "Are you going to change?" she asks.

"No," he answers.

"It's January," she says, and looks for some acknowledgement.

"Yeah."

"You're wearing shorts. I mean even in July those shorts might be too much." She's teasing him, but he doesn't seem to understand. The shorts are lime green with whales on them.

He grabs a coat and offers her one. It's the softest leather she's ever felt. "This is nice," she says as she rubs it. "Really nice. Is this real leather?" she asks. "It feels like some kind of new, crazy soft material."

"Yes, leather," he answers.

As he opens the door to leave, she reaches out her hand. "I'm Teresa."

They shake hands. "I'm Jack. I'm pleased to meet you."

They walk two blocks to a diner. It's a casual spot where they find a booth and sit down.

"Maybe you think I'm a terrible person," she begins. "Crashing your party and sleeping with you on our first night?"

"No, I hadn't thought that," he answers. "You just looked like a girl who might need help. I've never interfered like that before, but it felt like I should do something."

The waitress brings him a large Mountain Dew and her a glass of water. "Come here often?" Teresa asks, recognizing that the waitress knew what he wanted.

"I wasn't sure what was going to happen," Jack continues, "so I guess I did abduct you. Maybe I should be apologizing. There are some really weird guys at school." He smiles again and shakes his head.

He's got a great smile, she thinks. He has perfect teeth and dimples appear when he smiles.

"I slept on the couch," he adds.

Teresa has been sizing him up. Jack is six foot one and might weigh a hundred and seventy pounds. His light brown hair is full and long. It grows forward and covers his face. He has blue eyes and almost no facial hair. *I wonder if he shaves*, she thinks.

"Well, thank you," she says. "Know what?" she begins and leans forward, "when I first woke up, I thought you might be a crazy person. Maybe you were going to make me your sex slave or something." She then leans back and finishes, "but I'm not worried about you now."

"No?" he questions.

"Nope, I'm not afraid of anyone that makes paper models and wears shorts like that."

Jack has been painfully shy most of his life, especially around girls. Things feel differently with Teresa. She's outgoing and does most of the talking. Being with her is easy, comfortable.

4

New York, New York

Leaders of Gene's wealth management team assemble at 9:00 a.m. The team is responsible for managing the wealth of approximately one hundred families. Positions on the team are coveted because they provide a career track to managing director roles where annual compensation begins at over ten million dollars.

Most of the bank's clients prefer monthly statements, quarterly meetings, and one annual review to discuss investment performance and cash requirements for the coming year.

Morgan Sachs provides newsletters with insights from their top investment officers. They host events for their most important clients where they can meet and interact with economists, world leaders, and celebrities. Spend a long weekend at a five-star resort with a former Prime Minister, respected economist, or rock star. It's one of the benefits of investing over thirty million dollars with the bank.

#

The group is sitting when Gene enters the room and says, "Good morning."

Peter answers, "Good morning. Gene, the group would like to add an agenda item to this morning's meeting. They'd like to revisit the topic of adding more clients to the list we currently serve."

Gene takes his seat. For over two years, he has consistently turned down this request. "I see," Gene begins. "I suppose that will be a decision for you to make. I have two announcements this morning. First, I will be leaving this group. Peter will assume my responsibilities. This is a continuation of the same trend that has been going on the past few years. You know that I have a great deal of confidence in this group. I'm counting on you to carry on the same level of excellence going forward. Peter will be re-assigning responsibilities within the group and yes, it means promotions and raises for several of you. Are there any questions?"

Gene looks around the room to make sure the group understands. This is a group of extremely ambitious young people. They've all made significant personal sacrifices to be at this table. They have two reactions: they're shocked by the news and anxious to get details from Peter. Anxious about what it means to them personally.

"You know," Gene explains, "that I've consistently turned down this request and for a simple reason. Wealth in America is concentrated in the hands of a small number at the very top. Forget about politicians saying 96% of the country's wealth is in the top 1%. All the wealth is in the top 5% of the 1%. How do you want to spend your time? Assume you work fifteen hours a day seven days a week. You need to use all of that time to provide superior service to those few people. Like it or not, their wealth translates to power. You need to be their trusted advisors so that you know what's going on, what important decisions are being made. I never cared about managing things for wealthy families even if it could make me rich. I wanted to make a difference. Serving those few at the very top led us here at the bank to finance China's economic expansion, to have the inside track on the largest mergers and acquisitions and avoid the past two financial collapses. We've provided the capital for developing countries to become part of the worldwide supply chain and improve the lives of their people. You choose your own path, but for me it was an easy decision to focus on only the very wealthiest. My first announcement is that I'm leaving the group and will only focus on my most important clients, just seven families."

The group turns quiet and reflects on their own goals and the future strategic direction of the group.

Peter breaks the silence by asking, "And your second announcement, Gene?"

Gene nods and replies, "I expect my sons to come to work here at the bank in the near future. Some of you have met my son, Gene, Jr., during his internships. I have a younger son named Jack. I need a training program designed specifically for them, an accelerated course if you will. This is very important to me. I've already got a couple of men working on this. The bank's Chief Operating Officer (COO) now wants another person added to the group."

Gene looks around the room, making eye contact with each team member.

They will all compete hard for this assignment. Something "very important" to Gene means it's even more important to them and their careers.

"Peter?" Gene turns to Peter Hollingsworth.

Peter distributes a memo and explains, "Here are our thoughts on the goals and the curriculum. For those interested, please get me your thoughts by the close of business Wednesday. All of the bank's resources will be at your disposal."

The team understands that "all of the bank's resources" means that you'll have a blank check to train Gene's kids. Nothing like this has ever come up before.

"Any questions?" Peter asks. There's no response.

#

Gene sent an email to the team the previous day after seeing a news story concerning the Internal Revenue Service (IRS). Once sent, he knows this group will work hard to outdo one another preparing for today's meeting. Such is the nature of this ultra-competitive environment.

Gene begins, "It appears an IRS Supervisor denied not-for-profit applications to conservative groups. The report is a congressman was behind it. He was worried about the large amount of money raised by conservatives. What are your thoughts?"

Peter asks, "Did she break any laws?"

"Yes," is the first answer to come from the team. Paul Lovett, sounding like the lawyer he is, responds. "I should say it's unclear if she broke a law since all we have are allegations and damage control spun by their public relations people. They claimed it was isolated to a regional office, but everyone knows it originated in Washington. The IRS slowed approvals for conservative groups and accelerated approvals for liberal groups. It's all political. Her biggest problem is that she leaked personal information about American citizens—from their own tax returns—to outside parties. That's a felony."

Another member of the group, Suzanne Gentile, has been looking to contribute to these conversations. "Right," she adds. "They actually cross-referenced the tax returns of individuals to the applications of companies bidding on government contracts. Let's say you own a company or a stake in a company and you donate to a conservative cause. They disqualified your company from getting government contracts. Priority was given to business owners of the president's own party. More government contracts translate to more donations in the future. It's all about payoffs, rewarding people of your political view with government contracts."

Peter's disgusted. He shakes his head before adding, "Another example of how our government can't perform its duties. Every single part of our bureaucracy is getting politicized. Watch, the other party will likely do something even worse when they come to power again. It's a dangerous cycle that drags us all down."

"Well," Gene continues, "can anyone tell us what this means?"

Paul Lovett provides an answer. "It means that the IRS supervisor should go to jail. They'll stonewall, plead the fifth, the media will make it more complicated than it is, Americans will lose interest. The IRS will suspend her with pay for the rest of her career—like a paid vacation for screwing up. There's no accountability in our government. There should be a law saying if you accept government employment, then you can't plead the fifth in your own defence. Americans would support that."

"No," Doug Snyder interrupts. "It means that we need to get access to the IRS files. If the government is going to use the information for political purposes, then they shouldn't have a problem giving us access. We need to search tax returns for new clients. That's why Gene sent us the email. The IRS database should be a goldmine of new information for the bank."

“Thank you,” Gene responds. “I’m particularly interested in identifying the ‘up-and-comers,’ the newly rich. Is it possible we’ve missed business owners of unusually profitable, privately-held companies?”

Karl Simon is filling in this morning for his boss. *The IRS shouldn’t be political*, he thinks to himself. *How can this happen? The scumbags behind this corruption should be sent to prison. All Americans, including those here in this group, should be outraged. Instead, they view it as a business opportunity?*

“Peter,” Gene continues, “do we still have that former IRS commissioner working here at the bank? He was helping clients with tax settlements, wasn’t he?”

“Yes, and he’s still here.”

“Maybe he’d be a good starting point,” Gene suggests.

“Isn’t our using the data as bad as what they’ve done?” Karl asks. “We’d be using Americans’ most confidential information to target them for our purposes.”

Doug answers so that Gene or Peter don’t have to. “No one is making a value judgment, Karl. No one is using the words ‘good’ or ‘bad’. The simple point is that if the data is available, then we should use it. We should also think about what other databases might be available to us. Maybe we get access to the FBI’s database or the healthcare database with medical records.”

“Very good,” Gene replies.

Karl bites his lip. The government has the moral obligation to keep the information it collects confidential. It even assures the American people that it will be kept private. That doesn’t happen. If the bank can get access, others can too.

5

Boston, Massachusetts

"So, how did you end up at our party?" Jack asks Teresa. "I mean, where did you come from?"

She has a mouth full of food when he asks. She covers her mouth with a napkin and gulps it down. "Well, I went on a date last night with my boyfriend Roberto," she begins. "We've been going together for a few years; since high school. Sometimes off and on but mostly on. Last night was our anniversary, kind of; it was a get-back-together anniversary."

Jack's thinking that she has difficulty getting to the point, but he's enjoying looking and listening. She uses her hands and arms a lot when talking. He considers that she might have difficulty on the telephone without these added forms of communication.

"Anyway, he's a jerk. A real jerk and I knew it, but I kept hoping something was gonna change." She doesn't know Jack well enough to reveal all the details. "My friends told me he's a jerk, but I kept giving him chances. I'm an idiot, right?"

He wants to nod his head acknowledging "Yes," but "Yes, you're an idiot," doesn't seem right.

She continues, "Anyway, he's a jerk. I've given him a hundred chances and I've been good to him, but that's it. I'm done with him." She makes a hand signal like waving him good-bye.

"So, how did you end up at our party?" Jack repeats his original question. Both find that a little funny.

"I was getting to that," she says with a smile. "We were out to dinner and it didn't go well. I threw my glass of wine in his face and walked out. I figured I'd walk to the T and take the subway home." She shrugs her shoulders. "I hadn't figured on the high heels, slippery sidewalks, and that it was so freaking cold. Anyway, I'm walking and I'm freezing and that's when I walk up to your doorstep. I didn't know there were fraternities there. Next thing I know I wake up in this strange guy's room."

Jack's eating and not reacting to what she's saying.

"Who were all those girls at your party anyway?" she asks.

"There are girls' schools around. Predominantly girls' schools or used to be all girls' schools. Anyway, our school sponsors parties and buses girls in so everyone can meet. Those girls were from Wellesley College."

"Girls are bused in?" she replies. "I guess that makes it easy for you."

The waitress delivers their check and Jack puts down a credit card.

"A black American Express card?" she asks. "I've seen green, gold, and I know there's a platinum one too. I've never seen a black card. How does a student get a credit card anyway? Parents?"

"I guess. I've had it for a while now," Jack answers without thinking about it.

"Well, thank you for breakfast," she says. "I'll get these clothes back to you soon."

"Sure, anytime," he answers.

"I could drop them off, or you could take me out sometime and I'll bring them with me," she suggests.

Jack nods but doesn't say anything. He's happy with the way the morning is going, but feels frozen. He doesn't want to mess this up.

She's a little unsure of how to interpret Jack's behaviour. "Hand me your phone," she instructs. She inserts her name and number in his phone. "If you ever want to see your clothes again, you'll call me." She looks at him. "Ok?"

"Ok," he answers. He's thankful that he didn't have to ask for her number. "What are you doing today?" he asks.

"My family gets together every Sunday for dinner. Aunts, uncles, cousins. I'm going to go help my mom cook. We mostly just hang out together. What about you?" she asks.

"I'm gonna get some schoolwork done and then go see my folks for dinner. They live in New York."

"New York?" she says excitedly. "I've never been there. It looks so great on television. Are you going to New York City? Is that what you mean?"

"Yeah, the city," he answers.

"You're lucky. That must be exciting, so much to do."

They get up and leave. "Maybe I should walk you to the T," he offers, thinking of the proper etiquette.

"Are you worried I'll end up at another party?" she asks.

"No, no," he answers, thinking that he may have offended her. "I just meant…"

"I'm kidding," she says. "But thank you, and that won't ever happen again. Thank you for rescuing me. I really mean that and thanks for breakfast. I'm feeling better with some food in me." She flashes a smile that feels like it touches Jack's soul. She turns and walks off.

He intends to say "good-bye," but nothing comes out. His heart is pounding. That was the most successful encounter he's ever had with a woman.

6

Watertown, Massachusetts

The house is quiet when Teresa gets home. Her mother's name is Mary. Teresa finds her mother in the kitchen. The fact that Mary isn't saying anything signals that she's upset.

"What do you have on? What is this?" her mother asks after seeing the sweatpants and leather coat. "What is the matter with you young lady?" Despite being upset, she keeps her voice down.

Teresa gives her mother a hug. The two are very close.

"Don't hug me. What's going on?"

"I know Mom. I'm sorry." Teresa takes off the coat and begins peeling a pile of potatoes beside the sink. "Where's Daddy?" Teresa asks.

"He's upstairs taking a nap. He got home this morning after a long bus ride from Detroit," Mary answers.

Teresa takes a deep breath and explains, "Last night started off great with Roberto. The restaurant was nice. We had wine. It was crowded. He was being so sweet and then out of nowhere he asks me if I'll do a three-way with him."

"No," Mary says, "You mean three people having sex together?"

"That's what he asked."

Mary puts her hands to her mouth. "Another girl joining the two of you?"

"Yeah, Mom. He pulled out his phone to show me a picture of this girl named Sammy." Teresa is shaking her head. "Couldn't believe it, and after I've already taken him back a dozen times. He's such an asshole. You were right. Everyone was right about him."

"I was right," Mary says. After a moment, she says "Carrots" to her daughter. She means peel the carrots next. "What did you say to him?"

"Nothing, I threw my wine at him and left the restaurant. Walked right out and headed for the T."

"Good, but why didn't you call me? How many times have I told you to call me?" her mother complains. "A million times I've told you call me, call me."

"I know Mom and I'm sorry, but guess what happens?" Teresa asks.

"Guess what happens after your boyfriend asks you about a three-way?"

Teresa continues, "I start walking to the T, but it's so cold and it took me longer than I figured. I was so upset when I left the restaurant. You know how Daddy says you never have to walk far to get to the T? He wouldn't say that if he ever walked in high heels. I start walking. I'm freezing. The sidewalks are a mess. These guys are standing outside one of those nice brownstones in the Back Bay. They invite me in to their party."

Mary blesses herself, "Oh, my God, you didn't go inside?"

"I did Mom but wait," Teresa continues. "I only went in to get warm before calling you. I was so cold. Anyway, some asshole put something in my drink. I was completely knocked out."

Mary asks, "Should I wake your father?"

"No, no. I wake up and this guy has rescued me from whatever trouble I might have been in. He carried me off to safety. He gave me these clothes and took me out to breakfast. He's really nice, good looking too, I mean, other than the long hair."

Mary can't believe what she's hearing. "You go out to dinner with one boy and he asks about a three-way. You come home after spending the night with some other boy? You've got to get your head on straight. I told you Roberto was no good and neither is this boy. And you missed church this morning." Mary emphasizes her last point, thinking her daughter's behaviour is related to missing mass.

"I know, Mom. I'll go to the 5 o'clock service and I didn't do anything wrong. Maybe it's a blessing because I agree with you. Roberto was no good for me. I see that now."

#

Teresa's last name is Rossi. The family lives in Watertown, Massachusetts which is just outside of Boston. The extended family gets together every Sunday for a large meal that can last for hours. Families take turns hosting the meal. This week is their turn.

#

Teresa's father, Joe, wakes up at 1:30 p.m. He comes downstairs and sits in the living room.

Her younger brother Nick enters the kitchen through the back door. Joe overhears Nick ask, "Mom, do I got time to go to the gym?"

"No," Mary answers, "and why do you have to go to the gym every day? Go wake your father and wash your hands for dinner."

"Ma, I can be back in less than an hour," Nick appeals to his mother.

Joe speaks up, "I'm awake, honey. I'm in here. Nick, don't ever talk back to your mother."

Teresa enters the living room. "Hi, Daddy. You want to go to the 5 o'clock mass with me?"

"Hi, sweetheart. How come you didn't go earlier? With your mother?" Joe asks.

"I got caught up with friends," Teresa answers innocently. She sits next to her father.

"How come you had to go to Detroit?" she asks. Joe works for the T as an assistant general manager.

"Oh, you know. The union calls and we go." Joe sounds tired.

"Do you get paid for these trips?" Teresa asks.

The question surprises Joe. "Yeah, we get paid. The T pays us. We get overtime on weekends. You know."

Teresa wonders why the T, the state's Transportation Authority, would pay expenses for a trip to Detroit. Massachusetts taxpayers fund the T. "That seems weird," Teresa adds innocently.

Joe would like her to understand how things work. "It's not weird, honey, it's just how things get done. It's like when someone from your office gets paid to drive around to check everyone's homes at election time. You know, make sure they have signs in their front lawns with the politician's name. The guy driving around is working for the state, but they're really working to help the politicians. State car, state gas, on the clock, ya know. It's how stuff gets done. No sign in front of your house, then no job. You take care of the people who take care of you."

Teresa nods and lets it go. "You want me to bring you something to eat in here?" she asks.

Joe is busy changing television channels. "No thanks. I'll go to the 5 o'clock mass with ya."

Both know that dinner will start and they won't speak of attending mass again.

7

New York, New York

At 2 p.m., an executive assistant opens the door to Gene's office and escorts a group of men in. Leon Washington is an aide to the president of the United States. Ed Sweeney is a lawyer for Morgan Sachs. Bob "Slugger" Brigham is a lobbyist hired by the bank. Gene's style is to make visitors feel like honoured guests in his office.

"Thank you for your time today gentlemen," Gene begins. "I have a few objectives for today's meeting. I think we can address them in fairly short order. First, Leon, I can confirm that the fundraiser you requested is set to go. We'll hold it at Metropolitan Museum of Art, the "Met," here in New York on the evening requested in April. There will be three hundred guests at a cost of $25,000 per plate. I'm sure the president can find a use for the seven-and-a-half million dollars." Gene looks towards Leon for acknowledgement.

Leon Washington is an articulate young man with a Harvard law degree. He joined the president during his second campaign. "That's great," he answers. "The president will be glad to hear that. It's nice to see that people continue to show this kind of support for the man and his policies."

Gene's no longer surprised by the arrogance of staffers like Leon. They think it's easy to find people willing to write $25,000 checks. The truth is that Gene and the president's political party had to exert their influence. The attendees either work for the bank, count on the bank for business, or rely on the political party getting them government contracts. The meal is just another cost of doing business for insiders. This president, like others before him, has lost the support of his "true believers" during his second term in office. Supporters don't donate the way they once did because the president hasn't been effective in office. The other party has kept him from making progress on his campaign promises. It's the same tactics repeated over and over by the party not occupying the White House. They stunt progress even when it's in the country's best interests. To them, that's preferable to seeing the opposing party gain in popularity.

"Second," Gene continues, "Here's a folder with a list of requests." Gene hands Leon a manila folder. It would have been more accurate for Gene to say, 'Here is a list of favours I need for my clients. I know that some are outrageous but get them done.'

Leon wants to impress upon Gene how much he is asking. "Gene, I don't know if I can pass all of these along. What I mean is that some of these requests require, well, I don't even know what. And these lists get longer and more challenging."

Gene smiles and politely explains, "I understand. I expect there will be another list next month and the month after that. I also expect there to be another request for fundraisers from the president and others in his party. I can also imagine the next president will send a nice young person to sit in that same seat and this pattern will repeat. Get back to Peter with progress reports. Some of these are time sensitive."

"The third agenda," Gene moves on, "is an update of the proposed banking regulations. Ed?" Gene turns his attention to Ed Sweeney.

"Thanks, Gene," Ed begins. "Leon, we've gone through the latest draft of the new regulations in front of Congress. The banking committees in the House and Senate are now on the same page. I don't know how long that will last. We have some revisions and we're counting on the president's support. The changes are just a lot of detailed legal and finance stuff, very boring. Treasury Secretary Martin supports the changes. We'd like this passed and signed by the president by the end of next week. We're talking immediately. No delays."

"Slugger?" Ned turns the group's attention to Bob Brigham. Bob's in his early fifties, but could pass as much younger. He gave himself the nickname "Slugger" years ago to market himself better. He's a former congressman and now a partner with the most influential lobbying firm in Washington,

D.C. He charges the bank a fortune for his services and the bank gets its money's worth.

"Nothing new here guys," Slugger begins. "As Ed said, the votes are lined up. We've also prepared a script of talking points for both Democrats and Republicans. It's how they can explain their support to their constituents and show their willingness to work in a bipartisan way." Slugger smiles at Leon and adds, "Like I told you, this is done and the president will get all the credit for passing bank reform. It's a huge win for him. But, like Ed said, we must move now while we have support from both sides. No time for screwing around with conference committees and negotiations. It's gotta be now."

Leon nods his head in agreement. Bank reform legislation is important to the president and he needs a public win right now.

#

The discussion goes on for a short while before Gene asks Leon for a few moments alone. Ed and Slugger leave the office.

"You know, Leon, I like you," Gene starts. "You've done a marvellous job representing the president. You have a great work ethic. Perhaps you'll consider running for office yourself one day?"

Leon would welcome Gene's support if he were to run for office.

Gene continues, "I know that a job like yours can require financial sacrifice. I understand your annual salary is $200,000. I'm thinking that a talented young man like yourself finds it difficult making ends meet in Washington, especially in the crowd you like to run with."

Leon smiles. "More like impossible to make ends meet and have any kind of life."

"I'm thinking that we set you up to work for a charitable foundation as a part time thing," Gene suggests. "We start you with an annual salary of maybe three hundred thousand dollars. You attend a few meetings each year. That's it. Everyone in government is doing this now; getting a second or third paycheck. This would allow you to live the life you deserve. In return, I'd like to know what the president is planning or thinking about on certain issues."

Gene's offer was once illegal, but Congress changed the laws. Many Washington insiders now have several sources of income to supplement their full-time jobs with the government. Thanks to Congress, the income doesn't have to be reported.

Leon nods before answering. "Thank you. I really appreciate it, but I can't accept. I can't talk about it."

Gene suggests an improved offer. "What if we were to double the amount?"

"Thank you again, but no, and I really can't talk about it."

Gene knows what that means. Leon already has a similar arrangement with someone else. Leon is beholden to someone else.

"I understand," Gene replies. "You'll let me know if that changes. One more thing, I'll need fifteen minutes alone with the president at the fund-raiser. The fifteen minutes will occur before the event starts. I have a message for the president that I need you to relay to him directly. I want you to remind the president he needs to address the points that I've talked with him about fiscal and monetary policy. The two need to work together. He needs to provide me with a financial plan. The consequences of not providing a plan will be catastrophic for his administration and the country." Gene looks squarely into Leon's eyes. "Do you understand what I've said?"

Leon heard it clearly. "I don't know if I can use that kind of language with the president. I mean, no one uses that kind of language." The truth is no one tells the president anything that he doesn't want to hear.

"Yes," Gene responds firmly. "That's precisely the language that I need you to use with the president. There can be no misunderstanding."

8

Watertown, Massachusetts

Members of the Rossi family arrive for dinner. Joe's younger brother and sister arrive with their spouses. Mary's two sisters arrive with their husbands. Everyone has brought food and drink. Nieces and nephews come and go throughout the afternoon. The weekly celebration is familiar and comfortable for all.

Regardless of the house they assemble in, most of the conversation happens in the kitchen. Meal preparation goes on while people drink wine and nibble on food.

Mary's a terrific cook. She's made a pot roast with red wine sauce. The house smells wonderful. It's a hearty meal for a cold winter day.

Joe's brother Anthony tells Mary he can't wait to eat because everything smells so good. He asks, "What kind of sauce is that?"

Anthony gets the answer he wanted when Mary replies, "Your triple knot special, Anthony."

Joe and Anthony carry on a family tradition of making their own wine. Their father and his two brothers began making a wine they called "Triple Knot." One knot for each brother. They had their own label created of a rope with three knots. Under the rope are the words "Triple Knot" and the subtitle, "Not a too sweet, Not a too dry, Not a too good."

Soon after they sit down for dinner, Anthony asks Joe, "What happened in Detroit? Sounds like you lost control of your guys."

Mary cringes. Anthony loves getting under the skin of his older brother.

"Nothin' happened," Joe answers. Joe clearly doesn't want to talk about it.

Anthony continues. He's having fun. "That's not what I heard. I heard you dressed your guys up in Boston Bruins uniforms. It's hard to pass as a bunch of locals from Detroit when they look more like the Boston Bruins hockey team. Maybe your guys will be on ESPN, Joe. Huh?" Anthony is enjoying himself. Family members look to Joe for an explanation.

Joe sits back. He shakes his head. He may be annoyed but he sees the humour in it. He takes a gulp of wine, looks around the table, and explains. "I was asked to bring a bus load of guys to Detroit. Their local union of mass transit workers is on strike and we went to show support. We were supposed to blend in and look like locals. I spread some money around for our guys to go out and buy stuff. The idea was to buy Detroit Red Wings sweaters or Michigan State University sweatshirts, something local. Instead, our guys figured they'd buy Boston Bruins sweaters so they can wear them back here too." Joe shakes his head and takes another gulp of wine.

"Next thing I know," Joe continues, "the union boss out there asks me what the hell is wrong with you guys?" Joe is now smiling and shaking his head in disbelief. "Anyway, I didn't know what he was talking about. He points out Tom Murphy who is trying to get on television. He's talking to a reporter from a local television network and in his deepest Boston accent he's saying 'it's unfaya what they're offerin, it's completely unfaya.' I look over and twenty of our guys are standing together in Boston Bruins sweaters. I couldn't believe it. Murph's accent was a dead giveaway too. Everyone knew immediately we were all from Boston. Idiots."

"Are you in trouble with the union?" Mary asks.

"No, no, nothing like that."

Anthony then says, "Murph might be in trouble with Joe. Did Murphy get on the news? I didn't know that part."

"No, the television people cover up stuff like that for us. Anyway, I should have paid closer attention to them," Joe admits. "It was freezing cold and some of our guys were drinking whiskey to stay warm. I should have supervised their shopping spree, but I couldn't imagine anyone being so stupid."

Teresa has heard similar stories from her father. She asks, “So when you go to these places you pretend to be from there?”

“Sometimes, honey,” Joe answers. “Guys come here if we need ‘em and vice versa. All for one and one for all kind of thing for the union. Bigger crowds suggest more public support. Like maybe a lot of people care about an issue when maybe there really isn’t much support. Most people are against the fare hikes we want for higher wages and retirement benefits. You know?” After a pause, he asks, “Where’s Roberto?”

“Oh, he’s not coming Daddy,” Teresa answers.

9

New York, New York

It's 5:15 p.m. when Gene's assistant tells him that his sons will be arriving shortly. Gene ends his meeting.

His sons are standing beside a limousine when Gene arrives in the underground garage. Gene gives each of them a big hug.

Jack is wearing a blue blazer, button-down shirt, and khaki pants. While the khakis are not intended for winter, he looks nice, and it's an improvement for him.

Jack's older brother Gene, Jr., is wearing a navy-blue pinstripe suit and a black, cashmere winter coat. Gene, Jr. is six feet tall and has an athletic build that he maintains with daily workouts. He likes to remind people that he played football at Harvard. While true, he was their third string quarterback and only saw action in the final game of his senior year.

Gene, Jr., is known as "JR" among family and friends, short for Junior. He likes the nickname.

They get in the limousine and ride to Gene's apartment. Once there, they go upstairs to escort Gene's wife, Grace, to the car. They wouldn't think of asking her to come downstairs on her own. Raised as a southern lady, the boy's mother would prefer to wait upstairs all evening than not to be escorted.

Grace isn't ready when they get home. She's in the master bedroom suite. They understand the routine. They'll wait patiently for her.

Eventually, the door opens and she makes her entrance. Grace O'Neil is especially good at making entrances. Grace is five feet six inches tall, has long blond hair, crystal blue eyes, and a tan every day of the year. She's thin even by New York City standards.

Jack inherited his mother's features including her high cheekbones and eye colour. Gene, Jr., resembles his father, with shared features including dark hair, darker skin, and a square jawline. They're common features among those known as 'black Irish.'

Jack is closest to his mother when she enters. They give each other a hug before she hugs JR and kisses her husband. Grace returns to Jack and instructs him to take off his jacket.

"Heavens, Jack are you eating anything at all?" she asks. "I think you've lost weight. Eugene, look at your son."

Grace's mothering instincts are on constant alert with Jack. As a boy, Jack required extra attention. He was born premature and required extra medical attention.

Gene and JR look at each other. They smile. "I'm fine, Mother," JR says.

Grace glances at JR and waves her hand as if to dismiss the comment.

"Jack, are you eating the food we're sending you?" She's feeling Jack's midsection, which makes him uncomfortable. She adds, "We should have you see a doctor while you're in town."

"They're only in town for a few hours, sweetheart," Gene reminds her. "The plane is taking them back tonight, so if we're ready, let's get moving." Gene takes his wife's arm and escorts her out.

#

They go out to one of Grace's favourite restaurants.

"Thank you, boys, for coming," Gene says as they settle in at a table. "I have something important to talk with you about." The boys were expecting news. It's unusual for Gene to send his private plane to bring them home.

"Changes are coming," Gene begins. "Big changes are coming and I want you to be prepared for them. I want you to understand why things are happening. World events, politics, everything. I see a clash coming between powerful forces. I want to make sure you're prepared. I want you to enjoy the very best that life has to offer and for a long time." Gene looks into the eyes of his sons to make sure they're following him. "I'd like you both to come to work with me at the bank at the end of this school year. I want to teach you some important lessons and prepare you for what's coming. Lessons few people know or understand."

JR is in his second year at the Harvard Business School. He has been planning to come to work for his father for the past twenty years. Jack, on the other hand, doesn't want any part of the bank or working in business. Both sons are stunned to hear their father request that Jack leave his studies to work at the bank.

JR speaks first. "Of course, Dad, whatever you need. What are these changes you're talking about?"

JR's response was predictable. Grace and Gene are looking at Jack for his reaction.

Jack is staring at the saltshaker. He's not moving.

"Jack?" Gene asks.

Grace takes one of Jack's hands to comfort him. "Of course, you don't have to work there if you don't want to," she tells him. "This is merely a suggestion, a proposal. Let's call it a proposal."

Jack feels betrayed, and that his studies aren't appreciated by his father. His father simply doesn't understand the importance of the work he has in mind. *Banking*, Jack thinks to himself. *How could anyone want to work in a bank?* He considers it a waste of his time and abilities.

Grace shoots Gene a look. He knows it means, "do something to comfort your son."

The news is hitting Jack harder than Gene expected. "Son, I want you to think about this. When you go back to Boston, I want you to think about it. It might be something you actually enjoy."

There are thousands of young people begging for the opportunity Gene is offering his son. Gene had to work his way up from nothing. He's annoyed by his son's lack of appreciation.

"And you don't have to if that's your preference," his mother adds a second time. "We'll all just think about it for a little while." Grace can turn up her southern accent when she chooses. The words "a little while" seem to float off her tongue.

There's an awkward silence before Jack announces, "I'm going to the men's room." He leaves the table.

Grace then says in a scolding tone, "He's not able to do that, Eugene. Leave him to his schoolwork. He's better off there. He's happy there. Copes better there."

JR sees an opportunity. "Dad, are you sure we need him? I mean if he doesn't want to work there and if he's better off at school then…"

Gene has often talked about what he calls 'intellectual horsepower.' He means superior intelligence and the ability to understand things that others can't. See things that others can't without explanation or assistance. JR knows that Jack has those rare abilities. He'd prefer to not compete with Jack. He'd prefer to be the only son of Eugene O'Neil at the bank.

Ten minutes pass before Jack returns to the table.

"Are you ok, honey?" his mother asks.

Jack nods his head.

"Jackson," his father begins. "I'm asking you to think about it, ok?" Gene is looking at his son.

Jack is looking down at his hands.

"Think about it and we'll talk again in a few weeks," Gene states. "Does that sound reasonable?"

Jack nods his head.

#

After dinner, the boys return to Boston via a limousine and Gene's plane. A different limousine takes Grace and Gene home.

On the ride home Grace asks, "Eugene, what could possibly be so important that you'd tell Jack that he needs to come to work for you?"

Gene would prefer not to get into details. "You know me, honey. I've had a dream of working with my boys. I can see changes coming and I'd feel a whole lot better if they understood how the world works. It's very different than it appears. It's very different from what we teach in schools or gets reported in the press."

"Not everyone is cut out to do your kind of work," Grace replies. "JR, yes. Jack, no. Best to leave him be."

10

New York, New York

Gene's first appointment Monday morning is at 5:30 a.m. with a personal trainer. The bank has a gym in the building. His trainer starts Gene on a forty-minute workout consisting of cardio exercises and weights. Gene has lost twenty pounds since going on his diet. Shortly after beginning the diet, he added exercise. While he finds the workouts boring, he loves the improvement in his energy level and appearance.

He completes his workout, takes a shower, and dresses for the workday. As he walks towards the elevator, he runs into one of his partners, Bernie Schwartz, walking in the same direction.

"How about this?" Bernie starts. "Two old farts like us working out." Bernie is a long-time friend who has been at the bank a couple years longer than Gene. Bernie's conversations often turn into a list of complaints. That's fine with Gene. The two have always gotten along well and have had each other's backs during conflicts involving office politics.

"Know what's fucked up?" Bernie asks. "We're working out so that we can work even harder and longer. But you've got these lazy bastards on unemployment and food stamps, unwed mothers on welfare. They're sleeping in. They got no interest in real work. People like to complain about the top one percent, but the top one percent does ninety-nine percent of the work."

Gene smiles.

"I know you agree with me," Bernie continues. "These leeches are taking government handouts, getting fat, drunk, smoking cigarettes and marijuana. They'll develop health problems from their own life choices and will be the first ones in line for free healthcare. Hard working Americans paying the insurance costs for those making bad life choices. They don't need free healthcare; they need a kick in the ass. Stop eating Big Macs, turn off the television, video games, get a job or two." The elevator reaches the trading floor where Bernie will get out.

Bernie is a legend at the bank. He's treated like royalty on the trading floor. He's made the bank billions of dollars in profits over his career.

Gene admires Bernie's fair treatment for those that work for him. Only hard work and results lead to pay increases and promotions. It doesn't matter who you are or where you came from.

Bernie takes a step out of the elevator and turns towards Gene. "And another thing about free healthcare and these handouts."

Gene holds up his hand. "Bernie, this is the guy you wanted as president. We've talked about this."

"I know, Gene, but this isn't what I thought we were getting." The elevator door closes. Bernie waves his hand in disgust.

11

Washington, D.C.

Leon Washington attends a meeting in the White House. The group includes senior political advisors and members of the president's Cabinet. The meeting is fast paced. Every issue runs through political advisors who understand the political implications of decisions even when they don't fully understand the subject matter.

Bobby Ferguson is the president's top political advisor. He is directing the meeting. When Leon's turn arrives, he begins, "I met with Gene O'Neil yesterday, Mr. President. A few points of interest; first, he was able to confirm the April fundraiser and the $7.5 million figure."

The president looks at Bobby with a big smile.

"We should have asked for more," Bobby replies.

Leon continues. "Gene passed along this folder of favours he wants our help with."

The president points to Bobby, who points to Will Duffy. Will is another "political advisor" and he handles the president's dirty work. This same sequence has played out in previous meetings. The folder is passed down the table to Duffy with each hand treating it as if it were radioactive.

Leon adds, "Gene asks that we get back to him with updates through Peter Hollingsworth. Also, they've revised the new bank regulations. Slugger Brigham has provided talking points, his ideas on how to provide cover for everyone voting in favour. He says they have the votes in the House and

Senate. They'd like to get this done immediately—a real rush job. Passed and signed by the end of next week."

The president's happy to hear it and adds, "That's fast alright but good news."

"And finally, Mr. President, he made two other points. He wants fifteen minutes of your time alone before the fundraiser." The president nods. Everyone asks for fifteen minutes. "And, he said he wanted a plan from you on a more coordinated monetary and fiscal policy along the lines that he says he discussed with you." Leon looks up to watch the president's reaction. Leon doesn't know what Gene discussed with the president.

The president sits up. His eyes are looking down at the table in front of him.

"He wanted me to say, Mr. President," Leon takes a big gulp, "and I'm simply quoting, that failure to follow up would be catastrophic for the administration and the country." Leon feels a sense of relief once the words are out of his mouth.

After a pause, the president shows his trademark smile. "So our Wall Street banker friend wants me to work on things, huh?" The president's tone reeks of sarcasm. Bobby Ferguson and Will Duffy smile and laugh on cue. They've learned when the president expects his "yes men" to respond and they're happy to oblige.

"Well, I guess I should say 'Yes, sir, Gene, let me get right on that.'" Others in the room smile. "How about that now Doug?" The president turns to Treasury Secretary Doug Martin.

"Mr. President," Doug answers.

Doug Martin is not a political type. He's a veteran of Wall Street who was brought in to the administration to help build a bridge between the government and Wall Street. One of his goals was to help put some teeth behind bank regulations. Everyone understood that new regulations were required following the last financial crisis. Unfortunately, he's seen too many congressmen weaken his legislation in return for donations to their own campaigns. Nothing has been done to address the flaws in the system. He understands that another crisis is likely and that it could cause more damage and suffering than the last one.

Doug knew people go to Wall Street to make money. He thought people came to Washington to make a difference. He was wrong. Money controls

Washington. Politicians from both political parties are interested in their own self-enrichment. Money flows in from everywhere to buy influence. Congressmen treat their offices like their own private business.

"Gene wants us to get busy." The president is talking directly to him. "Do you have any thoughts to share?"

Doug understands that it's the president's show. He feels a responsibility to state his honest opinion. "Mr. President, I think Gene and others believe that we can't continue to spend and borrow money the way we've been doing. They're concerned with the size of the nation's debt and believe the country needs a long-term economic plan."

His response increases the tension to the room.

"Deficits and spending," the president starts. "I could hire a hundred economists. Fifty would say we need to cut the deficit and fifty would say we need more spending and larger deficits. And not just a little bit. They'd tell me I have to spend a whole lot more money." He's shaking his head and holding his arms out to the side to show frustration. "I know there are people out there in this great country that need the support we're providing. Wall Street bankers don't give a shit about them. I need to stand up for ordinary Americans and get them the help they need."

The president is acting up in front of his handpicked audience. No one dares interrupt. "Doesn't Gene know that I've got a job to do? I can't let bankers get in my way. Heck, I've got an army? I've even got a navy and an air force?" The president has the group revved up. He's been using these lines frequently. "What's he got? Doesn't he know we could shut down his bank if we wanted to? That's what's wrong with this great country. His type sits in the office towers of their big banks and they're confused about who's running things. Leon, can you please let Gene know I'll do the best I can with the fifteen minutes. Same thing with this change in policy. Tell him I'll give it serious consideration."

The group understands that "I'll give it serious consideration," usually means the president intends to do nothing about Gene's request.

"Of course, Mr. President," Leon responds.

"With all due respect, Mr. President, I wouldn't do that." It's Doug Martin voicing an objection. "I've known Gene a long time. I don't think it's wise to disregard his requests or placate him."

People in the room are shocked. It's rare for anyone to object once the president has stated a course of action. The president doesn't like objections. People that voice objections don't last in this administration.

"All I'm saying, Mr. President," Doug continues, "is that it won't be received well."

Bobby Ferguson steps in to diffuse the situation. "Mr. President, it seems wise to meet with Gene, but I don't think you want to go without a better idea of the agenda. Perhaps the treasury secretary could talk with Gene first to prepare you better." This is typical Bobby. He shrugs his shoulders and adds, "Hey, you give him fifteen minutes and he gives you seven and a half million dollars."

Bobby's comment breaks the tension. The president smiles to show he's won this round with the banker. "Fifteen minutes. Seven and one-half million dollars. That's why I like you, Bobby. OK." The president turns to Doug. "Talk with Gene and update us at our next meeting?" The president doesn't wait for a response, "What's next Bobby?"

12

Boston, Massachusetts

Teresa waited for a phone call from Jack that didn't come. She took the initiative and sent him a text. She told him she'll be close to his apartment and can drop his clothes off. They agree to meet at a coffee shop.

Jack finds it odd. Here's this beautiful girl that shows up out of nowhere. She's different than other girls he's met. She makes him feel good about himself rather than socially awkward.

As he approaches, he sees her inside the coffee shop looking at her phone.

She tends to get places early and stresses when others aren't on time. She sees him approach. His hair is dishevelled. He's wearing a down coat, blue jeans, and boots instead of shorts and sneakers, more appropriate for a cold evening with snow in the forecast.

As he gets to the entrance, she presents him with a trash bag filled with his things. "See, I wasn't after you for your clothes," she says with a smile.

"Hi," he begins.

"I did keep a T-shirt," she admits.

He's quiet.

Her mind races and worries that maybe he didn't care to see her. Maybe he really just wanted his clothes back.

Jack asks, "Do you want to get something here or maybe go somewhere?"

"Sure. I'll do anything. Did you have something in mind?" she asks.

"Ah, no, not really, I guess," Jack answers. Neither are excited about remaining here.

"I know," Teresa says. "We could go to Sam's. It's just down the street. Ever been there?"

"No. Never heard of it."

She explains, "It's called Play it Again Sam's. It's a restaurant, bar, movie house. You sit at your table. You can eat and drink. They play old movies. It's fun. People laugh and talk through the movies. They're playing romantic comedies leading up to Valentine's Day."

His only reaction is a slight nod.

She inquires, "Is that a yes, Jacky?"

"Yes," he says.

She makes things easy for him.

#

They have a fun evening together. They're both suckers for love stories with happy endings. Quirky characters are their favourites. They talk about which characters resemble themselves and why. They find comfort in each other's company.

For most of Jack's life, he has been a social misfit. He's always been much younger than his classmates. He tried to fit in and when that didn't work, he gave up trying.

Jack is unlike other young men Teresa has known. He's secure in who he is. He knows where he's headed in life. He's low-key, not at all aggressive with her and more interested in talking about her than himself. Getting him to talk about himself is a challenge.

She keeps a watchful eye on the time. "I gotta get going if I'm going to catch the T," she tells him. "Last one leaves at 12:10 a.m."

He's disappointed that the evening is ending. "Ok, but should I get you a cab or a limo?" he asks. He's thinking that he has the responsibility to get her home safely.

"A limo?" she laughs. "Yes, that's exactly what you should do and have them pull up right here. I don't want to take another step." She pauses, "No, thank you Jacky."

They begin walking to the T station. It's snowing; large, puffy snowflakes are falling. *I should have kissed her*, Jack thinks to himself. *Sam's was the perfect place. Maybe I should put my arm around her. Maybe she doesn't want me to*. He's overthinking things.

They come to an intersection. She stops, crosses her arms, and points in opposite directions. "I'm going this way. You're going that way."

"Well, I'll walk you to the T station, anyway," Jack says. She accepts and puts her arms around his forearm. When they reach the subway, they stop and face each other.

"Thanks, Jacky. I had fun," she tells him.

He's smiling but having difficulty saying anything. She looks beautiful with the snowflakes in her hair. He feels lucky to be out with her.

"You know what they said in the movies?" she asks.

He shakes his head. "What's that?"

She leans forward and speaks softly in his ear. "If you don't kiss me, we'll turn out to be just friends. Do you want to be just friends?"

He immediately leans forward and kisses her. He presses his lips hard against hers.

Right answer, she thinks, *awkward kiss but right answer*. As they separate, she says, "Good night." She turns and walks down a flight of stairs into the subway station.

Jack watches her walk away and focuses on every detail in order to remember it later. She's wearing tight jeans and knee-high boots. Her dark hair ends halfway down her back.

When she reaches the subway entrance, she sees his reflection in the subway door. He hasn't moved. He's standing under a streetlight watching her. *Good*, she thinks. *He's interested. Hopefully, he likes what he sees.*

13

Boston, Massachusetts

Gene phones his older son and arranges a meeting in Boston. He instructs JR to come to the airport. They'll meet on Gene's plane.

JR follows his instructions. There's an area of the airport reserved for private jets. A strikingly beautiful flight attendant named Elsa welcomes JR.

Gene is seated, talking on the phone, when JR enters. He moves some papers aside and motions for JR to sit on a couch next to him.

"Thank you for coming," Gene begins.

"Sure, Dad. Is this a new plane? It's a lot bigger isn't it?" he asks.

"Yes, it's new and bigger. Planes or jets these days are amazing. It's got a much longer range than the old one. I can get almost anywhere now. It's a lot more comfortable on those long flights."

JR admires the plane and custom detailing before asking, "So what's up, Dad? Was this stop just for me?"

"Yes," Gene begins, "it's about your brother. I want you to reach out to him. I think I shocked him over dinner. That upset your mother." Gene rolls his eyes to convey frustration. "I want you to talk with him about coming to work with you and me. I want you to explain to him what a great opportunity this is."

"I can talk with him," JR replies "but I don't think he's going to change his mind." JR's real goal is to talk his father out of the idea. "What's going on anyway? I mean, you talked about big changes coming and then sprung the idea of Jack working at the bank. It shocked all of us."

Gene nods his head. "Well, as I said at dinner, I need to get you guys trained. I need you both to understand how things work and where you fit in the big picture."

"Dad, I'm graduating from Harvard Business School," JR begins. "I've done two internships at the bank. I don't need more training. I'm ready to go, but Jack? I can talk to him, but he has no interest in business. I doubt he's ever taken a business course. I don't think his school even offers one. What's really going on?"

#

Gene takes a deep breath. "I understand that you're well educated. It reminds me of Mark Twain's comment about 'never let schooling get in the way of your education.'" Gene smiles. "Let me tell you a story. It's a great story. The greatest business story of all time. One of the reasons it's such a great story is because it's true and yet very few people know it or could even imagine it.

"Back in October 1913, President Woodrow Wilson passed the United States Revenue Act," Gene starts slowly. "For the first time in the history of our country, Americans were required to pay federal income taxes. The taxes were low, but this was new and unpopular. It probably wasn't even constitutional because the states voting in favour of the amendment voted on different versions of the law. They never agreed on the same language. Leaders in various states agreed to pass it based on the promise that there would be a Constitutional Convention. Everything would be renegotiated before it became law. That never happened. Powerful men supporting the bill skipped the Convention. Renegotiating a final version meant risking that it wouldn't pass. Money was passed around and there was no convention. The bill became law."

Gene stands and gets a bottle of water from the refrigerator. He gets one for JR and hands it to him.

"Under the new law, wealthy Americans had to pay one percent of their income to the federal government. One percent." Gene shakes his head. "It's funny how far the country has come with taxes, huh?" He returns to his seat. "But that's not the story. Two months later; in December 1913, the president signed the Federal Reserve Act which created our central bank." Gene is hoping his son is beginning to put things together. "Now, as you say, you're about to graduate from Harvard Business School. You attended Harvard for your undergraduate degree. You've completed our internship program and you're eager to get started. So tell me, why pass these two bills and why pass them in that order?"

Gene waits patiently, hoping for a well thought out response.

"Well," JR begins, "the income tax allows the government to grow. More dollars or more tax dollars coming in as revenue means more spending and power. Politicians love bigger budgets." He hesitates. "The Federal Reserve sets our money supply and interest rates." Then a long pause. He fails to put the pieces together and stops.

"Let me help you out a little bit," his father says. "Certain men got together and put money behind Woodrow Wilson. Teddy Roosevelt ran as an Independent candidate and split the vote of the Republican Party. That created the perfect opportunity for big money to buy the presidency and they did. They bought the presidency for Woodrow Wilson."

JR is confused. *They bought the presidency?* he thinks.

Gene continues at a faster pace. "A small group of very wealthy men got together and bought the presidency in order to create a central bank in America, just as they had done in European countries. You'd recognize the names of these men; Rothschild, Rockefeller, JP Morgan, Vanderbilt, Kuhn, Loeb, and Winthrop. They created our Federal Reserve Bank and were the original owners. My guess is that Woodrow Wilson never understood what they were really up to but that doesn't matter." Gene is looking at his son and trying to ascertain if he's keeping up.

JR leans forward. He's keenly interested and trying to put the pieces together.

"It's simple," Gene continues. "What does a bank want from the people that it's lending money to? It wants collateral and it wants the borrower to be able to repay that debt. Lenders want borrowers to have a predictable stream of future income to pay them back. A bank gives someone a home mortgage based, in part, on their income."

JR nods.

Gene stands and stretches. "The Federal Reserve Bank, or 'Fed' as it's known, is going to manage the country's money supply. It's going to lend money to the United States government. Before the Fed will lend money to the government, they need to know the government has the ability to pay them back. Where is that money going to come from? Taxes. It has to come from the taxes that our government imposes on the American people. That's why you needed to have an income tax before you could create the Federal Reserve Bank. It's all part of the same scheme. It's the same system they created in Europe. Are you following me?" Gene asks.

"Yes, Dad. I'm following."

"Good," Gene answers. "There's a lot of intrigue behind it, but they got it done. They passed the bank bill on December 23, 1913, when most of Congress had left Washington for the holiday. They probably paid enough members to hang around long enough to vote. Congress could probably be bought as cheaply then as they can be today."

"But, Dad, they're lending money to the government. Whose money is it anyway? Isn't it the government's money? The people's money?" JR is confused.

"Well, that's a good question," Gene answers. "Whose money is it? Our government or our politicians sold control of our money supply to a small group of very wealthy men. American citizens have been paying interest to this small group and their heirs since 1913. Like it or not, it's their money. Look at your money. Seriously, look at it." Gene takes a twenty dollar bill out of his wallet. He points to the top of the bill and says, "Right there, see, it says 'Federal Reserve Note' right on it."

Gene wants to help his son understand. "I'm sure it sounds like fantasy but that's the story. They bought the presidency and he gave them control over our country's money supply. They promised him economic stability and growth. They lied about that."

"How come no one knows about this?" JR asks. "None of this is taught in school."

Gene rubs his hands together before answering. "Well, I suppose it comes down to incompetent media, a bad education system, lazy citizens, but let's get you up to date. Ownership in the bank has passed down through several generations. That's where I come in. I work for these people. Yes, I work for Morgan Sachs, but I work for these men and women too. I look after their interests. I advise them. They're my clients."

The pilot enters the cabin and knocks on the wall. "Mr. O'Neil?" he says.

"Yes, John, what is it?" Gene answers.

"We have that bad weather moving in that we talked about," he explains. "We'll need to leave soon if we want to get out today."

"Understood, thank you John," Gene answers.

Gene turns back to JR. "I work for them. Their net worth is in the trillions of dollars. They can have whatever they want, but what they want most is security and anonymity. They don't want anyone to know this story. That's why you'll never tell anyone—ever."

JR now sees an opportunity for himself. This is where he belongs. He needs to meet these people, join their inner circle.

"Now as to changes coming," Gene continues. "We're at a crossroads. I've been trying to work with the United States government on a fiscally responsible path. The bank's owners are tired of the government printing money and spending it irresponsibly. The debt is too high. It's not backed by anything, like gold. Cryptocurrency is a new risk to the status quo and something we don't yet control. The two sides are frustrated with each other. It's never been this bad. It's coming to a head. That's why I want you and Jack close to me." Gene is sitting directly in front of and facing his son. "Talk to your brother. He looks up to you. Don't talk about this story. Get him to come to the bank. It's very important. Can you do this for me?"

"Of course, Dad."

After quick "good-byes," Gene's plane takes off ahead of the weather. His next stop is London.

14

Boston, Massachusetts

The relationship between Teresa and Jack develops quickly. They're spending a lot of time together. When they're apart, they look forward to the next time they'll see each other.

Teresa works in an administrative job for the Commonwealth of Massachusetts. Her work hours are from 8:30 a.m. to 5:00 p.m. with a half hour for lunch. She takes a course at a community college one night a week. Most evenings, she hangs out at Jack's apartment while he studies. She spends her time talking on the phone, doing her own schoolwork, and following entertainment news. She's surprised by how much time Jack devotes to his studies.

Daylight hours in Boston this time of year are short. They experience three major snowstorms in two weeks. Two young people find it easy to settle indoors and get to know one another. Jack's gaining confidence in himself.

#

"How old are you?" Teresa asks one evening. She's been telling friends about Jack. They've asked questions that she doesn't have answers to.

"I'm 18, how old are you?" he answers.

"18? Really?" She's surprised. "I'm older than you? I'm a cradle robber." She pauses and considers it. "I guess I like younger men." They're lying in his bed. He's reading a book. She's browsing an entertainment news magazine.

"How old are you?" he asks again.

"I'm 20," Teresa answers. She's looking for a reaction but doesn't get one. "Are you ok being involved with an older woman?"

"As long as it's you," he responds, without taking his eyes off the book.

She loves his gentle sweetness.

"So, if you're 18 then what year are you in? In college I mean?" she asks.

"I'm a senior."

"What, you can't be a senior at 18!" she exclaims. "Did you skip some years?"

He smiles. "Kind of but yes, I'm a senior. I'm actually taking mostly graduate courses now."

"Graduate school here?" she asks.

"That's the plan. I guess I could go somewhere else."

"So," she continues, "you're 18, you're a senior, and when you finish school you're going to keep going to school here?"

"Yeah, I think so," Jack answers. "I'd like to get a Masters, PhD, more, maybe help teach, you know. There's so much to get done." There's an excitement in his voice when he talks about his studies.

She turns quiet, reflective.

Several moments pass. "What's the matter?" he asks.

"Nothing," she answers. She wishes she felt the same passion for something in her life, something with a future. She became concerned when he said he was a senior, concerned that he might be leaving Boston at the end of the semester. She's glad to hear he'll be here for the foreseeable future.

"You are going to get out and get a job at some point, right?" she asks.

"Yes," he smiles. "I'm going to get a job. I'll contribute to society, hopefully in a meaningful way."

"I don't think I've ever seen anyone work as hard as you," Teresa says. "I don't know how you get by with so little sleep, four hours a night maybe. How do you do that and why do you work so hard?"

"It doesn't feel like work," he answers. "It's kind of a privilege to learn what the great minds thought. What did they discover? How did they do it? What does it mean? How can each breakthrough lead to the next?" He's talking fast. "See, each great man, woman, stands on the shoulders of the ones that preceded him. Each one's contribution leads to the next one's breakthrough. I want to be a part of that chain. The harder you work, the more you can achieve, and the richer and fuller your life can be."

"Wow, I wish someone taught me that years ago. How do you pay for all this? I mean, this has to be really expensive."

"I'm kind of on a scholarship," Jack answers. He pauses because he doesn't know. "I mean, I know I've got some scholarship money and I know my dad pays for some of it. I guess I don't know the breakdown exactly."

"Did you take out student loans?" she asks.

He shakes his head. "No. I've never talked with anyone about loans."

This is all strange to Teresa. When she entered the frat house, she had no idea that she was stepping into a completely different world.

"You don't know how much it costs. You don't know how much your scholarship is or how much your father is paying?" She shakes her head. "Nice life, Jacky." She puts her head on his chest and struggles with a deep sense of unfairness between their lives.

15

London, England

Gene flies to London to meet with some of the owners of the Federal Reserve. The owners refer to themselves as the "shareholders." Gene's objective is to make sure that the people directing him are certain of their goals and how far they're willing to go. The last thing he wants to do is to alienate powerful people—like the president of the United States—and then not have their full support.

Originally, there were seven shareholders. Now, one hundred and ninety-seven people own shares that have passed through several generations. Managing this group is almost impossible due to its size and the fact that many of them have very little appreciation for the real world.

Gene's strategy is twofold. First, he has tried to convince each family to consolidate their votes in the hands of a small number of people, ideally one person. The Rothschild family has 17 family members, but Madeline ("Maddy") Rothschild speaks for the entire family. Second, he's identified those shareholders with the most influence over the others. Maddy is the most respected shareholder followed by David Rockefeller, William Vanderbilt, James Loeb, and Peter Morgan. Gene relies on Maddy to help manage the others.

#

The group begins the day by having breakfast together at 8:00 a.m. They'll transition to their business meeting when everyone completes their meal.

It's customary for Gene to run the meetings.

"As you all know," Gene begins the meeting, "I continue to push the American president for a plan. I'll be meeting with him again soon. Unfortunately, he's acting like most politicians. He hopes to leave office before we force him to do anything. He'd prefer to leave any difficult decisions to the next man or woman."

"Unacceptable," Maddy states.

"Agreed," David adds.

"Gene," James Loeb begins, "this president simply doesn't understand that we've run out of patience and his policies are precisely the kinds of things he promised not to do. He has gone back on his word. The way I see it is that we've been more than fair; more than patient."

"I understand," Gene answers as he distributes a document to each member of the group. "You asked me to come up with a plan. I'm suggesting a series of steps to force the president and Congress to act. I've outlined the strategy in this document. I've designed a plan so that each step is of increasing power or impact on the economy. Hopefully, we won't have to go too far down this list before they agree to our demands."

Gene takes a deep breath before continuing. "I'd like to take you through these steps. I want to explain each step and why I've put them in this order. I want you to think carefully about this before we begin. I need to make sure that we're all in full agreement. If we agree, then I will introduce the highlights of this plan to all the shareholders at our next meeting."

Peter Morgan offers his support. "Sounds good, Gene."

"Please understand," Gene continues, "that these actions are significant. Not even we hold the power to control events should things spiral out of control unexpectedly." He pauses for effect. "There are risks here. Each of you need to understand and accept those risks."

"Yes," Maddy answers for the group. "We understand and appreciate your asking, but this is our duty. American politicians have gone further than anyone in history to pile up a mountain of debt. It's a time bomb for the entire world. America needs a wakeup call and it needs to understand its one-hundred-year reign as a world superpower may be over. They need to understand that their reckless spending was their own undoing."

16

Boston, Massachusetts

JR follows up on his father's request to talk to Jack. They agree to meet for dinner. Jack suggested the same place where he had breakfast with Teresa. He likes the comfort of familiar surroundings.

Even though the brothers live just a couple miles apart, they rarely see one another. Their relationship is odd even by the high standards of the Irish. Jack has always looked up to his older brother. JR doesn't know what to make of Jack. He loves him, but Jack was weak and quiet as a child. He didn't play sports. He was nonverbal for the first few years of his life. Any interaction was challenging. It was Jack's lack of speech that led his parents to having him tested, and it was those early tests that first revealed Jack's unusually high intelligence.

JR enters to find Jack sitting, halfway through his dinner. He thought Jack would have waited for him before ordering.

JR walks over to the table and begins, "Hey, little brother."

Jack looks up with a big smile. "Hi, JR."

"It's good to see you," JR begins. "We should get together more often."

Jack smiles, but doesn't say anything.

JR sits down. "That was quite a bombshell Dad dropped on us, huh?"

Jack nods and raises his eyebrows. "I met a girl," he says. He'd like to impress his older brother and maybe get some advice.

"That's great," JR replies. "You know, it would be great for the two of us to work with Dad at the bank. We'd be back in the city, in his building, working in finance and done with school." JR lists the things that Jack doesn't want to hear.

"She's really nice. I think you'd like her," Jack replies. He'd prefer to talk about Teresa.

JR wants Jack focused on the reason for their meeting. "I'm sure she's great, but she's just another broad. When we get to the city there will be hundreds of them."

Jack's feelings are hurt. He's been with a woman. He had hoped to get some congratulations or encouragement. Teresa is not "just another broad."

A waitress arrives. Jack has finished his meal. JR orders coffee and a sandwich to go.

"What are you thinking?" JR asks. "Do you want to go to work for Dad or would you prefer to stay here? Whatever you choose, the family will support your decision. If you'd prefer to work on math and science stuff, I mean if that's where your heart is, then you should do it. Mom and Dad will see that. I know Dad will support whatever you choose. It's your life after all."

Jack nods before asking, "Do you remember when Uncle Dave would tell us how Grandpa was gonna change the world?"

"Yeah, sure Jacky, I remember. I guess Grandpa said it all the time."

"That's what I want to do," Jack says. He sits up straight, "I want to make a difference. We're close to breakthroughs now. String theory isn't a theory, it's the basis of all matter. We can apply one breakthrough to many other fields; nanotechnologies, medical sciences, everything. I want to focus on what's important and push boundaries. I want to show how the smallest pieces of matter are energy and from there everything is possible. I can see how it all comes together. I can change the world. I can make improvements in the lives of billions of people alive and not yet born."

JR sees the enthusiasm and confidence in his brother. He wants to believe him even if he doesn't understand what he's talking about.

Jack puts his head down and shakes it from side to side. "A bank," he says dejectedly. "A bank!" he repeats and mocks the idea. "How do you spend a moment of your precious time on earth worrying about money or looking after other people's money? Put on a suit? Sit in an office? For what, just money?"

JR has mixed emotions. Dinner was successful because Jack won't be coming to the bank. He feels a little insulted that Jack believes his own pursuit of money is shallow. What about Jack? Is Jack delusional about his own pursuits or is he really on to something? JR focuses on what's most important to him. He assures Jack, "I understand little brother. This is where you need to be. I think you're gonna change the world alright. Just like Grandpa."

"You really think Dad will be ok with that decision?"

"I'm sure he'll be ok with it," JR answers. "You just gotta be firm when you tell him."

After a little more conversation, the waitress delivers JR's sandwich in a paper bag to go. The brothers hug one another and say goodbye.

17

Iero, Greece

When Gene's business concludes in London, he flies to the island of Iero. It's a stunningly beautiful island in the Aegean Sea. The shareholders acquired the island from the Catholic Church in the 1990s. The island was completely undeveloped at the time. The only structure was a convent. After its acquisition, Gene worked with a team to build a self-sustaining community. They built estates for each of the shareholders' families. Homes for the workers needed to support the community were also built. The island now has a farm, hospital, airport, schools, and its own law enforcement. It looks and feels like paradise.

Aides welcome Gene and collect his luggage. They escort him to his quarters and offer whatever he'd like in the way of food, drink, and companionship. They inform him that they'll take him to the Winthrop estate at 6:45 p.m. While this family has always been kind and supportive of Gene, they make it clear that Gene is their employee. He works for the Federal Reserve Bank. They are owners. They are, therefore, in a social class and standing superior to Gene.

Gene settles into his quarters and lays out his papers. He connects to the internet and begins making phone calls from his satellite phone. Gene's phone is of military quality. He can be reached anywhere in the world at any time.

#

There's a knock on the door at 6:45 p.m. Gene opens the door to see a young man who announces it's time to leave. They ride in a golf cart to one of the family's homes.

Gene is escorted to the library and told to wait. He's familiar with the routine. He wonders how many times they'll remind him that the family is a direct descendant of John Winthrop who founded the Massachusetts Bay Colony in the late 1600s. He served as its first governor. To hear the family tell it, America wouldn't exist without their contributions.

Twenty minutes later, Edward "Ned" Winthrop arrives to greet him. Gene thinks back to previous visits. He believes that Ned has always kept him waiting in this same spot for twenty minutes.

There will be fourteen for dinner, including Gene. Ned likes to have family members speak directly with Gene about their ideas. Meeting with the entire family like this occurs once a year.

#

Dinner is served outdoors on a veranda overlooking the water at sunset. They sit at a table with six on either side and one at each end of the table. Gene sits in the middle of the table with his back to the water.

Conversation is all over the place and they cover many topics. All thirteen family members have strong opinions and different perspectives. No family member seems to agree with another on anything.

Gene prepares for these meetings by reviewing photographs and biographies of each person. Addressing them by name is a challenge. Eleven of the thirteen family members are women in their seventies and eighties. They bear a strong family resemblance and dress alike. Gene is never quite sure to whom he's speaking.

#

"Mr. O'Neil," a woman to Gene's left begins, "it occurs to me that things run more smoothly under monarchies. One clear voice with unquestioned authority may be better than everyone having a vote. Perhaps democracy has been a bad thing."

Gene nods his head respectfully.

"I mean," she continues, "think of how inefficiently the world runs today. We pay good money to get things done. Others are paying the same politicians to do the opposite. Politicians put money in their pockets and get rich, but nothing gets done. They blame their political opponents for the gridlock and tell us they need more money. We should just have a monarch or dictator. When we pay them, things get done." She looks again at Gene for an answer.

"Well," Gene begins. He'd prefer to not guess her name. "You have a point." Gene smiles, hoping that it will disarm his audience. "The system in democratic societies is grossly inefficient. It requires you to invest a lot of money to have influence. Keep in mind, however, that has been to our advantage. We have more money than anyone else—or you do, you have more money and, therefore, should be able to buy more influence." Gene realizes he may have offended his hosts by overstepping his bounds. He didn't mean to say "we." He's sure Ned caught it.

Gene continues, "Now it's important for the shareholders to unite with a clear vision of what they want to accomplish. I'll get these politicians to fall in line. What I really need from you are your thoughts on our proposed agenda."

"Well, I think everyone should return to monarchies," she repeats. "Then, we'll only have to pay one person and we know things will get done. That's my vote."

#

The woman sitting directly across from Gene has been waiting her turn. She begins, "In terms of priorities, I feel we all need to love one another. We must draw closer together. All human beings need to unite under God and with the understanding that there is only one God. All these other quasi-religions need to stop preaching Muhammad or Buddha or Jews. The world needs one religion so that we can all move forward together with a common understanding of what's truly important."

Gene had hoped this year's visit would be different. He'll spend the evening sitting quietly and listening to each person's thoughts. They may not make sense. They may not be actionable by the bank. The good news for Gene is that he'll return to the United States tomorrow and spend the weekend with his wife.

"I know what I want," another woman takes her turn. "I want the United States to be a stronger leader, to be respected in the world again and to maintain a consistent foreign policy. I want them to stop letting the Russians and Chinese do whatever they want. And the Middle East? You Americans elect presidents that are either too weak or too aggressive. You change presidents and the world waits to see what American foreign policy will be. Countries test your presidents to see what they can get away with. One president claimed to have proof of weapons of mass destruction when he didn't and invaded a sovereign country. That was the worst thing you could have done. Another drew a line in the sand and countries walked all over it because they didn't respect him. You allowed terrorists to take over oil fields that generated millions of dollars of cash each day. You sold uranium to Russia and gave seven billion dollars of untraceable cash to Iran. Iran buys that uranium with that money and trades with North Korea. Both countries get raw material and technology. How much did your president get in kickbacks from all that cash? God sakes, your baby boomer presidents have been catastrophes. Build a strong military and stick with a foreign policy that your allies and enemies all know and understand."

#

In the morning, Ned arrives at Gene's quarters with an assistant. They load Gene's belongings into a limousine and drive to the airport.

"Thank you for making the trip," Ned begins. "I appreciate your meetings with the family. They enjoy talking with you."

"Not at all, Ned. I always enjoy spending time with you and your family."

"Well, I know they must seem like a handful, but they are wonderful people. Big hearts and good ideas too, I think." Ned is showing his age. He is eighty-four years old. "What do you think of them, Gene?"

"I think your family members are creative and broad minded," Gene answers. "As I've told you, however, before we get together at the next shareholders meeting, I need to know if you support our agenda. Your family has wonderful ideas, but they're not actionable by the bank. Religion, monarchies all very interesting, but not anything to do with the bank's charter."

Both men are frustrated. Ned has come to previous meetings with a list of concerns deemed unworthy of discussion by the larger group. His family is unable to contribute in any meaningful way. It's a difficult pill to swallow for a proud family.

"Ned, I understand that the world is a very different place than the one you grew up in. Things are changing. I'm sorry that the other shareholders have a different view of where we should focus our efforts."

Ned raises his eyebrows and shakes his head. He has a tear in his left eye.

Gene re-introduces another topic, "Perhaps it's time to reconsider what we've talked about. Maybe your family would prefer to sell their shares in the bank. I can work with you to set up a trust fund. It would provide anything your family members desire during their lifetime. It would provide donations to all the causes that your family cares so deeply about. Gifts would continue for many years after your death. I'm talking about education, the arts, and medical research. It would preserve your family name forever."

Ned nods his head. "Maybe we've come to that."

The two men are standing beside Gene's plane. Gene puts his left hand on Ned's right shoulder as they shake hands. "The reason I raise this issue again is your family looks up to you. Should anything happen to you, I don't know how they'll make decisions. We should take steps now and do what's best for them while we can."

"Give me time to think it over. This is hard. You have to understand our family history. We founded the Massachusetts Bay Colony. The United States has depended on us. Selling shares would mark the end of our involvement, our leadership."

Gene nods his head, "I understand. The country owes your family an enormous debt. Thank you again for your hospitality. I enjoyed seeing you all."

"Have a safe flight," Ned replies.

Gene was not expecting anything from the family on this trip. The fact that they may be willing to sell their shares is enormously significant. In the history of the bank, no one has sold shares. Now, two families could do so.

He boards his jet. Next stop is Charleston, South Carolina.

18

Boston, Massachusetts

Teresa has been saying she needs new jeans. Jack has objected because he loves the way she looks in her jeans. He's joked about coming up with a mathematical formula to describe the perfection of her ass.

"Let's go shopping," she says. "It'll be fun."

He doesn't like to shop. "Why not just order them from your guy?" Jack asks.

"My guy?" she answers. "Who's my guy?"

"You know, your guy, your tailor, whoever does your clothes," Jack explains.

"Oh my God, do you have a guy Jacky?"

He smiles and shakes his head.

She's just getting started. "Just how far up that skinny little ass of yours is that silver spoon? I guess it must be way up there." She grabs his ass.

"How about if we just go online?" he asks. "My treat." He'd prefer to get some schoolwork done. He'd prefer anything to shopping.

"Don't be silly. We could go to the mall, but since you're such a silver spoon, I'll take you to where my dad goes. You'll see. They're jeans. You have to try them on. You can't do that on the internet."

He agrees to go. He wants to spend time with her.

#

They take her car to East Boston, past a yard where containers from cargo ships are stored along the waterfront. They make their way to a warehouse with no signs. Teresa recognizes a man at the door and he buzzes her in. She gets a hug and he asks, "How you doing, Honey? How's Rock?"

She answers, "I'm good. He's great, thanks. How are you?"

Jack gets a cold reception from the man.

"Who's Rock?" Jack asks.

"That's my dad. It's his nickname from high school, built like a rock."

There are tables and large boxes overflowing with merchandise. Sneakers, sunglasses, umbrellas, raincoats, and more. There's a pallet with a large pile of new Nike T-shirts. A sign written with magic marker says '$4.00 a shirt.'

Teresa reaches the area for women's jeans. There are several tables with piles of jeans.

"This is crazy," Jack says. "These prices are great. How is this even possible? Four dollars for a Nike shirt, ten for sneakers? Maybe I should pick up some things?"

"This stuff fell off a truck," she explains. "That's why it's so cheap." She collects four pairs of jeans and begins walking towards the dressing rooms.

"Fell off a truck? Don't you just put them back on the truck?" he asks.

"Figure of speech. It means all this stuff was stolen by the guys operating the trucks or the ships or the guys unloading the containers. They take a piece for themselves. It's part of the cost of getting stuff from somewhere else here. They keep some and sell it. Cash only. Capiche?" This is a lesson taught to her by her father.

He's struggling with the idea that she's buying stolen merchandise. He's also realizing that he needs to learn more about the real world.

He stands still.

"What's wrong?" she asks.

"Who does this?"

"You mean the guy that buzzed us in?" Teresa replies. "His name is Don Giatrelis. He's a cop, works for the city. He's on disability. Been on disability as long as I've known him."

"That's not what I meant. It's not right to pay people for stealing stuff. It rewards them, encourages them, like we're an accomplice to a crime. This stealing must raise the costs for everyone else." Jack doesn't want to offend her, but he can't support it.

She looks disappointed and responds harshly. "It's easy to be high-minded when you just plunk down your black credit card for anything you want. The rest of us look for deals and ways to get by. We can't afford to act like you." She twirls around with her hair flying and stomps off to the dressing rooms.

He feels badly and retreats to the exit.

#

Twenty-five minutes go by before Teresa appears. She's not carrying anything.

"I'm sorry," Jack says.

"Don't be," she answers. "You're right. I didn't mean to criticize you. Buying from them is not stealing technically, but it's not right either. I guess I never thought it through or didn't want to think about it." She pauses before adding, "So, I'm sorry."

They walk out together. Teresa waves to Mr. Giatrelis and he lets them out.

"Who keeps an eye on you?" she asks.

"What do you mean?"

"Well, you kept me from doing something wrong. Who makes sure you don't do anything wrong?" she asks.

He smiles. "I don't know. I guess no one now. My mom when I was little."

"Well, you have someone now," she says. "How about you keep an eye on me and I'll keep an eye on you? We'll keep each other from doing anything wrong?"

"Best offer I've ever had," he answers.

A simple promise, but one that implies they'll be together to fulfill it.

19

Charleston, South Carolina

Grace O'Neil enjoys spending time in Charleston, South Carolina. She traced her family history back to the city. Her relatives often talked about their roots in the Deep South, even if they didn't have any proof of it.

Grace hired a historian to authenticate the family history. Sure enough, the historian was been able to connect Grace to several highly respected families. Gene is sceptical. His view is that you just have to pay enough money to the right historian to create the past you'd like.

Grace bought a home in Charleston's most prestigious neighbourhood. The home features traditional antebellum architecture. She put together a team that included members of the historical society to bring the house back to its glory. The renovations were massive. Master artisans were hired to perform as much of the construction as possible by hand. They used tools from the time period of the original construction.

#

When Gene arrives at the house, he has to look twice. He's unsure if he's at the correct address.

Grace waves to him from the front door.

"It's really beautiful honey," he tells her.

Grace kisses him and takes him by the hand. "I think you're going to love it," she says.

She gives him a tour of the house. She loves explaining the details behind the work done and believes her ancestors would be pleased.

While Grace appreciates that the cost was significant, the subject doesn't come up. The couple hasn't talked about money in years.

While walking up the main staircase, Grace stops to point out a portrait she had done of her mother. Gene admires it before asking, "Is there a painting of you anywhere in here?"

"No, nothing of me." While she would like to have that done, she feels awkward initiating it.

"I think that would be appropriate," he comments, and makes a mental note to take care of it.

"I did have a portrait done of my ancestor Colonel Anderson. It's in the library. I told you my family fought in the War Between the States. The archives proved it," Grace says proudly.

"You have told me that."

"We should do the same kind of research on your family," Grace suggests. "Understand more about your family history."

"No. No need of that. I understand they escaped Ireland during the potato famine and were just glad to get to America. Find survival and then opportunity. If they fought in that war it was likely against their will."

Gene's mother told him of an ancestor who was killed during the rioting that broke out when immigrants were rounded up and forced to fight for the North. He figures there's no need to research that further.

#

They enjoy a relaxing dinner in downtown Charleston. He answers two phone calls during the meal. These interruptions used to annoy Grace. She's come to accept that everything in life has a price. The price of her lifestyle—including the Charleston home—is sharing Gene's time.

When they return home, they discover the electricity has gone out. Gene asks, "Did you have one of those generators from the 1700s installed somewhere around here?"

She thought she'd planned for everything. Storms track up the Carolina coast out of Florida and this may be common. She'll have a generator installed.

"Do you want to get a hotel room?" he asks.

"No, we have candles. Let's climb under the blankets together."

As they prepare for bed she asks, "I've been meaning to ask you about your comments over dinner with the boys. You said some clash was coming and you wanted the boys close to you. The more I've thought about it, the more ominous it sounded."

Gene doesn't talk business, but this involves their sons. "Powerful forces are at odds with one another right now. It's unclear how it will all play out. Negotiating a compromise will be a challenge and the stakes are high. I want our sons to understand how the world works, to be prepared for the worst and for when I'm gone."

"When you're gone? What are you talking about? We're going to enjoy many years together in retirement. You promised you'd retire. You once told me that sixty would be a good time to retire. Do you remember telling me that?"

"I remember," he answers. "I don't plan on dying at my desk like some men, but people are living longer and working longer. I've seen families accumulate wealth over generations that dwarfs everyone else. I want our sons to build on what we've started. Think of how blessed we've been and how much we've been able to help others." Gene is referring to the many millions of dollars they've donated to charity.

"It is in giving that we receive," Grace says. "I understand and I believe in giving. I don't understand why we have to do it anonymously. We're judged in our social circle by how much we give away. It raises our standing. I hate it when others put their names to their contributions and flaunt it. We're giving a lot more than them, but I can't tell anyone."

Gene doesn't respond. He believes it's not giving if done for another reason.

"Promise me something," Grace says.

"What's that?"

"Two things, actually. First, promise me that you won't work too much longer and that we come up with a date for your retirement," she says. "Later than you first planned, but let's set a date. Second, promise me that you'll be sensitive about Jack. He's not you. Promise me that you're not going to push Jack into something that's not right for him. His ability to cope with the world could slip backwards again. I couldn't bear that."

"I promise to look out for him. You can trust me on that."

"And a retirement date," Grace adds to make sure she's clear, "without a satellite phone. I love you. Goodnight."

20

New York, New York

Gene returns to New York. His partners at Morgan Sachs have been getting anxious about the news he's provided about the Federal Reserve and the president.

The term "partner" is no longer accurate at Morgan Sachs, but it's still the way that these executives refer to one another. For most of the bank's history, it was a partnership. Individual partners were personally liable for the debts of the partnership. They could be sued for the mistakes made by one another. The bank didn't take on a lot of risk because partners could lose everything, including their homes and savings. They operated in a traditional role of banker by providing services for a fee.

Gene began work at the bank right out of college. He became a partner in just eight years, one of the fastest partner tracks in the bank's history.

Fourteen years later, the partnership changed its legal status to a corporation. That meant two monumental changes. First, partners were no longer personally liable for the mistakes by another partner. The bank could be sued, but the personal assets of the partners were no longer at risk. Secondly, the corporation could issue ownership shares of stock to the public.

The bank went public in what is known as an Initial Public Offering ("IPO"). The shares of stock that Gene had accumulated were worth over $1 billion. He had been doing very well with his salary and annual bonuses. The IPO created a large windfall for him, with tax benefits.

The bank began taking a lot more risks. They were no longer risking their own wealth: they were risking other people's money (referred to as "OPM" on Wall Street).

Prior to the IPO, retiring partners were turning over their ownership share to younger men in a slow, orderly manner. These transitions had been going on since the bank's founding. Partners could have done an IPO at any time in the bank's history, but chose not to. It was viewed as a betrayal of their core values. The IPO caused a split within the bank between young and old. Personal relationships among partners ended bitterly.

Gene felt conflicted. He sympathized with the older partners and was grateful for what they built. He recommended that the younger men set aside "a few billion dollars" for the older men and their heirs. The younger partners never considered it.

Gene put forty percent of his shares into a charitable trust. He asked older partners to serve on the board of his trust. In that way, money could be directed to their favourite causes.

The older partners recognized and appreciated Gene's actions. They began directing clients and business to Gene. It was also a backhanded way of taking business away from the others who treated them poorly.

The bank had to go public. All of its competitors had transitioned from partnerships to corporations. It was the only way to compete in the global economy.

#

At 9 a.m. Monday morning, Gene meets with the executive leadership team. There are seven people in this group. David Sandler is the bank's CEO and is the public face of the bank. He is a member of this team and directs these meetings. He is no more senior in rank than any one of the others. Gene is a member of the group.

Gene enters the room and takes his customary seat around a small conference table. This meeting occurs every other week at this time. Following the meeting is another meeting with approximately one hundred managing directors. The men and women that run each of the bank's operating units are present for that meeting.

David Sandler begins the meeting by going through the highlights of the bank's most recent results. He covers their assets, operating results, and "valuations at risk." Nothing is particularly unusual this day. Major currencies are trading within predictable ranges. The bank's capital and reserve requirements are adequate given their risk models. Revenues and operating expenses are running close to budget. Fifteen minutes go by before David pauses and asks if there are any questions. There aren't any.

He moves on, "Ok, then, Gene, can you give us an update on what's been going on and your insight into what's next?"

Gene uses these meetings to keep the bank's leadership informed. He explains the status of negotiations and the lack of progress with the president. He also explains the position of the shareholders and their unwillingness to accept further delays. He outlines in broad terms the options being considered by the shareholders.

Henry Lodge is the oldest member of the executive leadership group. He asks, "Gene, is there any way that the president or congressional leaders will view Morgan Sachs negatively based on your role with the bank?"

"I don't think so, but it could be an issue for some," Gene answers. "You know that someone from our bank has held my position for decades. Overall, it's been a very good thing for this bank. I don't think we'd want to lose my spot."

David Sandler is very supportive of Gene. Knowledge on Wall Street is power. Gene's insight into the Fed has meant knowing things before his competitors.

Brad Nardella, the bank's chief operating officer, is another member of the group. He asks, "Gene, should things start to go badly, then you'll let us know in advance, won't you? By that I mean we may have certain holdings that we'd prefer to liquidate in advance of any serious drop in prices."

Nardella often disappoints the group. Rather than understand the significance of these issues, he's most concerned about his own investments.

David responds, "Brad, you might think of this differently. There are going to be many opportunities for profitable trading for you—and for your clients. Gene will keep us informed. I don't think we want to get into any more details at this time."

David is concerned about how much information Gene shares. If things go badly, then members of this group may need to testify before

Congress. It's best to leave some things unsaid. David and Gene speak frequently and privately. Neither man trusts email.

21

Scituate, Massachusetts

Teresa and Jack wake up together on a Sunday morning in March. The temperature is expected to reach the mid-70s. They have no plans and each one asks the other, “What do you want to do?”

It’s likely there will be more weeks of cold temperatures before winter is over. Teresa wants to get outside and enjoy the weather.

“We could go to South Boston and watch the Saint Patrick’s Day parade,” she suggests.

Jack appears deep in thought. He’s not saying anything.

“No, not more schoolwork,” she begs.

“No. I want to take you somewhere,” he says.

“Really? Where?”

“You’ll see when we get there,” he answers.

Jack drives since only he knows where they’re going.

She loves surprises. She starts asking questions until Jack reveals more information. He begins sharing more than ever before.

“You know I grew up in New York, right?” he begins. She nods yes. “Well, I have a great uncle who lives in Scituate, Massachusetts. My mom and dad used to send me and my brother there each summer. It’s south. I mean Scituate is south of Boston, about 40 minutes from here.” Teresa has heard of the town, but never been there.

"Anyway," Jack continues, "I'd spend time with my aunts, uncles, and cousins. Mostly I'd spend time with my Uncle Dave. He was always good to me and I loved coming here. He took me out to Yellowstone and Yosemite, the national parks." Teresa likes that Jack's been becoming more and more talkative.

His driving makes her nervous. "You do have a license, Jacky, right?" she asks.

Jack keeps talking. "Me and him camped out a few times, out there in the parks. He used to say that Europe might have the Louvre, the Parthenon, Sistine Chapel, whatever, but America has this. He figured we were better off. We have this unspoiled magnificence all around America. He loved the outdoors. You'd agree if you ever went with him. I'd like to get back there. Nature will touch your soul."

"Maybe we could go there," Teresa suggests. "You can show me. So, he's your great uncle. How's that work, I mean, which side of the family?"

"He's my father's, father's brother, or the brother of my grandfather on my father's side." Jack struggles with the car's directional signals as he exits the highway. More than half of the trip will be on back roads. Jack continues providing more background. "My uncle taught at M.I.T. He's been retired a long time now."

"M.I.T. again huh? So, he's another geek. Is that what you're telling me? You're from a long line of geeks?" Teresa is enjoying the drive and the sunshine. She has her window down and her head is part way out. Her hair is flying in the wind.

"No, nothing like that. Not too many geeks. Uncle Dave used to say that M.I.T. hired him because they thought they were getting someone like his brother, my grandfather. People have always told me that he was a really smart guy." Jack is looking around at the new stores along the route and points. "A lot of this is new, in the past four or five years I mean."

"My God, it's a beautiful day," Teresa says. "So, we're going to meet your great uncle. Did you tell him we're coming?"

"No." Jack looks down at his phone and considers calling. "I don't think he gets out much. He should be there. If not, I can introduce you to others, or we just go to the beach, lighthouse, or get lunch if you want. Are you ok missing your family dinner this week?"

"Yes, one week isn't a big deal. So, there's more than just an old uncle."

The roads are getting narrower with sharp turns.

"Jacky, you know you only get half the road, right?"

"I like my half in the middle," he answers with a smile. He follows that up quickly with, "I'm sorry. I'll be more careful. Yeah, my dad also has a sister and a brother who live there too. My dad built a house next to Uncle Dave for them. It's nice. You'll see."

"This story keeps getting bigger and bigger, Jacky." She pulls her head inside the car and begins looking through her bag. She wants to fix herself up before meeting anyone. "Jacky, you can't do this. You have to tell me when we're meeting people and especially family." She looks in the mirror. "Oh my God, I look like shit. They're going to think you found me on the side of the road."

"They're not 'people' they're family," Jack replies. "My dad has an older brother Steve or Stevie, and an older sister Connie. Stevie has intellectual disabilities. Aunt Connie and her husband, Tom Murray, care for him. They have two boys of their own. I mean, Connie and Tom do. Connie has looked after Stevie forever. My dad helps with money and Connie looks after him." Jack stops at a red light. "Confused?" Jack asks as he takes his hands off the steering wheel and stretches.

"No, I'm following," she answers while putting on mascara. "Intellectual disabilities? You know I'm taking courses and I'd like to teach. I've thought about teaching special education."

"Yeah, I know. My folks started a charity," Jack says. "Stevie and others go to a place every day to learn social skills, real world stuff, and it provides them with work. Local companies hire them to file stuff, stock shelves, do mailings, whatever."

Teresa is focused on making herself look better. "I would have put on something much nicer than this." Teresa means her T-shirt and jeans. "I love surprises, but you have to tell me if the surprise involves meeting people." She wants to add, "What is the matter with you?" but doesn't.

"You look great," Jack assures her. "Really, you always look so beautiful."

God, he's hard to be mad at, she thinks.

#

As they drive over a hill, the ocean comes into view directly in front of them. They smell the salt air and see seagulls flying overhead. The temperature is in the mid 70s. It feels liberating after having spent most of the past four months indoors.

The town of Scituate is a small town well off the beaten path. It's known as the "Irish Riviera" because a large number of Boston's Irish population migrated here as soon as they could afford to move out of the city.

Jack slows down on the main road before turning. "Years ago, these were all summer homes," Jack says while pointing. "They've been 'winterized' and so there are more 'year rounders' now. It's a term Uncle Dave uses to describe people. I think he liked it more when the summer people left after Labour Day."

Jack turns left onto a side street. They pass five homes on each side of the road. They're small, approximately 1,400 square feet each. On the left side of the road is a large home. It's got a circular drive and doesn't appear to fit with the others. Jack pulls in the driveway.

#

Jack escorts Teresa to the front door and rings the doorbell. A woman in her sixties answers the door. Aunt Connie immediately gives Jack a big hug. "Jacky, Jacky, Jacky, so good to see you. We miss you around here. You look good." Connie has an obvious soft spot for Jack. "Why didn't you call? Tommy and the boys will be upset they missed you. And what is this you brought with you?"

Jack introduces Teresa. Connie reaches out to shake Teresa's hand.

"I'm sorry Aunt Connie," Jack says, "We just kind of took a ride out of Boston and ended up here."

Connie and Teresa introduce themselves.

Jack asks, "Is anyone else here?"

"Well, the boys are at the parade, obviously." Connie looks at Teresa, "St. Pat's, ya know," thinking she might need to explain. "Tom went out to run errands. Likely got a little side-tracked." Connie rolls her eyes and motions her hand to her mouth, pretending to drink a beer.

"You have a beautiful home," Teresa says.

"Come in, come in, you haven't seen anything," Connie instructs as she begins pushing them down a hallway and into a large room. It's a combined kitchen and family room with high ceilings. There's a fireplace, sky lights, and sliding doors that lead out to a deck. About one hundred yards in front of them is a rocky beach and the Atlantic Ocean.

"Oh my God it's beautiful," Teresa says.

"It's nice. It's nice," Connie says. "We like it. Thanks to Gene."

Teresa notices that Connie seems to repeat herself and talks very fast.

"What can I get you?" Connie asks.

Jack smiles. All his memories of Aunt Connie involve her asking someone, "What can I get you?"

"Jacky, what can I get you? Answer me now," Connie says. "You're skin and bones boy. I've got corned beef and cabbage for the holiday. How's that sound? Good? Good? You go outside and say 'hi' to Stevie. He'll be glad to see you, and then fetch your Uncle Dave. We can all sit down to a meal good and proper." Connie has her arms out to the side as if to demonstrate that it's a wonderful idea and that's the end of it.

Teresa is enjoying the view of the ocean. There's a large grass lawn, pool, gardens, and an entertainment area surrounding a fire pit. A man in his 60s is pacing back and forth in the yard. This must be Stevie.

"Well, thanks Aunt Connie, I appreciate it, but I don't know," Jack replies. He's looking to Teresa to find out what she wants to do. Teresa is just staring outside.

"We had a big breakfast," Jack adds.

Teresa turns and raises her eyebrows at Jack's fib. "Well, our breakfast wasn't really that big Jacky," she teases. They haven't eaten anything and they've been keeping each other honest, even when it comes to little things.

"Ok, I'm going to say 'hi' to Stevie and we'll get Uncle Dave," Jack says. "Lunch sounds great and thank you."

Teresa follows him outside.

#

"Hi, Uncle Steve, how are you doing?" Jack asks.

Steve is five feet ten inches tall and weighs approximately two hundred pounds. His light brown hair needs to be combed. He's wearing a long-sleeved polo shirt and corduroy pants that need ironing. He doesn't maintain eye contact during conversation.

"Hi," Steve answers, followed by, "Good." Steve pauses before asking, "Who are you?" to Teresa.

"I'm Teresa," she answers.

"I'm Steve." He reaches out to shake Teresa's hand. "Are you Jack's girlfriend?"

"Yes, I am," she answers, followed by, "Has he brought a lot of girlfriends here?"

"Yes," Steve answers.

Teresa is surprised. "He has, huh?"

"No," Steve replies.

"It's a beautiful day, Uncle Steve," Jack states. "Have you been outside for long?"

"No, I don't think too long."

"Well," Jack says, "we're going to have lunch with you. We're going next door to see if Uncle Dave will join us. Do you want to come with us?"

"No," Steve answers. "I'm ok."

"Alright, we'll be back in a few minutes," Jack says.

Teresa and Jack walk next door.

#

"Oh, my gosh," Teresa says, "this is really nice. You can hear the waves crashing on the beach."

There's a small house next to Connie's home.

Jack smiles. "It is nice. We used to run up and down this street as kids. It dead ends at the water and there's no public parking. You never got much traffic."

They walk next door and ring the doorbell. They hear it ring inside but there's no response. They hear the telephone ring and answered. Jack turns to Teresa, "That's Connie calling to wake up Uncle Dave I bet." He adds, "Sorry about lunch. I mean, I didn't want to put you on the spot or make you stay if you didn't want to."

Teresa appreciates the fact that he cares enough to say it. "No, thanks, I'm glad to stay for lunch."

"I learned to ride a bicycle right here," Jack says, pointing.

"Was that last year?" Teresa jokes at every opportunity about Jack being younger than her.

The door opens. Uncle Dave opens his arms and hugs Jack. Dave stands about five foot eight and uses a walker. Seeing Jack brings a huge smile.

Jack begins, "It's good to see you Uncle Dave." Dave is slow to let go of Jack. "I have someone to introduce you to," Jack tells him.

Uncle Dave struggles to maintain his balance as he lets go of Jack. He extends his hand to Teresa. "Pleased to meet you, dear," he says. They go indoors.

The house is small, a two-bedroom cape. The bedrooms are upstairs to the left and right of the stairway. Windows sit in dormers upstairs. There's one full bathroom downstairs. The dining room has been turned into a bedroom so that Dave doesn't have to use the stairs.

Dave settles into a reclining chair in his living room.

Jack asks questions about Dave's health. Dave wants to know about Jack's studies.

Jack is standing, looking out a window. "Uncle Dave, what happened to the Esposito's house and the Finnegan house? They're gone."

Dave smiles, "Your Dad. He bought 'em. Tore 'em down. He wanted the family to have more room and a better view. Paid a lot I guess. That printing press of his is still going strong."

Teresa doesn't understand. Jack turns to her "When I was little, I asked Uncle Dave where all the money comes from. We seemed to have more than everyone else." Jack looks at his uncle, "He told me that my dad had a printing press. He just printed as much money as he needed."

Teresa's eyes widen. "I'd like to get one of those," she says.

Teresa and Jack take turns using the bathroom. Teresa goes first.

"She's very pretty," Dave states.

Jack seems pleased. "You think so?"

"I do. She's lovely, but it doesn't matter what me or anyone else thinks. Only matters what you think." Dave almost called him son. He caught himself, but he thinks of Jack as a son.

"You look good, Jack, so big and all grown up. No longer afraid of the dark anymore?" Dave asks. His mind is running through hundreds of memories. "Your folks would be so proud of you." Dave is thinking of Jack's grandparents.

Dave looks old and frail. It's hard for Jack to see him like this. Dave was a combination of father figure and best friend during his childhood.

"Can I get you anything?" Jack asks.

"No, no thank you," Dave answers.

"Have you read anything good lately?" Jack asks. Dave has been an avid reader his entire life.

"No. I suppose I've read everything there is to read. I've been watching a lot of television lately. News mostly." Jack notices thick eyeglasses on the coffee table.

There's a bond between the two. Just sitting together feels comforting to them both. When Jack was very young, he hardly spoke. They'd sit together quietly for extended periods of time. Both content.

#

It's Jack's turn to use the bathroom. Teresa sits briefly before her curiosity gets the better of her. She begins walking around the room, looking at the pictures on display.

"Can I get you anything?" Dave asks. It looks as though he's making a small effort to get up. She sees that it's not much of an effort, but appreciates his asking.

"No, thank you, sir. Nothing for me." She's looking at pictures lined up along the fireplace mantle. "This is your wife?" Teresa points to a large picture.

"It is. Love of my life." Dave smiles. "We were good together."

Teresa turns to Dave, "She's very pretty."

"Is this you?" Teresa is now pointing to a picture of a young man in uniform. "You were in the service?"

Dave nods his head again. "Yup, we were all in the service. The country called and we all signed up. Didn't matter how old you were or what you were doing."

Teresa notices a series of pictures, seven in all. They are in a long, vertical frame that could hold eight pictures. On the bottom is a picture of a young boy and older man sitting on a pier with fishing poles. The boy has a big smile and no front teeth. As you move up the series of pictures, the boy is getting bigger, growing up. They're in the same location and in the same pose. There's a tackle box and a bucket for the fish they catch. "Is this you?" she asks. She looks more closely and with some excitement asks, "Is this you and Jack?"

"Yup, that's us. Me and my buddy," Dave says. "We did a lot of fishing. Did a lot of everything. A lot of just hanging out together." After a few moments, Dave adds, "He's got the gift you know. Same gift his grandpa had. I've seen it. I know it."

Teresa doesn't know what he's talking about. She moves to another picture.

"Who's this?" Teresa is pointing to a picture of Jack, Uncle Dave, and another boy that's bigger than Jack.

"That's Jack's older brother Gene, Jr.," Dave answers. "There used to be a lot of boys on this road. JR was kind of a ringleader when he was around. The boys would spend all day at the beach, lighthouse, docks, wherever. They'd find mischief wherever they went. Kids' stuff ya know."

#

As Jack returns from the bathroom, Connie is coming through the front door. She announces that she's got the meal ready and orders them back to her house.

Teresa asks, "What can I do to help?"

"Nothing to do. Nothing to do. Just come on and make yourselves comfortable. Jack, help your uncle," Connie instructs. They make their way back to the house and enjoy a lovely meal together. Teresa fits in easily. She's interested in hearing more about the family and especially more about Jack. She finds an eager storyteller in Connie.

#

After dinner, they say their goodbyes. Connie tells them "Now don't be strangers. Come back soon. Come back soon, but give us some notice next time."

Teresa assures her they'll be back. She takes the keys from Jack.

"This was really great, Jacky," Teresa tells him. "Thank you so much for bringing me here. I loved it."

Jack doesn't say anything. He's thinking of Uncle Dave.

"So your father bought all this?" she asks.

"Yeah," Jacks answers. "Stevie is the oldest, then Connie, and then my dad. My dad's father died at a young age from a heart attack. My Grand-mother was a schoolteacher and gave piano lessons. Dad went to work on Wall Street after college and started sending money home, you know, to help."

Teresa is looking back and forth between the road and the ocean until she can no longer see the water.

Realizing that Uncle Dave may not have much time remaining, Jack considers when he might get back here again.

"So earlier," Teresa begins "you said something about your Uncle Dave taught at M.I.T. but they thought they were getting his brother. What did you mean?"

Jack clears his throat. "Well, my grandfather's name was Frank. He and Dave were both in the war. Uncle Dave fought on D-Day. There's not many of those guys around anymore. My granddad was put in this intelligence unit where they worked on cracking the German codes. The Germans sent out radio transmissions and our side had men trying to crack their code. The allies figured they needed a machine to crack the codes. People just couldn't do it in time. They invented the first computer. It cracked the German code. It must have been amazing. I imagine the machine was big and slow, but to be first had to be thrilling."

Jack stops the story to ask, "Did you get enough to eat?"

"Yeah, I'm stuffed," Teresa answers. "So that was your grandfather doing that?"

"Yup," Jack continues, "that's what he did. After the war, the United States government owns all this stuff, doesn't need it, and doesn't know what to do with it. My granddad comes home, starts a family, teaches at M.I.T. and starts a computer company. Dave used to say my granddad was the smartest guy he ever knew."

"Wow," Teresa says. "And he died at a young age."

"I guess he was complaining of chest pains," Jack answers. "He left work and went to the doctor's office. The doctor told him to take a couple aspirin and go home and rest. He goes home, lies down, and has a massive heart attack. He died a couple hours after seeing the doctor. My dad was the one that found him. Found him dead on the floor I mean. That must have been very hard."

There's a pause when neither says anything.

Teresa breaks the silence. "That picture of you and Dave. Those pictures of you guys together fishing; there are seven of them. How come you stopped? That frame still has one open spot."

Jack's face turns sad. "Uncle Dave was in the hospital that summer." Teresa notices Jack has tears in his eyes. Jack turns to his right to look away from her. "Uncle Dave was my best friend when I was a kid; only friend really. He used to tell me 'you've got it, Jacky. You got the gift your Grandpa had. You're gonna change the world.' He used to tell me that all the time. It made me feel better about myself. He made me believe that studying and hard work would pay off."

Teresa tries to comfort him. "That's great. He said that to me, but I didn't know what he was talking about. He must know better than anyone. I guess that means you will change the world."

"We'll see," Jack says. "My Grandpa led people. He led that team that created the first computer and he led people when he started a computer company. He was a natural born leader. JR's more like that than me."

Teresa reaches out and holds Jack's left hand. "You will," Teresa tells him. "You'll lead when your time comes."

22

New York, New York

Treasury Secretary Doug Martin requested a meeting with Gene. It's a follow up to his meeting with the president. He joins Gene in his office.

"Mr. Secretary," Gene offers a smile and a handshake to welcome his friend. "It's great to see you."

Doug is happy to be back on Wall Street and in the offices of Morgan Sachs. "Thank you for seeing me, Gene." They swap small talk about wives and family for several minutes.

"Gene, you caused quite a stir with the president at our last meeting. Leon updated the group and communicated your warning. I'm here on a reconnaissance mission to prep the president for your meeting at the fundraiser. What can you tell me?"

Gene has always appreciated Doug's straightforward approach.

"Well, what's going on is that some of us are growing impatient with the president and Congress," Gene answers. "When we funded the president's campaign, he made us promises about spending and borrowing. Now," Gene shrugs his shoulders, "I understand candidates lie, but they don't lie to me."

"Ok," Doug replies.

"I've been asking the president," Gene continues, "for help on this matter for years, and he continues to delay. He spends money in all sorts of ways with his real goal of just buying votes. His policies are killing American business, and he continues to borrow as if there are no consequences. The country needs an economic plan, and that plan needs to address the national debt. Maybe you can tell me, what's his plan?"

"I understand your point, but this isn't easy," Doug explains. "You know what he inherited. The Congress just—" Gene holds up his hand in a motion to stop. Doug is slightly offended. "Gene, seriously, the Congress—" but Gene puts up his hand again. An awkward silence ensues. As treasury secretary, Doug would prefer Gene not hold up his hand as a stop sign when he's talking.

"Doug," Gene begins, "we go back a long way. I like you. Always have. I wanted you in the Secretary's job. I'd like to have you join us here at the bank when you're done in Washington. I understand Congress is fucked up. I don't care. That's not my problem."

Doug nods his head.

Gene continues, "The president inherited challenges, but that was some time ago. He has brought most of these problems with Congress on himself. I simply don't care about guessing at who is more to blame than the other. It's not productive. I can't help you with your reconnaissance mission. Sharing information with you today would only put you in a more difficult position. I don't want to do that to you."

"I suppose I should say thank you," Doug answers. "The problem is that I can't go back empty handed. Can you tell me anything about how to prepare the president for your meeting?"

Doug looks tired. He was an all-American hockey player during college and has always kept himself in great condition. On this day, however, he looks tired. Gene figures the job is wearing on him.

"Maybe we can help each other," Gene offers. "Help me understand what's going on because I've never seen things so bad. The country has always had challenges, but people have pulled together to get things done for the good of the country. I don't see that anymore."

"I wouldn't have believed the dysfunction in Washington if I hadn't seen it with my own eyes." Doug shakes his head. "Political donations in exchange for favours have always existed. I get it, but it's gotten crazy. It's all that happens in Washington and money flows in on both sides. Congress creates a tax code and then corporations rush in to pay for loopholes. You know, it's all a scam for insiders to make money. There's no serious intellectual debate on priorities and problem solving. No one seems to care what's right or best for the country. This group can't solve the national debt; they can't solve anything and they don't even try. There's no plan for the debt." Doug spoke passionately and from the heart. He didn't expect to end with his last sentence.

Gene appreciates his honesty.

Doug has a great deal of respect for Gene. He may be a powerful figure on Wall Street but he's still just a banker. "I understand you're concerned. A lot of us are, but I don't understand where you're going with all this."

"Doug," Gene begins, "you should explain to the president that his line of credit is under review. He needs to get together with Congress and create a financial plan for the country. No more irresponsible spending and borrowing. I'd like to think we can control a good deal of what goes on, but events could quickly and easily spiral out of anyone's control."

"What do mean?" Doug asks. "If you don't want to lend us money, then there are plenty of other bankers and countries that will. I just don't see what you're trying to accomplish."

"Doug, please carry the message. Be clear with the president," Gene instructs.

A frustrated Doug tries one last time. "Gene, the president sent me here to get answers and specifics. I don't want to simply repeat Leon's warning about catastrophic consequences."

Gene stands and takes a step towards the door to communicate the end of this meeting. "Do your best. Carry the message and I'll provide specifics for the president when we meet at the fundraiser. Tell him changes are coming and the sooner he gets on board, the less painful it will be for everyone."

23

Boston, Massachusetts

On a quiet weekday evening, Jack receives a phone call from his mother. He's doing schoolwork at his desk. Teresa is lying on the couch watching television. "Hi, Mom," Jack answers.

Teresa is interested.

"I'm sorry about that, Mom but I've been really busy with everything." He follows that up with another, "I know, I'm really sorry, I'll do better."

Wow, Teresa thinks. She gets up and writes "Mama's Boy" on a sheet of paper in front of Jack.

Another pause before Jack says, "I think it's great that Dad wants me to come to the bank. I just don't think it's for me. I hope he understands." Jack is doing more listening than talking.

"I met a girl, Mom," Jack reveals to his mother.

Teresa's eyes light up.

"She's really great. You'd like her." Pause. "No, she's not a student here, she's from the area. We met at a party." More pauses. "Ok." Pause. "I understand." Again, Jack is quiet for long periods as his mother is doing the talking. The call ends with, "I love you too and I miss you. I'll do better about calling. Love to Dad too. See you soon."

Jack turns to see that Teresa has a big smile on her face.

"So, you told your mother about me," Teresa says.

"No. That? I was talking about another girl."
"What did she say? Is she happy for you?" Teresa is beaming.
"She says that she hopes we're practicing safe sex."

24

New York, New York

Gene is up and off to the gym for his morning workout. The sun rises a little earlier each morning this time of year.

He's on the treadmill for cardio work. The goal is to get his heart pumping at its maximum rate by working out hard for ninety seconds at a time. His trainer explains that "interval training" will lead to his body burning more calories throughout the day.

Gene completes the workout in twenty-four minutes. He's drenched in sweat and exhausted after his final push. He sits on the edge of the treadmill to catch his breath. He's not paying any attention to the words of encouragement from his trainer.

While Gene is looking down at the floor, a pair of black wingtip shoes appears. He looks up to see Bernie Schwartz standing in front of him.

"Good workout?" Bernie asks.

"Yes, good morning, Bernie."

"Twenty-five thousand dollars?" Bernie says in a disgruntled tone.

"Oh, yes, Bernie. Yes, I'd very much appreciate your presence at a dinner with the president," Gene answers with a sarcastic smile.

"Twenty-five thousand dollars," Bernie says again, followed by, "Can I pay fifty thousand not to come?"

“No, thank you Bernie and it’s fifty thousand dollars as we’d really like to have the pleasure of your wife’s company too. You two will sit with me and Grace so we can enjoy the evening together.”

Bernie lets out a deep breath to register his disgust. “You want us to bring our two dogs for another fifty thousand?”

25

Watertown, Massachusetts

Teresa gets two fifteen-minute breaks per day at her job. She finds the timekeeping part of her job odd. She can spend eight hours a day and not accomplish anything; that's acceptable. Coming in late or leaving early, however, gets you called into your supervisor's office. You could be the most productive person in the office and it doesn't matter. Everyone knows today's government is broken, but nothing is ever done about it. If her group is unproductive then the solution is to hire more people.

She walks one block to a pharmacy during lunch. She picks up a pregnancy kit and returns to work. Her body knows it before the test confirms a positive result. She spends the rest of the day trying to control her emotions and thinking about next steps.

She's not ready to talk with Jack or her mother. Her best friend is Molly McCann, but they haven't been speaking much lately. Molly is close with the circle of friends that includes her former boyfriend Roberto.

#

Teresa texts Molly and asks if they can get together tonight.

Teresa goes to the McCann house that evening. She's been coming here since the two were in kindergarten together. After saying "Hi" to the family, Teresa and Molly go upstairs. Teresa flops on Molly's bed. Before she knows it, her emotions begin pouring out of her. She tells Molly that she's fallen in love, she's pregnant, and Jack will likely want nothing to do with her.

"You remember Katy Federico from school?" Molly asks. "She had an abortion. Told me all about it. She went to the clinic on Commonwealth Avenue. The government paid for it all. Go down there. They'll take care of everything. It's your body, your choice."

Molly cracks a window open slightly and lights a cigarette. She pulls a chair over to the window and holds the cigarette outside.

"I don't know," Teresa says.

Molly's thinking, *Wait until everyone hears this. Roberto is going to freak out. He's been telling people that Teresa is going to come crawling back to him. He'll want to kill this new guy.*

"Terri, what do you want to do?" Molly asks Teresa. "What's in your heart? Do you want the kid? If this guy marries you and has money or a job, then that would work. If he doesn't have money or you're not getting married, then you're going to have to rely on the government. In that case you'll want to have more kids, like four. The more kids, the more money from the government, and easier it is on you."

Molly is trying to comfort Teresa, but it's having the opposite effect. Molly continues, "Government pays rent, food, all your healthcare, they'll pay your heat in the winter. They'll give you an allowance for clothes. They pay for cars, gas, your cell phone. It's all based on the number of kids you have. You gotta learn to take advantage of the system."

"I don't know," Teresa answers. "Have children just to get money from the government? I'd be dependent on the government, other people. I don't want to get on a track where I'm relying on someone else and a burden on others. That would feel so weird."

"Course the guy should be forced to pay child support," Molly continues. "It's the same guys causing these pregnancies because they don't like using condoms. Everyone else pays for their children's upbringing. They should be forced to pay. DNA test ya' know and jail if they don't pay. That would stop the pregnancies and save taxpayers a fortune."

"The government would pay for everything wouldn't they?" Teresa asks.

"Of course, they would. Government pays everything. You've seen it." Molly lights up another cigarette. "They're all around. Mary McGee has three kids now and what's she, 22 years old? She moved out of her parent's house. She began renting but the government says she should have her own home. They gave her a mortgage and she doesn't have a job. Her new boyfriend moved in with her so he's living rent free. Not supposed to, but you could do that. You gotta learn how to get the most out of the system. There's a Muslim family here now right down the street. They're new citizens. The guy has three wives, ten kids, and the government pays him like $180 thousand per year. Free money and he's never even had a job in this country. That's how it works."

Teresa knows the statistics from her work at the State. Over ninety percent of the poorest Americans come from families with unwed mothers. The cycle of welfare goes on for generations. On that track, her children have a greater chance of going to prison than college.

The two talk for hours. Molly keeps coming back to the question, "What do you want to do?" She tells Teresa that she doesn't have to tell anyone for a while. She needs to figure it out for herself first.

#

Teresa's thoughts continuously return to Jack. She's worried that Jack won't want anything to do with her. He just started having sex and a girlfriend for the first time. He's enjoying himself and can't get enough. He'll want to date other girls. She's got nothing to offer.

#

Teresa knows in her heart what she wants. She tells her mother of the pregnancy the next day. She tells her all about Jack and their relationship.

Mary's not surprised about Teresa's feelings. She's seen a noticeable change in her daughter.

"Have you told him yet?" Mary asks.

"No," Teresa answers.

"What's he going to say?"

"I don't know, Mom."

Mary nods. "You'll need a lot of help with or without him. We'll raise the child and give it all the love and support it needs." She pauses before adding, "You go talk to him, huh?"

Teresa nods and adds, "Yuh."

"Whatever he says," Mary adds, "everything will be ok. You'll be ok," Mary states strongly. "The baby will be ok. We'll raise him here. Love. Values. Christian."

"I think the state," Teresa begins, "offers money or support programs to young mothers to help with expenses. It's something I could look into."

"No," Mary replies. "Why would you do that? We work for what we've got. We're not like those who aren't willing to work. That's no way to live. They have no pride and feel no shame. No," she shakes her head.

The challenge is breaking the news to Teresa's father. Mary suggests that they invite Jack to a Sunday dinner. It will provide an opportunity to introduce the two men. There will be no talk of the pregnancy. They'll enjoy a nice meal and the two can get know one another.

"Are you sure? Teresa asks.

"Sure," Mary answers, "how bad could it get?"

26

New York, New York

Gene arranges a video conference call with the five leaders of the shareholders. "Thank you for joining me on such short notice," he begins. "I have news that I wanted to share with you. I met with the Winthrop family following our meeting in London. I have been suggesting to Ned for some time that it might be in his family's best interest to sell their shares in the bank. I spoke with him this morning. He'd like to begin the process."

"That's great," David Rockefeller responds excitedly. "What do you have in mind and how would it impact our acquisition of the Kuhn family shares?"

"Good questions," Gene answers. "While I've made progress on the Kuhn transaction, it could still get messy because the family doesn't have anyone with the capacity to understand it all."

"They used to think," William Vanderbilt begins, "that marrying cousins off to one another would make them stronger and keep their ownership shares limited to a very small number. They were nuts."

Gene continues, "My approach is to acquire the Winthrop shares at a low number and use that transaction as proof that it's fair market value in any dispute with the Kuhns. We buy out the shares from the two families for a total of only $400 billion."

"That's absurdly low," Madeline Rothschild answers. "Do you think Ned will accept only $200 billion for their shares?"

"I do," Gene answers. "I think I can get him to agree to it. They have no heirs and their existing net worth is already enormous. It's all going to be gifted to others. Ned is even concerned that the size of their gifts may look unseemly. I'll get that deal done and then I'll use that value to get the Kuhn transaction done. I'll have the trust agreements governing everything updated. I'm good with trusts."

David speaks up again, "That's great. How would we finance this?"

"I suppose it doesn't really matter when you think about it. I'm thinking half in cash and half in a note from the Federal Reserve for bookkeeping purposes. I can take care of the details," Gene answers.

James Loeb asks, "So each of the remaining five families gets an increase in their ownership from over fourteen percent to twenty percent. Do I understand that correctly?"

"Well," Gene begins carefully, "you'll recall that I was supposed to receive some interest in the bank if I could get the Kuhn transaction done. I was hoping this group would also consider some portion of the Winthrop transaction now as well."

"You're talking getting ownership shares for yourself, Gene? We're back to that topic again?" Peter Morgan asks. He's clearly annoyed.

"What do you have in mind?" David Rockefeller asks.

"Ten percent," Gene replies. He knows that you don't get if you don't ask.

"Whoa, Gene, ten percent? You can't be serious," David protests. "We all know the value of these shares. I know you're good at what you do and this is great news but ten percent is outrageous. You're just managing things for us after all."

"Yes, David, I'm managing things," Gene answers sternly. "I'm creating wealth. I'm getting you shares at a huge discount and I'm putting myself in personal jeopardy with the president of the United States."

Gene's last remark stops the conversation.

After several uncomfortable moments of silence, Maddy speaks up. "Gene, I think this is a conversation we should have among the five shareholders. We'll discuss it. I'll get back to you. It's in all our best interest to make sure you're properly compensated. We greatly appreciate what you're doing for us and we understand the risks you're taking. We'll leave things at that for now and thank you for the update with the Winthrops. You're doing a great job and we appreciate it."

27

Boston, Massachusetts

Jack's been texting Teresa about when they'll see each other again. Teresa has avoided him for a couple days. She calls to say she'll come over to his apartment this evening.

They sit on the couch together. She's pictured some very negative outcomes to the conversation they're about to have.

She looks in Jack's eyes and tells him she's pregnant. There's no reaction, but that's not uncommon for him. He seems to be processing the information. Seconds pass that feel like minutes. *He's not going to want anything to do with me*, she thinks. She's quickly losing control of her emotions.

"What are you thinking?" he asks.

"I'm going to have the baby."

Jack continues to show no emotion. Teresa's heart sinks.

She puts her hands over her face and leans forward. Her head is down to the top of her knees. Tears well up in her eyes.

"Ya think we should get married?" he asks.

Her emotions prevent her from thinking clearly. *Did he just say marriage?* she thinks.

"Well, this is ok," he concludes. "Maybe we should get a place together, I guess. Right? Is that what you think? Maybe that's what we should talk about." He seems calm, not especially happy, but calm and rational. "That would give us time. I mean time to be together. Time to get ready for the baby."

She sits up and looks at him. She's fighting back tears. "You're not mad at me?" she asks. "You're not running for the door?"

"Mad? Um no, not mad. Shaken. Surprised. Not mad. Kind of out of the blue, ya know?" Jack answers.

Jack wants to ask why birth control didn't work. He figures it's best to ask that question later.

Teresa needs to keep talking, to get more from Jack. "You're not mad?"

He shakes his head, "No, I'm not mad."

"Jack, I love you," Teresa says. "Not because of this. I really love you."

Their first 'I love you.' Jack says it too. They comfort each other. They'll consider getting a place together. They'll hold off on talk of marriage. She invites Jack to Sunday dinner at her family's home.

Jack doesn't consider discontinuing his education. There has always been enough money for everything. They'll get a place together and his life and studies will go on uninterrupted. He thinks of the graduate students that he's seen around campus with their children. That doesn't look so bad.

28

New York, New York

The Dean of the Harvard Business School, Heather Douglas, scheduled a phone call with Gene. The two know each other well.

The conversation begins with each asking about the other's spouse. Heather thanks Gene for his very thoughtful anniversary gift. Gene sends a card each year to commemorate the dean's promotion to her position. The card includes tickets to Wimbledon's centre court for the championship tennis matches. The dean and her husband are tennis enthusiasts.

Heather explains, "Gene, we've had an unfortunate incident. It appears that Gene, Jr., has passed in schoolwork completed by another person. As I understand it, he purchased a paper, not realizing that the same paper had been submitted once before. When questioned, he said he wanted to talk with his lawyer."

Twenty seconds go by before either says a word. Heather asks, "Gene, are you still there?"

"I'm here," Gene answers. "This is terribly unfortunate. I assume that you'll leave this up to me to speak directly to my son. I'm also assuming that he'll graduate with his class."

"I haven't made up my mind on next steps. As you know, this is not the first time that he's been in trouble here. Perhaps he can re-submit the assignment. I don't know about graduation. Maybe keeping him out of all graduation activities would be the appropriate punishment. I just wanted to call you as a courtesy and let you know of the incident."

"I understand the difficult position he's put you in, but any punitive action against him would jeopardize his entire future. Not being allowed to graduate or not participating in the graduation ceremony would break Grace's heart. It would amount to a public humiliation. I would consider this an enormous personal favour if you'd allow me to handle this discreetly and directly with my son."

At the end of the conversation, the two agree on a plan. Gene, Jr., will re-submit the assignment, participate in graduation ceremonies, and graduate as planned. Gene will address the matter with his son. Gene will also fund a tennis scholarship in the name of the Douglas family.

Gene has bailed JR out of so many situations that it makes him sick. Gene saw other young men like JR when he himself attended Harvard, the rich kid who couldn't be touched. Gene himself had nothing in common with them. He drove a cab part-time and sold Sunday morning newspapers at St. Peter's Church in Cambridge to make ends meet. He leans back in his chair with his hands folded behind his head. He looks at a family picture on his credenza. He, Grace, JR, and Jack are standing in the White House Rose Garden. Gene focuses squarely now on Jack. His grand plans for JR are shifting to Jack's direction.

29

Watertown, Massachusetts

Teresa drives her car to Jack's apartment on Sunday morning. She'll bring him home for their family meal. It will only be the immediate Rossi family and Jack. It will not include the larger, extended family. Teresa has keys to his apartment. Before she inserts her key in the door, it opens and a young man is on his way out.

"Hi," he says. "It's nice to finally meet you in person." He moves his backpack from his right shoulder to his left in order to shake her hand.

"Yes, it is," Teresa says with a smile. "I've only met you on video calls with Jack. They call you 'Cheese' right?"

"Right. I don't know why they think that nickname for a Chinese person is so funny. I do love cheese." He shakes his head. "He's head over heels for you ya know? Never seen him like this," Cheese continues talking as he walks away. "Be careful. He's in rough shape this morning."

She enters the apartment to see Jack sleeping on the couch. His hair has been cut. His hair is in some odd, patchwork pattern. She wakes him.

Jack explains that he and some friends took turns giving each other haircuts last night.

Oh my God, she thinks to herself. *This is going to be the father of my child? He's a child himself. What a stupid thing to do and now he's going to meet my family?*

"Really?" is the first word out of Teresa's mouth. "Were you drinking last night?" Jack rarely drinks alcohol.

Jack answers, but his speech is slower than normal and he looks to be in pain. "I did drink. We drank shots actually, all different kinds." He stops, but she wants more details and stands over him with her arms folded.

"Yeah, um, we played this game of hacking into computer networks. Four two-man teams. Me and Cheese never lose. We pick targets and you have to break into the system of a supermarket company, utility, bank, government agency, whatever."

Teresa is staggered. Most young men go out, meet girls, and try to get laid. These guys hang around playing on computers. "You break into computer networks? What does that even mean? Do you steal stuff?"

"No. Well. We could," Jack answers. "We wouldn't. It's really just an intellectual exercise. Show we can do it. Computers are no more than math when you get right down to it. Security is always changing and it's a challenge." It seems harmless the way Jack describes it. "We'd never steal from anyone."

"You can break into computer networks and then what do you do? And what if they catch you?"

Jack takes two Tylenol and drinks a large glass of water. "It feels like there is this giant wad of cotton in my mouth," he says.

"It's called dry mouth," Teresa explains. "Your body is dehydrated from the alcohol."

"We can break into just about anything. Cheese and me have been the champs since we got here. You need two guys; one does the hacking and the other stays on watch for defensive measures in case someone is watching you. We ruled last night. The target was a bank. Another team got three hours and couldn't break in so we took it. We were in, got a list of depositors, account balances, addresses, and pin numbers in one hour and forty-two minutes."

"'Family Feud' for geeks," Teresa says.

Jack doesn't understand the reference to the television game show. He adds, "Anyway, we ripped it up. We even broke into a country's intelligence agency this morning." Jack's excited about his victory.

"And you drink while you play?" Teresa asks.

"Yeah," Jack answers. "We did shots. We gave each other haircuts because there's some waiting around too."

Teresa has heard enough. She wants Jack focused on today's dinner. "What are we going to do about your hair?" she asks. It's short in some areas but long, untouched in others.

"I'll wear a hat," he answers.

"A hat? A freaking hat? You think you're going to wear a hat to my parent's home? Meet them? Have dinner with my father with a hat on?" She's getting emotional. "This is crazy," she says. "Why is it that smart people are so dumb? Do you have a comb and scissors?"

Teresa gives him a haircut. She's watched her mother give hundreds of haircuts.

In a few minutes, she thinks this may have been a blessing. "This is better," she says. "This is much better. You're going to look like a marine, a skinny marine, but good."

#

The drive from Jack's place to the Rossi home takes fifteen minutes. Teresa confirms that her mother knows of the pregnancy, but they haven't told her father. "And we're not going to tell him today. This is just about you meeting my family."

They arrive at the Rossi home at 1:50 p.m. Diner is scheduled for 2:00 p.m. Teresa is glad that they're almost ready to sit down. They enter the home and Teresa introduces Jack to her father, mother, and brother Nicholas.

"Call me Nick," he tells Jack.

Joe finds it odd that they didn't simply add Jack to the family dinner. Mary explained that this will give them more time to get to know Jack.

The group sits at the dining room table. Mary has tried to follow the proper etiquette in terms of seating arrangements. Joe and Mary will sit at the ends of the table. Jack will sit directly to Joe's right. Teresa will sit beside Jack and Nick on the opposite side of the table. She thinks she has it correct, but it means Jack will be next to Joe, within arm's reach of Joe.

#

The dinner conversation is strained at first. Joe can turn on his personality and light up the room when he chooses, but that's not happening.

Teresa's been seeing Roberto for years. Now this new guy shows up. *What's going on?* he thinks to himself.

Mary tries to get the conversation going. "So, Jack, Teresa tells us that you're from New York and that you go to school at M.I.T."

"Yes, Ma'am," Jack answers. Teresa cringes inside. She hopes it's not going to be a day where he provides short answers followed by long periods of silence. Her family likes to talk. They prefer noise. The more noise the better. She was hoping Nick would help with the conversation, but he's as quiet as a church mouse.

"New York, huh?" Joe says. "That mean you're a Yankees fan? Jets fan?"

"I don't know," Jack answers. "I'm not really into sports."

Joe and Nick exchange a look of disapproval.

"You're from New York, though?" Joe states. "Where?"

"My family lives in the city, sir, Manhattan," Jack answers politely.

Mary serves dinner family style. She has placed the meal around the table in various trays. Everyone serves themselves and passes the trays from one to another.

"Manhattan. What do your folks do?" Joe asks.

"My dad works at a bank. My mom does charity work mostly," Jack answers. Joe might have a plan for his questions, but Jack doesn't recognize it. He's simply enjoying the meal. Eating is helping his hangover.

Teresa is feeling powerless to stop what feels like a train wreck. She can see her father processing the information. Jack is from New York City, not into sports, and his father is a banker; three strikes. Jack doesn't know it, but he's already struck out with her father.

Jack surprises her by saying, "You have a beautiful home, Mr. and Mrs. Rossi, and thank you for this meal. It's delicious. The sauce has a deep, rich flavour."

"Well, thank you," Mary says. "We have a vegetable garden in the backyard. We make our own marinara sauce from the tomatoes. It's an old family recipe. Isn't that right dear?" Mary directs the question to Joe.

"Yup. Been doing it for years. We add the family wine too," Joe adds.

"And that's your family coat of arms up there isn't it?" Jack points to the wall behind Joe.

"Yup," Joe answers. "How'd you know that?"

"I looked it up online. I was just looking up the origin of the name 'Rossi.' I came across that coat of arms. Are you both Italian?" Jack asks.

"I'm Italian. Mary is Portuguese," Joe says. "A lot of us here in Watertown," (Joe means both Italians and Portuguese). Jack has noticed that Teresa has her mother's good looks and similar features: long limbs, narrow hips, and beautiful dark eyes.

The group eases into an easy, casual conversation. Jack is asking a lot of questions about Teresa. He wants to hear details of her growing up. Joe and Mary are proud of their children and enjoy talking about them. The Rossi's are more boisterous than Jack's family. They enjoy laughing, especially when it's directed at themselves.

#

When the group is finished eating, Jack helps Mary and Teresa clear the table. Joe and Nick don't move. They believe that's a woman's job. Mary and Teresa serve dessert and coffee. They're pleased the meal was a success.

Teresa begins to plan their escape.

"Are you Catholic, Jack? Are your folks Catholic?" Joe asks.

Oh, no, Teresa thinks to herself, but it's too late.

"Yes, sir. Well, I was raised Catholic. I don't know. Maybe I am. My dad is Catholic. Mom is a Southern Baptist, a Christian," Jack answers.

"But you're not sure you're a Catholic?" Joe asks.

"Well," Jack begins "I believe in God. I think that mathematics, our galaxy, all matter is too well-organized, too perfect to think it all happened randomly. I'd like to think there is a God. I don't believe all those stories in the Bible though."

Jack eats desert and drinks a second glass of Mountain Dew. Teresa must have told Mary of his preference.

"So you believe in God, but you're not Catholic is what you mean?" Joe asks. For Joe, it's a simple yes or no question.

Mary is thinking of how to change the subject.

Teresa realizes that she should have warned Jack to expect the question.

"Well, I read an interesting book about five years ago that linked astronomy to religion. I don't know if you want to hear about that," Jack says.

"No, go ahead," Joe encourages.

"Well, the premise was that religion is based on the calendar and not on events which actually happened." Jack shrugs his shoulders adding, "I don't know. Mrs. Rossi, the desert is delicious, thank you."

"What do ya mean? The calendar?" Joe asks with a confused look.

Jack explains, "The story of Jesus is identical to the story of Horus, the Sun God from Egypt around 3,000 B.C. He was born on December 25th to a virgin mother, three kings followed him, he was a teacher, had twelve disciples, after three days he rose from the dead. Besides Horus, there are the eight other identical figures and stories from all over the ancient world. India, Persia, Greece all had the same story with a different person in Jesus's place. Some stories date back to thousands of years before Jesus."

Jack is talking as though he's in school and this is open speech. The Rossi family look at him with blank stares.

"From astrology," Jack continues, "we know that the sun is at its low point in the sky on December 22nd each year. At that time, there are three stars called the three kings from Orion's belt. They line up with the star 'Sirius', the brightest star in the sky. The four stars point to where the sun will rise on December 25th. From December 22nd to the 25th the sun doesn't move, it remains on what is called 'the Southern Cross', a grouping of stars. The idea is the sun dies for three days and arises on December 25th. So the story of Jesus is the latest version of a story that dates back thousands of years and is based on astrology. That's all I meant, or that was the premise of that book."

Nick loves the story. It might be sacrilegious to others at the table, but it's new and interesting. "That's awesome," he says. No one has ever talked liked that in this family.

"That's all very interesting, dear," Mary says. "I think we'd like to hear more about your family, Jack. First, can I get anyone anything else to eat or drink? Joe, would you like a beer, wine, coffee?"

"No, no, Mom," Teresa says, "Jack and I should probably get going. He's got to get back to school."

"Woah, woah, wait a minute," Joe stops them. "So, is that what you believe?"

"I don't know. I find the concepts interesting," Jack answers. "Do you want to hear more?"

Joe raises his eyebrows and nods. He's surprised there's more.

A voice inside Teresa is screaming *No!*

"Definitely," Nick says with encouragement. Nick thinks his father is going to explode at any moment.

Teresa shoots Nick a look as if to say, *Thanks a lot.*

"Well," Jack continues, "we all know it takes the earth about 26,000 years to go around the sun and end up in the same place. The earth sits on an axis and wobbles. There are twelve constellations, twelve months, and twelve disciples. Each constellation represents a new age, which lasts about 2,200 years. Jesus issues in the age of Pisces, he's a fisherman. The previous age was Taurus the bull, and we know the story of men worshipping the false God of the golden bull. Aquarius will be next. We know the story when Luke asks Jesus about the last Passover, Jesus tells him to follow the man with a pitcher of water. He's referring to the next age, which is Aquarius. Again, all based on a calendar. Ancient people used the stars as their calendar and needed to know when to plant and when to harvest."

"Again, that's very interesting, Jack," Mary says. "That's probably enough talk of religion for today."

"There's another explanation," Teresa says. "Maybe God set it all up that way for a reason. He created it all this way so all the world's people would repeat the story of His greatness. His story is written in the stars."

Jack turns to her. "Maybe that's right," he says. "Maybe that's the answer." They look each other in the eyes and share big smiles.

Joe and Mary recognize the way Teresa and Jack look at each other. In that moment, neither Joe nor Mary could care less about what Jack just said. The look tells Joe the relationship is more serious than he thought.

There's a pause before Joe declares, "Well we're Catholic in this house, Jack. I don't know about all that astrological, cosmological stuff. We're Catholic. That's how I was brought up. That's how our kids were brought up." Joe is pointing his right index finger down into the table. He's doesn't appear angry, but he's making his point firmly.

After pleasant "good-byes", Teresa gives Jack a ride back in town.

#

After Teresa and Jack leave, Mary asks Joe, "What do you think?"

"I don't know," Joe starts, "he's just a kid. What happened to Roberto?"

"You never liked Roberto."

"She has more in common with Roberto. At least he's from around here. This kid? He's from New York. His father's a banker. He doesn't know if he's Catholic. They got nothing in common. It's a waste of time." Joe swats the air as if there were a fly in front of him.

"She likes him, Joe. She really likes him."

"He's got a good haircut and good manners," Joe says. "I'll say that for him. It shows he respects this house."

Mary smiles. Teresa told her about her giving Jack the haircut this morning.

Joe then asks, "Do you know what he was talking about with Aquarius and the calendar and the earth going around the sun in 20,000 years and all that?"

"I didn't really follow all of that," Mary admits.

"The kid reads something five years ago and can remember all that?" Joe's impressed. "Go figure, huh?"

#

As they drive away in the car, Teresa and Jack have a similar conversation. Teresa asks, "What do you think?"

"I think they're great. They're really nice people. I can see where you get it from." He follows that up with, "and your mom is beautiful, hot actually."

Teresa punches him in the arm.

Jack then asks, "Did you see your father's finger when he was pointing down at the table? That's the biggest finger I've ever seen. I thought his finger might go right through the table."

The subject of her father's hands has come up many times over the years. She smiles and explains, "When he got his wedding ring, the jeweller said it was the second biggest ring he's ever made. I should have warned you about his handshake."

"I hoped they liked me," Jack says.

"Of course, they did. Who wouldn't like you?"

30

Washington, DC

Treasury Secretary Doug Martin is back in the president's meeting of senior advisors. Bobby Ferguson provided an agenda. He's running the meeting and jumping from one topic to another in a random order. It's keeping everyone on their toes.

Doug's anxious because his report is not what the president wants to hear.

News reports have come in over the past few days about armed engagements in the Middle East. Some members of the press have been critical of the president's 'foreign policy shortcomings.' The topic dominates the news cycle.

One of the reasons Doug dislikes Washington is people are more concerned about 'spinning the news' than fixing a problem. "Spinning the news" once meant casting events in the most favourable light possible. Now, it means lying to the extent that your political opponents can't prove otherwise. The administration pays dozens of people to do nothing but spin the news and leak information, even classified information, to journalists supportive of their agenda.

While they talk about the Middle East, political advisors outnumber the foreign policy experts in the room by two to one. They have more influence over the president than the experts.

How did we get so messed up? Doug thinks to himself. He realizes it's the same when they discuss his area of expertise. These advisors know almost nothing about the economy, yet they have more influence over the president than he does.

He's grateful they're spending time on the Middle East. The meeting will last two hours. Every minute discussing foreign policy means there's less time for him. There's a chance they won't even get to him.

His hopes end abruptly when Bobby says, "That brings us to our treasury secretary. Mr. Secretary, three agenda items for you today; an update on the housing numbers, any suggestions or edits for the president's speech, and a status report on Mr. O'Neil. In light of our time constraints let's just talk about Mr. O'Neil."

Doug begins, "I met with Gene. The meeting went well, but he is insistent that we provide him with a plan for addressing the nation's debt. He's concerned about the level of spending, its impact on hurting economic growth and adding even more debt." Doug hasn't said anything that the group doesn't already know. The president is underwhelmed.

Bobby will play the role of bulldog. "Mr. Secretary, what specifically does he want? That's what you were going to find out for us."

"He believes that this administration and Congress are both to blame for the problems. He said that our credit is under review and we will not be able to spend and borrow like we've been doing. He said we owe him a plan."

Both the president and Bobby are frustrated that Doug didn't get more details.

"Mr. Secretary, Doug," the president begins, "What does that mean? We have nations all around the world willing to lend us money at cheap interest rates. It sounds to me like our old friend Gene O'Neil is starting to lose it."

"I apologize, Mr. President, that I didn't get more from him," Doug responds. "He said that he'd address the specifics with you at the fundraiser."

The president is not pleased. He shakes his head to show his frustration and gives Bobby a hand signal to say, "Let's move to the next topic."

31

Boston, Massachusetts

The pregnancy has changed the relationship between Teresa and Jack. It brings them closer together, but adds stress. Despite strong feelings for one another, they've only known each other a short period of time. The relationship hasn't had time to develop.

While Jack has completed all the requirements to graduate, he has one additional assignment, a paper that he needs to complete.

Teresa will continue to work through the pregnancy. She won't tell anyone at work until it's necessary. They'll begin looking for a place together after Jack's graduation.

They'll break the news of the pregnancy to their parents over the Easter holiday. Each will talk with their parents alone.

32

New York, New York

Jack takes the train from Boston to New York on the Friday afternoon of Easter weekend. The plan is to meet his parents for dinner. The family typically drives out to their summer home in the Hamptons and spends the Easter weekend together.

Grace and Gene arrive at the restaurant a short while before Jack. They're seated and looking over the menu when Jack arrives. Gene stands and greets his son with a hug and kiss on the cheek. "How are you, Jackson? You look great. I like the short hair."

Grace thinks, *He's no longer hiding behind his hair.* She remains seated. "I like it too, very much," she says. "You should keep it that way.

Jack walks to her, kisses her cheek and says, "Hi, Mom."

Jack wants to tell them of the pregnancy immediately. It's difficult, but he goes through his rehearsed remarks without pausing or stopping. "Mom, Dad, I met a girl. Her name is Teresa Rossi. We've been seeing each other. She's pregnant. I'm in love with her. She's from Boston, twenty years old, works for the State or, Commonwealth of Massachusetts and goes to night school at a community college. We're planning on getting a place together, to live together starting this summer, after graduation I mean. We don't know about marriage, or we're not doing that now." Jack says it all with rapid-fire efficiency and without emotion.

His parents were not prepared. They just said 'hello.' Grace appears to be in pain. The plan was to have a nice, relaxing dinner with their two sons. She puts her hands to her stomach and then to her head. Her body stiffens. Her jaw is clenched.

She inquires, "I'm sorry, but who is this girl and how long have you known her? What about her family? Who are they and what do they do?" She is talking faster than normal. As soon as Jack can answer one question, she asks another. When she asks, "What does she want from you?" she offends her son.

"Mom, what do you mean 'what does she want?' She's in love with me too. You know that's possible." Jack hoped his mother would be more understanding.

His mother has always very protective. "I'm sorry. I didn't mean that. You just can't be too careful these days."

Grace instructs Gene to get a waiter. She searches her purse for an anxiety pill.

"Jackson," Gene begins, "this is a very big step. There are important decisions that the two of you need to make. Only you and Teresa can make them. We'll offer our thoughts, but these are your decisions that you need to live with for the rest of your lives. You know how I feel. I believe children need the love and support that only a family can provide. A mother and a father, that is. A married mother and father is what I mean to say."

While Gene maintains his composure in all situations, his mind is in motion. Opportunity knocks.

There's an uneasy silence overhanging the table. Grace is not pleased with either the news or Gene's response.

"I'd like to propose a toast," Gene announces. "Here's to love. If you've found true love at your age, then you're a very lucky man."

Grace isn't interested in a toast. The news is not something to celebrate. She joins in the toast only because it allows her to take her pill.

Gene takes a drink of whiskey and declares, "You know, I've seen many talented young men waste years looking for the right woman. They're looking for something before they even know who they are." He pauses and looks towards Jack. "I hope you'll be as lucky as I've been with the choice you make." Gene looks affectionately towards his wife. Grace is cold, detached, and not interested in returning his affection.

#

They order dinner. Gene and Jack talk about school. Grace remains quiet, lost in her own thoughts. She and Jack have enjoyed a close relationship. For years, the two talked daily on the phone. Lately, their calls have been much less frequent. She asks herself, *When did that stop? Is this new girl the reason?*

Grace orders a salad and fish. She's drinking vodka martinis instead of her usual, white wine.

The men enjoy steaks. Gene doesn't drink alcohol when he associates with businesspeople. He enjoys drinking with family and friends.

"Jack," Grace begins, "didn't I tell you to use birth control? How did she get pregnant? What I mean is, do you think that she wanted to get pregnant?"

Jack doesn't answer.

"Now, Grace," Gene says, "These things can just happen sometimes."

"No, they don't, Eugene," Grace responds. "They happen when a woman sets her sights on someone. This girl decided she was going to take advantage of Jack and cash in. She can see that Jack's a good person. He's naive and a perfect target. Eugene, you're going to have to take care of this."

Grace carries on, unaware of how her comments are hurting her son.

Grace had dreams for her sons. They were going to marry the right girls from the right families. Their weddings would be the talk of the city. Her boys would be the two most eligible men in the city. Half that dream just vanished. The combination of disappointment, alcohol, and medication is affecting her behaviour.

"I know this is difficult, Mom," Jack begins. "It's difficult for me too. I thought that after you had time to think about it, you'd be happy for me. Happy that I've found a great girl and fallen in love."

Grace knows it's her responsibility to contact the girl and her family. *How undignified*, she thinks.

"Did you say she goes to school in Boston? Harvard was it?" Grace asks.

Grace heard Jack's description very clearly. It's her not so subtle way of saying that Teresa doesn't go to a four-year school let alone one of the right schools. Both Gene and Jack understood her point.

"No, Mom," Jack answers. "She's taking evening courses at a community college. I think you'll like her. She's a really good person."

Grace's look at Gene communicates her message, 'Are you hearing this?'

Gene orders another whiskey. His mind is in motion about his own goals. He turns to his son and says, "I'm sure we'll both like her a lot. Your happiness is what we're most interested in. We'll need some time to talk about plans and next steps, ok?"

Jack is pleased by his father's reaction. He seems genuinely happy for him.

"You have to give me the girl's name and contact information, her mother's too," Grace instructs. "I'll be up there as soon as I can to meet the girl and her family. Your father will come too. We must not talk about this with anyone else. We should keep this quiet. Do you both understand? This is just between us for now."

After several moments pass, Grace turns and says, "Jack, you have a wonderful, kind heart. You have always believed that people are good—as good as you are. Unfortunately, you should believe the opposite. Focus on people's motivations, their greedy aspirations to fix their unfulfilling lives. People are bad. They're not good. They act only in their own self-interest. You must change your thinking. People only show you what they choose to reveal and they hide the ugliness. Understand their motives; think the worst of them and you'll better understand them. You'll be able to predict what they'll do next."

Jack is shocked by his mother's comments. He's never heard her talk like this. He turns to his father. "Is that what you think too, Dad?"

"Well," Gene begins. "I like to think the best of people first, but I'm often disappointed. I agree you should consider other people's motives, but consider what's most important to you in a relationship or a transaction. From there, figure out how to make it work for both parties, and with a profit. Every event represents an opportunity, so figure out how to make it work for you. But, and I mean this, if anyone tries to ever hurt you or a loved one, then you need to destroy them. Don't wait to find out how far an enemy will go. Once they've shown their hand then go right for their jugular. Inflict maximum damage without mercy."

33

New York, New York

On Saturday morning, Gene is up early and working in his study at home.

Jack wakes, pours himself a cup of coffee, and joins his father.

Gene welcomes him, “Good morning, Jackson.”

“Hi, Dad.”

Gene invites him to “Sit down, make yourself comfortable. I imagine your mother will sleep for another couple of hours. I figured I’d get some work done. Do you want to go out to breakfast? It’s been a while since we’ve done that together.”

Jack sits. “No thanks, Dad, just coffee.”

“That was some news you brought us,” Gene begins.

“I know. I hope you’re not disappointed in me.”

“No, I’m not disappointed. Surprised is all. Young people have sex. Some young women get pregnant. I understand,” Gene says in a comforting tone. “But this means making some important decisions about your future and about what comes next. It’s no longer just you that you need to think about. It’s about your child and it’s about Teresa.”

“I know, Dad, we’re trying to figure it out,” Jack replies. Jack may be eighteen years old, but he looks like he could pass for sixteen. It’s difficult for Gene to see him as a father.

"Well, have you thought about where you're going to live?" Gene asks. "Have you thought about your education, health insurance, medical costs, day care—is Teresa going to work? Is the child going to take your last name?"

"Not exactly, Dad, I mean we haven't gotten to all that yet."

"Being a father is the best thing that can happen to you, but it's an enormous responsibility."

Jack nods his head and drinks his coffee.

"Well, let me say that you'll continue to have the full support of your family," Gene states clearly. "By support I mean our unconditional love and whatever financial and other help you need." Jack is relieved to hear his father say it. "But I do have a favour or issue to resolve; have you thought any more about coming to work with me at the bank?"

Oh, shit! Jack thinks. This is the one topic he hoped wouldn't come up. "No, Dad, or, I thought about it. I'm not sure it's right for me." Jack is feeling very uncomfortable.

"Well, you now have new responsibilities, and you've brought those on yourself. You really have to consider this differently now."

Jack is looking down and from side to side. He doesn't say anything.

"I imagine you're not going to come out to the Hamptons with us today. Is that correct?"

"Yeah, Dad. I was gonna take the train back to Boston. I mean if that's ok with you and Mom."

Gene nods. "I understand and it's ok with me, but not before you say 'good-bye' to your mother, right?"

"Right, Dad, of course."

"And make sure you go to church at some point this weekend. By the way, have you heard from your brother?" Gene asks. "He was supposed to join us last night. I never heard from him. Have you?"

Jack shakes his head "No, I haven't heard anything."

Gene tells his son, "I want you to think about coming to work with me after graduation. We'll get you and Teresa a nice place to live here in the city. You come to the bank for one year. If at the end of that year you don't want to stay, then that's it. You go back to school in Boston, or wherever you want, and we won't ever talk about banking again. One year, that's all I'm asking."

Jack doesn't move or say anything.

Gene pulls his chair a little closer to his son. "Jack," he begins. Jack looks up into his father's eyes. "I think this is the first time in our lives that I've ever asked you for anything."

"I know, Dad. I think it is too." Jack doesn't know how to answer. Leaving his studies for a year to work at the bank would be just horrible. The voice inside Jack is telling him to say no to his father, but he can't get the word out.

Gene doesn't want to say anything more. Silence is a powerful tool in negotiating. He allows time to pass. A good amount of time before adding, "I'm asking you to consider it and get back to me. Go back to Boston. Talk with Teresa. Explain that it's only one year and then you're free to do whatever you'd like with my full blessing. It may surprise you. You might enjoy it. There's a lot going on right now that you need to learn. I believe it's in your best interest and the best interests of your new family. I'm talking about all of your best long-term interests."

Jack agrees to talk with Teresa about it.

34

Watertown, Massachusetts

The Rossi family attends the 11 a.m. mass on Easter morning. They'll have dinner at the home of Joe's parents. It's tradition. Between church and dinner, they stop at home to pick up some things.

When they enter their home, Mary tells Joe that Teresa has some news. They need to talk. The three of them sit down in the living room. Teresa starts to break the news but immediately breaks down in tears. She can't get it out. Mary tells Joe of the pregnancy.

A rage wells up inside of him immediately. There's nowhere for Joe to direct his anger.

"You knew about this?" Joe asks Mary. Mary nods her head. "You knew about this before that boy came to have dinner in our home?" Again, Mary nods. "You didn't tell me. Nobody told me. In my home and no one tells me." Joe stands and begins to pace back and forth. "That boy should have told me. He should have had the decency to look me in the eye and tell me." That boy is now the target for Joe's anger. "What a piece of shit."

Mary interrupts, "Joe, it's not his fault."

"You should have been watching her more closely," he tells Mary harshly.

"That boy's gotta pay," Joe says threateningly. "That boy's gotta pay for this." Joe continues to pace. Veins are now bulging from Joe's temples. His face is dark red. "I gotta go," Joe says. "I gotta get out of here."

"Go? Go where?" Mary asks.

"I gotta go to the club. They need me down there." He turns and quickly walks out the front door.

The women have seen this before. When put in a difficult situation, people choose fight or flight. This involves Mary and Teresa, so he can't fight. He leaves for the comfort of the Elks Lodge where he's a member. It's his "club" and open 365 days a year. He has escaped there during similar situations. Joe is predictable.

"What about your family, dinner at their house?" Mary asks from the front door as Joe gets in his pick-up truck.

Joe heard her, but doesn't respond or slow down. He drives away quickly.

Mary knows the pattern. He'll go to the Elks Lodge and have a few beers. Hopefully, not too many beers, and calm down. There's nothing for her to do.

Teresa hasn't said a word.

They'll go to Joe's parents' house and explain that Joe is helping at the club. While they'll find it odd, they won't ask questions.

#

Teresa and Mary enjoy a wonderful time at dinner. While they'd prefer to have Joe with them, they enjoy being with family. Breaking the news to Joe feels like they've unloaded a giant weight from their shoulders.

Joe arrives around 5:00 p.m. Teresa didn't see him until he was right in front of her. He gives Teresa a big hug and holds her tightly. He whispers, "I love you, Princess," in her ear.

"I love you too, Daddy," she replies.

Joe's brother Anthony yells to him, "Hey, that's your daughter, not your wife you big drunk." The men are seated on lawn chairs in a large circle.

"That's a close family," Joe hears, followed by, "There are laws against that Joe." The men are cracking themselves up. Joe turns so that Teresa's back is towards the group of men. He raises his middle finger towards them.

A short while later Joe sits beside Mary. They hold hands. "Hey, me and you don't have secrets," he says.

"I know. I'm sorry. This is hard." Mary felt dual loyalties.

"What about marriage?" Joe asks in a whisper. "They should get married don't ya think?"

"Yeah. I don't know. We'll see. I hope so."

35

Boston, Massachusetts

Teresa visits Jack that evening. They sit and update each other on their meetings with their parents. While breaking the news was difficult, it reinforces a new dynamic to their relationship. They begin to think of themselves as a new family; a family unit separate and apart from their old ones.

Jack tells Teresa of his father's request again to come work with him. The new offer is for just one year. "We can't do that," Teresa answers. "We need to be together, and I have my job. I have the security of working for the government. You can't go because you have school here. Is this your father's way of breaking us up?"

"I don't think so," Jack answers. "See, my dad was happy for me, happier than my mom. He offered a toast at dinner right away. He said I'm very lucky if I've found the right woman at my age."

"I don't know anyone in New York," Teresa says. "I've never even been there. I wouldn't be home for Sunday dinners."

"I know. He asked me to think about it. Come to work with him at the bank for one year he said. After that, I could come back to Boston or go to school wherever I wanted. No questions asked. Then he said he's never asked me for anything before, but he's asking me now. He said it's in our best long-term interests, yours and mine, that is. It makes it hard to say no. I think he does want the best for us. I don't know if I can say no."

Teresa can see that Jack is considering it. She wonders if the State would allow her to take a year off from her job.

"Your mom called my mom today," Teresa says. "They're making plans for getting our families together. A dinner here in Boston."

They look in each other's eyes, smile, and Jack replies, "Oh boy."

36

New York, New York

The evening of the fundraiser arrives. A crowd of three hundred guests put on their finest evening wear. The event is at New York's Metropolitan Museum of Art (the "Met"). The bank's CEO, David Sandler, will introduce the president and welcome the guests. While Gene arranged everything, he'll remain behind the scenes.

Security is tight. Guests are required to go through metal detectors. It's an odd-looking sight. The wait staff serves appetizers, champagne, and cocktails to guests before and after they go through screening.

The president's entourage includes many Secret Service agents, limousines, and dozens of support vehicles. Traffic will grind to a crawl all over the city. Highway entrances and exits are closed between the airport and the Met. Hundreds of men and women are involved in security. More than one person will question why the taxpayer is paying for the security of a political party's fundraiser or a politician who won't run for office again.

Gene's meeting with the president will occur in a small room behind the podium. Once the meeting is completed, the president will have a short walk to the stage. He'll enter, the band will play "Hail to the Chief," and guests will stand and applaud. After the speech, there will be time for the guests to meet the president and have a picture taken with him. Twenty-five thousand dollars buys you a picture standing with the president. Donations of this kind are mandatory for anyone seeking influence with the bank, the political party, and contracts with the government. Money buys access.

#

Gene is seated in the small room when the president and Bobby Ferguson enter. He stands to greet the president. The president gives Gene a big, warm handshake with both hands. He flashes his perfect smile and thanks Gene for the evening.

The president re-introduces Bobby by saying, "Gene, you know Bobby." It's clear the president wishes Bobby to stay for the meeting. The president sits down in one of two, high-backed chairs set out for the meeting. He rubs his hands together and asks, "So, Gene, what do you want to talk about?"

Bobby stands behind the president's chair.

The president and Gene both look down at their watches and make a mental note that their time starts now.

Gene begins by showing respect to the office, "It's good to see you, Mr. President. I'm glad to be of service to you this evening. Thank you for our fifteen minutes alone." Gene doesn't look up at Bobby, but wanted to make the point that they're not alone. "As you know, I've been urging you to work more closely with Congress and to come up with a plan for the economy. We need to address what I'll refer to as the out-of-control spending and borrowing that's been going on. The people that have been lending money to the United States government are very concerned. I'd like to help, but you need to produce a plan. The country's debt is simply too large."

The president begins his typical sales pitch. "Gene? Come on. You know better than anyone the problems I inherited. We're making great progress. Look at the stock market. Look at the progress we're making on jobs. Look at—" Gene raises his hand in a stop gesture. The president pulls back with obvious agitation. No one puts their hand up to the president in a motion to stop him.

"Respectfully, Mr. President, we only have fifteen minutes," Gene explains.

The president starts up again. "Me and you have come a long way since we first met. I appreciate all you've done for me. I really want us to see this through together. We're doing great things for the American people. We can't stop now." The president is in full sales mode and he's very good at it.

Gene is concerned that if he lets the president talk, then he'll take up the entire fifteen minutes. It's difficult to interrupt the President, but he needs to make good use of this time. He speaks over the president. "You're right, Mr. President, we have come a long way. I've been glad to help. When we first met, we made mutual promises. I got you the money you needed, but you haven't honoured your end of our bargain. In fact, your presidency has made things worse. You made a promise to cut our deficit in half and instead you more than doubled it." Gene is steadfast and efficient.

The president tries again. "I know, and I remember that proposal, but times have changed, and as president I need to be flexible in my approach. My economists are telling me to stay the course. They're confident that we're taking the right steps."

"Mr. President, do you know why your economists work for you and not me?"

"Why's that?"

"Last year thirty-eight men on Wall Street made over a billion dollars each," Gene answers. Bobby Ferguson's eyebrows shoot up. "Good economists on Wall Street can make a fortune. We don't hire your guys because your guys don't know shit. Your guys live with their heads in the clouds. They give you the answers you want to hear. They provide you with 'credentialed'," Gene uses air-quotes, "experts for cover on your policies. You and I both know it's a load of crap."

"Well," the president replies, "I understand and maybe you're right about some of this. You and I aren't that far apart. Let's get together this summer, maybe play some golf. We can talk about any small differences we have and come up with a plan." The president sounds reasonable, but it's no more than a bid to buy time. The president's charm has worked for years. His political success is due to his likability and not any accomplishments.

"Again, Mr. President," Gene begins, "I have heard you. Let me be clear in our remaining time together. I need you to show your creditors that you understand the seriousness of this issue. You have eight weeks from tonight to get me your plan. That's a deadline. It's a firm deadline. Do you understand?"

"Gene?" The president looks for support from Bobby. "Or what?" He begins to take a more aggressive posture. He sits up on the edge of his chair with his back straight up and shoulders back. "I'm the president, Gene. What are you going to do? You gonna stop throwing fundraisers? You gonna stop paying for the bank regulations you want or favours for your best clients? I don't think so. I have a job to do. We can help each other if you'd like, but if not, that's fine with me. I can find others to raise the money I need, the money that I deserve."

"Mr. President, I told my clients that you wouldn't be willing to listen to a final appeal. I told them that we'd need to demonstrate the seriousness of the situation. I was hoping it wouldn't come to that."

Bobby doesn't like where this is going. He looks at his watch. Soon, he'll interrupt the two men.

"Is that a threat? Bobby, did you just hear him threaten the president of the United States? Gene, I got an army. I got a navy. I got a Justice Department and I even got an FBI and National Guard. What do you got? What do fancy Wall Street bankers have?" The president is grinning. He is enjoying mocking Gene. "I've got people that watch over banks and can turn yours inside out. What do you got?" The president has puffed out his chest. He has put the world-famous banker in his place. The president looks at his watch, stands, and turns his back to leave. That's enough he figures. This meeting is over.

"Interest, Mr. President," Gene answers.

The president gets a chill. The hair on the back of his neck stands up.

"You don't seem to understand. I'm not here on behalf of Morgan Sachs," Gene explains. "I'm here on behalf of my clients, the owners of the Federal Reserve Bank of the United States of America. Your credit is under review. No, we don't have armies. We don't have navies or a National Guard. I have your money. My weapons are far more powerful than anything in your arsenal. I believe it was Albert Einstein that said compound interest is the most powerful force in the universe?"

The president looks confused.

Gene stands, adjusts his suit and looks at his watch. "You only have an army or a navy if I lend you the money to pay for it. I decide if your stock market goes up or down, the value of the U.S. dollar relative to other world currencies, and the interest rate on your $24 trillion debt. I decide if this country has a recession, depression, or prosperity. No one will lend you money unless I allow it. I own your money. You have eight weeks to get me your plan. Use the time wisely."

There is protocol to these meetings. Gene is supposed to allow the president to exit the room first. Gene walks past the president and out of the room.

#

"What the fuck is he talking about, Bobby?" the president asks.

"I don't know, Mr. President. Maybe he is losing it. You appoint the chairman of the Federal Reserve," Bobby fumbles for an answer.

"Find out fast," the president instructs.

The president is agitated. He pauses to brush it off and get himself pumped up for his entrance to the dinner.

Bobby immediately calls Treasury Secretary Martin.

"Doug," Bobby begins. "I'm at the fundraiser with the president. He had his meeting with Gene. Know what he told us?"

"No, Bobby, I don't know." Doug is relaxing at home with family.

"He told us that he's not talking to us as a banker from Morgan Sachs. He's talking to us on behalf of the owners of our Federal Reserve Bank. He says we've got eight weeks to give him our plan."

"The Federal Reserve?" Doug asks.

"Yes, the Federal Reserve Bank. Is that possible? Who the fuck owns the Federal Reserve? Don't we own it?"

"No, Bobby, we don't own it. It's a third party, but I don't know who the actual owners are, I mean technically."

"Well, find the fuck out fast and get back to me. You need to be all over this shit."

#

The dinner proceeds successfully. The president is all smiles. He delivers a short but passionate speech on topics considered "safe." He talks about the environment, education, and America's infrastructure. The speech includes jokes aimed at political opponents and bankers. After the speech, the president walks over to every table and mingles with the attendees. He is charming.

Eventually, the president gets to Gene's table. Grace and Gene are seated with Bernie Schwartz, Bernie's wife, and members of the Met's Board of Trustees. The president thanks everyone for their support. He thanks Gene for making the evening possible and adds "Actually for making my entire presidency possible." Successful politicians, like the president, find it easy to say what is required for any occasion.

#

Bobby Ferguson approaches Gene and asks him for a few minutes alone. They walk outside of the main dining area and Bobby asks, "Gene, what's the Fed got to do with this?"

Gene isn't surprised by Bobby's efforts, but he has no interest in the conversation.

He answers, "I don't understand your question. I've given the president eight weeks. What else would you like to talk about?"

"What happens if he doesn't get you a plan? What are you going to do if we can't move that fast? I'm trying to help." Bobby has a drink in his hand and he's spilling it as he moves his arms about. "Maybe we need more time. We have shit blowing up on us everywhere right now. It's been a bad month. It looks like our policies are gonna need more time and money to work. The other party is killing our efforts to make progress on anything. Nothing is going according to plan and we can't afford another problem."

Gene answers calmly. "You have one crisis and only one crisis. Treat this like the only thing on your plate. Fix this and I can take care of all the rest. Believe me when I tell you that everything else is minor compared to this. I don't know what's going to happen if you don't address it. I'm not responsible if events spiral out of control. Once a match is lit, you're never sure how bad the fire might get."

It's up to the president. Both men keenly understand that leaving important matters in the hands of a politician is never a good thing.

37

McLean, Virginia

Shortly after the phone call with Bobby, Doug arranges a Saturday morning meeting with the Federal Reserve Chairman. His name is Sam Fredrick. The two men have met several times, but don't know each other well.

Doug travels to the chairman's home and they sit down for coffee on his back porch. The meeting begins around 9 a.m.

"Thank you for agreeing to see me on such short notice," Doug begins.

"Of course, Mr. Secretary, what can I do for you?"

"Please call me Doug. This may sound like an odd question." He takes a deep breath and asks, "Who owns the Federal Reserve Bank of the United States of America?"

"Call me Sam. You don't know?"

Doug shakes his head. "I know it's independent but no, I don't know."

"Please understand that I don't mean anything by asking you that question. It's just interesting how few people know or even ask. A small group of very wealthy men founded the Federal Reserve in 1913. I did some research of my own years ago. It's fascinating. There were seven men in all and you'd recognize the names. There were famous robber barons: J.P. Morgan, John D. Rockefeller, and Cornelius Vanderbilt. There was Senator Winthrop to give the group legitimacy and a political insider. There were also three very wealthy European bankers: Rothschild, Loeb, and Kuhn. Those three knew how to do it and its value because they were part owners of several European central banks. Did I get all seven names?"

"Yes," Doug answers. "You listed seven. One of them was a senator?"

"You look surprised, Doug. I was too."

"Yes, I'm surprised. Who owns the bank now?"

"Well, that's a good question," the chairman answers. "I don't know the makeup of the ownership today, or their names, and who owns how many shares. You see, the original owners created a trust agreement and it's kept in secret. The only people that would know that are the shareholders themselves."

"Do you hear from them? I mean, are they involved in managing the Federal Reserve Bank today?" Doug asks.

Sam sips his coffee before answering. "To the best of my knowledge, I've never met one of the owners. I deal with a trustee. The shareholders put him in control of everything. I meet with him regularly and take direction from him. He would know all about the ownership."

"Who's the trustee?"

"I'm sorry," Sam answers. "I'm not permitted to share that information with you."

Doug becomes frustrated, "What do you mean, I'm the treasury secretary of the United States of America!"

"Terms of the trust is all I mean. Your predecessors agreed that the information would remain private."

"That's crazy. It's Gene O'Neil isn't it?" Doug asks. "He's the trustee."

"It appears that you already knew the answer."

"So," Doug begins, "Gene O'Neil tells you which way to move interest rates, money supply, reserve requirements, and so forth?"

"We have a dialogue. Me and the other members of the Federal Reserve Board meet and we make recommendations. Gene has always been fair and open-minded. He usually follows our recommendations. I'd say we have a very good working relationship."

"Usually?" Doug replies. "To be clear though, does he have the final say over these matters?"

"Yes. He or the shareholders have the authority to dictate policy on all those issues. They have complete control."

"Does it strike you as just crazy that this could have happened?" Doug asks.

"Maybe," Sam answers, "but fortunately for us, Gene has been reasonable. He hasn't wielded the power he possesses."

#

Doug gets in his limousine and calls Bobby. "I met with our Fed Chairman this morning. A small group of very wealthy men were the original owners of our Federal Reserve. The chairman doesn't know who owns the bank because he only meets with a trustee. The trustee speaks for the owners. They have complete control over everything."

"And the trustee is Gene O'Neil?" Bobby finishes Doug's message.

"Yup," Doug confirms. "I guess J.P. Morgan himself was one of the original owners. Maybe someone from that bank has always been the trustee. It gets you thinking doesn't it?"

Bobby isn't interested in a history lesson. He responds curtly, "I don't know how you could have missed this. You better get your ass to your office as soon as possible and figure out next steps. You should have warned us about this." Bobby ends the call. It's clear Bobby wants someone to blame.

38

Boston, Massachusetts

Dinner arrangements were made for the meeting between the O'Neil and Rossi families. They'll dine at the Harvard Club in Boston. The club has several suites to allow alumni to stay overnight. Grace and Gene are staying in one of them.

While Grace prepares for dinner, Gene is sitting on a couch. She asks, "What is that you're reading, Eugene?"

"Nothing really, just some information on the Rossi family."

"What does that mean?" she asks.

"These are files on the Rossi family. It's background checks, tax returns, criminal records, a summary of their spending on credit cards, anything interesting in the way of phone calls, text messages, stuff like that."

"Excuse me. You have all that?" Grace asks.

"Yes."

"What does it say? What's it say about Teresa?"

"There's not much here, actually, Gene answers. "Joe has two assault and battery charges from years ago. He's had one job all his life with the Massachusetts Bay Transportation Authority. It appears he's a tough guy who works for the union. He travels around to where the union needs him, helps with political elections, demonstrations, union organizing rallies, and such. Mary cuts hair, works in a hair salon. They don't make any money. Teresa works for the state of Massachusetts and doesn't make any money either."

"What were Teresa's grades in school, Eugene?" Grace asks. "What about boyfriends or medical records?"

"I'm sorry," Gene answers, "I don't have that information. I could probably get it if you'd like."

"No." After a pause, she asks, "Have you considered learning about people through the art of conversation?"

#

Teresa is nervous about meeting Jack's parents. She keeps thinking back to Jack's mother cautioning him to practice safe sex. Does Grace think she intended to get pregnant?

Mary and Teresa worry Joe will cause problems. Joe doesn't like New Yorkers and he doesn't like business types. He believes that Jack is responsible for the 'problem' and needs to pay for his mistake. The women are hoping to enjoy their first meeting without incident. Mary made Joe promise to be on his best behaviour.

The Harvard Club is located in the center of Boston.

Joe drives them in town in his pick-up truck. It's large with front and back seats. They pick up Jack on the way. He could have easily walked the short distance from his apartment to the club. Mary and Teresa thought it best if he rode with them. It would make the introductions easier.

Joe drives towards a parking lot underneath the Boston Common. The Common is a park in the center of town much like Central Park in New York.

Jack's confused, "I think the Harvard Club is that way, Mr. Rossi," Jack points. It doesn't occur to him that they wouldn't use the valet.

"I know where it is," Joe answers. "Parking's gotta be expensive there. It's six bucks here if you pull in after 6 o'clock." Joe figures he's teaching Jack the value of thrift. He's also not going to drop the ladies off at the front door, which is a breach of etiquette to Jack.

The group enters the club and they're escorted to the dining area. They ask the maître de for a reservation under the name O'Neil and they're escorted to a small, private dining room.

As they enter, Mary sees Jack make eye contact with his mother. Grace looks beautiful in a gold dress. Grace's hair is pulled back and up. Her blonde hair, tanned skin, and matching dress colour make it appear she's made of gold.

Jack handles the introductions.

Gene is wearing a dark pinstriped suit, white shirt, purple tie, Italian leather shoes, and a gold watch. He has black hair with touches of gray. His presence gives off the feeling that he's taller than his actual height of five feet ten inches.

The waiter arrives, welcomes the Rossi family, and explains the dinner options. Gene suggests they let the sommelier select the wine for the evening. Joe orders a Budweiser "to get started."

Mary is concerned that they're not dressed as formally as they should be. She and Teresa are wearing black dresses. Joe is wearing gray pants with a blue blazer and tie. One problem dressing Joe is his unusually thick neck. Ties never look quite right. They appear short on him.

#

The group settles into polite small talk. They tell each other how nice it is to meet each other's children. The Rossis say this is their first time at the Harvard Club. Mary adds, "I didn't even know this place existed and it's huge."

They make their dinner selections. Grace and Mary will be drinking wine. Gene takes some time to decide if he will be drinking alcohol this evening. He orders whiskey, which is followed by a look from Grace that he chooses to ignore. Grace knows that his personality changes when he drinks; it's the "Irish curse." He becomes more talkative, sometimes too talkative for her liking.

Drinks are served and the mood lightens.

#

Joe begins, "So you guys are from New York?"

"Yes," Grace answers. "We live in the city. I understand you all live just outside of Boston." Grace is sitting upright with her shoulders back. She could give lessons on posture.

"We live in Watertown," Mary answers, and points in the direction she thinks Watertown is. "It's just outside of Boston, like fifteen minutes without traffic."

"That's convenient," Grace responds. "Do you come in town often?"

"No, not much at all really." Mary shakes her head. "We spend most of our time right in Watertown with family and friends. Course Joe comes in for work every day."

"Have you lived in Watertown long?" Grace asks.

"All my life," Mary answers. "Joe too. We're 'townies', that's what they call us anyway. What about you? Have you lived in New York City all your life?" Mary asks.

Grace looks at Gene and replies, "We've lived in the city now for over thirty years."

Gene adds, "Almost forty for me."

"Are you from New York originally?" Mary asks. "You don't sound like a New Yorker, Grace."

"No. Heavens, no," Grace responds. "I'm from the South originally and Eugene is from here, Boston."

"The South?" Teresa asks.

"Boston? You're from Boston?" Joe asks, while another bottle of Budweiser arrives. Each time the waiter delivers a bottle, he asks if Joe would prefer a glass. Joe declines.

Gene smiles, "Yes, sir, I'm from West Roxbury."

Joe's puzzled. "Jack came to our home for dinner and said his folks were from New York. I guess I assumed that you were from New York originally."

"Well, I've been in New York a long time but, yes, my roots are here in Boston," Gene replies, "and we still have family here."

"Whereabouts in West Roxbury are you from?" Joe continues.

"Right behind St. Teresa's Church. Do you know the area?"

West Roxbury is one of the many neighbourhoods that make up the city of Boston. St. Teresa's is a large, well-known Catholic parish.

"Sure, I know the area," Joe answers, "everyone does. How'd you get from St. Teresa's to New York?"

"It's pretty simple actually," Gene begins. "I was an altar boy at St. Teresa's and I went to school there. We lived in a two-family home about a block from church. The pastor liked my family. I had good grades. One day my mom tells me I'll be going to Roxbury Latin or RL next year. It's a highly regarded preparatory school for young men and abuts St. Teresa's property. The school gives out one scholarship a year to a local boy who shows promise. I was lucky to get it. That same kind of dumb luck got me from RL to Harvard and then New York."

Grace interrupts, "Eugene is being modest. He graduated first in his class at Roxbury Latin. That's how he got to Harvard." She nods as if to add an exclamation point.

Gene's not comfortable talking about himself. "I think they were trying to help us out really, my family I mean. I've always appreciated that. My father passed away at a young age, so the scholarships were a blessing. I may not have gotten anywhere in life without them."

Joe's surprised. He didn't plan on liking this guy. The guy comes from a two-family home in West Roxbury. His father died at a young age. It's easy to hate a faceless banker from New York City. It's harder to dislike a guy that came from a similar background or started with less than you.

#

The privacy provided by the room is helpful. Food is served and it's delicious.

Mary declares, "You know, this is the best meal I've ever eaten. I don't know if it's the food or the chef, but I've never tasted anything like this. It's like tasting food for the first time."

The O'Neil family members understand, but don't say anything.

Joe is feeling more and more comfortable. His questions become more aggressive. He asks, "Gene, if you don't mind. I want to ask you something?"

"Of course, what's that?" Gene replies.

"Well, how come we go through this financial mess? The stock market drops. A lot of people lose their jobs or get screwed. The Wall Street banks get bailed out. A lot of people get massacred and the government bails out the banks. You guys are behind the mess, but you end up making a ton of money."

Gene is chewing on his meal.

Joe continues, "Taxpayer bailouts going right into the pockets of bankers. I guess my question is how come nobody went to jail?"

Grace is appalled. She believes that Gene's character is above reproach. She understands that Wall Street has many corrupt people. She's heard stories. Her husband, however, is above it all. Joe should apologize immediately. She stares coldly at Joe.

"Well, Joe, yes something is wrong," Gene replies, not the least bit upset by the question. "People should have gone to jail. People lied. Some broke laws. I agree with you if that was your point. I suppose the reason no one went to jail is because our government didn't want to expose problems, didn't want anyone to go to jail."

Joe is speechless. He expected Gene to defend the bank and the government.

Gene recognizes that his response has caught Joe off guard. "I don't think my bank did anything wrong. When the government told us we had to take the money, we told them we didn't want it and we didn't need it. The president said all the banks had to take it. If the government gave money to only some banks, then everyone would know which banks were in trouble. We took the bailout money and we paid it back with interest as soon as the government allowed us to."

The table is quiet. Perhaps it's the whiskey that has loosened Gene's tongue. He continues. "All Americans should be upset, Joe. Why didn't bankers go to jail? Because our Justice Department is filled with incompetent people and political hacks. You can google what I'm going to tell you. The lead prosecutor for the state of New York gave a speech to his bar association. He said he didn't prosecute people because he was afraid that the prosecution would weaken the banks. The fellow responsible for prosecuting crimes decided he wasn't going to do his job. It's outrageous, and from a Justice Department whose top guy called Americans 'cowards'. I think he got that backwards."

Jack and Teresa are mildly interested in the conversation. They don't know anything about the most recent financial collapse.

"But what about you guys?" Joe asks again. "Wasn't your bank part of creating the mess?"

The question further upsets Grace and she announces that she needs to get some air. Joe's questions aren't proper. Mary says she'll join her and

Teresa goes along as well. Gene and Jack stand as the three women leave the room.

"What about us? Yes, we bought mortgage-backed securities. We bought CDOs. We traded in every security and made the market in many of them. Still do. We recognized that the mortgages backing up the bonds were crap. The people owing money on their mortgages were never going to be able to pay it back. It was a house of cards. We sold them. We sold them to others who eventually needed government bailouts. Is that our fault? I don't think so. It's our job to be smarter than the other guys and we were."

As Gene finishes, Joe is out of questions. Joe had pictured him as the villain. Gene left out the part about salespersons at his bank lying about how good the securities were when they sold them to other banks. He left out the fact that his bank paid a large fine for those "misrepresentations."

"Let's face it, Joe," Gene continues, "the group of people that dreamt up this stuff never understood banking in the first place. They were trying to allow banks to make loans and eliminate risk. That's impossible. You can't eliminate risk; you can only move it around. Rather than show the world they were some brilliant breed of young, hotshot bankers, they showed us that they didn't understand banking in the first place."

Jack is following the conversation, but losing interest. He has enjoyed an insulated world where he can focus on academics. He begins trying to solve an origami puzzle with his napkin.

"You might ask a better question." Gene pushes his dinner plate aside as he finishes his meal. "You might ask why our government promotes home ownership to people that can't afford them in the first place. Why is the average taxpayer paying for these programs? These problems go back to the 1990s when the Department of Housing and Urban Development decided every American should be given a home. They asked bankers to help find a way to pay for everything. That was your government. People didn't need to work and save for a home; the government will just give it to you. It became another entitlement program or another basic human right. That was the real crime. Vote us into office and we'll give everyone a home as a payoff for your vote. It's preposterous or call it what it is, communism."

#

Gene and Joe continue to go back and forth. Both men are enjoying the conversation. Talking politics and religion are often discouraged, but not in Boston.

Joe says, "You know your boy came to our house and tells us he doesn't believe in God. He thinks religion is based on the calendar, the moon and the stars. Is that what you think?"

Jack is shocked. "That's not what I said Mr. Rossi."

Gene answers calmly. "I don't know anything about that. I suppose it's only natural for a young person to have questions about their faith. I did. I questioned just about everything as a young man. Ultimately, I hope he values his faith as I do. It's a gift. It allows me to keep things in perspective and focus on what's most important. There are people who attribute part of our great country's decline on a lack of morals and the inability to apply values in everyday life."

"Mr. Rossi, I was just sharing a perspective that I thought was interesting," Jack explains.

"Are you a religious man?" Gene asks.

"I am."

"Well, something else we have in common." Gene raises his glass in a small toast.

#

Grace, Mary, and Teresa settle in on a porch overlooking the Boston Common. The Harvard Club was built on this very spot almost four hundred years ago. It wasn't long after its completion that the Common was protected from any development. The Club has enjoyed a privileged view ever since.

The women sit on heated benches. Patio heaters surround them and provide comfort.

Grace lights up a cigarette. Teresa moves one bench away to avoid the smoke. She offers Mary a cigarette and Mary accepts.

"How did you and Gene meet?" Mary asks.

Grace relaxes. She has told the story many times, but it rekindles fond memories and she loves retelling it. "My father arranged for me to meet Eugene," Grace begins. Grace can turn up her southern accent when she chooses. "My father was the general counsel for the Coca-Cola Company in Atlanta.

Their top lawyer. He tells my mother and me about this young man who has so impressed the company's chairman and chief executive officer."

Grace looks skyward as she continues. "Coca-Cola was interested in expanding and needed money to do it. Three banks were competing for the business and they just couldn't decide which bank to choose. Rufus Wallingford was the CEO at Coca-Cola and he tells each bank to send people down to stay with him and his wife. They had a second home up in the Smoky Mountains. Rufus loved the outdoors."

Grace lights another cigarette. "Each bank could send as many as three people to Rufus's home for two days with an overnight. He and his wife would listen to their sales pitch. Ed Pendergast was the Co-CEO of Morgan Sachs at the time. Ed liked Eugene and asked him to make the pitch on behalf of the bank. Eugene made the trip. A week goes by and no one heard anything. The people at Morgan Sachs figured they didn't get the business and they'd find out through a press release. You know, an announcement from another bank saying they won the business because they were the greatest bankers in the world."

Grace pauses and takes a deep breath before continuing. "One day Ed gets a call from Rufus. He tells Ed that Morgan Sachs won the business. Ed thanks him and begins to arrange next steps but Rufus interrupts him. He asks 'don't you want to know why you won our business?' Ed answers, 'Sure I'd love to know.' 'Well, that boy you sent down here,' Rufus says. Eugene was so young, and Rufus called just about everyone boy. 'My wife likes him. I like him. All you bankers said the exact same things, but your boy brought flowers for my wife. He made his bed in the morning. He cleared the table and offered to do the dishes. He sent handwritten thank you notes to us with a small present. He sent a handwritten note and flowers to our housekeeper. That was very thoughtful and pretty damned good for a Yankee." Grace smiles.

"You know, I heard that story from Rufus," Grace says, "and I heard Ed tell it the same way, so it must be so. Eugene manages it all and everyone was pleased. A few months go by and Eugene calls Rufus to ask if he could come by for lunch. Eugene shows up with a man who invites Rufus to join the Augusta National Golf Club." Grace looks at Mary to see if she understands the significance of the invitation. "It's a high honour to join that particular club. Rufus was pleased as punch, and from that day on, Rufus became

Eugene's best salesman. He told every chief executive that would listen to use Eugene for all their banking needs. Eugene is always helping others and they end up helping him. It's like an inner circle of important people all helping each other." Grace looks to Mary and Teresa and tilts her head. "I apologize for going on like that. Damned near talked your ears off didn't I."

Mary and Teresa both say, "No, we enjoyed hearing it."

"So, to answer your question, it was my father that found Eugene and figured he'd be a good catch. He arranged for us to sit together at a black-tie event in Atlanta. We've been good together. There's the obvious age difference, older than me I mean, but he's a very, very good man and a good father." Grace emphasized "good man" based on her perceived insults from Joe. Neither Mary nor Teresa understand her subtlety.

#

"Your turn," Grace says to Mary. "How'd you meet Joe?"

"Joe was a year older than me in school. Back in high school, he was the big man on campus. He was captain of the football team and kind of ran our high school with his friends."

Neither woman is smoking now, so Teresa moves closer. A waiter has come by and taken a drink order from them. Grace and Mary order another glass of wine.

"I didn't think he even knew who I was," Mary continues. "I didn't hang out with the cool kids. One day we got paired together in biology class after Joe and a friend were fooling around with bunsen burners. I was Joe's punishment and became his lab partner. Next thing I know, he's hanging around my locker and just showing up when I get out of classes. He asked me to prom. Joe was the first man I was with. The only man I've ever been with."

Grace has heard other women make that claim. This time she believes it.

"Months go by before I asked him what he thought was my best feature. He said, 'your eyes.' When I said 'really' he shook his head 'no.' He told me from that first day in biology class he couldn't take his eyes off my ass. Lucky for me I guess."

Joe and Mary have a good marriage. They've had to work at it, but they've been devoted to one another. Their marriage is exactly what Teresa is hoping for.

Mary is worried that Joe is unlike the people Grace knows in New York. With an apologetic tone she explains, "Joe's a good man. He's a little gruff but he's a pussycat underneath. This pregnancy has been a shock to him. Teresa is his little girl. He's always been protective of her. The pregnancy upsets him and he doesn't know how to deal with it. I think he hoped that Teresa would find a nice young man from our neighbourhood or close by, maybe someone more like the people we know."

Grace can see Mary is sweet. She'd like to ask more questions and learn more about Teresa, but not now. She'd also like to share what her dreams were for Jack before the pregnancy. They were very different than this.

#

When the women return to the table, the men are in good spirits. They're sampling four different desserts and at least that many liqueurs. Their ties are loose and the top buttons of their shirts are undone.

Gene and Jack stand as the women re-enter the room. Joe seems surprised by their standing again. Grace is tempted to remain standing until Joe gets up.

As the ladies enter the room, they hear Gene ask, "What about you, Joe? You've been asking me a lot of questions. Here's my question; why are you in a union?"

Joe seems puzzled.

Mary cringes. That's like asking Joe why he's American.

"What are you talking about?" Joe asks.

"Don't get me wrong. I think there was a time in our history when our country desperately needed unions. But now?" Gene shrugs his shoulders.

"Why am I in a union? You know as good as anybody that there's been a clash between labour and capital for centuries. The rich have all the money and power. They've exploited the working man. Workers have to stick together because there's power in numbers. Without a union, rich people and big companies would run all over them."

Gene nods thoughtfully before responding. “Well, Joe, I like you and might agree with some of that, but I have bad news. In the battle between labour and capital, capital won years ago. It’s over. We have challenges, but your union isn’t helping the working man. It’s hurting him.”

Mary is concerned about Joe’s drinking. She sits beside him and places a glass of water in front of him.

“What? No, of course the union’s helping,” Joe objects.

“All I’m saying,” Gene replies, “is that I know your union leaders. My bank manages your pension and all the union’s finances. I’m only suggesting you think about it. Maybe they’re looking after themselves and after politicians a lot more than their own members. We know unions kill productivity trying to save jobs. That hurts growth, stops investment and the creation of new and better jobs. Unions are responsible for pushing jobs overseas.”

Teresa and Jack are only watching. They are sitting next to one another holding hands. “You ok?” she asks about Jack’s drinking.

“Yeah, I’m good,” he answers. “You?”

She nods. “Yes.”

“No. Wait. What?” Joe asks.

“The only purpose of unions today is to funnel money to a political party. I believe we needed unions years ago. They helped workers get better pay, lower hours, improved workplace safety, added more days off, fought discrimination, and more. But everything the unions did for workers is now done by the federal government and its bureaucracies. The only purpose of unions now is to collect your dues and push a political agenda that’s actually hurting you.”

Joe feels a loyalty to stand up for the union. “They help us with jobs. They add jobs and keep our jobs safe. You must be a Republican looking down on the working man.”

Mary puts her watch in front of Joe and points to it in order to get his attention. She wants to conclude the evening.

“I apologize, Joe,” Gene replies. “I didn’t mean to offend you, and if I did I’m very sorry. I’m not a Republican or Democrat. I’ve raised more money for Democrats lately, but that’s a business decision. The truth is, Joe, that politicians from both parties are killing our country.”

Grace interrupts, “Well, I’d like to say thank you Teresa, Mary, and Joe. It’s been a pleasure meeting you all. I look forward to getting to know you better. I think that's enough for me. I'm going to call it an evening and go upstairs."

Joe and Gene look at each other and smile. They recognize they carried on too long.

"I want to thank the Rossi family too," Genes adds. "Teresa, you are lovely and I'm glad to have met you. I think that you and Jack are lucky because your futures are going to be spectacular. I want to offer you a toast and best wishes until we see you again." Gene raises his glass and others do the same.

The toast excites Mary. "Do you really think their futures are going to be spectacular?"

"I know it," Gene says. "It's not about labour and capital. It's about intelligence, mobility, globalization. These forces will drive world events. If you're on the right side of things, then you'll have more opportunity than at any time in all of human history. You can do and have anything you want in the world."

The group stands and begins to exit the room.

"Joe, Mary, you've got to come visit us this summer," Gene adds. "I'd like to invite you to our place in the Hamptons. Early August. We go every year for two weeks. I hope you'll come for one of those weeks."

Mary and Joe look at each other. Mary answers, "Yes, we'd love to, and thank you."

The invitation is a surprise to Grace, and not a welcome one. Gene rarely invites anyone, and never before checking with her.

#

When they reach Joe's truck, Mary says it would be best if she drove. Joe immediately climbs into the passenger seat.

After dropping off Jack, Mary asks, "What did you think?"

"They're ok," Joe says.

"Ok, Daddy? They're wonderful, aren't they?" Teresa says excitedly. "I mean did you see her? Her dress, jewellery, hair, her accent. Oh my God."

Mary smiles. "Did you notice that not one of them have an ounce of body fat. How's that possible? They must have great genes."

"I hope we measured up ok," Teresa adds. "I mean I hope they liked us."

"Measured up?" Joe perks up. "Of course, you measured up. You're as good as anybody in this world. Don't ever think otherwise."

"You shouldn't have had so much to drink," Mary begins, "and why get into politics? We talked about this. I asked you not to and you promised."

Joe shrugs his shoulders.

Mary asks, "What do you think about what Gene said about the union?"

"You mean, Eugene?" Joe asks playfully, mimicking Grace's accent. They all think that's funny. Joe adds, "The union? He doesn't know what he's talking about."

"Well, you heard him. Maybe it's not doing us any good? You've complained for years about how hard it is to get anything done, and all this money going to politicians." Mary wants Joe to consider it.

"He's full of shit," Joe replies. "Just because he's rich and goes to the Harvard Club doesn't mean he knows everything."

"Did you hear that they have a place in the Hamptons?" Teresa asks. "The Hamptons! Do you think we'll really go there? Wouldn't that be unbelievable?"

"Yeah, yeah, yeah. The Hamptons," Joe answers.

"Do you see what I mean, Mom?" Teresa asks. "I bet they have millions."

"It would be something to see what it's like in the Hamptons," Mary says. "I bet there are celebrities everywhere." She looks into the rear-view mirror to share her smile with Teresa.

#

Grace and Gene return to their suite. "What did you think of them?" Grace asks.

"I thought they were delightful, honey," Gene answers. "Very nice. You?"

"I really wish you'd be serious."

"I think both Mary and Teresa are lovely, very pretty. Joe's a little rough, but a good man. Teresa didn't say much, but she was probably nervous." Gene knows his wife. She can be a snob, but she has a good heart. She may have hoped for an elaborate wedding to a well-to-do family. That's less important to him.

"You know what she told me," Grace begins. "She told me that Jack took her to Scituate and she met your family. Jack's probably been saying too much. She probably figured Jack has money. How do you get pregnant these days? And I can't believe you invited them to the Hamptons. You didn't even check with me. I've made plans. I don't know if I can fit them in or if we even want them."

"I'm sorry. We'll figure it out." Gene gives her a kiss.

"And how dare that man question you on government bailouts and such things. He brought it up right there at dinner in front of me." Grace prefers the manners and customs of the home where she grew up. "I don't understand why you didn't just take care of this and make this whole thing go away. You should make this go away, make them go away. You need to mind what I'm telling you."

"We'll figure this all out, honey," he repeats. "Good night, I love you."

39

Boston, Massachusetts

Grace and Gene enjoy breakfast together at the Harvard Club the following morning. She'll return to New York. Gene will begin a trip around the world. He gave the president eight weeks for a plan. It's unclear how the president will respond. Gene needs to prepare for all possible scenarios. He'll fly around the world and meet with leaders of the largest economies. Appointments are set up in London, Paris, Berlin, Moscow, Riyadh, Beijing, and Tokyo.

In each country, Gene first meets with the person managing things for Morgan Sachs. These men and women are extremely knowledgeable and useful.

Gene's developed a trust among the leaders in these countries. They rely on him to raise billions of dollars through the sale of bonds, primarily for long-term investments in infrastructure, including roads, electric plants, and airports.

World leaders are supportive of Gene's initiative. United States economic policy is hurting international trade. It's causing inflation and social unrest around the world. Political leaders use the term "social unrest" to mean the population is getting agitated. After agitation comes violence, possible change in governments, or civil war. Using the term "social unrest" communicates a serious warning.

Sheiks in Saudi Arabia blame the United States for the uprisings in Tunisia, Libya, Syria, and other countries. The majority of their population live in poverty. The United States, through the Federal Reserve, followed a policy called "quantitative easing" and exported inflation from the United States to this region. Food prices skyrocketed. Millions of men became desperate when they were unable to feed their families. Reasonable men followed religious extremists based on their promises of food and safety. A financial policy designed to make politicians popular in the United States transferred inflation to an area of the world that could least afford it. The result was violence in the streets and the recruitment of terrorists. It was the worst possible outcome. World leaders are relying on Gene's help for changes in American policies.

#

Gene understood quantitative easing would lead to problems. He didn't know how bad it would get. He thinks back to his warning to Bobby, "You can light a match and start a fire, but you're never sure how bad the fire might get." Quantitative easing led to worse outcomes than expected, and faster than anyone could have predicted. Such is the nature of our tightly integrated world of politics and finance.

The gulf between rich and poor is wide in the United States. It's worse in other countries. Worse by catastrophic proportions. The suffering of the world's poorest is grossly unfair. Americans have no idea what real poverty looks like; it's not being deprived of a cell phone. He thinks back to his days studying the classics at Harvard and a quote from Thucydides; "The strong do what they can and the weak suffer what they must." Can these differences be explained as part of man's nature?

Looking down from his private jet, he thinks of how to improve the allocation of the world's limited resources. Is it possible to create cooperation among people on a massive scale to share things more equally? What would have to change? Political leaders operate in their own interests and the interests of their people over others. What would have to change? Tyrants and majorities acting as tyrants can't create long-term, sustainable change. They only create resentment. What would have to happen to get the people of the world to work together?

While Gene doesn't regret his career choices, he realizes there may have been a better use of his time. He spent his career enriching the wealthiest people on earth. Was that selfish? Should he have spent more time considering the least fortunate? He didn't contemplate the question as a young man. He was busy building a career and caring for family. Is it too late to make a difference? Where is that opportunity?

#

Gene sleeps on the plane when he can. It's an exhausting trip and the changes in time zones create a challenge.

Of particular interest to Gene on this trip were the decision makers overseeing the world's largest sovereign wealth funds. They're a relatively new power in the world's financial landscape. They control enormous wealth and influence.

He's able to secure the cooperation he was after. The trip is a success.

#

The jet has a crew to look after Gene's needs, including a flight attendant, Elsa, who looks a lot like Grace did years ago. On the long flight home Gene asks, "Can you please pour me a glass of whiskey? Pour one for yourself too if you'd like."

His satellite phone rings. It's Jack.

"Hi, Dad, I know you're probably busy," Jack begins.

"No. Not at all, Jackson. What's up?" Gene asks.

"Well, I've been talking with Teresa," he answers. "We'll come to New York for a year like you asked. I'm only committing to a year. If it doesn't work out, then I can continue with school and no questions asked. We'll never talk about banking again. I mean, that's our agreement, right?"

Elsa delivers Gene's drink. She's carrying one for herself.

Gene leans back in his chair and smiles. "That's right, one year. That's the agreement. But don't be surprised if you like it and decide to stay longer."

"I wouldn't count on that, Dad," Jack answers.

"Welcome to the bank. You've made the right decision."

40

Boston, Massachusetts

Jack and Teresa return to his apartment after eating dinner out. Cheese is sitting on Jack's couch eating pizza and watching television.

"Hey," Jack says nonchalantly as they enter.

Teresa is getting used to Cheese letting himself in, making himself at home, and even buying food deliveries on Jack's credit card. She understands that her relationship with Jack has meant less time for Jack and Cheese to spend together.

"Guys," Cheese says excitedly, "zombie movie is just starting and it's a good one."

Jack sits down next to his friend and says, "Buddy, I got a present for you."

"Great," Cheese answers, "Love it."

"I'd hand you my keys to the apartment but…" Jack stops. Cheese already has keys. "Teresa and I are moving to New York for a year. My lease here is paid through the end of December. I'm not sure what to do with all this furniture but, well, would you like to have the apartment 'til the end of the lease?"

"What the fuck are you talking about?" Cheese responds. "New York? Dude, we were going to hang out here for the rest of our lives. Teach, research, breakthroughs together? What do you mean? Are you serious?"

"I know, but it's only for a year," Jack explains. "I promised my dad that I'd come to work with him at the bank. Then I'm free to come back here. I can do whatever I want after that." Jack feels he's betrayed his closest friend.

"Your dad? The bank? What the fuck, man?" Cheese puts down his slice of pizza, grabs his backpack, and starts walking towards the door.

"I'm sorry. My dad wants me to come. It's the first time he ever asked me for anything. I figure I owe it to him," Jack continues to explain as Cheese walks out.

Jack sits back, shakes his head, and feels horrible. He and Cheese had talked about working together in and around MIT for years to come.

Ten minutes pass before Cheese texts, "I understand. I'll take the apartment."

Jack replies, "It's just one year, then I'll be back."

41

London, England

Madeline Rothschild has organized a call among the leaders of the shareholders.

"Gentlemen," she begins. "I want to discuss Gene's proposal for ten percent ownership interest in the bank. After giving this some consideration, I believe that five percent is appropriate. Does anyone have thoughts on the matter?"

"I thought ten percent was outrageous," David Rockefeller responds. "I thought that maybe one percent would be fair."

Peter Morgan objects, "I still don't know why we should give him any ownership interest. Let's just give him a billion dollars or two."

James Loeb weighs in, "Madeline, I know you like Gene, but I'm also in favour of paying him in dollars rather than shares in the bank. He is only an employee after all."

There is an uneasy silence before Madeline speaks again. "You all have very short and convenient memories, don't you?" Her tone resembles a mother scolding her sons. "Do you forget how dysfunctional this group was? Do you remember oil prices in the 1970s? Do you remember America's prime interest rate over eighteen percent? Nothing was being handled correctly. Our families were continuously at odds and it put everything in jeopardy. I stepped in. I found Gene and we fixed things and we've kept them right. Now, he's putting his life on the line for us. We've seen how leaders respond when confronted with their debts. This may get ugly. I expect nothing less than your complete loyalty and support. You owe me. You owe him. I trust I'm making myself clear."

There's a pause before William Vanderbilt says, "I'm ok with five percent."

"I'll put it to a vote," she says. "All in favour say aye."

She hears 'aye,' but is unsure if everyone participated in the vote. "Are there any nays?"

Silence.

"Good," she answers.

42

New York, New York

The transition from business school to New York is easy for JR. He's planned it for years. Despite his mother's urgings to live at home, JR rents an apartment in order to have his freedom.

JR wasn't putting much effort into school and was getting even less out of it. All he wanted from Harvard Business School was a diploma and a network of contacts, not unusual for Harvard students. The network alone justifies the costs.

His transition is efficient. JR tells a realtor exactly what he wants. The search of properties consists of selecting from four apartments. He chooses one and hires an interior decorator to furnish the apartment. It's a "turnkey" operation, meaning JR merely needs to show up and turn the key. Everything will be in place for him, right down to connecting electronics, new sheets on beds, and kitchenware in drawers and cabinets.

#

Leaving school is more difficult for Jack. He loves school. He's identified himself by his academic success and he's less comfortable in the real world. M.I.T. provided the opportunity to learn from great professors. Mathematics and science provide an order and beauty Jack craves. He once corrected his father when Gene referred to mathematics as one of man's greatest inventions. Jack believes man discovered mathematics as it's too perfect for him to invent.

The move to New York itself will be easy. Like JR, he can hire people to help where needed.

Teresa is anxious. She's never lived anywhere except the house she grew up in. She's enjoyed a close network of family and friends for support.

Joe Rossi is against the move. He called in favours to get her a job with the State. Giving up the long-term security of government employment with great benefits is risky. "What if things don't work out?" he asks. "You're giving up a job for life with medical benefits and a pension. You don't even have to work hard. You just have to show up and not make trouble."

Mary and Joe think marriage should be a prerequisite of the move. Teresa ignores them. She's putting her faith and trust in her relationship with Jack.

#

Grace selected an apartment for Teresa and Jack. It's two blocks from the O'Neil home. It has three bedrooms and 3,200 square feet. It's considered very large in the city.

Grace invites Mary and Teresa to New York. She shows them the apartment and invites them shopping. She's also invited an interior decorator along.

According to Grace, today's plan is to "collect the basics." Before Teresa and Mary know it, Grace is not only buying "basics," she's buying furniture, rugs, lamps, and more. Grace and the decorator carry a floor plan with a list of their needs.

Mary can't believe the prices or volume of things Grace is buying. She objects to some purchases because she can find much better bargains elsewhere. Grace isn't paying attention.

Teresa tells Grace that she wants to have "a few pieces of furniture" brought to New York from their Watertown home. They have sentimental value to her.

By the end of their shopping spree, Mary believes they've bought more than can fit in the apartment.

At day's end, Mary and Teresa board a bus back to Boston. They sit next to each other and are glad to catch their breath. They look at each other and shake their heads in unison. "Do you believe that?" Mary asks.

"No, Mom. I've never seen anything like it. The people. The prices. The chaos. Grace. The way she just kept asking that decorator for her thoughts and buying more shit."

"She should have asked us for more of our thoughts," Mary says. "She didn't seem to pay any attention to our suggestions. Did you notice the way the decorator bought everything? I bet the decorator marks up every purchase and Grace could care less."

"She asked for our opinions," Teresa answers, "and then kind of ignored them. Maybe she figures that since she's buying everything, she can make all the decisions."

"She's nice and very generous, but you're going to have your hands full there."

"Yeah," Teresa agrees. "But can you believe that apartment? Can you believe where I'm going to be living?"

"No, I really can't believe it," Mary answers. "It's bigger than our home and the view is incredible. Central Park is right in front of you."

"It's quiet too, huh?" Teresa says. "I mean I was thinking everything in New York is noisy, but it's high up, or it's the construction, but it was really quiet."

"Security," Mary says. "You've got security in the building. I was worried about safety, but I guess everything has been taken care of. Maybe money can't buy happiness, but it buys a lot."

#

Joe is waiting for them at the bus station in Boston. He drops Teresa at Jack's place and brings Mary home.

Teresa tells Jack of the trip. He's glad that his mom was able to help, especially if it makes Teresa feel better about the move.

To Joe, the shopping spree is an ominous sign. He's worried his daughter will be spending more time with the O'Neils and less time with his side of the family. She'll grow closer to them and might be influenced by their money and lifestyle. He decides that he'll deliver the pieces of furniture that Teresa asked for. He'd like to see things for himself.

43

Washington, D.C.

Doug Martin continues to attend the president's weekly meetings. Three weeks go by without being called on. His phone calls and emails to the White House go unanswered. Doug forces the opportunity to speak with Bobby Ferguson by cornering him after a meeting.

"Bobby, what's going on?" Doug asks.

"Mr. Secretary, good morning. What do you mean?" Bobby replies casually.

"You haven't called on me in the meetings," Doug begins. "You haven't answered my calls or responded to emails. Gene gave us eight weeks to come up with a plan. I've sent the president my ideas. I haven't heard anything back. Can you tell me what's going on?"

"Nothing, Mr. Secretary," Bobby answers. "We've read your suggestions and they're very good. We're considering all options, but we've got a lot going on right now. Do you have thoughts on how we might stop him or delay things? I mean maybe until the end of the president's term? Do we have any legal actions we could take against the Fed to take away their powers? Does Gene have any weaknesses we might exploit? You know, skeletons in his closet that would compromise him? We need to run every option down."

"What? I don't know about legal actions. I could research that. Weaknesses? None that I know of but that's really not the point. The country needs a long-term financial plan."

"Ok," Bobby answers. "Do some research. Think of every possible option. We'll get back with you soon." He turns and walks away.

44

Cambridge, Massachusetts

The O'Neil family has two graduation ceremonies; JR from the Harvard Business School, and Jack from M.I.T. The ceremonies occur on the schools' campuses.

Grace, Gene, and Jack attend JR's ceremony that concludes in the late afternoon. JR's preference is to get an early dinner in order to get back and celebrate with friends. He'd prefer to skip the events recognizing students who graduated with distinction.

JR invites his girlfriend, Jennifer Furash, to join them for dinner. She's a first year in the business school. Her mother and Grace are very close and part of the same social circles in the city. She is the type of young lady that Grace would prefer her sons to marry.

They dine on Italian food in Boston's North End. Grace makes sure to get plenty of photographs of the day. She's very proud of her son.

#

Grace, Gene, and JR attend Jack's graduation along with Teresa, Mary, and Joe Rossi. Jack's aunt and uncles, Connie and Tom Murray and Steve O'Neil, also attend. Connie explains that Uncle Dave wanted to come but "wasn't able to."

Jack graduates with a perfect grade point average. M.I.T. doesn't recognize a valedictorian. One other student also achieves a perfect grade point average and both are recognized during the ceremony.

Teresa invites everyone to participate in a dinner celebration. She keeps the location secret as long as possible—until they're almost there. The location is the diner where Jack is most comfortable.

They join several tables together to create seating for everyone. The men settle in to one end and the women on the other. Joe Rossi sits across the table from Gene. He jokes, "I was kind of hoping for the Harvard Club."

Gene smiles. "This feels more appropriate, huh?"

Connie puts her mouth to Grace's ear to confide in her. She tells her "I love this boy. We all love him. He's come such a long way, huh? Isn't it a blessing, just a wonderful blessing?"

"Louder," her husband Tom replies. "I don't think they heard you across the street."

Connie's whispers are loud enough for everyone to hear. The group gets a good laugh.

JR meets Teresa and the Rossi family for the first time.

Cheese shows up for the celebration. "I knew you wouldn't miss a free meal," Teresa says. She introduces him to the group. "Everyone, this is Jack's best friend in the whole world, Li Jie. They all call him 'Cheese' and I still don't understand that nickname."

Jack stands and gives Cheese a big hug. Teresa directs them to put their graduation caps and gowns back on in order to get a picture. They stand with their arms around each other's shoulders, huge smiles.

45

New York, New York

Gene calls Maddy with an update. He tells her the good news regarding progress on his trip around the world. Things are in place for the first phase if the president fails to act.

"Congratulations, that's really great work, Gene. Do you think they'll all keep their commitments?"

"That'll be the hard part, but so far so good," he answers.

"And you still don't think the president is going to do anything until he's forced to?" Maddy asks.

"We know that politicians are untrustworthy, but they're predictable. I'm ready to act. I need to know the shareholders are on board."

"We are. You'll have our unwavering support. You have my word on it," Maddy answers.

"That's good to hear. You should know that I'm being followed."

"Are you sure? Do you know who it is, Gene?"

"Yes, I'm sure because the bank's security team watches over me. They have video evidence of it, but no, I don't know who it is. Easy guess that it's the president's men."

"Be careful," she cautions. "The stakes couldn't be any higher. We can buy whatever security you need."

"Thank you. I think I'm ok for now. I just wanted to let you know. Maybe they're just watching or maybe they're trying to intimidate me." Gene switches topics, "How was my request for an ownership interest received by the shareholders?"

"I'll be honest," Madeline begins, which feels unnecessary. She's always brutally honest. "The ten percent number shocked everyone, including me. You're getting ownership but not ten percent. I'd prefer to talk with you in person rather than over the phone. I'll come out to your place in the Hamptons this summer. I also want to talk with you about a succession plan. You and I both need to identify people for our positions and get them trained. They'll need time."

"I understand. I've got someone in mind for my position," Gene answers.

46

Watertown, Massachusetts

Teresa's friends arrange a going-away party for her. It was supposed to be a surprise, but no one can keep a secret in their neighbourhood. The party will be at Molly McCann's home. They'll spend their time between the kitchen, backyard, and basement. There's a staircase linking the basement to the backyard.

Teresa is moved by the gesture. Despite her recent estrangement from the group, she cares deeply for these friends. They've enjoyed good times and made memories that will last a lifetime. She's worried that Jack may not appreciate the close bond she shares with the group. He's never been a part of a large, close circle of friends.

Teresa has ignored Roberto's attempts to speak with her since their dinner together. He texted and called. While she'd like to see him, she prefers that he not come to the party. He's not invited.

Teresa and Jack have spent most of their time together in and around M.I.T. This will be the first time Jack will meet her friends. She's told them a lot about him and their expectations are high.

#

The four McCann children are home for the party. Molly's parents have put out appetizers, a keg of beer, and a cooler with soft drinks. Everyone enjoys getting together here. The family is made up of two boys and two girls that are close in age. The parents and children are all naturally outgoing.

People start showing up around 7:00 p.m. Mr. McCann wants things to wrap up by midnight. He's a firefighter in town and figures that's late enough in their neighbourhood.

Mrs. McCann has pulled out old pictures and created several large collages. They're displayed on poster boards in the living room. The pictures begin with the group in pre-school, and follows them through to today.

Teresa and Jack arrive and the group quickly embraces Teresa. She introduces Jack, but he is on the outside of most conversations. He's socially awkward in most settings; tonight is more challenging because he doesn't know anyone. The group reminisces about shared experiences that don't include him.

The crowd is split between those that are at least twenty-one years old and legally able to consume alcohol, and those under twenty-one. Age isn't an issue. Almost everyone seems to have a beer in their hands. Music is playing. It's a fun atmosphere.

At one point, Jack joins a circle of people and tries to fit in. The group is huddled at the end of the driveway. A young man is bragging about punching a homosexual.

Jack doesn't understand. "You hit him because he's gay?" Jack asks. The crowd turns towards Jack. Jack is wearing a light blue, button-down Ralph Lauren shirt and salmon coloured shorts.

Jim or 'Jocko' Bonistalli was the one talking. "Yeah" he answers, "he was gay and I smacked him. What's it to you?" he asks aggressively.

This makes no sense, Jack thinks to himself. Jack turns and retreats back to the house. He hears Jocko laughing and assumes it's directed towards him. Jack wishes he were invisible.

A couple minutes go by before another fellow who witnessed the incident finds Jack. He introduces himself as Paul and says, "Don't worry about him. You did the right thing. Jocko is the world's biggest asshole. Always has been. Every neighbourhood has one, right?"

Teresa is the center of attention. They serve cake and sing "Happy Going-Away to You" in the melody of Happy Birthday. The singing is terrible. Everyone is laughing.

Jack begins thinking that Teresa is being inconsiderate of him. Perhaps he should just leave. It's not like anyone cares if he's here or not.

#

Paul's girlfriend Maureen and their friend Lucy approach them. They're wearing jeans, high heels, and tube tops with their navels exposed.

Paul handles the introductions before Lucy says, "You're really smart, huh? Say something smart."

Jack shies away but they encourage him. "Ok," he relents. "How about this? Let's say you're travelling in a spaceship at a great distance from the planet Earth. You're travelling at almost the speed of light and moving away from Earth. You look backwards through a powerful telescope at Earth, what do you see?"

Jack waits for an answer but only gets blank stares. After a few moments, Lucy answers, "Earth?"

"Right, you see Earth but what do you really see?" Jack asks again.

They're not following. Lucy tries again, "Earth, right? I said the Earth and you said right."

Jack replies, "Yes, you see Earth, but not in your time. You're looking back in time. You're a great distance from Earth and it takes light time to get to you. You see the past. Now, here's the fun part; you turn your spaceship around and now travel at the same speed towards Earth. What do you see now?" Again, Jack sees blank stares and waits briefly before answering himself. "You see Earth, but now you're seeing Earth in the future. Einstein proposed the concept as a part the space-time continuum. See, perhaps there's only one time with many dimensions and that leads to a lot more possibilities."

There's a long pause before Lucy asks, "Didn't guys from your school figure out how to count cards in Las Vegas and win like millions of dollars? We should do that."

Maureen gets excited about the idea. "Yeah, you should teach us how to do that or we could just go out there and watch you."

Jack goes inside the house.

#

After using the bathroom, Jack joins Molly's father, mother, two younger brothers, and guests in the living room. His plan is to thank Molly's parents for the party and leave.

The group is fighting over who gets control of a new, smart television the family purchased today. There's some debate over what the television can do. Jack offers help and they're glad to accept it.

He takes the controls, begins working, and says, "You need to be careful about the settings because companies use the television to gather information about you."

Only Mr. McCann seems to have heard him. "What are you talking about?" he asks.

"I'll show you." Jack has the living room projected on the television set. The living room and the people sitting around are now on television. Jack initiated the camera lens in the television.

"Hey, how'd you do that?" Mrs. McCann asks.

"The same way you watch television is the same way that telemarketers can watch you," Jack tells them. "Basic technology on televisions, computers, and phones are gathering information about you all the time."

"Wait, they can watch us while we're watching television or when we're on our computers and phones?" Mr. McCann asks. He and his wife are looking at each other.

"Anything with a lens means they can see you. Anything with a microphone means they can hear you," Jack explains. "Maybe it's marketing people interested in knowing who's watching their shows and commercials. They can use facial recognition and speech software to track your emotions. The problem is that it could also be a bad guy interested in seeing if anyone is home. It could be a government, ours or another one. It's easy. Anyone can do it."

There's silence in the room as the parents consider that information. Other people have noticed the family on the television set and have crowded into the living room.

"I'm just saying you want to be careful. I changed your settings," Jack adds.

"Perps could be watching, right?" Mr. McCann asks.

"Sure," Jack answers. Jack then gets on the internet from the television and goes to Teresa's Facebook page. Her page is now projected on the television screen. He clicks on a picture of Teresa just uploaded, showing the McCann's backyard. Teresa has a big smile and is drinking water through a penis-shaped straw. "This picture was uploaded by Suzie Thompkins at 9:41 p.m." Various screens are quickly popping up and down on the television. "Suzie lives at 14 Bradford Street in Watertown. If you want to know more about Susie you can go to her social media posts here." Up pop multiple pages.

"You know where she lives?" Mr. McCann asks, and, "You know where she is now?"

"Yeah," Jack answers. "You can find out just about anything and link this information to her phone, current location." Jack gives the television controller back to Mr. McCann.

Jack hears someone yell out the back door, "Hey Susie, this guy is checking you out online."

"Good. Send him my way," she yells back.

Jack thanks his hosts for their hospitality and tells them he's leaving. He goes out the back door to find Teresa to let her know. Girls seem more interested in him now. He surmises that television tricks are more impressive than Einstein.

#

Jack can't find Teresa anywhere. She's not in the backyard or the basement. She's not in the driveway or the front of the house. He continues to look and spots her. She's standing on the side of the house opposite the driveway. As Jack walks towards her, he can see that she's with someone. They're standing in the shadows.

They see Jack approaching. Jack can see it's a guy; he's about five feet ten inches tall. He's wearing a T-shirt a few sizes too small. It accentuates his muscular upper body. *Oh no,* Jack thinks *what now*?

"Hey, Jack," Teresa says. "This is Roberto, an old friend."

Jack's got his hands buried deep in his pockets. *Not another asshole like Jocko?* he wonders.

"Hi. It's good to meet you," Roberto says, and reaches out to shake Jack's hand. "You've got a really great girl here."

"Hi. Yeah," Jack answers.

"We were just catching up. Kind of saying good-byes," Teresa tells Jack.

Jack's feeling awkward, out of place, jealous.

"Actually, I think we're done," Roberto says. He reaches out and gives Teresa a hug. "It was great to see you and good luck with everything," he says. "Good luck in New York."

"Hey, break that up, what's going on?" comes a woman's voice. It's Roberto's girlfriend who's been looking for him. She didn't like their hug.

"Teresa, I don't think you ever met Sammy," Roberto says with a smile.

"No," Teresa answers. "I don't think we ever met, but I've seen pictures of you."

"Wow, you look so familiar," Sammy says.

"The collages," Roberto explains, "the pictures I showed you in the living room, the big collages?"

"Oh, yeah," Sammy answers.

Jack tells Teresa he's going to leave and they can catch up tomorrow.

"No. Wherever you go. I go," she tells him. She's ready to leave.

Teresa says her 'goodbyes' and 'thanks' to everyone. She leaves with Jack.

#

As they drive away, Teresa asks, "What did you do with the television that got everyone so excited?"

"Nothing, really," Jack says. "I just showed them how people can use technology to spy on you. Companies come to school all the time and pay us to help build whatever they need. They call it 'rent-a-brain.' The pay is good."

Teresa is surprised because here's a job that Jack could get. "Wait," she says, "companies come to M.I.T. and to pay you to do stuff for televisions and computers?"

"Yeah," Jack answers.

"Well, maybe that's the kind of job you should get when we come back in a year. You could go to school at night maybe." To Teresa, people around here would kill for that kind of job.

"It's pretty mindless stuff," Jack answers. "I'd be bored to death. Breaking into classified networks is more challenging and fun, but none of it compares to what I want to do."

"When you say breaking into classified networks, you mean the stuff you and Cheese like to do together? Your competitions? How many networks have you broken into anyway?"

"I'm not saying I did and I'm not saying I didn't," Jack answers. "I'll say two things. First, I bet there isn't a system I can't break into. Second, you have to remember that people could be listening or recording our conversation right now by picking up keywords. They can listen through our cell phones even when they're turned off. That's how it works."

"You're paranoid," she answers. "You're talking about a ridiculous amount of information. No one can do all that."

"Of course they can. I've worked on it," Jack explains. "It's what big data is all about. Big tech companies capture everything there is to know about you. They sell it to marketers and they share it with the government."

"You know they track all this stuff for sure?" she asks.

"Yes."

"Why would a tech company share information with the government?"

"They told me," Jack explains "that some in Congress were threatening to pass laws over big tech like they did in Europe. You know, limit what information they could collect. They cut a deal. The government wouldn't pass any laws; they'd let big tech collect everything on Americans under two conditions. First, they had to share everything with the government, and second, they had to pay campaign contributions to the congressmen on the committee overseeing tech. I don't know if that's right, but that's what I heard."

"That's crazy," Teresa says.

"It's why tech companies are worth so much money. It's not because they do internet search for you or let you post pictures. It's because they know everything about you and they sell it." There's a pause for a moment before Jack asks, "Do you remember the Boston Marathon bombing?"

"Yeah, of course," Teresa answers. "They caught the guy real close to here. I could show you."

"No," Jack answers, "that's ok. They knew who did it within minutes of the bombing. Our government knew. They had the information by going through metadata files of every single phone call, email, text, credit card transaction, and web post."

"I guess it's good they caught them," Teresa says, "but I don't want people knowing everything about me. I want my privacy or I want to choose what gets shared. Are you saying people are making money off my personal information?"

"Yes," Jack answers, "a lot of money."

#

A couple minutes pass as they drive in town. Jack asks, "Did you have fun?"

"I did. It was great seeing everyone. They were all so nice. Did you see Molly? She was getting wasted on Jello shots." Teresa is laughing. "It was good to end things with Roberto too. I hadn't seen him or talked with him." She pauses. "There's something I didn't tell you about the night we met. The night I walked out on my date with Roberto. See, he asked me to join him and another girl in a three-way. The girl was Sammy and he had naked pictures of her on his phone. He showed them to me. That's why I said she looked familiar. I was kidding around."

"Wow," Jack says.

"Yeah, wow," Teresa responds. "What do you think of that?"

"I think it's genius."

"You guys are all alike. What about you? Did you have fun?" Teresa asks.

"I don't know. I didn't know anyone. Felt awkward, you know."

"What are you talking about? You were a big hit. The girls thought you were so sweet. When you offer to get people drinks, when you say 'God Bless You' after a sneeze or open doors for others. People love that about you. It shows you're considerate, polite. You could just stand there and smile and people would like you."

This comes as a surprise. Conversations didn't go well. He didn't connect with anyone. He almost got beat up. He sees a former boyfriend hug Teresa. *People like me*, he thinks. He continues to gain confidence in himself. Teresa fits in his life. She's more helpful than she could possibly know.

After another minute, Jack says, "I've got to get one of those super tight T-shirts that Roberto was wearing."

"Jealous?" Teresa asks. "First, you've got to get muscles."

Having fun comes easy for them. Leaving the party and close friends was surprisingly easy for her. She has something with Jack that's infinitely more important to her.

47

Washington, D.C.

Both Gene and Doug suspect they're under surveillance by the president's men. They'd like to meet.

The chairman of the Federal Reserve Bank meets with Congress regularly. He provides updates on monetary policy and answers questions. It's reasonable for both men to attend the event. They arrange to use a senator's private office during the chairman's meeting to maintain secrecy.

#

Gene asks, "How are you and the president making out with a plan?"

"Honestly, I don't know," Doug answers. "They've kind of frozen me out. I've provided them with a plan, but I haven't gotten any feedback. They may be doing nothing; they may be working on their own plan. I'm sorry. I just don't know."

"I see."

Doug opens up. "Bobby asked if you had any weaknesses they could exploit. Play dirty tricks I imagine, or publicize something that you'd prefer to remain private. They'd like to find a way to stop you, or at least delay things until the end of the president's term."

Gene nods his head.

Doug continues. "My guess is they've hired dozens of people, private investigator types, to look into your background. Maybe even the FBI, even though that would be illegal. Are you upset?"

"No, not upset really," Gene replies. "I don't know if it's arrogance, incompetence, or something else. They just can't seem to do their jobs. They're so focused on politics, power, and bullshit rather than their real jobs." After a pause, Gene adds, "I'm being followed. Do you know anything about that?"

"No, but that sounds like them," Doug answers. "They're watching me too, even if it's disguised as my security. It's Bobby Ferguson and Will Duffy. They're horrible human beings. I worry their types will stop at nothing to get what they want. And by 'their types,' I mean the president too."

"I understand. What about your plan? Do you have something that would work?"

"Yes. It turns out many in government had some great ideas. They've had the same warnings for years. Everyone knows what has to be done to cut spending. We just don't have the political leadership to do anything. Leadership doesn't have any incentive to change. Their goal is to resist change, remain in their offices, and keep raking in money. Their incentives aren't aligned with the people."

48

Boston, Massachusetts

Jack wakes up about 8 a.m. on the day of their move to New York City. He stayed up late completing his final paper.

Teresa is in the bathroom talking on the phone with her mother. She was talking quietly to let Jack sleep. He knocks before entering.

They kiss good morning. "Did you finish your paper?" she asks.

"All done," Jack announces. "I emailed it to Professor Hildebrand around three this morning."

"Remind me again," Teresa asks, "why you wrote a paper when you've already graduated."

"It lays out the foundation for the graduate work I want to do back here in a year. I'm explaining what I'd like to do with my dissertation that will hopefully allow me to get a doctorate."

"Well, congratulations," Teresa says, and gives him a hug.

"Thank you," Jack answers followed by, "I guess we can hit the road now."

"I'm ready," she answers, "but I do have one errand to run that's kind of on the way."

"Oh, no," he says. He figures "one errand" could mean all day.

"Trust me," she tells him. "You'll like it."

#

In a short while, they're in the car headed out of town. Teresa is driving. She's driving back to Scituate.

"What's going on?" Jack asks.

Teresa answers, "You'll see."

He trusts her. He feels liberated with no schoolwork to think about. He's got a few days to kick back and relax before starting at the bank.

They make their way to Scituate and she parks in Uncle Dave's driveway. Aunt Connie and Uncle Stevie are sitting on the front steps.

Teresa calls out, "Good morning. I told you we'd be back. Are you ready?"

"Everything's in Tom's truck, everything but Uncle Dave. We're ready to go, ready to go," Connie answers.

Tom comes out of Uncle Dave's home. He helps Dave into his truck. Connie and Stevie get in the back seat of the truck. Teresa and Jack follow in her car. They drive to the town pier.

Teresa takes a lot of pictures of Dave and Jack. She sends them via email to a local drugstore for printing. It will take about an hour to get hard copies produced.

Everyone thinks it's a marvellous gesture. Uncle Dave and Jack are moved to tears.

Tom suggests they eat at Kiely's Pub while they wait for the pictures. Kiely's sits on the water in Scituate Harbour. They can watch boats come and go during their meal.

Teresa sits next to Uncle Dave. She begins asking him about Jack's grandfather.

Dave's energy level is high and he's unusually talkative.

"He was a great man," Dave says of Jack's grandfather. "His own man. He always did the right thing, every time, no matter what."

"And he was really smart?" Teresa asks.

Dave smiles. "Smartest guy I ever saw. He could just see things and get to the answer faster than anyone else. It didn't matter what the subject or question. He'd get there first. He was great at explaining complex things in a very simple way."

"And that's how it was with computers for him?" Teresa asks.

"Yeah, that was one thing," Dave begins. "But he could do anything. Always said he was 'gonna change the world.' I guess he knew that computers was one way to do that."

She then asks, "Do you remember telling me that Jack was a lot like him?" Teresa is unsure if Uncle Dave remembers much of their last visit.

"He's a lot like him. Jack's got the gift alright. No doubt about it. Maybe smarter even. He's got a great big heart too." Dave looks at Jack with a smile.

Others aren't paying attention to their conversation. They're discussing what they'll order for their meals.

"I don't really want to go to New York," Teresa confesses to him.

"Yeah, I understand. I do. I'll tell you something I know to be true. It's not where you are that's important or the key to happiness. It's who you're with."

#

Following the meal, they walk to the drugstore. Tom chooses to stay behind. He tells the group, "I'm gonna stay here a while and make sure Kiely's doesn't wash out to sea." He'll get a ride home from one of his friends sitting around the bar.

"Awful good of you, Tom, awful good of ya," Connie says playfully.

Teresa figures it isn't the first time that Tom has used the line to remain with friends.

They get the pictures, return to Dave's house, and insert one in the eighth and final spot of the frame. The little boy missing his two front teeth is now fully grown. In the first seven pictures, Jack was seated and looking up at his uncle. In today's picture they're both standing. They've got their arms around each other's shoulders. They're holding fishing poles; the tackle box and pail are at their feet. Both men are smiling.

Teresa gets a sincere "thank you" from each member of the family.

Jack takes a copy and with tears in his eyes tells her, "First picture for our new home. Thank you so much. This was great, really just so thoughtful. I can't believe you did this. I love it. I love you for doing this."

49

New York, New York

It takes Teresa and Jack four hours to drive from Scituate to New York. While Jack has travelled back and forth many times, this trip feels different.

They enter the apartment and Jack looks around. Teresa is waiting for him to show the same exuberance that she's feeling. All the items bought on the shopping spree with Grace are now in place. It's so beautiful that Teresa thinks pictures of the apartment should be in a magazine.

Grace had flowers delivered.

There's a manila folder with paperwork and a handwritten note. The note reads:

Welcome. I hope you'll be comfortable and happy in your new home. The lease is for one year. There's an option to purchase should you choose to stay longer. I can't wait to see you both.

Love always and forever, Dad.

Jack reads the card and puts it back down without any reaction.

"Really?" Teresa asks. "Are you not blown away by all this? I mean just look at all this, look at this furniture."

Jack answers, "Nah, this stuff probably just fell off a truck."

Teresa smiles, gives him a hug and asks, "Do you like it?"

"I do. It's nice. Do you?" He's calm, maddeningly calm she thinks.

Teresa is amazed by the luxury they'll be enjoying. She gives him a tour and finds a few surprises. Grace has made changes to her original plan. There are televisions, baby monitors, a changing table, and more. "Your mother is amazing, Jack. It looks like she's thought of everything."

The final room they visit is the master bedroom. Jack looks and says, "I'll need to set up a little space with a computer. You know a work area, a desk? How'd you guys forget a desk?"

Jack reads a note from his mother that she left on the bed. It reads:

I hope you like it. We've stocked the refrigerator and your chef will be there at 8:00 a.m. tomorrow morning. Teresa can tell him her meal preferences. I've provided him with a list of yours.

All my love, Mom.

Teresa reads the note after Jack. "Jesus Christ" she says. "Un freaking believable, a chef?"

Teresa attributes Jack's calmness to the fact that he's always enjoyed this kind of lifestyle.

They open the doors to their walk-in closet. New suits hang on what will be Jack's side. It appears "Jack's guy", his tailor, has already delivered suits, shirts, ties, shoes, and more. She doesn't have to ask if they'll fit. Her side is empty. Not one thing.

50

New York, New York

The first day of work at the bank arrives. Gene arranged to meet his sons in the bank's executive dining room at 7:30 a.m. for breakfast. He arrives early and reads the morning newspapers.

Jack arrives next wearing one of his new suits. Gene beams with pride at the sight of him.

Jack sits down and orders a large breakfast.

"Good morning, Jackson. You look great. Are you anxious to get started?"

"Good morning, Dad. Sure," Jack answers.

Gene then asks, "Do you need a comb son?" Jack's hair is dishevelled. Employees at the bank are meticulous about their appearance.

Peter Hollingsworth joins next, followed shortly by JR and then Jarrett Washburn. Jarrett works at the bank and is a little older than JR.

Gene handles the introductions. "Boys, you both know Peter Hollingsworth." Peter shakes their hands. "I've also invited Jarrett Washburn to join us for breakfast." The boys introduce themselves and shake Jarrett's hand.

"As you know," Gene continues, "Peter and I have been close since I joined the bank. We've worked together on your training program. He put together a team to take you through it. Jarrett, here, has been a late addition to the team by our chief operating officer. Let him know if you have questions or need additional help, clarification, anything. I expect you boys to give this your best efforts. We're devoting a good deal of time and expense and it's solely for your benefit."

Jack's thinking this is for his father's benefit.

Gene continues, "Keep an open mind. Don't rush to judgement. There's good and bad in everything whether it's banking, capitalism, government. Keep an open mind. At your ages, some of what you'll learn might seem exploitive or predatory. Take your time and consider all perspectives."

Jack's thinking his father sounds defensive.

"In a short while, we'll talk about why this training is so important now." Gene's tone is serious. "Our system has worked extremely well. Americans enjoy a miraculously high standard of living, we're secure and free. None of these things came cheaply or easily. You'll get trained and then we'll talk about where we go from here. All right then. I can't tell you how excited I am about getting you both here. Remember, keep an open mind, work hard, ask for help; we'll talk soon." Gene collects his things, wishes them luck, and leaves.

It sounds slightly ominous, but Jack will "keep an open mind" as his father requests.

JR orders a light breakfast. He's fighting a hangover and would prefer to keep quiet. Jack needs this training, after all. Not him.

#

After breakfast, Peter leads them to a conference room on the tenth floor. It's room number 1001. There are two young men sitting at the table awaiting their arrival. Peter begins, "Gentlemen, allow me to introduce you to Steve Johnson and Billy Wong." Peter sits at the head of the table while they all shake hands and introduce themselves.

"We know," Peter continues, "why we're here. There's a lot of material for you to cover." He turns to JR and Jack, "Steve and Billy were handpicked for this task. They are highly regarded here. They will be able to provide a good deal of the training. Where additional resources are required, either they or you need to let me know. Everything will be at your disposal. Is that clear to everyone?" Peter looks around the room. There are a few audible "Yes, sirs."

"We have never done anything like this before," Peter explains. "I'll be doing periodic progress reports to test your understanding and retention of the material. We are expecting you to learn every bit of it. It's more important that you understand everything than how long it takes. Do you understand that?"

JR and Jack both nod, "Yes."

"In the same way that you'll be tested, your teachers are also being tested. Your success or failure reflects on their performance. I trust I've covered that sufficiently?" Peter is looking at the instructors. Steve and Billy nod their heads.

"Very well then," Peter says. "Jarrett here is from the operations end of the bank and reports up a chain of command to our chief operating office. I guess Nardella wanted to see what's going on here. Steve and Billy work for your father."

JR is annoyed by the idea that he could learn anything from Steve and Billy. They look younger than he is. He'd prefer to be doing something productive, something that involves making money.

Before Peter leaves, he adds, "Let me know what I can do. Ask questions. Ask a lot of questions. Help your instructors so that they can target the training to meet your needs."

Peter hands his business card to JR and Jack. On the back of the card is Peter's satellite cell phone number. He makes a point of stressing that he is reachable on that number "at any time." Peter leaves the room.

#

"Ok," says Jarrett while rubbing his hands together. "Let's get started."

JR immediately interrupts him, "What was that?"

Jarrett understands. "That? That's just Peter being Peter. He can't help himself." JR likes Jarrett immediately. Jarrett is a little over six feet tall with an athletic build.

"So, again, I'm Jarrett Washburn, I've been with the bank six years. I've only recently met Steve and Billy. They've been here three and four years now. They've been working on this project for about six months."

JR and Jack realize that they began preparing this training before either of them knew about it.

Jarrett continues, "The bank is broken up into a bunch of different departments. A lot of guys move around in their first years until they find something they want to specialize in. The bigger departments include Investment Banking, Wealth Management, Trading, Merchant Banking, Research, Mergers and Acquisitions." Jarrett is talking quickly. "We'll cover all the departments, what they do, who runs them, and so forth. Sometimes a managing director will get hold of a young person and ride them hard with an unspoken promise that they'll help them get ahead at the bank. Sometimes they're sincere and will help them get ahead. Other times they're not and they'll burn you out and drop you. Steve, Billy, why don't you guys introduce yourselves and provide a little background." Jarrett stands and gets himself water and fruit.

On one side of the room is a credenza with refreshments. Bagels, donuts, fruit, coffee, juices, and bottled water are available. There is a bookcase above the credenza completely filled with books. On the other side of the room is a giant whiteboard. The entire wall is a whiteboard where you can make notes with erasable markers. Opposite the door's side of the room is a window that stretches from the floor to the ceiling.

Steve and Billy look at one another. Billy nods as if to say, "Go ahead."

Steve begins, "My name is Steve Johnson. I'm originally from a small town in Texas, Beeville. I went to the University of Texas in Austin and started here four years ago. I'm not sure about graduate school right now." Steve talks more slowly than Jarrett, with a slight accent and at an even pace. He has a kind face and an easy-going way about him. He's over six feet tall and lean.

Texas, JR considers. *How smart can the smartest guy in Texas be?*

Billy begins, "My name is He Wong. People call me Billy. I'm from San Francisco originally and I went to Yale. I was an economics major. I'm also considering graduate school. I'm not sure. We'll see." Billy is about five feet nine inches tall.

"Were you an economics major too?" Jack asks. His question is directed at Steve.

"No, I had a double major in history and literature," Steve answers.

"Peter gave us bios on you two," Jarrett is speaking again. "Why don't you guys give us a little background and tell us what you're looking to do at the bank."

JR wastes no time answering first. "I'm Eugene O'Neil, Jr.," he declares proudly. "I went to Harvard for undergraduate and business school. I played football for Harvard. I did two internships here at the bank. I'm not sure what I want to do at the bank but I want it to be big, important." He nods his head confidently.

"What do we call you?" Jarrett asks. "I mean the bank already has a Gene O'Neil."

"Most people call me JR, short for junior," Gene answers. He'd like people to refer to him that way as a constant reminder of who he is.

Jack volunteers, "Some people call him Gino." Childhood friends gave him the nickname years ago. JR hates it.

Jarrett nods to Jack as if to say, "Your turn."

"My name is Jack O'Neil or John is my real name. I went to M.I.T. I'm here to learn. I have no idea what those departments are that you listed. I expect that I'll be here for a year." Jack shrugs his shoulders slightly. He'd prefer not to add 'I really don't want to be here but my dad is making me do this.'

"Some people call him Squirt," JR adds.

"Ok, Gino and Squirt," Jarrett says. "We really don't have any rules other than the rules that we agree on. All we have to do is get you guys up to speed. We could fill the room with booze and broads as long as we get the job done. This place values results and results only. If we work our balls off round the clock and don't get the job done, then we failed. There are no awards for effort." Jarrett looks at them quickly and doesn't wait for any acknowledgement. "We train you. We get our gold stars from your dad and we all move on."

"What about you?" JR asks of Jarrett. "What's your background? You kind of skipped over that."

"Sorry, you're right," Jarrett apologizes. "My name is Jarrett Washburn. UPenn for undergraduate and graduate schools, Wharton. I played football too. Not well. Go Quakers." Jarrett raises his fist to mock enthusiasm. "I fucking love this place. The Bank. The City. I can't imagine being anywhere else in the world. I've moved around a little bit within Operations. My grandfather and uncle worked here at the bank their whole careers."

Jarrett continues talking fast. It appears he doesn't slow down to even take breaths. "I know teachers need to figure out how students learn. Everyone learns differently. You might be visual learners, you might prefer to read shit on your own, or audio might be your thing. Let me know what you need. This place is fucking crazy. Whatever it is you need, we'll get it. If you need someone to read to you while you get a pedicure, we'll get it." Jarrett looks at them both for confirmation. "Ok?"

Both JR and Jack nod before Jarrett continues. "JR, you'd know this from your internships. Jack, the bank has everything. There's a gymnasium downstairs with a sauna, steam, masseuse, everything. Any kind of administrative support help you need, there's an admin assistant just outside this door. There are three dining areas, including the Executive Dining Room where we met this morning. There's also a kitchen that's open twenty-four hours a day and serves anything you want. Pick up the phone and call for delivery. The bank supports offices all around the world so it never sleeps. This place is always open for business. You'll see people sleeping here and all sorts of crazy shit, but don't worry about it. Don't worry about anything except producing your own results. Questions?"

Neither JR nor Jack have a question.

#

One of Gene's executive assistants opens the door and walks in. She steps aside as Teresa walks in behind her, carrying a box of donuts. Teresa is wearing a jacket, white sweater, and black leggings.

Jack's glad to see her. While he had encouraged her to visit, he's a little surprised that she took him up on the suggestion, and so quickly. He handles the introductions.

Teresa notices the credenza filled with food and drinks. "I'm sorry, I thought you guys might want a little snack to help with your work."

"It's sweet of you and thanks," Jack responds. He instructs Teresa to sit next to him.

"I brought us lunches too," she tells him, "from our new cook, ah, chef. He's really nice."

Steve and Billy aren't sure what Teresa's presence means. Steve asks, "Do we want to take a break?"

"Teresa, are you going to be joining us?" Jarrett asks.

"Yes, if that's ok I guess, maybe for a little while." Teresa doesn't know anyone in the city and doesn't yet know what to do with her time.

"Ok with us. Your timing is perfect. We were about to get started." Jarrett begins to collect his belongings.

JR can't believe what he's seeing. Teresa is now going to participate in the same training program as him? That's not going to happen.

#

Jarrett has his things under one arm. It's clear he intends to leave.

"Steve, you're starting and with the Goldsmith's tale? Is that right?" Jarrett asks.

Steve nods his head and answers, "Yes."

"Ok, good luck, call if I'm needed," Jarrett says. "Teresa, it was very nice to meet you." Jarrett exits the room.

"Creating a plan for this training was a challenge," Steve begins "because one of you knows a lot about banking, but it's all new to the other one, or two," Steve says, referring to Teresa's addition. "We're going to start slowly and go as fast as y'all can go. We're going to approach banking as solving the needs of a society. It will make its creation and development easier to understand. Before I forget, we've got a considerable amount of reading material for you." Steve looks to Billy, who nods and points to the bookcase above the credenza.

JR is bored. "Reading material? Seriously?" *Where'd Jarrett go?* he thinks. He excuses himself and leaves the room.

Steve's unsure how to interpret JR's departure. He focuses his attention on Jack and Teresa. "Banking is at the heart of everything, business obviously, but also governing and maintaining order in society. We'll start at the beginning and you'll see how it's all connected. Many years ago, there were these goldsmiths. They were like blacksmiths who worked with gold and other metals. They had a place to keep gold safe, a vault with guards if you will. People chose to store their gold and valuables with the goldsmith. It was safer than in their own homes. People turned over their gold in return for a receipt from the goldsmith confirming the amount on deposit. Simple."

He continues. "It's helpful to think of banking as solving some of society's basic needs. Keep in mind that banking evolved over centuries. No one woke up one day with all the answers. Its evolution required trial and error, and some errors were disasters that caused terrible human suffering. You can think of the Great Depression in our country, or the poverty and inflation that destabilized Germany in the 1930s and led to World War II. Those were the result of errors caused by bankers. Also, we continue to evolve. We continue to try new things and continue to make costly errors, like some recurring problems here in the United States."

Steve gets up and refills his coffee cup while talking. "Ok, so the first benefit for ordinary people is there's a safe place to store gold or wealth. The second benefit is that you have the beginning of paper currency. You can take that receipt from the goldsmith and endorse it or turn over your claim to someone else. You'd simply write 'pay to Teresa Rossi' on your receipt and sign your name." Steve is using his hands to pretend he's signing a check. "Right? Simple. You endorse your receipt and now that other person has the claim to what was your gold.

"This is where the expression 'good as gold' comes from," Steve says. "Your receipt evolves into paper money and it is in fact as good as gold. Your receipt can be exchanged for gold by presenting it to the goldsmiths. Again, simple, right?"

Jack and Teresa answer "Yes," at the same time.

Teresa says, "Jinx."

Steve doesn't know what that means.

Teresa explains. "It's what you say when two people say the same thing at the same time. And what you said wasn't boring. Sorry, most people think of banking as really boring."

Steve nods. "If you hang in here with us and learn these lessons, you'll never think of banking as boring again. Far from it."

"Well," Billy interrupts. "Some of it is boring, but not where we're going. You'll see."

#

"Using paper money," Billy says, "is a huge improvement. We're talking about the year 1200 A.D. It's impossible to put yourself back in those times, but people had to swap goods and services to survive. You've heard of barter. People might swap a day's labour for food. They'd trade chickens for nails, corn for fertilizer. It was horribly inefficient. It prevented trade from happening on any meaningful scale and slowed the advancement of civilization. The move to paper money is one of man's greatest advancements. It creates markets and prices. Trade explodes. Prices for goods and services become rational. You're no longer limited by what your trading partner needs. The lives of ordinary people improve immediately."

Steve says, "Let's stick with the mechanics for now. People now have all these receipts in circulation with all these endorsements. Practically speaking, you end up with a lot of endorsements on one receipt from the goldsmith. You endorse it to another person, and they endorse it to the next, and so on and so on. This leads to another improvement where the goldsmith gives you a receipt payable only to 'bearer.' Whoever presents the receipt can collect the gold. It doesn't need to say payable to 'Teresa Rossi" anymore. Also, you can break up your deposit into any denominations; call them hundred-dollar bills, five-dollar bills, or a one-dollar bill. It all started this simply. It was a huge improvement and fairly efficient. The goldsmiths charged fees for storing gold and clearing checks. Any questions?"

"Nope," Jack answers. Teresa shakes her head no.

"People like to complain about banking," Billy adds, "but civilization depends on it. We couldn't last a day without it."

#

JR left the conference room in search of Jarrett. He finds him in his office.

JR begins by saying, "Sorry about that, dude. I can't believe she showed up here." JR is referring to Teresa. "I guess she thinks she's joining the training."

Jarrett treats it as nothing. "It's fine. Results only, and that's all anyone cares about. I could care less how many people you and your brother want to add to the room."

JR is surprised, as he expected a different response. He had hoped Jarrett would instruct Teresa to leave. He pauses before saying, "UPenn, huh?"

"Yeah," Jarrett answers with a smile. "There are a lot of us here. Not as many as you Harvard guys, but a lot of us."

"Guys still get together for drinks after work?" JR asks. He understands that while he may not be as smart as others, he can network the hell out of Wall Street to get ahead.

"Oh, yeah. Our group usually starts at Fitzgerald's. I'll be there tonight with some of the guys. Bobby Fitzgerald is the owner. Good guy, shitty food, a lot of girls. Come by. I'll introduce you around."

JR smiles. "Sounds good. I'll look for you there."

JR decides not to return to the conference room. He'll take some time to look up friends.

#

Lunch is delivered to the conference room; steak and potatoes with their choice of salads and vegetables. They push their work off to the side in order to eat on the conference table. Teresa and Jack enjoy the lunch prepared by their chef.

"Here's a book that you need to read," Steve tells Jack. He hands him a book titled *The Wealth of Nations*. "It's a famous book by Adam Smith. He introduces his theory of the 'invisible hand.' He believes that markets or business works efficiently and that government interference is generally bad for business. Governments and regulations create more harm than good. He describes it as if there's an invisible hand that keep the gears of business working efficiently without interference. Less interference allows business to create wealth for the largest number of people. We can debate his points. You need to read it. I bring it up because your father's known here as 'the invisible hand.'"

Teresa thinks it's funny. "Ooohh, the invisible hand," she says, mocking the term as if it's scary.

"Yeah," Steve smiles. "He's the hand that keeps everything moving or makes sure the bank makes the right moves, like avoiding the last financial crisis. His reputation is that he always knows which way the market is moving. He's always right and always first."

Jack picks up the book says, "Thanks," and begins looking at it. He looks back at the bookcase. There are a lot of books and two copies of each one. Apparently one for him and one for JR.

"See, I think," Billy adds, "that the nickname is appropriate because of the invisible part. I mean the fact that he's invisible to the press, never in any news story. The bank doesn't even show him on the website." Billy has his hands on the table with his palms up. "How can that be? Not on our website, not in our annual report, and yet he's the most powerful person at the bank. He's invisible."

Teresa jokes, "I guess it's better than a lot of other nicknames."

#

They make good progress on their first day. Steve wraps things up a little after 4 p.m. "I'm thinking that we'll stop here today. You've got reading material tonight."

Billy adds, "We also want you to read newspapers and magazines; *The Wall Street Journal, New York Times, The Economist,* and others. Would you prefer to get them digitally or in hard copy?"

"Digitally, I guess, online," Jack answers.

"And we want you to watch the news on television, different channels; we'll discuss news events, various perspectives, and its reporting," Steve says.

"Why all the news when we're talking about banking?" Teresa asks.

"The entire world is connected," Steve answers. "You can't talk about any issue in isolation and banking is at the center of it all. Money connects everything and everyone."

Billy adds, "Here's your first assignment." Billy hands Jack two books and points, "We'll talk about this one tomorrow."

Really? Teresa thinks, looking down at the books. She considers that it might take her a week to read one book, and they want to talk about it tomorrow?

"Teresa," Billy says. "Would you like us to order copies of the reading material for you?"

"No thanks. I'll read his or I'll just ask him what it says."

51

New York, New York

"Really?" Teresa asks Jack as they exit the bank. "The first day and they expect you to spend the night reading?"

Jack would prefer to go home and begin reading. He dreads the thought of having to justify time for work. He's told Teresa that he'll need to devote as much time to working as he did with school. His father was rarely home when he grew up, and there was never a word about it. Work is a priority and the cost of success.

"I have a job now. Do you remember when you asked if I'd ever get out of school and get a job?"

"I know. I know, but it's so nice out, and you worked all day. Can we at least walk around a little bit?" Teresa asks. She often uses a whiney tone when asking for things.

"Yeah, sure, of course, we can walk around, or we can go out to dinner if you'd like. There's plenty of restaurants to choose from."

Teresa places her arms around Jack's forearm and they begin walking. "We don't have to go out to a restaurant. Just a walk would be nice. You know that lunch our chef made today was ridiculously good. I can't believe I just said, 'our chef.' That's crazy isn't' it? The food reminds me of the meal at the Harvard Club. Best food I've ever eaten."

"I'll let you in on a secret, but you probably shouldn't share it with others," Jack begins.

"Ok," she replies.

"My folks have the food we eat flown in from a specific farm," he begins. "See, I think the reason it tastes so good is that it's all natural, organic, there's no manipulation of the food in any way. You see, everyone is eating genetically altered foods, like mass-produced chickens. They grow the chickens super-fast, but they're basically mutants. They have oversized breasts, meaty areas, and undersized organs. They have about a quarter of the life expectancy of a normal chicken. People aren't eating normal, healthy chickens."

"What?" Teresa asks.

"Yeah, same with everything else we eat; beef, and even fruits and vegetables," Jack continues. "Food companies have re-engineered food in order to maximize their profits. I don't know all the details, but my mom is seriously into it. She says the food companies are treating everyone like guinea pigs to see how far they can go with all this. The stuff they're selling is bad for us."

"Seriously?" she asks.

Jack continues, "Sugar too. According to my mom, our government allows food companies to add sugar to everything. Sugar, in all sorts of names and forms, is in almost everything people eat. It improves the taste, but doesn't satisfy your hunger, so you end up eating more. Eat more, buy more, and food companies profit more. I guess they've paid off people in our government that are supposed to be looking out for us. Americans are getting fat and sick because of our food. Health issues like obesity and diabetes are building up in a lot of us."

"That's freaking crazy. So rich people eat healthy while others are eating shitty food or food altered in some way that's bad for them? Makes them fat, sick?"

"I don't know all the details. My folks are into it for the health benefits. If you eat these foods, you won't believe how much better you'll feel. You won't get sick nearly as often. You'll keep your weight down at an optimal level and you'll have more energy than you can imagine. Do you remember you'd say that I study all the time and don't need much sleep? It's the food. My mom did a ton of research. Dad arranged talks for her with scientists, lobbyists, everyone. The more she dug into it, the more pissed off she got. She insisted we all go healthy and grow our own food or pay others to grow it."

"My mom said that none of you have an ounce of fat on you, I mean you and your parents after dinner at the Harvard Club. She thought you all must have great genes."

"Well, I eat other food too, but I'm eighteen," Jack replies. "My folks lost a lot of weight. I think it's impossible to be overweight eating like this."

"How many people know this secret? I mean, do all rich people eat like this?"

"No, or I don't know. I don't know how many get this food or where it actually comes from."

"That's why you've never needed much sleep?" Teresa asks as she processes the information.

"Right. Healthier and a lot more energy. I'm sure that's why Mom got the chef. It will be great for your pregnancy. The baby will be healthier."

She smiles, "That's a hell of a secret. Let's walk a little, but we'll eat at home. You know my dad is really against big business. He thinks they're all bad and figures our government needs to keep watch over them."

"Maybe," Jack replies "but it's really messed up if we're paying to be protected, but they don't do their jobs."

As they continue to walk, Teresa adds, "This is really selfish when you think about it. Maybe we need to do something about this. It's not fair to eat like this and watch others eat themselves towards sickness and death. My parents are eating that food. Do you know how many women want this option? They don't understand that it's the food itself that's causing their weight issues. There's a lot of unhappy women fighting low self-esteem and depression."

There's an uncomfortable silence before Jack replies, "Honestly, I hadn't thought about that until now. Wrong of me, I guess. Bigger world to consider. Sometimes I think I've been living my life in a bubble. Focused on just me and school."

52

New York, New York

JR gets to Fitzgerald's around 8:00 p.m. He expects to run into Jarrett. He's also arranged to catch up with a couple of friends who graduated a year earlier from business school. He sees them standing together at the bar when he enters.

JR approaches, "Mocha, T-Bone. How the hell are you guys?" They shake hands and their handshakes turn into mini-hugs. Ed Tyler, aka "Mocha," works at Morgan Sachs, and Tim Maher, aka "T-Bone," works for a competitor. They use nicknames around each other.

"Good," both friends answer.

"How are you?" Mocha starts. "You graduated and at the bank now?"

"Yup, graduated, I'm in a training program my dad set up. It might be all bullshit."

"Right, a training program your dad set up," Mocha replies. "Don't bullshit us. That's gonna lead you into some perfect setup. Hell, you'll probably be my boss soon."

"What's going on with you, Mocha, you still in Mergers & Acquisitions?" JR asks.

"Of course, what else would I do? It's not like I've got any real skills."

"He was just telling me," T-Bone says, "about his trip to Amsterdam, ripped it up with his entire team from your bank.

"Is that right?" JR asks.

"Fucking sick," Mocha replies. "I don't know how many broads were there taking care of my guys. All young, all beautiful. Closed a big deal and flew out the same day to celebrate. We spent four days there. We've been on a roll lately. Maybe you should join us."

"Don't even think about it," T-Bone warns. "You'll both end up in jail."

"Fuck you T-Bone," Mocha says. "You're jealous and bored."

"I'm just saying," he replies, "you keep trading on inside information and eventually it's going to catch up with you."

JR is staring at Mocha, hoping for an explanation.

"We've got this team of guys," Mocha explains. "Some spend their entire time trying to figure out who should buy who or who should sell their company or a division or something. My job is to approach their CEO or a board member to float ideas by them. I figure out their level of interest. If they're interested, great, if not then I might start a rumour about who's in play. I'm everyone's best friend on the street. Everyone wants to know what I know so people throw shit at me left and right."

"You mean investors looking for a quick profit on a stock run-up?" JR asks.

"Sure, investors and lenders who want to finance the transaction. The law firms that want to represent one of the parties. Everyone wants to know who might be in play."

"When you say people are throwing shit at you, do you mean money?"

"Money. Tickets, invitations to everything, and they'll swap information they have," Mocha continues. "I like to think I know everything going on."

"You know it or you make it up," T-Bone adds.

"We all got our scams," Mocha protests. "You're jealous that I'm making a fucking killing while you're bored to shit in wealth management."

"Maybe a little bored," Tim responds ,"but it's an annuity. I keep growing the principle and I'll cash checks for the rest of my life."

"Funny," JR says. "I used to think of M&A as a place I'd like to be, but now I'm thinking about wealth management."

"Don't do that," Mocha objects. "You'll both be sucking up to rich people for a measly one percent of their wealth that you have to split with the bank."

"A lot more than that," T-Bone replies.

"What's that mean?" JR asks.

"Like he said, we all got our scams."

"Give it up," JR asks, "What are you not saying?"

"We tell the clients that we only charge them one percent," T-Bone explains. "We tell them that we're aligned with their interests because the way we make money is to grow their assets, but that's not entirely true. You see, the investment companies pay us for directing money into their funds, ETFs, or other investments. Yes, we get the one percent that our clients know about. We earn even more that the clients don't see or know about."

"What's that work out to?" JR asks. "I mean, how much money do you end up making on a portfolio, the percentage I mean?"

"My book of business is about four hundred million dollars," Tim answers. "I know that's not huge, but I didn't start with your connections and I'm only one year out of school. We charge the clients one percent and I split that with the bank, so I get two million. I can get a point from the investment houses easy, keep all of it, and my clients don't know about. I could get more if I wanted to push it. All told, that's an easy six million a year and I'll keep growing it."

JR is running numbers in his head. His dad talked about trillions of dollars of wealth controlled by the Federal Reserve owners. He starts to think about Tim's numbers applied to that sum.

"Scraps and boring," Mocha replies. "I'll make three times that one deal, not even a big one."

T-Bone looks at Mocha and says, "Look, if you promise not to be an asshole then maybe I'll manage your money for you."

"Would that mean," Mocha answers, "that I can call you every day and say fuck you?" The group laughs at that line. Mocha turns to JR. "Find your niche. That's what the street is all about. Legal or close to it, find it and cash in as long and as hard as you can."

#

JR walks over to Jarrett, who is enjoying himself with a group of people. Jarrett handles introductions.

"You know Mocha?" Jarrett asks

"Yeah," JR answers, "I met him during an internship. He was trying to figure out what he was going to do at the bank. Do you know him?"

"Only by reputation," Jarrett answers. "The guy is becoming a legend, crazy bastard I hear." After a pause, he asks "JR, you got a girlfriend?"

"No, you?"

"No. No girlfriend, no wife for now."

A stocky fellow carrying three drinks walking behind Jarrett overhears him. He turns his head and says, "Jarrett has a girlfriend, his best friend. Her name is Money and Jarrett loves his best friend." The fellow then makes the sound of kisses.

Jarrett and JR are similar creatures. Fitzgerald's is not crowded, but there are attractive young women hanging around. In no time, both Jarrett and JR are making new friends. "This is awesome and it's only Monday, so much better than Boston," he says.

The bar has many televisions. The channels are set to Sports and Financial News. At 11 p.m., a financial news show begins. A very attractive, young, female news anchor named Lynn LaRoyo comes on to host the show. Each night's show includes her interviewing a prominent Wall Street figure or CEO.

Men stop and toast Lynn as the show begins. It appears to be a nightly ritual. Several men add, "I love you Lynn" to their toast.

JR asks, "What's this all about?"

Jarrett answers, "Everyone loves Lynn. She's the one we'd all like to get to know. There's something so freaking sexy about these curvy Spanish, er Mexican broads. There was a bet last year about the first one to sleep with her. I don't think anybody won. I never heard anything."

JR is watching the television closely. Lynn is a strikingly beautiful woman. Her guest tonight is a well-known hedge fund manager.

That's it then, he thinks to himself. *This is her lucky day because she's going to meet Eugene O'Neil, Jr.*

53

New York, New York

Steve, Billy, Teresa, and Jack meet in the conference room the next day. There's no word from JR.

"Let's move on," Steve says. "It may sound boring at first, Teresa, but it's important. We need to cover some basics before we blow you away. Ok?" He looks at Teresa for acknowledgement.

She smiles and nods.

He continues, "Now, if you could transport yourself back in time, you might be able to anticipate what happens next. Let's go back to the goldsmiths. Townspeople turn over their gold in exchange for receipts. People exchange their receipts among one another as a form of payment. It's all going well. The goldsmiths notice that very few people ever come back to collect their gold. People are satisfied that the receipts can be turned into gold whenever they want, but they rarely come get it." He looks at Jack and asks, "What do you think the goldsmiths do next?"

Steve and Lee wait for an answer. Jack shrugs his shoulders.

"Well, think about it," Steve continues. "They've got this pile of gold, but they only need a small amount of it." Steve pauses again for an answer but neither Teresa nor Jack responds. "The goldsmiths make loans. They make loans and charge interest on the loans. They transact the loan in one of two ways. First, they take gold from their vault and give it to the lender. The second way is to give the lender a receipt for gold so that the lender can use it like real money."

"Wait, what?" Jack replies, "In either case there are more claims to the gold than there is actual gold in their vault?"

"Right," Steve answers.

"If they use your first method and give out gold to the person taking the loan, could that gold end up in the vault of another goldsmith?" Jack asks.

Billy answers. "Yes. The loans are great for the goldsmiths' businesses. They take gold from people and charge them storage. Then they create loans to people and charge interest on the loans. They're loaning money that they're creating out of thin air. The goldsmiths begin making enormous profits."

"But in either case you're creating more claims to gold than actual gold. Isn't that illegal?" Teresa asks.

"Paper money is no longer backed one hundred percent by the gold in their vaults," Billy answers. "Forget legal for a minute. Business always moves faster than lawmakers can keep up with. There are no laws at this point."

"Jack, what you said is important," Steve says. "There's more than one goldsmith. One of them gives out gold from his vault that ends up in another's vault. Some make loans that turn out ok while others made bad or risky loans that can't be repaid. Goldsmiths are all working independently of one another and there are no standards for loans and little understanding of risk."

"Sooner or later," Billy states, "one of the goldsmiths makes too many bad loans. What happens? A depositor shows up to take out some gold, maybe take out a lot of gold. The goldsmith can't repay him. Word spreads throughout town. Everyone shows up to get their gold. That's known as a 'bank run.' The goldsmith or bank can't repay its depositors from their gold or cash on hand."

"The first goldsmiths," Steve adds, "weren't treated well when an angry mob showed up."

"People came to understand what the goldsmiths were doing," Steve continues. "Improvement to the business model was needed. Let's start calling them banks from now on, not goldsmiths."

Steve walks around the room. "They learn that in order for a bank to be successful, they need to create the feeling of trust with their depositors. Banks will continue to make loans. They keep enough cash on hand to satisfy short term needs. They stop charging a storage fee and instead pay interest to depositors to attract money into their bank. The more deposits, the more loans a bank can make. Size becomes important. Size allows banks to make more loans and charge more interest. Size also allows them to spread loans in more places, which reduces the risk of losses."

Teresa has heard her father talk negatively about bankers her entire life. She starts, "Let's say I'm a banker. I take someone else's money. I make a big, risky loan and I charge them a high interest rate. If they pay me back, then I make a lot of money on interest. If they can't pay me back, then I go to the government and they bail me out? Is that it? It's a no-lose situation for the bankers?"

Billy answers, "Well, no, and you're getting ahead of us by a few centuries. Governments aren't involved at this stage."

Steve then explains, "Keep in mind that back then there was almost no middle class. There were rich landowners and people that worked for them, mostly farmers. People were very poor. You might have read Shakespeare's *Merchant of Venice* where there was a banker named Shylock. Bankers were unscrupulous people demanding a pound of flesh for not repaying debts. Literally, a pound of flesh. It was a horrible business. That changed when a professional class of bankers emerged and made banking legitimate."

Billy begins writing on their whiteboard. 'Banking. Store your wealth safely. Write checks. Don't carry your wealth with you. Earn interest on savings. Accumulate wealth.' "You can't underestimate the impact of these changes. This is huge for the common man. People begin saving money and interest helps them grow their savings. That savings helps a middle class to develop. The savings funds loans in the way of home mortgages and entrepreneurs to start small businesses. Upward advancement within society becomes possible."

Steve retrieves two copies of the same book from the bookcase. He hands one to Teresa and one to Jack.

Steve explains, "This book is about the Medici family, who were the first professional bankers. They create a network, or bank branches, over a vast territory beginning in Italy. Deposits are safe; the Knights Templar guard them. The family creates their own gold coin called the 'florin.' It becomes the basis for trade throughout Europe. They create banking in the way we think of it today. The family makes a fortune and they use it to finance the Renaissance. They commission Michelangelo, Leonardo Da Vinci, and others to create fabulous works of art. Developments in banking literally move man out of the Middle Ages."

54

New York, New York

Lynn LaRoyo is working at her metal desk in her five-foot square cubicle within her network's newsroom. The room itself is a massive space that's broken up into tiny cubicles that feel dehumanizing. Telephones ring twenty-four hours a day in an environment that appears like total chaos to an untrained eye. She receives a phone call. Caller ID shows it's coming from Morgan Sachs.

A woman says, "Good afternoon, Miss LaRoyo, this is Eugene O'Neil's office from Morgan Sachs. We'd like to arrange a lunch meeting between you and Mr. O'Neil to talk about an appearance on your television show."

Lynn's heartbeat accelerates with enthusiasm. "Excuse me. Mr. O'Neil would like to be interviewed?"

"That's correct Miss LaRoyo. Would a Thursday lunch meeting this week work for you?"

They arrange the time and place. Lynn is excited. She's had many guests on the show, but no one as important as Gene O'Neil. His appearance would be a big boost for the show and her career. She knows Gene doesn't do interviews and this would be a real coup.

Lynn thanks the woman and hangs up. She allows herself a fist pump and congratulates herself for the hard work and long hours she's put in.

Back at Morgan Sachs, the woman who made the call works for Jarrett. She's sitting at her desk with JR standing beside her. She confirms the time and place for lunch. JR thanks her and hands her a $100 bill.

55

New York, New York

Joe Rossi and his friend Nick Lucenta drive from Watertown to New York. They'll deliver the furniture that Teresa requested.

Joe could handle the trip himself, but having Nick along makes it easier. They begin the trip a little after 7 a.m. to avoid some of the rush hour traffic in Connecticut and New York.

Joe calls Teresa as soon as they enter New York State. She's running late at a doctor's appointment and won't be home until later than planned. Teresa instructs her father to drive into the building's garage. Teresa will call the doorman with instructions to let Joe into the apartment.

Joe Rossi follows her instructions. The building's doorman assists, escorts Joe and Nick to the apartment and unlocks the door.

Joe and Nick enter. A man is standing directly in front of them when they enter. He's wearing an apron and holding a knife.

"Who are you?" Joe asks.

"I'm Paul, the O'Neils' chef. Who are you?"

"Chef?" Joe asks.

"Hey, Chef, I'm Nick Lucenta, nice to meet you." Nick has a huge smile as he walks in and shakes Paul's hand. "Terry's got a fucking chef, Rock, how 'bout that?"

"I'm Joe Rossi, Teresa's father," Joe explains and shakes Paul's hand. "We have some pieces of furniture that we're delivering."

"It's nice to meet you both", Paul replies. "I'm going to be working in the kitchen for another hour or so. I'd be glad to make you something if you'd like."

"No, thanks," Joe answers. He and Nick tour the apartment.

"This is fucking unbelievable, Rock, huh?" Nick says as he looks around. "Maybe you should move in with them. You'd have a chef."

They make their way through the rooms. They locate the nursery and place the furniture where they think it looks best. They make two trips back to the truck to get everything. The furniture doesn't match the other pieces, but Joe likes seeing them here. He's glad Teresa wanted reminders of home.

There's a picture of Teresa with her parents in the nursery. It was taken the evening of Teresa's graduation from high school. She's wearing her graduation cap and gown. Joe has fond memories of that night.

Nick excuses himself, saying he's going to use a bathroom. Joe contemplates turning on the television, but his curiosity gets the better of him and he looks around. In the master bedroom is a desk with books, papers, and envelopes. He begins looking through things after checking to make sure Paul isn't watching him. He justifies his snooping as protecting his daughter's interests.

There's a manila folder with the title "NYC Apartment." Joe looks inside and sees the note left by Gene. There's a sales brochure listing all the amenities offered in the building. There's an option to buy the apartment. The purchase price is $14.9 million. He sits in the desk chair and stares at the number. After a pause, he continues searching. There's a direct deposit slip to John J. O'Neil from Morgan Sachs. He examines a pay stub to see the gross amount of the check is $19,230.77. He examines it to determine the time period. He then uses the calculator on his phone to determine Jack's annual pay of $500,000. *How is that possible?* he thinks. He checks the pay period and calculates it again. While he wants the best for his daughter, rich people, rotten banker types are the problem with the world. He doesn't want Teresa becoming like them.

A few minutes pass before he hears Nick's voice. "Hey, Rock, you gotta see this. They got a bidet. It shoots warm water at your ass, shocked the hell out of me." Hearing Nick jolts Joe back to the present moment. Joe then hears Teresa's voice say "hello" as she enters the apartment. He puts the papers down and joins the others.

#

"Hi, Daddy," Teresa says. She hugs him. "Thank you for coming and bringing everything. These pieces mean a lot to me. I'm gonna love seeing them every day."

"Yeah, I'm glad to do it, glad you wanted them," Rock says. "You remember Mr. Lucenta," Joe says.

"Of course, hi," Teresa says. "How do you like the place?"

"It's unbelievable," they both say.

"I asked Paul to make us some lunch, is that ok?" she asks.

"Yeah, sure, great," Joe answers.

"This view, Teresa," Nick says. "It's unbelievable, I don't know what else to call it." They're looking directly over Central Park. "Wait till I tell everyone back home about this."

They sit down and enjoy lunch together.

During lunch Joe asks, "So Dave Giatrelis tells me you and Jack showed up to do some shopping at the warehouse. You didn't buy anything. He says you guys didn't look like you were talking much. Is everything ok?"

"Oh yeah, Daddy. They really didn't have much that day. How is Mr. Giatrelis?"

"Good, I guess," Joe answers. "I understand he went back to work for a few days before he hurt his back again."

"Oh, that's awful," Teresa says.

"No, it's expected, planned," Nick says.

Joe explains, "He was out of work for eight years collecting on his injury. The wages for his job went up during that time. He went back to work, re-injures himself, and now collects at a higher rate. You know, based on today's wages. He went back to work for four days and almost doubles his disability income. A lot of guys do it."

"I guess I should have picked up on that faster," Teresa replies.

Joe's surprised she didn't immediately recognize the scam.

"Dad," Teresa says. "You and Mom should go see a movie. Grace told me to see it. There's this high cost of not doing anything or watching others do the wrong thing. According to the movie, people inside our country's Center for Disease Control know our vaccines for children are causing our autism epidemic. People inside the government have been trying to tell the truth, but their bosses have covered it all up. Drug companies have paid them off. The total cost of all these scams is enormous, and not just in dollars, but how it hurts people. The movie will shock the hell out of you. I don't know if it's accurate, but we all have to start doing the right thing and expose wrongs, whether it's Giatrelis or the Center for Disease Control. There are so many bad people or weak people that take advantage of the system. It hurts us all."

Joe recognizes a big change in his little girl. He wants to say "you gotta get your share," but doesn't.

She finishes with, "People only seem to care about getting their share. It makes me sick." She wants her father to recognize that all the scams he's taught her are not in society's best interests.

56

New York, New York

Steve, Bill, Teresa, and Jack continue with their training in the conference room.

"Teresa," Steve begins, "I think you're going to like today."

"Why is that?" she answers.

"Just a hunch. How far did you both get with last night's reading?"

Jack answers, "Good, I finished it."

"I didn't get too far," she admits.

"I have some questions about it," Jack says.

"Go ahead," Billy instructs.

Jack starts, "Well, bankers take in deposits and pay interest. They make loans, charge interest, and keep enough cash to meet short term needs. They can make more loans than the actual assets they have or capital in the bank. Their assets might be only ten percent of the loans they make." Jack looks at Teresa to make sure she's following. "Let's say that I go to a bank and take out a loan for one million dollars. I deposit that money into a second bank. That second bank now counts my loan as their asset and can make loans based on my deposit, right?"

"That's right," Steve answers.

Jack continues. "Bank number two keeps ten percent of that as a reserve and can make new loans of nine hundred thousand dollars. They keep ten percent in reserves. The cycle continues with bank three who counts the loan from bank number two and so on. There's a multiplier effect. The cycle of creating a loan and making a deposit with these reserve requirements means that you're creating new money. After ten loans you've created about six times the original loan value in new money."

"Wait, what?" Teresa asks.

"That's right," Billy answers. "There's a multiplier effect. Many people have been against it since the beginning of our banking system."

"And this is how new money is created?" Jack asks.

"It's one way," Steve answers. "The reverse can also be done, shrinking the money supply by increasing the reserve requirements. Loans get reduced or become due immediately. In that way you can shrink the total amount of money in the system quickly. It all depends on those reserve requirements. They're an incredibly powerful force over our economy."

"Wait, they're not fixed? They can change?" Jack asks.

"Yes, they can be changed," Steve answers.

Jack asks, "By whom?"

"You've lost me," Teresa says.

"The Federal Reserve Bank of the United States sets the reserve requirements," Steve answers. "They have the power to change them. Let's talk a little bit about history and how we got here. Teresa, this will make things clear and I think you're going to like it."

#

"This is important," Steve begins. "Loans are made, but there's not just one bank. The loans made by one bank go into other banks. Those other banks are going to make loans, and they'll likely make bad loans or loans that can't get repaid. The key is that bad loans will happen and will put other banks at risk. The guy that owes you money has his money in another bank that might go out of business. It's a system that requires some oversight. Are you following, Teresa?"

"Yup, they're all connected and share risks whether they like it or not," she answers.

"Right," Steve says. "So, let's talk about our existing system."

Steve draws ten rectangles on the whiteboard.

"Jack, you mentioned ten banks," he begins. "Each of these rectangles represents a bank. We're in England and the year is about 1690, by the way. There are ten banks and business is going well, but each bank is always worried about the others. All ten banks take in deposits and make loans." Underneath the rectangles, Steve writes "Deposits & Loans." He draws figures of people, homes, and factories representing individuals and business loans. Steve likes to draw as he talks.

"Money is moving back and forth among the banks," he continues. "This first bank on the far left is the largest bank. Its name is the Bank of England." He writes "BOE" in the middle of the rectangle. "It's owned by a small group of wealthy men. Each bank needed a charter from the king, so you had to be well connected in society, from the right family, a landowner."

"Figures," Teresa says and rolls her eyes.

"These guys here in the biggest bank are worried about their smaller competitors, worried about the loans they'll make and the impact they'll have on their own bank. What do you think they do?"

"Well, they would want to take over everything," Teresa suggests. "They'd try and get all the deposits and loans. They'll drive the others out of business."

"Good," Steve answers, "but wrong."

"Well," Teresa tries again, "they'd buy their competition or threaten to take their business away if they don't sell to them."

"Another good guess, but wrong again unfortunately," Steve answers.

"Mostly wrong," Billy interrupts.

Jack is smiling at Teresa's obvious low opinion of bankers.

Billy notices Jack's smile and says, "Teresa, maybe you've seen too many Wall Street movies."

"Jack," Steve asks, "any guesses?"

Jack shakes his head no.

Steve explains, "They approach the other banks. They tell them 'we're not interested in running you out of business but we all know we have a problem. We're all concerned about the loans others make because we all share in some of that risk. We have a deal for you and it has two parts. You're going to put your deposits into our bank and open your books to us. In return, we won't run you out of business and we'll even guarantee all the deposits to your customers.' There's more but essentially that's it." Steve writes these points on the whiteboard and says, "Now, this was too good a deal for these banks to turn down. All deposits are guaranteed, they'll remain in business, they'll continue to make good money, their jobs are secure, freaking awesome, huh?"

"Most of the other banks recognize it's a great deal," Billy says. "They immediately comply and begin putting their deposits into the Bank of England." He then puts an "X" through the three rectangles on the right side. "There were some banks that didn't like the arrangement. They didn't accept the deal and these others conspired to push them out of business."

"I was right," Teresa says.

Jack asks, "The Bank of England would then know the total amount of deposits and loans in the entire system?"

"Right," Steve replies. "They know the numbers for all the banks and they set the reserve requirements. They create rules for how to make loans, how to limit risks, that kind of thing. Our Federal Reserve Bank in the United States fills that same role here. They monitor all the deposits and loans. Only they know all the numbers."

"Does our government own the Federal Reserve Bank?" Jack asks.

"No," Steve answers. "We'll come back. For now, let's stay with the Bank of England. You can see that it was a very good deal for the smaller banks. It turns out to be an even better deal for the Bank of England. This bank grows larger and more profitable than anyone could have imagined. I think they stumbled onto the world's greatest money-making machine. I don't think anyone understood how profitable this was going to be or how much power this would create for them. It's staggering."

"I was struck by a quote from a banker in last night's reading," Jack says. He pulls the book from his backpack, turns to the page, and reads the following:

Banking was conceived in iniquity and was born in sin. The Bankers own the Earth. Take it away from them, but leave them the power to create deposits, and with the flick of the pen they will create enough deposits to buy it back again. However, take it away from them, and all the great fortunes like mine will disappear, and they ought to disappear, for this would be a happier and better world to live in. But if you wish to remain the slaves of Bankers and pay the cost of your own slavery, let them continue to create deposits."

Sir Josiah Stamp (Born 1880, Died 1941)
President of the Bank of England

Jack continues, "This guy Stamp becomes crazy rich. He's a banker and believes this system is hurting the average guy." Jack turns towards Teresa. "He believes it makes slaves of all us."

"Remember," Steve's talking, "that Stamp is talking about central banks, not commercial banks. The Bank of England and the Federal Reserve Bank of the United States are central banks."

"Well, shouldn't we change the system?" Jack asks.

"Well, maybe. I mean it depends," Steve answers. "We'll get to that, but for now you just need to understand that's how this all works."

Jack's unsatisfied by the answer. He makes a mental note of the questions Steve and Billy don't answer. He realizes he needs to do his own research.

57

New York, New York

Lynn LaRoyo is nervous about her lunch date with Gene. She arrives at the restaurant at exactly 1:00 p.m. She knows the time because she was thirty minutes early. She's been walking around a clothing store across the street. She's been watching for Gene's arrival, but never spotted him.

She enters the restaurant. The maître de asks, "How may I help you?" She scans the room, but doesn't see Gene.

She smiles and is pleased to say, "I'm looking for Gene O'Neil's table." She's escorted to a booth in the far corner of the restaurant. There's a young man sitting alone. There are a dozen roses on the table.

She's puzzled and turns to the maître de, "I'm sorry, I said Gene O'Neil's table."

The maître de nods his head, turns and walks away.

"Hi." JR stands to greet her and hands her the flowers. "I'm Eugene O'Neil, Jr., of Morgan Sachs. Please sit down. I was looking for a way to meet you." His ego tells him that she'll find him very attractive and be flattered by his stunt.

She sits down. "Are you really Gene O'Neil, Jr.? Is your father Gene O'Neil of Morgan Sachs?"

"Yes and yes," he answers. He's smiling. She isn't.

"Let me see your driver's license," she instructs.

He takes it out of his wallet and hands it to her. She's more beautiful in person than on television.

She feels hurt. Her hopes were high. Having Gene on the show would be great for her career. Instead, it's just another guy looking to hook up.

"I'm sorry for the false pretence," JR explains. "I wanted to meet you and I understand that you're a hard girl to get a hold of."

"What's that mean?" she asks.

"Nothing really," JR answers. "I mean, I understand some of the guys from Morgan Sachs tried to date you and were unsuccessful."

"Is that why you wanted to meet me? Because I turned down other guys?"

"No, not at all," JR begins. "I saw you on television and thought I'd like to get to know you. I've just gotten back in town, just graduated from Harvard Business School and joined the bank."

Another Harvard guy that mentions it during the first moments of a conversation, she thinks. *So predictable and so obnoxious.*

A waiter arrives and asks if he can get them something to drink. He hands them menus and announces the lunch specials.

"I'm not hungry," Lynn says. She's thinking of her boss. She told him that she was having lunch with Gene O'Neil. "I have to get back to work," she says.

"No, wait," JR replies. "Please stay. I'm sorry. I didn't mean to offend you."

"I know, but next time you ask a woman out, use your own name." She stands and walks towards the front door.

"Wait, let me walk you out." JR stands.

She doesn't turn around or slow down.

JR notices that almost all the heads of the men in the room have turned to watch her. The fact that others find Lynn so attractive is a turn on for him.

#

Lynn returns to work and walks past her boss. He's anxious to get an update. "How'd your lunch go with Mr. Big Shot? You're back early."

She answers, "There was a mix-up with communications. I didn't get my lunch today. It's been pushed back."

"Mix-up? I told you that was never going to happen."

"No, I'll get it," she answers confidently. "I just had to establish some ground rules. Let him know who's in charge."

58

New York, New York

Gene is spending the day in his office. He concludes a phone call and has twenty minutes before his next meeting. He walks to his conference table and sits down in front of a large pile of cards requiring his signature.

For years, Gene has spent lavishly on gifts for his clients and potential clients. It's another way of differentiating himself from the large herd of bankers. Everyone appreciates a card and gift on a birthday or the anniversary of a significant event in their lives.

Gene sits down and begins signing cards. An assistant, Natasha McVey, has provided him with a list of people, occasion, gift description, and its significance. She even provides her thoughts on what personal message he might write on the card. The more important the client, the more expensive the gift. Today's gifts include a diamond necklace, gold watch, set of golf clubs, a shotgun, and an all-expense paid vacation. There are dozens of cards to sign.

#

Twenty minutes later, Gene begins his call with the five leaders of the shareholders.

"How did it go with the president at the fundraiser?" David Rockefeller asks.

"It went exactly as expected," Gene answers. "The president seemed to be in shock and unsure of next steps. He didn't understand what I was talking about. I'm sure his team was trying to figure it out as soon as our meeting ended."

"Have they reached out to you since?" James Loeb asks.

"No, not yet, but I imagine that's coming. They'll stall for time," Gene answers. "They're not responding to the treasury secretary either."

"And what about last week? Your trip around the world. If we understood Madeline correctly, the trip was a success?" David asks.

"The meetings went very well," Gene begins. "They understand the direction we're moving and they're all trying to position themselves for an improved standing in what may be a new world order. Bankers, businesspeople, are a lot more rational than politicians. Madeline predicted this outcome and, as usual, she was correct."

"That sounds promising," David responds.

"Maddy, I had the feeling you had already paved the road for me in some of my meetings. Everyone seemed prepared by the time I got there," Gene states.

"Well," she answers, "we don't just control the Federal Reserve Bank in the United States, we control the central banks in Europe. That gives us leverage with the Saudis, Russians, Chinese, everyone. Don't sell yourself short, Gene. Your influence and relationships with world leaders and their bankers are valuable assets for us. You did a great job."

"Thank you, Maddy," Gene replies.

David brings the group back to the purpose of the call. "So, we'll continue with your plan and move to the next step? Are they ready for the bond auction?"

"Yes," Gene answers. "I have their assurances that they will all play their part. There will likely be smaller players that try to muck things up, but their efforts won't amount to anything. We've tied up all the big players. Hopefully, the president gets the message."

59

Washington, D.C.

Doug Martin receives a phone call from Bobby Ferguson. He's invited to the White House where he joins the president, Bobby, Will Duffy, and Leon Washington.

"Ok, Doug," the president begins, "can you give us an update?"

"Our lawyers have reviewed all of the documents and contracts concerning the Fed," Doug begins. "The contracts are legal and enforceable. They have complete control over our money supply, interest rates, everything."

The president doesn't care for details. "Forget about contracts or the law right now. Assume for a moment that we can get around the law, any law. What are we going to do about Gene O'Neil?"

Doug repeats what he has been saying in his emails and reports. "I think we need to come up with the plan that he's been asking for, Mr. President. While painful in the short term, a financial plan or budget for the country will be a very good thing. It's sorely needed and long overdue."

The president and his team are frustrated. The treasury secretary doesn't understand how politics work. Politics is all about the short-term, the next election. That's all that matters and all the American people understand. Politics is about winning elections, not solving problems.

"Bobby?" the president says.

"Well, we can't agree to slow down spending. I think that maybe we need to create an incident that would convince Gene to give us more time. Something big, but short of a war, or not a real war anyway."

"They got our money," Will Duffy says. "What if we create a new supply of money that would replace the old? We create a new dollar to replace the old ones that they control?"

The president appears interested in the suggestion. He turns to Doug.

"That wouldn't work, Mr. President, and doesn't address the problem. Two presidents have tried alternatives. Prior to the creation of our Federal Reserve, Abraham Lincoln printed new money they called 'greenbacks' because of the bright green ink on the back. It helped him pay for the Civil War. Lincoln hated bankers because they were charging him high interest rates. Lincoln took those greenbacks out of circulation right after the war. Those extra dollars would have crippled a normal economy."

"And the second time?" Bobby asks.

"Kennedy," Doug answers. Doug pulls a dollar bill from his wallet. "You see how all our money says 'Federal Reserve Note' on it. Well, Kennedy's money said, 'United States Note' and had red serial numbers. The story is that Kennedy's father understood the role of the Federal Reserve. He made a fortune on Wall Street and he knew some of the owners of the Fed. He resented them and wanted to transfer their powers to his son."

"Two presidents tried it and both were assassinated?" the president asks.

"In any case," Doug continues, "Kennedy's vision was to back the new currency with silver rather than gold. The bankers controlled the gold supply. He thought the government might be able to control silver. Then in the 1970s the United States changed its policy altogether and we no longer back our dollar with gold. We don't back it with anything. Mr. President, there is no way for us to print new or replacement dollars, and it wouldn't address the problem anyway."

There's a long pause.

Doug appeals to the president again. "Mr. President, we have a system in place. We simply need to work with Gene and others in a more responsible manner. We need a financial plan for the country."

The president thanks Doug for all his work. He compliments him on the plan he's created. "Talk with Gene about your plan and check with the

Congressional Budget Office (CBO) to make sure the numbers add up. I'll agree to the plan if Gene agrees and if the numbers are right."

"Of course, Mr. President. I'll keep you posted." Doug leaves the office, encouraged that a deal is within reach.

#

The atmosphere in the room changes as soon as Doug leaves.

Bobby asks the president "Do you think he believed you?"

The president grins. "Yes. People want to believe their president. What's Gene up to these days?"

Will Duffy answers, "We don't have a baseline to compare his behaviour to. I suppose maybe there's nothing unusual for either him or his wife. They have two sons who have come to work with him in the bank recently. There's Eugene, Jr., who graduated from Harvard Business School. He's been running around New York with a lot of girls and having himself a good time. His second son just graduated from M.I.T. He's kind of a computer nerd. He spends most of his time reading, studying. He's got a pregnant girlfriend and they're living together close to the bank's offices."

"What about criminal records, emails, phone calls, texts?" the president asks.

"Nothing unusual," Will begins, "that we can tell, but we can't follow the younger one. His name is Jack. We can't access his computer or his phone."

"We don't know?" Bobby asks in frustration. "What do you mean we don't know? Get the fucking CIA or NSA to get you access."

"We did. They can't crack into his computer," Will answers. "Like I said, the kid's a computer nerd. The NSA actually hired him a couple times for his help. He has some encryption that they haven't been able to break."

"Look guys," the president begins, "let me be clear here. I wanted a view into their personal lives in order to dig up dirt. Does Gene have a secret or a weakness that we can exploit? Is there something that would make him vulnerable? If we can't find a weakness then create one. Create a lie that will stick to him. You guys are the best in the world at this. Turn your arsenal on Gene like you've done to those you've destroyed in political campaigns. Use every agency of this government if you have to, but get me shit or create shit on him and his family. I want to be able to put him in his place. In the meantime, let Doug work with him on his plan. Hopefully, he can convince Gene that we're working hard and that'll buy us time."

60

New York, New York

Lynn arrives at the newsroom around 1 p.m. She'll work until about 1:00 a.m. including an hour on air.

There's a stack of mail sitting on her desk. On top of the pile are a dozen tulips and a letter that stands out. It's larger than standard mail. It's on bonded paper with raised letters and elegant calligraphy. She opens the letter and reads the following note:

Dear Lynn,

I apologize for not being truthful in my attempt to meet you. I saw you on television and thought you were someone that I'd very much like to get to know. I find your reporting to be interesting and intelligent.

I'd like to take you out to dinner. I will call your office in hopes of setting up a date.

Please accept this apology. I'm sending tulips with this note as I figured maybe you don't like roses.

Sincerely,
Eugene O'Neil, Jr.

Mission accomplished, she thinks to herself.

61

New York, New York

Another day of training begins, but with a twist. Jarrett shows up at 7:30 a.m. Steve, Billy, Teresa, and Jack were about to get started. He announces, "Guys, we've got a change in plans. I got a call from upstairs. Jack, you and JR need to learn about bonds immediately. Have you guys covered that yet?"

Billy answers, "No. We got the same call."

"Ok," Jarrett says, "Where's JR?"

"We don't know," Steve answers. "We haven't seen him in a while."

Jarrett takes out his phone and calls JR. The group hears Jarrett's side of the conversation. Jarrett tells him to get in here now; his father has sent orders about what he needs to know and fast. Jarrett is firm and direct.

After ending the call, Jarrett sits and says, "Ok, get going. JR will catch up or you'll redo the lesson for him."

Billy stands and grabs a marker. He writes the following on the whiteboard:

"*Bonds rule the world.*"

He steps back and says, "That pretty much tells you about bonds." He begins pacing the length of the conference room and explaining what he means. "James Carville was the top advisor to President Clinton back in the

1990s. Those are his words. He was a brilliant political strategist. Clinton was elected in 1992, but his party got beat badly in the 1994 Congressional mid-term elections. Clinton ran for president on the slogan 'it's the economy stupid,' but then his economic policies were a disaster. He was a smart politician and knew he had to change course and listen to people from Wall Street. They focused on the bond market in order to help the economy. Jobs and growth became his priority. He gave up his liberal agenda on social programs and healthcare reform. It worked. His policies created jobs and those jobs turned into votes. He got a second term as president."

While talking, Billy added a second quote to their whiteboard:

"I used to think that if there was reincarnation, I wanted to come back as the President or the Pope or a .400 baseball hitter. But now I want to come back as the bond market. You can intimidate everybody."

"That's Carville, too, when he realized how things work, even if you're the president of the United States. The bond market rules everything. You know that bonds are debt," Billy explains. "They're like a mortgage. You get money today for the promise to pay it back with interest later. Think of them as long-term loans, like twenty years. Corporations borrow money by issuing bonds. They borrow money today to build a factory or something that will produce profits over the term of the bonds. A factory is a long-term investment and the bond is long-term debt. You have to match the useful life of an asset with the time period that you pay the debt off. If you don't, then you have real problems. Straightforward, right?" Billy asks.

Jack answers, "Yeah, I guess."

"It's governments, however, that are the biggest issuers of bonds. They're the biggest borrowers by far," Billy continues.

Teresa interrupts. "Wait. Governments? They shouldn't need to borrow money. They should be flush."

Billy nods his head and continues. "Governments borrow more money than anyone. A lot more. Let's go back and talk about history and how we got here. Back to the beginning. Kings borrowed money to build up their armies. Their economies were agrarian, based on farming. The only way to grow in power and influence was to acquire more land or take land from others. Feuds or wars went on for centuries between rival countries or city-states.

Kings borrowed all the money they could in order to pay for wars and get more land. Wars require soldiers and weapons. Kings wanted as many soldiers as possible—more than the other side. So, how do you think they paid for all this?" Billy pauses so Jack and Teresa can think about it.

"Governments have only a few options," Billy continues. "First, a government might just print money, but that's the worst thing they can do because their money becomes worthless. Second, they might offer to pay soldiers with IOUs or promises to pay them in the future. Think about that from the soldier's perspective; would you agree to that? No, you could get killed in the war or your side could lose. A promise to pay you in the future would be worthless. If you're a soldier, you want something of value regardless of which side wins. The only thing in this world with guaranteed value was gold. You'll fight in a war, but you need to be paid in gold before you enter any battles."

Steve then adds, "That's how wars were fought."

Jack turns to Steve and says, "On our first day, did you say you had a dual major; economics and history?"

Steve smiles and says, "Yes, that's right. The funny thing about history is that most of it is incomplete. They never tell the business side of history, and yet that's the most important part. Money. History comes down to everyday people and the power of economics over them. What will ordinary people do and how far will they go to protect their own interests? That's the history of man."

Billy continues. "Generals, leadership, military strategy are all part of the story. But wars are about who can get the most soldiers, most firepower, most resources on their side of the battlefield. And who can get the most resources? The side that can convince bankers to lend to them the most money. Convince the bankers they have the best chance of winning and are the best bet for bankers to make money. Bankers decide who's going to win the war before any shots are fired. They're the only ones that can pay for everything."

"Whoa," Teresa says. "Bankers determine who wins and loses wars?" She doesn't believe it. "Aren't you overstating the importance of bankers? Sounds like you're going way, way too far."

"This system has existed for centuries. We can talk specific examples," Billy replies. "Think about the famous Battle of Waterloo in 1815 between the English and the French. The banker that determines the outcome is

Nathan Rothschild. The Rothschild family is the greatest banking family of all time."

Steve grabs a two-volume set of books on the Rothschild family and hands them to Jack. He explains, "The Rothschild family grows out of a Jewish ghetto in Germany to become the richest men in the world. Richest by far. There are four brothers. Each of them manages a branch of the bank in the largest cities in the world. How do they become so rich? Bonds. They invent the modern-day bond market and how our central banks work."

Billy speaks again. "They're true bankers with a network of contacts and the best communication system in the world. They provide the gold to governments, who then pay their soldiers. Governments give them a bond or a promise to repay the Rothschilds with interest. The relationship between bankers and governments grows closer and closer over time. They need one another."

"But," Jack begins, "there is still the risk that a government could lose the war and their bonds would be worthless. They can't repay the debt. You said so yourself."

"Good point," Steve answers "and here's how they get around that. Two governments go to war. Both sides issue bonds or take out loans with the Rothschilds. The Rothschilds make both sides promise that if they win, they'll pay off the total debts of both countries. They can charge enormous fees to these governments because for them it's life or death. And remember, the more debt there is, the better it is for bankers. They make interest on their loans."

"Wait," Teresa says with obvious surprise. "They're the bankers for both sides? Both countries agree to pay off the debt or total cost of the war? So they act like the house, you know, a casino. Bookies make money by taking bets on the action regardless of who wins? They get a piece of the action. That's what banks do with governments over war?"

"Yes, Teresa," Steve answers "and that's a good comparison."

"How is this possible?" Jack asks. "I mean, we all learn about our government and history in high school, but nobody ever talked about this. How is it possible that there is this side to the story that no one knows?"

Teresa looks at him without knowing what to say. To her, this is the same scam she's seen many times before. This is just a far bigger scale and somehow legitimate.

"Maybe it's our education system," Billy suggests. "Our schools do a horrible job of telling the truth about history. Everything has to be politically correct at the expense of the truth."

"But what about the gold?" Jack asks. "Where does the gold come from and why would people swap gold for bonds?"

"They get the gold from all over the world," Billy answers. "That includes other governments, kings, the church, wealthy individuals—their network. Why exchange your gold for bonds? Simple. Gold is great, but it doesn't earn you any interest or dividends. There's no cash coming in every year. Gold sits in your vaults and you hope that it's worth more next year and the year after that. Bonds, on the other hand, have the promise to repay you both the principal and interest. Interest is something that gold doesn't give you. So, if you're wealthy and own gold, it's likely you'd prefer to exchange some of that gold for bonds. You get annual interest payments."

"You also buy influence with the royal families," Steve says. "Influence, government contracts, status."

Billy and Steve continue to explain as Jack and Teresa are processing the information.

"The Rothschilds earn a fee on the issuance of the bonds. They earn fees when they buy and sell bonds, on currency exchanges every time wealth moves to another denomination. They create these markets or actually monopolize them. It's the biggest game in the world. Do a Google search of the homes built by the Rothschilds. Seriously," Steve is instructing Teresa, who has her laptop open, "look at them."

Teresa follows his instructions and begins viewing images of the most magnificent homes she's ever seen. "Oh, my God. I've never heard of the Rothschilds."

Jack then turns to the other side of the transaction and asks, "But these bonds are just promises to repay the debt after the war is fought. How are the countries going to repay the debt plus interest?"

"Taxes," Steve says.

Jack now sees it fit together. "Governments owe money to bankers. The only way for a country to repay all this debt is from the collection of taxes in the future. In order to have debt, you need to have taxes. You need to have some future stream of money coming into the government. So, bankers lend money to countries based on how much future taxes they expect that government to be able to collect. The bigger the economy, the more growth, then the more money that bankers will allow you to borrow."

Jack stands and retrieves a book from JR's pile of required reading. His own copy of the book is at home. "This is why Napoleon despised bankers. Why he blamed the bankers for his military failure." Jack reads the following quote from Napoleon Bonaparte:

"When a government is dependent upon bankers for money, they and not the leaders of the government control the situation, since the hand that gives is above the hand that takes... Money has no motherland; financiers are without patriotism and without decency; their sole object is gain."

Napoleon Bonaparte, 1815

"I didn't know you'd gotten that far," Billy answers.

"There are a few points that I take from that quote," Steve says. "Governments rely on bankers obviously. 'The hand that gives is above the hand that receives.' Napoleon believes bankers are more powerful than the leaders of government. Keep in mind that he was the Emperor of France. But, 'financiers are without decency,' I don't think so. It's not that they're without decency as much as they don't have a dog in the fight. Like Teresa said, they're like a casino or bookie and they make money on the competition. I don't think bankers are bad. They're providing a service and it happens to make them a shitload of money."

"There's another quote that I like from that book," Billy says. He takes the book from Jack and begins searching for it. As he searches, he explains, "You have to understand just how powerful the Rothschilds were. I mean if you were to combine the largest ten banks in the world today, you'd approximate their size in terms of wealth and influence. Think of that, and they were owned by one family." Billy finds it. "Here's the quote from the mother of the four Rothschild brothers:"

"If my sons did not want wars, there would be none."

Gutle Schnaper Rothschild

"There were periods of peace. Extended periods. Why?" Steve asks before answering his own question. "Wars didn't make economic sense. Governments were paying back their debts from previous wars. There's a limit on the amount of loans that bankers are willing to make. It comes back to the value of the future tax collections that a government can get from their own people. Bankers set limits because the crazy monarchs might just keep waging war forever."

"Leading up to Waterloo," Jack considers, "England would be a better bet than France. France was still an agrarian society. England was going through the industrial revolution and their prospects for growth, prosperity, and therefore, future tax revenue, were far greater. They would have been able to borrow a hell of a lot more money than France."

"Exactly," Steve answers. "It probably helped that Napoleon was crazy too."

#

"That's one example and maybe it's right. It's plausible, but what about others?" Jack asks.

Billy answers, "Ok, Jack and Teresa. You give me an event, something significant, and we'll put it into the context of how bankers and the bond market determined the course of history."

"It sounds like a challenge," Jack says as he looks to Teresa. "Any suggestions?" he asks her.

She thinks for a moment, "Our Civil War."

"Ok," Steve answers with some excitement in his voice. "First, let's talk about the strategy for the South. They didn't have the industry of the North. They didn't have the factories, railroads, or transportation network. What they had was cotton. They controlled most of the world's cotton production, and that was an extremely valuable asset. Cotton was shipped from our ports in the south to England where it could be turned into clothing, linens, everything." Steve stands and creates another diagram on the whiteboard.

He continues, "The South needs to pay for a war. How do they do it? They sell bonds because they need cash now. They sell their future production of cotton years out into the future in exchange for cash now. Investors buy the bonds because there's a profit. Manufacturers who will need the cotton can buy it now at a discount several years into the future. They secure the raw material they'll need in advance and more cheaply."

Billy adds, "It's still how the commodities market works today. You can buy coffee, corn, soybeans, or anything today in advance of when they're ready to come to the market."

"Things go well for the South," Steve continues and he adds to his diagram. "They sell bonds all over Europe successfully in exchange for cash. They pay their soldiers and buy the supplies required."

"What's the North's strategy and why?" Steve asks.

"They go to war to free the slaves," Teresa answers.

"Right, or we can come back to why," Steve responds. "The North understands the South's weak spot. Their strategy includes a naval blockade of the southern ports. They take New Orleans. They shut down the ports because they need to stop the flow of cotton to Europe. If cotton doesn't get to Europe, then the South's promises to repay the bonds with cotton deliveries become worthless. Stopping the flow of cotton means stopping the sale of bonds and the South's ability to get cash. The North succeeds with its blockade. The South can't win because there's no money to pay for what they need."

"Back to Napoleon's quote," Jack says, "or Shakespeare for that matter. If you borrow money from someone else then that person has control or influence over you. We don't want anyone having influence over our government. We don't want bankers having influence over our leaders or defining policy."

Steve and Billy stand still and without expression.

#

"You know," Billy adds, "this probably isn't relevant, but Teresa you said the North went to war to free the slaves. The reason for the Civil war was actually the mineral riches found in the American West. You know of the California Gold Rush of 1849. The North was content to let the South have slavery in the southern states. Wealthy businessmen in the North and South both wanted to get rich off what was believed to be huge deposits of gold and silver out west. The war was about the fact that the South had an advantage over the North at getting to those riches. They had cheaper labour—slaves.

Northerners weren't going to let the South keep that advantage. I mean the Supreme Court of the United States even found a way to say slavery is ok in one area, but not another. That made no sense. It was shameful. Our court today might be even worse."

"Billy, please don't get started on the courts," Steve begs.

"It's true," Billy answers. "Today's court is full of political appointees with their own extreme views. Citizens United might be their worst decision ever. Were they paid off, or are they high minded idealists with no clue of how the real world operates? How did they ever conclude that you can be taxed for not buying something? The court's become too political. Too many judges are out of control."

Steve interrupts, "We got off on a tangent here. Remember that bonds rule the world and every event in history can best be explained through economics. People will do what's in their own best economic interest."

62

New York, New York

It's been eight weeks since the president's fundraiser. Gene has a reminder on his calendar to call the President. Instead, Doug Martin calls on the president's behalf.

Doug explains, "You can probably guess why I'm calling. It's been eight weeks since your meeting with the president. We've made a lot of progress. I've been working on the plan that I've been sharing with you. I've seen your edits. The president is still waiting for the Congressional Budget Office for their input. You know, model out the numbers. The bottom line is that we need more time."

There is a long pause.

"Gene are you still there?" Doug asks.

"Yes, Doug, I'm here" Gene answers. "I'm supposed to believe that the president can't get the budget office to move faster?"

"Well, yes," Doug answers. "I think we can get there, but it's a process. Things take time in Washington, a couple more weeks maybe."

"Thank you for the call, Mr. Secretary."

"Wait," Doug interrupts anxiously. "What are you saying? Is this acceptable?"

"No, I did not say it's acceptable. I told the president that the deadline was firm. It has come and gone. Thank you for your efforts. Have a nice day."

Gene hangs up the phone. He writes the following email to the leaders of the shareholders:

"As expected, the president did not provide a plan. The deadline has passed. We will move forward on Monday. I will provide you with a progress report at the conclusion of the auction."

63

New York, New York

Jack and others are in the conference room enjoying their lunch break when Jack receives a video phone call from his friend Cheese. Jack answers the call on his laptop. Cheese is sitting in Jack's old apartment.

Teresa leans into camera view to say "hello" to Cheese. She sees posters of zombies covering the walls. "I love what you'd done with the place."

Cheese gives a thumbs-up signal.

Jack tells him, "I'm in a conference room on the tenth floor of the bank building. I'll spin the computer around to show you." Jack begins turning the computer and introducing people. He begins, "This is Steve Johnson, one of my instructors, from Texas originally," Steve waves. Jack continues until he has introduced everyone.

"Nice to meet you," Cheese says. As soon as the camera is back on Jack, Cheese says quietly, "That looks awful. You need to get the fuck out of there."

The group overhears him and thinks it's funny.

"What's going on?" Jack asks.

"I got a job for the summer. The pay is sick. Want to guess what I'm doing?"

"You're giving driver education lessons?" Jack asks.

"No, good guess kind of, and my driving is better than yours. You were on the right track. I'm writing code for a company that's working on driverless motor vehicles."

JR overhears Cheese. "That's great. Everyone wants a driverless car. It would be like the lone ranger when he whistles for his horse to come. You use an app to tell your car to come get you. You could do anything you want while the car drives itself."

"That's cool," Jack tells Cheese. "I mean there has to be a lot of variables to work out. It's got to be challenging."

"You'll like this part," Cheese says. "I had an interview with them. I didn't know shit about this stuff, so I broke into their computer network before the interview. I wanted to figure it out and see how much progress they'd made."

"You broke in without me?" Jack asks.

Conversation in the conference room stops. They're all interested in Jack's conversation.

"Yeah, good and bad about that too," Cheese answers. "They caught me."

"No shit," Jack says in obvious concern. "Hacking is a two-man job, you know that. I could have helped you."

"I know, but see," Cheese explains, "a few things. They caught me, but they were impressed that I could break in. By reviewing their programs, I saw how slow their program was. I could make it more efficient and usable. More efficient means faster, address more variables in the same time, make it better. They were upset at first, but they love me now. They want me full-time and to lead a team. They're paying me a ton of money and will pay me more if I can figure out some things."

"That's great buddy," Jack says.

Teresa leans her face in front of the compute and adds, "Congratulations."

"Thanks. Maybe I'll hire Jack," he answers. "Course, you'll need to apply and I'd have to interview you."

"Driverless cars, huh?" Jack says, "I've heard about that technology."

"Not cars, motor vehicles," Cheese corrects him. "Cars, yes, but buses and every truck on the road. I'm talking about small trucks like the postal service, parcel deliveries to large eighteen wheelers you see on the highway. The technology will work for every vehicle on the road."

The implications begin to hit the group.

"Who's paying for all this?" Steve asks.

"Who's paying?" Cheese repeats the question. He's a little caught off guard that others are eavesdropping. "Not sure, some private equity group. They're investing a whole lot of money. They've got teams working with computer companies, auto companies, and even the federal government, departments of Transportation and Defense. It's fucking huge."

"But," Jack begins, "doesn't that mean millions of people are going to lose their jobs? Everyone that drives trucks, buses, taxis, ubers? All those jobs will be replaced by this technology?"

"Yup, that's what's coming," Cheese answers.

"And," Jack continues, "the private equity guys, what's in it for them? Some kind of royalties or licensing deal?"

"I guess," Cheese replies.

"That's awful," Teresa says. "Think how many people will lose their jobs and families will lose pay checks. I have an uncle that drives a truck."

"Don't blame me," Cheese says defensively.

"I heard of driverless cars on the news," Teresa says, "but they never said it was going to replace all these jobs. Why don't they tell you that? I mean why doesn't the news tell you what stuff means to the lives of everyday people?"

There's a pause in the room while people contemplate the impact of the technology.

JR breaks the silence. He's unfazed. "That's just progress. It's gonna happen over and over again. Technology will keep replacing low end jobs. It's inevitable."

"Maybe it comes back to the split in our economy," Steve says. "Look at all the technology companies. They pay a lot of money to engineers and programmers in Silicon Valley and they outsource the manufacturing to China or others. You know; countries without minimum wage laws, government regulations, or environmental concerns. Highly skilled people become part of the top wage earners. Jobs that can be done more cheaply elsewhere are moved. The top and bottom and not many jobs in between."

"Globalization," Billy says.

"Yup," JR agrees. "Jobs move to whoever is willing to do it cheapest even if their government manipulates their currency in order to make it so."

Billy then adds, "Those governments know that jobs means keeping workers busy and not protesting against the government. A population with jobs means people have something to lose. It's easier for the government to have control over them."

"What do you mean by currency manipulation?" Teresa asks JR.

"It means," JR answers, "that the United States deals in dollars and other countries have their own currencies. Let's say one dollar equals one Chinese yuan. Let's say it costs one dollar to produce a pen in the United States and one yuan in China. The Chinese lower the value of the yuan to the dollar. Let's say they drop it in half, so instead of the pen costing a dollar when it's made in China, now it only costs fifty cents. People buy the pen made in China."

"Can they do that?" Teresa asks. "Every country's dollar should equal each other's or it's cheating."

"Yes, they can do that," Billy answers. "Countries do it all the time."

Teresa looks at Jack. "That feels wrong, doesn't it?"

"You guys are killing my buzz," Cheese says. "I'm out of here. Talk with you later, Jack."

Jack waves him a goodbye on the video and adds, "Congratulations, I'm happy for you."

"We'll get to currency manipulation," Billy says.

"America has enjoyed this wonderful period of wealth, prosperity and security," Steve says. "The whole world wants the same kind of standard of living. Think of it like a war. We're fighting with other countries over jobs and money or buying power. Technology like driverless vehicles will reduce the number of jobs. Robots and artificial intelligence are going to take away a lot more jobs. Every country will compete hard for the remaining jobs."

Teresa looks down towards the conference table and shakes her head. "It's just going to get harder and harder for the American worker and their families. We need some kind of plan, I mean, as a country. People need to understand what's at stake."

64

New York, New York

JR calls Jack with an invitation.

"I'm seeing this girl," JR begins, "and she wants to meet you and Teresa. I thought maybe we could do dinner on Saturday night. I told her you guys don't drink much or stay out late. I mean, the pregnancy and all."

"Sure. I'll check with Teresa and let you know," Jack answers. "Why does she want to meet us?"

"She said she wanted to meet my family. I told her about you two, you're happy together. She thinks all my friends are assholes, all the same basically, business school guys interested in money and what it can buy."

#

The two couples go to dinner. JR immediately brings up Lynn's television show and tells them all about it.

"That sounds exciting," Teresa says. "You're kind of a celebrity."

"No celebrity, but thanks. It's fun, but it's really just a lot of hard work," Lynn replies. "Very long hours, like everyone I suppose."

"JR and Jack are in this training program at the bank," Teresa begins. "You've probably heard about it. I join them some days. It's interesting and fun. The guys are really smart and the days go quickly. I'm learning just listening to them. Part of the training required us to watch different news channels and read all these newspapers. It's all new to me and Jack."

"What news do you watch on television?" Lynn asks.

"They gave us a list," Teresa replies. "The idea must have been for us to get different perspectives. I like it, but it's so odd. It's like the networks aren't even covering the same news or same world. The reporting is that different. The day's biggest story on one network isn't even covered on another one. So weird."

"What do you think?" Lynn asks Jack.

"The difference in reporting is obvious. They don't report news as much as they have five or six people on their sets telling you what to think. I don't want them to tell me what to think or how to interpret the news. I'll do that. I just want them to give me the facts." Jack pauses. "What strikes me though is how critical they are of people with opposing views. They look down and even make personal attacks. It's like they want you to get emotional, stir things up. I never expected that."

Teresa nods her head. "You know, they do get me riled up, and hadn't thought about it that way. I guess that's what they're trying to do. My other reaction is I don't want to watch the news."

"Look, we're in New York, people," JR weighs in. "We all know what needs to happen, let the smart people run the country. I'm not calling others deplorables or anything like that, but why would we let them run anything? That would be backwards. They should just thank us for being willing to manage things."

Lynn addresses Teresa and Jack, "I understand your points. I don't get into politics on my show. It's on at 11 p.m. weeknights. Watch it sometime and let me know what you think."

#

During a break to the ladies room, Lynn begins asking questions about Grace.

"She's been very generous with everything," Teresa tells her. "I mean the support they provide is unbelievable. It's like nothing I could have imagined."

The questions keep coming. "Do you like her? Do you guys talk? What's she really like? What does she do with her time? Who are her close friends? Is she happy?"

Teresa's unsure how much to share and unsure of Lynn's intentions. She doesn't want to appear rude, and she could use a friend. "I guess you'd say she's happy. I get the feeling she's lonely. I'm not sure what I'm sensing exactly. She doesn't let you get too close. I think family is the most important thing to her. Maybe the money's important to her too."

"New York," Lynn says. "There's a pecking order here. You don't socialize or initiate anything with people lower on the food chain than you. Don't get close with many people. The higher you move up, the lonelier it is, the smaller the group you can talk to. She's at the very top, so it must be very lonely or difficult. There's a lot of crazy shit that happens at the top and people love to hear the rumours."

"Really?" Teresa replies with interest.

"Sure. Sex, affairs, drugs, treating others like complete dog shit because you can. The city is nuts. You know, if you ever have information on Gene or Grace or pictures, then I could turn that into money. I mean, I know people in the press that pay big money for that kind of thing."

"No."

"Yeah, they pay a lot," Lynn explains.

"Well," Teresa answers, "I couldn't do that. I wouldn't betray anyone, ever."

"What about marriage?" Lynn asks. "I mean, I don't know if I'd agree to move away from home without the guy asking me to marry him."

"I know, I thought about it," Teresa answers. "My folks thought I should. It just didn't feel right. We ought to get back to the table."

65

New York, New York

Gene instructs his sons to come to his office no later than 8:45 a.m. Monday morning.

JR and Jack arrive to see several computers sitting on a wheeled cart in Gene's office. The computers are connected to a large flat screen television on the wall. The table in Gene's office has eight seats. The boys are directed to sit in two of them.

Two computer technicians are checking to make sure everything is in working order.

Bernie Schwartz enters Gene's office and says "good morning" to everyone. Gene welcomes Bernie and asks, "Bernie, I haven't told my boys what's going on here. Can you fill them in on what we're going to be looking at on this flat screen?"

"Sure", Bernie answers. "The United States government is going to sell bonds today. They're going to sell $100 billion of bonds. Investors will buy the bonds, which basically means they're giving money to the United States government today. The government will pay them back in one year plus interest. The government will sell the bonds and the price determines the interest rate. It's an auction; the government is borrowing money so they want the lowest interest rate they can get. You'll be able to watch it live here." Bernie points to the flat screen.

"Guys," Gene says to the technicians, "can you give Jack logins and passwords? Jack, you should learn how to drive these computers. It may come in handy one day." The computer technicians comply and Jack moves to the far end of the table.

"Both sites, please," Gene instructs the technicians. Jack is given his own authorizations to the Morgan Sachs account and the Federal Reserve account.

Bernie continues, "Let's say you're willing to buy all these bonds at $98 billion. You give the government $98 billion today and they will pay you back $100 billion in one year. You'll earn $2 billion on your investment of $98 billion or just over 2%." Bernie looks at the boys, who both understand. "Let's say someone else is looking at this investment and they'll accept a 1% return on their investment. They bid $99 billion. Again, they give the government $99 billion today and a year from now the government pays them back $100 billion. If I bid $98 billion and you bid $99 billion then you win and you get the bonds. You don't have to buy all $100 billion. Each auction is a little different, but generally you have to bid at least $10 million."

Gene asks, "Do you have any questions before Bernie explains the layout of the screen?" JR and Jack shake their heads no.

Bernie continues, "At the top of this screen is summary information about today's auction. You'll see the amount of $100 billion and the term of the bonds, one year. On the right-hand side, you'll see a list of banks and governments who are expected to bid on them. They're listed in the order of participation in previous auctions. 'CHN' here," Bernie points to the symbol on the screen, "is the Chinese. It's their sovereign wealth fund. 'JAP' is the Bank of Japan, and so on. FED is the Federal Reserve. Down here in about the ninth spot is us, 'MS' for Morgan Sachs." Bernie looks at the boys and then his watch.

Figuring he has a couple more minutes, Bernie continues. "You'll see there's nothing on the left-hand side of the screen yet. The people running the auction will begin things at 9:00 a.m. Everyone has five minutes to enter their bids. No one can see what the others are bidding." Bernie smiles and rubs his hands together before saying, "then the fun starts. The right-hand side of the screen lights up and everyone can see all of the bids. You can see where your bid is in relation to everyone else's. The government begins accepting bids and locks investors into contracts. The left-hand side displays all the transactions that are locked. That will go on until all $100 billion worth of bonds have been sold."

While Bernie is talking, David Sandler, the bank's CEO, enters the room and sits next to Gene.

Bernie adds, "This is all going to happen fast. We'll see this column of locked contracts fill up in no time. Buyers can change their bids or withdraw them unless the government locks them into a contract." Bernie is starting to get nervous because the time has come for them to enter a bid. He looks at Gene and asks, "Ok?"

Gene answers, "Bernie, one more thing. Explain why the rate is so important."

Bernie seems annoyed to get the question so close to the beginning of the auction. Instructions on the monitor read, "You may begin entering your bids. We'll begin locking in contracts at 9:05 a.m."

There is a digital clock on the screen that started with five minutes. It has begun counting down to zero.

"Well," Bernie says, "The interest rate drives everything. Markets all over the world are connected. U.S. government debt is the safest investment in the world. All other interest rates are based on that rate. If the rates on U.S. Government bonds go up then so do the interest rates on the bonds for every country and every company. If these rates go down, theirs will go down. U.S. debt is the standard from which everything else is measured."

The countdown clock ticks past one-minute remaining. Bernie turns to Gene and says, "We should enter our bid."

"Thank you," Gene says before instructing him, "Please enter $97.0874 for all $100 billion."

Bernie had a number in mind of $99.50 for $1 billion. Bernie doesn't believe Gene's instructions. "Gene, we can't do that. There's no time to talk about it." Bernie looks at Gene and then to David.

Gene repeats, "$97.0874 for all $100 billion please."

Bernie looks again to David, who nods his approval. Bernie enters the numbers and looks at the screen. He figures that these instructions can only mean that Morgan Sachs doesn't want any of these bonds. Why else would they bid such a ridiculously low price? And besides, the bank doesn't have $97 billion of cash to invest. They may have $2 billion at most.

The countdown clock ticks down to zero. There's nervous anticipation in the room. Bernie is scratching his head and hoping to get answers soon. In all his years of trading, he has never seen anything like this.

The right-hand side of the screen lights up. There's only one bid. At the top of the column, it shows "MS…$97.0874…$100B." All investors are listed, but there are no other bids.

Bernie can't believe what he's seeing. He turns to the technician responsible for the computers. "Something's wrong. We must have lost connection." Everyone in the room stares at the flat screen. "It's impossible, something's wrong," Bernie is talking quickly. "There's a screw-up someplace. Is it on our end or theirs?"

"Everything is in good working order," is the response from the technician.

Gene and David are calmly watching the screen. There's no activity. Time passes. Eights bids come in slowly for $10 million each. No other serious investor is bidding. Two minutes pass and then all activity stops.

#

It's a very different picture at the United States Treasury Office where they're running the auction. Bob White was left in charge of the auction. Bob is an assistant to an assistant. He was left in charge while more senior treasury officials are away at a training program in Florida. The government prefers to hold training meetings in the best places. On this particular day, his bosses are out on the golf course.

Bob was told that the auction would be routine. He's worked many auctions before, but never had the responsibility of managing the entire process. His role has been to lock in bids according to someone else's instructions.

While the auction is live, every second feels like minutes. Everyone at the treasury is shocked by the lack of bids and the price from Morgan Sachs. People are looking to Bob for answers. Do we sell the bonds to Morgan Sachs at this price? How long do we wait for more bids? There's a second screen that Bob's looking at which displays the interest rate that the government would pay based on the low price; three percent is staring back at him. That interest rate is extremely high in today's market. He prays for more bids.

The clock is ticking. After the digital clock counts down from five minutes to zero, it begins counting in the other direction. It usually takes about ten minutes to complete an auction. Bob can't accept the smaller, $10 million bids because Morgan Sachs's bid is for the entire lot and can't be broken up. Accepting those eight bids would only amount to $80 million, which is insignificant when you need $100 billion.

#

David Sandler speaks up. "Well, you did it, Gene. I'm not sure how you got the entire world to cooperate, but it looks like you did it. This is really something. How long before the treasury terminates the auction and reschedules it for another day?"

Gene puckers his lips. "I'd say any second now." Gene has picked up the *Wall Street Journal* and is scanning the headlines.

"I've never seen anything like this," Bernie says. "What's going on? Are you behind this, Gene? It must be a complete shit show at Treasury."

David gets up from his chair. He says his goodbyes to everyone and begins to leave the room.

#

Bob White knows that time is running out. He's been instructed to sell the bonds. The clock is ticking. He's been calling and texting his supervisors.

The group at the treasury is staring at Bob and waiting for his decision. The government is depending on that cash today. It needs to pay for the day-to-day operating expenses. $97 billion won't even pay for a week of spending by the United States government. An even larger auction is scheduled for next week. Accepting this bid, however, could trigger shockwaves into the financial system.

#

"Locked," Bernie declares. The group assembled in Gene's office looks up at the screen to see that the treasury has accepted Morgan Sachs's offer. They need to wire $97,087,400,000.00 to the treasury by the close of business today.

Silence. Disbelief. Shock.

David stops in his tracks. He turns and looks at Gene.

"Idiots," Gene says.

"How long before the president or treasury secretary calls?" David asks.

"How long before the markets tank?" Bernie asks.

Gene answers, "A few minutes for the phone call and immediately for the markets."

Gene switches the flat screen to television mode and a business channel. Live market updates are broadcasted. Stock prices decline sharply on the news.

"Gene, we're not prepared to wire $97 billion," David says anxiously.

JR and Jack are sitting still. The mood has changed dramatically since Bernie called out "locked." Jack's worried his father has made a colossal mistake and is in serious trouble.

"You gonna be able to fix this?" David asks.

"Yeah," Gene answers with obvious frustration.

David then looks at JR and Jack and says, "It was nice to see you boys. I hope your training is coming along well." David quickly exits the room.

Bernie asks, "You want help unloading these?" He means reselling the bonds at a loss.

"No, thank you Bernie. I'll take care of it," Gene answers.

"Call me if you need anything," Bernie offers. He then looks at JR and Jack on his way out of the office. "Your Dad's got some giant pair of balls."

#

Gene turns to his sons. "I wanted you to see this for yourselves."

"Are you in trouble, Dad?" Jack asks.

"No, not trouble exactly," Gene answers. "There's just a lot going on right now. There's a lot at stake."

"How can I help?" JR asks.

The voice of Gene's assistant comes on the speaker of Gene's desk phone. "Bobby Ferguson from the White House is on line one."

Gene puts the call on speaker to allow his sons to hear the conversation.

"What the fuck is going on, Gene?" Bobby is in a panic.

"Excuse me," Gene replies.

"What the hell have you done?" Bobby rants. "You bid our bonds at 3%? You've driven the stock market into a free fall. The Dow is down 800 points already. The president is fucking livid."

"Hi, Gene," comes another voice. "It's me, Doug, I'm on the line as well," says Doug Martin.

"Gentlemen," Gene begins. "Let me be very clear about a few things. First, the level of incompetence of our government is staggering. The folks running the auction at the treasury should never have accepted our bid. They should have terminated the auction. Second, Mr. Secretary, you're going to make an announcement immediately that there was a computer problem with the auction. You and Morgan Sachs will both issue press releases confirming the glitch. The results of today's auction will be voided. That will stabilize the markets. Third, I'll have the Federal Reserve wire you $100 billion today to meet your immediate cash requirements at 1% interest. Fourth and most importantly, do you people understand what it is you're playing with? I could just as easily have bid $96 or $94 billion today and crashed the stock market."

Gene pauses. He begins speaking, but more slowly and in a measured tone. "Now, I'm going to ask you two questions. Bobby, do you remember when I told you that once a fire is lit, there's no telling how badly it can burn. I told you that you'd be responsible. Do you remember me telling you that at the fundraiser?"

It takes a couple seconds before Bobby grudgingly answers, "I remember."

"I could let this fire burn, Bobby. I could add gasoline to it right now. My second question is when are you going to get me that plan for how you're going to repay this debt?"

There's no response.

"Why don't you fellows talk with your boss and get back to me."

"I'll get right on the press release, Gene." Doug tells him. "Do you want to see it before it goes out?"

"No. There's no time for that, just get it out fast."

"Alright then, I'm going to hang up," Doug says.

"Bobby are you still there?" Gene asks.

"Yes."

"Get back to me by the end of the day and don't ever ask me what the fuck is going on. That's the question I'm asking you and your boss. Did you forget that I gave you a deadline and I told you it was firm?"

"It's not easy, Gene," Bobby pleads. "This is the president's legacy we're talking about and—"

Gene hangs up the phone.

#

"How can I help?" JR asks. "Maybe it's time for me to meet people from the Federal Reserve?"

Gene shakes his head no.

"This is why you had us learn about bonds last week?" Jack asks his father.

"Yes. Again, these lessons are very important."

Jack follows up, "Can we spend some time together talking about all this? I mean, where this is all headed and why I'm here exactly. You certainly don't need me, and why would I need these passwords?"

"Yes, of course, and I'm sorry I haven't made time for that yet. I figured some classroom style training would be the best start. I knew we'd have time to get into all the details this summer. I'll give you both all the time you want out at the Hamptons. July and August vacations, you know? We'll have time. How's that sound?"

"Sounds great, Dad," JR answers.

Jack nods his head, "Sure."

66

New York, New York

Mary and Teresa talk several times a day by phone. Jack's been devoting all his time and energy to work. While Teresa visits Jack often, she spends a lot of time alone.

Mary arranges a three-day visit to New York City to spend time with her daughter. They'll go shopping for baby items. Mary invites Grace to join them.

Mary learned from her first trip that you have to be strategic about shopping in the city. She's done her homework and selected stores for this outing.

Grace joins them in a large clothing store in the SoHo area of Manhattan. Looking at outfits inspires good feelings among the women. They dream about the child's future.

After shopping together, they go off in different directions in search of items on their own. The store is crowded. Many languages are spoken.

Teresa meets up with Grace by accident at a clothing rack. She confides, "Jack told me about the food. About the special farms and the need to get food that hasn't been altered by the food companies. It's so good and I've begun noticing the health benefits. It's like a miracle drug. Thank you so much. I can't believe what the food companies get away with. That really angers me."

Grace's facial expression doesn't change. Teresa had been hoping for a bonding moment where they share a topic important to them both. Grace barely acknowledges her comments.

"I mean, is that how you stay so young looking and keep so thin?" Teresa asks.

"Thank you for the young-looking comment," Grace begins. "As for thin, we have to be thin. A man, a wealthy man, can look any way he chooses, but not us. We don't have that luxury. Yes, the food will keep you thin, healthy, and full of energy. The food in supermarkets is poison. I'm glad you like it."

"Is there any way," Teresa begins, "that we might be able to share some or I can buy some of this food for my parents? My dad is way overweight and that's probably going to develop more and more health issues as he ages."

"Perhaps," Grace answers, and moves away in the opposite direction.

#

A short while later, it's Mary and Teresa that meet up. Teresa smiles when she sees how many items her mother is carrying. They decide to look for Grace and get lunch.

As they begin their search, Mary thinks she overhears Grace in a dressing room. She overheard her crying. She gets to the dressing entrance and sees Grace through one side of a thin curtain. After a few moments, Grace looks up and makes eye contact with Mary. Grace has tears in her eyes. She's sitting in a metal folding chair. Mary moves the curtain aside and stands in the doorframe.

"I lost a baby girl," Grace confides. "Just before delivery." Grace has a tiny pink outfit on her lap.

Teresa is about twenty feet from Mary and approaches. Mary holds up her hand and shakes her head as if to say, "Stay back." Grace doesn't notice Teresa. She's looking down at the outfit.

Mary sits beside Grace in another chair and pulls the curtain closed.

"This outfit reminded me of one lying on our changing table when I got home from the hospital," Grace explains. "I picked it out for my baby girl." She's fighting back a lot of emotion.

Mary puts her hand on Grace's knee. "I'm sorry. I can't imagine how painful that must have been. I'm very sorry."

Grace nods her head and composes herself. "It took years, and then I had Jack. He was a blessing. He helped me out of my dark days. He was kind of a sickly child. He became my focus, you know? Getting him better. That helped me get better."

They sit quietly. After several minutes, Grace starts to compose herself. She stands, appears to stiffen up, and puts on her sunglasses. She thanks Mary and then says, "I should get going."

Mary hugs her and offers, "I'm so sorry. Let me know if you ever want to talk."

Grace leaves in the opposite direction of where Teresa is standing.

Teresa approaches. "What's wrong?" she asks.

"Nothing really. We all get hurt in this life," Mary answers. "She's no different than the rest of us."

67

Hauvers, Maryland

Gene's invited to Camp David to meet with the president and senior members of Congress. The president called the meeting.

Camp David is beautiful. It's approximately 60 miles from Washington, DC in a secluded area.

The group assembles around 9:00 a.m. in a building that resembles an ultra-luxurious hunting lodge. They sit on couches and high-backed chairs arranged in a large circle.

The president starts the meeting with a short statement. "First of all, I want to thank everyone for coming today. I thought it would be helpful to get everyone together." The president turns towards Gene and continues, "Gene, you should know that I've told this group about our discussions at a high level only. I have not gotten into details. They understand what occurred last week at the bond auction and why it's imperative to work with you and others. Our government needs access to capital at affordable rates. This is our moment, our chance to get the leadership of both parties to understand the situation and work together. With that said, Gene, let me ask you to take the floor and share your thoughts."

Gene begins, "Ladies and gentlemen, I'm not sure what more to say. You continue to ask for more money and more time. I think we can agree that at some point there's an end to all this borrowing. There are credit limits on people, companies, and governments. The ones who decide on those limits are the ones lending money. For centuries, this has been known as 'the golden rule.' Not the one that says, 'do unto others as you would have them do unto you.' This golden rule says whoever has the gold makes the rules."

Gene is seated at the end of one of the couches. He is speaking slowly, quietly. "There is a limit on borrowing and the people lending you money have decided your credit has reached its limits. You're the country's leaders. Leadership is about making tough choices. Make them. Come up with a plan. Work with the treasury secretary." Gene stops.

The room is quiet. It appears Gene is done. Several members of Congress have been on their portable devices and weren't even listening.

"Gene," the House Speaker begins, "what does this mean exactly and how'd we get here, I mean now? It feels like you just sprung this on us."

Gene responds, "All of you know I've been speaking about this debt for some time. I understand that many of you don't spend a lot of time on the topic. You've ignored it. You've ignored me or hoped the problem would go away. Let me put it this way. The United States federal government claims to have debt of $24 trillion, but that's understated. We'll come back to that. Do you understand the implications of that much debt?"

Gene looks around the room. "Let me help," he continues. "First, the Federal Reserve has been helping you by keeping interest rates at historically low rates for years. I promised the president low rates and he promised me a financial plan for the country. Instead, he increased spending, tripled the debt, and has no plan." Gene looks at the president, who looks away sheepishly.

"The first issue," Gene continues, "is that your interest rates are going to go up. Here's an easy way to think of it. Every 1% increase in the interest rate on $24 trillion means higher annual interest cost of $240 billion. There are 75 million Americans paying taxes. That means, on average, every taxpaying American needs to pay roughly $3,200 per year in taxes just to pay for that 1% increase." Gene shrugs his shoulders. "I want you to think about how well that's going to be received when you tell the average American who's making about $60,000 a year that he needs to pay $3,200 more in taxes just to cover interest. I may need to raise rates two or three times that number."

Gene knows he's hit a nerve. Tax increases end political careers. "And you ask me to lend you more money just to pay the interest on the money you already owe me? The answer is no, not without a repayment plan."

The Senate majority leader, one of the biggest proponents of deficits, speaks up. "I understand, but we need time to consider all options thoughtfully. Perhaps we should think about some kind of special commission to look into this."

"You're free to do whatever you'd like, senator," Gene replies, "just as your bankers are free to charge more interest starting today or stop lending you money altogether."

"Hold on now," the Senate minority leader speaks up. "We've studied our federal government's debt as a percentage of Gross National Product or GNP for years. The ratio is high, but we were at these levels right after World War II. We dug ourselves out of it." Several people in the group are nodding their heads in agreement. "It's one of the measures we look at to know how much debt is reasonable. We think we're ok."

"Senator," Gene begins, "you're right. At the end of World War II, the ratio of federal government debt to GNP was high. It was acceptable, short-term and attributable to the war. But think about it, there was almost no consumer debt and low corporate debt. There wasn't much debt at the state and city levels of government either. Now, several states are bankrupt. Over a dozen of our largest cities are bankrupt even if we don't officially recognize it. More importantly, you've created these massive unfunded pension liabilities to millions of government workers that aren't included in our debt. Do you want to talk about Medicare, Medicaid, and Social Security? You don't include those as debt, but you promised to pay medical costs to seventy million baby boomers for decades. Remember, you taxed them during their years of employment and you spent it. We had a president decide that we'll pay for prescriptions to all seniors. The next president added a health plan and lied to the American people. He'd cover forty million more people and it wouldn't cost us a penny? He lied. Food stamps for fifty million Americans? Our taxes and regulations make it harder for American business corporations to grow. Less growth means there's less future tax revenue for bankers and, therefore, we stop lending. You people have done everything you could to screw things up for our great country. We've seen this crisis building for forty years, or roughly the period of time that some of you have been in office."

Gene is careful not to show any emotion or political preference. "Yes, the ratio of debt to GNP appears to look like other time periods. The problem with your calculation is that it ignores all the debt in the system. When you add up all the debt, it's the highest it's ever been. Your debt is now roughly $320 trillion. It's over thirteen times greater than your official figure of $24 trillion. The ratio of debt to GNP is the highest in any country ever. Here's the worst part, you're the leaders and you don't even see a problem."

Silence.

#

The vice president speaks up and in a friendly tone begins, "What can we do here today? What are you really after? There's got to be an agreement that we can come to that meets the needs of everyone. I'm sure we can figure this out."

Gene understands his audience. Everyone is calculating how they might spin the news and blame this event on bankers or the other political party. They're wondering how they can turn the problem into an opportunity for themselves.

Gene answers, "We all understood this day would come if you didn't stop this obscene spending. It will be far less painful if you take steps than if you make your bankers do it. I understand our federal government owns 600,000 buildings and many aren't even used. Start selling the assets you don't need. If you wait for bankers to do it, then we'll sell anything that will raise cash. We'll sell buildings, land, national parks, and military assets like aircraft carriers to the highest bidders."

"Hold on, Gene," the House Speaker interrupts. "You're talking about America's defence." The Speaker is a conservative who has directed money to the defence budget for years. In return, defence contractors have made him a wealthy man.

"That's right, Mr. Speaker," Gene responds. "That's exactly what we're talking about. I guess the president won't be able to keep telling people, 'I have an army, I got a navy and an air force.' We're talking about cutting defence spending, social programs, government jobs, and all the bullshit that you waste money on to buy votes and keep yourselves in office. Sell assets, cut spending, and get the economy growing again."

Gene stands, buttons his suit jacket, and walks towards the exit. He cautions, "If members of this group begin using this for their own political advantage then you will all fail, and the country will feel the pain."

As he exits and the door closes behind him, he hears the vice president say loudly and clearly, "Fuck."

68

New York, New York

Jack continues to immerse himself in work. He works long hours and reads voraciously from every possible source. He's learning more on his own and relying less and less on Steve and Billy.

Teresa feels a little disconnected from him. She has more free time on her hands than she knows what to do with. She misses home and Sunday dinners with family.

Jack returns to their apartment one weekday around 8 p.m. They sit down for dinner together. He opens a book and reads during the meal. Teresa is talking. Jack tries to read and listen at the same time.

She raises her voice, "You haven't heard anything I've said."

"I'm sorry," he replies, "Yes, I have. What is it?"

"I miss everyone back home," she says. "I love you, but you're busy all the time and don't have time for me. I don't want to say anything because I don't want to be ungrateful about all this. Not saying anything doesn't make sense so I'm telling you. I'm struggling. I need to tell you that. I need you to hear me. I need time with you." Her emotions come pouring out.

He puts the book down.

"I feel like I don't have a life," she continues. "I hate to ask for money, but everything here is so expensive. My best days are when I go to work with you and we spend time together." She's glad to be sharing her feelings even if he doesn't want to hear it.

“Why don’t you come with me more often?” he asks. “I love it when you come.”

“I only have a few outfits good enough to wear to the bank or anyplace we go. I can’t keep wearing the same things over and over and over. Didn’t you ever notice?”

“No. I’m sorry. I didn’t notice. I suppose I should have been more thoughtful.”

“Maybe I shouldn’t say anything, be tougher,” Teresa answers. “But we walk into our apartment on our first day and you’ve got like twelve brand new tailored suits in your closet. They’re just ready and waiting for you. Shoes. Shirts. Freaking monogrammed gold cufflinks? Everyone at the bank has such beautiful things. I’m embarrassed by what I’ve got or don’t got.”

They’d been sitting on opposite sides of their dining table. Jack moves. He sits beside her. “I’m sorry. This is my fault and inconsiderate of me. I guess I was too focused on all this work. Everything is so new and different. The work. The pregnancy. Missing school. You know? I’m really sorry.”

He takes out his phone and calls Peter Hollingsworth. “Hi, Peter, it’s Jack. I have a favour or favours to ask of you.” Jack goes through a list of requests. He’ll need a credit card for Teresa, a stylist to help her with shopping, transportation by limousine and private jet to Boston on Sundays. He pauses to ask her, “Anything else?”

She shakes her head no.

“And thank you, Peter.” Jack ends the call.

She watches him text Steve and Billy that he’ll be taking the next two days off.

Tears had welled up in her eyes when she was explaining her feelings. Now, she sits on his lap and hugs him. “I can’t believe you just did that. Thank you for hearing me. Thank you for understanding. I’m sorry.”

“I should have done it earlier. I’m sorry. I wasn’t thinking,” Jack replies.

She kisses him softly.

“You just never learned how to be rich,” he says. “We can start tomorrow. I’ll show you.”

69

New York, New York

Two weeks pass. Jack receives an invitation from Peter Hollingsworth to go to lunch.

Teresa has joined Jack every day since her shopping spree and accompanies them. She's been doing all the reading and catching up with the lessons.

#

"Peter," Teresa begins the conversation, "I want to thank you for helping me fly up to Boston on Sundays. I can't believe how easy you've made everything. The private jet means I don't have to go through security at the airport. It's so easy."

"You're welcome, but those lines at the airport aren't about security," Peter answers.

"What's that mean?" she asks.

"The Transportation Security Administration or TSA is a jobs program. We could provide far better security for a fraction of the cost, but our government wanted to create a lot of jobs and they did. Our politicians created thousands of low-end jobs to buy votes and strengthen the unions; the union dues mean more payoffs back to the same politicians. It's terribly wasteful. It's the same cycle that happens with all these government jobs."

Peter notices that his comment caught them off guard. He adds, "I'm sorry. I meant to say you're welcome with regards to your transportation." He then asks, "Is that a new outfit?"

"Yes, we've done some shopping," Teresa answers with a very big smile. "Do you like it?"

"It's very nice," Peter answers. There's been a transformation of Teresa. The clothes, hairstyle, and makeup are new. She's seeing a personal trainer and eating healthy. She looks amazing and carries herself more confidently.

#

Peter begins asking questions. He asks specifics about all the topics covered in training. It's clear that Peter's objective is to test Jack's understanding of the materials covered thus far. Jack answers with short, efficient responses. Teresa adds details.

Once satisfied, Peter asks Jack, "Are you enjoying it?"

"I like it ok, but I don't think it's for me. I enjoy learning new things, but I can't see myself devoting my career to this. There's more to life." Jack is unapologetically honest. Peter feels slightly insulted.

"Peter, why do you think the world hates America?" Jack asks. "Is it just because we're richer than other countries?"

Teresa sits on the edge of her chair. Following the news is new to them both, but they're concerned about what they're learning.

"I suppose it's a lot of things." Peter is evasive. "Yes, America is richer than other countries and so there is some resentment. That richness, however, has been like a magnet in the sense that people from all over the world were attracted to America. They knew they could build a better life here for themselves and their families."

Jack had hoped for a better answer. "No, I'm really interested Peter. What's really behind it?"

There's a pause as if Peter didn't want to get into it. "I suppose, it's because we're a colonial power. Americans don't think of themselves that way, but the rest of the world does."

Jack gives Peter a puzzled look. "We're capitalists, but we're not colonialists. We don't take over other lands. Even when we've conquered countries in war, we don't seek to rule them, occupy them, or tax them. Quite the opposite; we give them their freedom. We spread democracy wherever we can."

"Well," Peter starts slowly, "we have conquered the world. No question about it. The combination of our corporations, our government, and our banks has conquered the world. That's why people hate us. They resent us terribly. It's also why our standard of living is so much higher than anywhere else. Higher than the world has ever known."

"What do you mean our corporations, government, and banks?" Teresa asks.

"Consider this part of your training I suppose." Peter takes a deep breath and looks around. "The way the world operates is quite simple. Let's say we, um Americans, find something we want or need in another country. It could be sugar from the Caribbean. It could be some newly discovered raw material for a medicine, or for a weapon for our military. The point is we want something and it resides in another country." Peter takes a drink of wine and a bite from his lunch.

"American corporations just buy it right?" Jack suggests.

"No, we send in the bankers," Peter answers.

That was the last thing they expected.

"We send in someone from the IMF or International Monetary Fund with an offer to help that country. The offer is too good to turn down. We tell them that the natural resources found in their country are likely worth many billions of dollars. We arrange for substantial loans from the IMF to that country. We say the loan is an advance on the raw materials that will be developed. The raw material is the collateral for the advances. The country might need clean water, hospitals, schools, or it's just political payoffs."

Neither Jack nor Teresa are eating.

Peter continues, "And so it begins. American corporations begin taking what they need and paying the country. After some time, the IMF comes along with some bad news. They say that they overestimated the value of those resources. Those raw materials aren't worth what they thought. The country has more debt than its resources can support. The country is in default on their debt and has a serious problem."

Peter takes another break to enjoy his lunch.

Neither Teresa nor Jack wants to interrupt.

"The IMF comes back with another offer. They'll say 'look, we'll rework your loans. You'll pay us a certain amount to satisfy your debt. It will take a lot longer than we thought. We'll need to increase your interest rate because this is riskier than we assumed.' The result is that we conspire to take their resources as cheaply as we can."

The news is disturbing to Teresa and Jack.

Peter uses his napkin to wipe his lips. "The loans from the IMF don't really end up in that country. Some of it does, but most of it supports our own corporations. Get the raw materials cheaply, kind of like a loan from the IMF to our own American corporations. And who is the International Monetary Fund, Jack?"

Jack turns to Teresa and answers, "The IMF is owned by the central banks. It's controlled by the Federal Reserve Bank of the United States and the Bank of England."

"Correct," Peter says.

Jack comes back to the original question. "People in these countries hear news about natural resources and it creates optimism for a new life and better future. Money flows into the country, but not as much as hoped for. Politicians grab some of it. Jobs are created to mine materials, build roads, and transports goods. They're jobs, but they're low paying jobs with no future. The ordinary person sees American corporations come and take their resources. The optimism for a better life dies at some point. The result is that their natural resources are gone and they're left owing us a bunch of money?"

"Correct," Peter says. "As I said, we're a colonial power. We've taken the riches of other countries. If the leader of a country doesn't like the offer, then we've used our military to intervene. Our diplomats talk foreign aid as bribes or threaten the use of our military if they don't agree. You have to understand that this can be a very nasty business. It is a system, however, that has also produced extraordinary progress for man. This system has meant less armed conflicts. It works exceptionally well."

Jack's not feeling very proud to be an American. He looks at Teresa and then off into the distance. Jack then says, "It isn't working well for everyone. Not for those in the countries we've exploited. We didn't fire any bullets and we didn't take their land. It's basically a more civilized form of warfare. It makes us a colonial power and hated."

"That's awful," Teresa says.

Peter looks at Jack. "You'll recall your father saying at our first breakfast to 'keep an open mind.' I think this is one of the moments that he expected."

Jack answers, "There are two ways to enslave a nation. One is by the sword. The other is by debt."

"Yes, that's well said," Peter compliments him.

"I didn't say it, John Adams did," Jack answers. Jack turns to Teresa, "John Adams was the second president of the United States."

"I know who John Adams is," Teresa answers, "from Massachusetts."

"There's something else you should think about," Peter adds. "Our country is now in a similar predicament. The United States has more debt than it can afford and the outlook is ominous. There was nothing underhanded or deceitful about the bank's methods. Our political leaders did it; both political parties. They've enjoyed the spending, power, and making themselves rich. It's gone way too far. Like other countries, our politicians found it easy to take out loans or cash, but the repayment can be very painful."

Jack nods, "I understand, Peter. Thank you for lunch. I got a lot out of this and I appreciate it."

"Keep an open mind," Peter responds. "Dig into your studies. It's terribly important. Banking is about a lot more than most people understand. It touches everything."

#

After leaving Peter, Teresa asks, "Jesus, Jacky, do you believe this? Do you think he's right about all of it?"

"No," Jack shakes his head. "Or yes, I mean. I know he's right about it. It's why my dad wanted us here now. The bond auction I told you about. It's all coming to a head now. The bank wants to stop lending or charge higher interest rates, or something else, but it's going to impact every American's finances or their entire lives."

Teresa confides, "You know, the more I learn about all this, the less I really want to know. Our country is better than this. We need some kind of change."

70

Washington, D.C.

As the president concludes a cabinet meeting, he's informed that a train carrying oil has had an accident in Ohio. There are casualties. The president huddles around a television with Bobby Ferguson, Leon Washington, and the attorney general ("AG").

"What a tragedy," his AG says.

The news anchor changes subject to the price of oil, which is up sharply on the news.

"Gene O'Neil," the president says. "He's behind this."

"Whoa, Mr. President. I don't see any connection there," his AG replies. The AG is a long-time friend of the president. Their close relationship allows her to say more to the president than others are comfortable sharing.

"No, I'm telling you," the president insists. "This is Gene O'Neil. I can see his fingerprints all over this. I bet he's making money hand over fist on this. He bought oil or futures, options, something, and he's making huge profits."

"Isn't it more likely, Mr. President, that this is the pattern of other accidents?" his AG asks. "We're transporting all this oil by rail because we didn't want to build pipelines. These accidents are caused by moving more oil by rail than the system was designed for."

"No," the president responds harshly. "We ran the decision about the pipelines through all our models. We talked with our supporters. Opposing the pipeline meant gaining more votes and raising more money. We had to do it, but I was never told anything about trains having these accidents or causing fatalities. This is some kind of industrial sabotage. Jesus, Bobby, in a battleground state like Ohio too? We need Ohio." He pauses. "Gene knew this was going to happen. Where are we with him anyway?"

Bobby answers, "Our treasury secretary is working on that plan to satisfy both you and him. We haven't found any dirt on him or his family yet. We've started work on the negative public relations campaign you requested. We'll make him look worse than any businessman in history."

The president has his arms folded and nods. "What about you?" he asks his AG. "Can we lock him up? Put him in jail?"

"There's no case here, Mr. President, no legal justification for anything like that. He hasn't broken any laws."

"No law?" the president responds harshly. "I am the law. You and me are the law. We've got to dig deeper here people. We're fighting a different kind of enemy here. We've got to ramp things up. We've got to get him. Don't you people understand?"

"Yes sir, Mr. President," Bobby answers.

Leon and the AG share a concerned look with one another.

71

"I got a call from MIT today," Jack tells Teresa excitedly.

"Oh, yeah, what was it about?" she asks.

"They liked my paper. Professor Hildebrand says he'd like to be my advisor when I return to pursue my doctorate."

"Congratulations, that's wonderful. I'm happy for you," she tells him.

"And he believes there's commercial application to one of the examples I used."

"What's that mean?" Teresa asks.

"I suggested," Jack explains, "you could create an application on your phone that linked facial recognition software with a database of people from social media and other sources. Basically, you point your phone at someone and it could tell you who they are."

"Really," Teresa responds. Now she's excited. "Women would love that. You could immediately know who you're talking to and identify the liars and creeps right away." She pauses before asking, "What about money, Jack? Are you going to make money off it?"

"I don't know. I hadn't thought of it," he answers. "Maybe the school would make money, or maybe me?"

"Jack?" Teresa is incredulous. She's thinking he may have given away rights to an application worth a lot of money.

"It was really just an example of computing power and not the point of the paper," Jack explains. "I used it to run the numbers on all the people on the planet, variables of facial features needed for positive identification, and the power to compute a positive match within five seconds."

"But you may have blown your chance to make some real money."

"I'm sorry. I wasn't thinking about that. I really just wanted access to MIT's supercomputer to work on things before I go back. The professor granted me security clearance, highest level. I can work on the formulas that I'll need for my dissertation. I suppose I could build that app too."

Teresa pauses and responds thoughtfully, "Look, it's great. I'm happy they liked your paper and you have access to whatever a supercomputer is. Maybe you can make money on it. You should ask, but if there's ever a next time for something like this, let's talk about it."

Jack nods and breaks out into a smile. "I've got access to a supercomputer," he says with excitement.

72

New York, New York

Peter and Gene are discussing a variety of topics when Gene asks for a progress report on his sons.

"I believe that JR is of the opinion that he knows all that he needs to know right now," Peter reports.

"Is that right?" Gene responds.

"Last week, he asked me when I was planning on retiring. He asked if I thought it would be a good idea for him to step into my role. His reasoning was that it would give him a first-hand view of your job. I guess he figures he'll start in my job and move to yours."

"Are you kidding me?" Gene asks. "Right to your job and mine. Skip the decades of learning shit, sometimes working for assholes but all the time working your ass off. Unbelievable. You know I get upset by people wanting to take from others? I get more pissed off at his type. I expected so much of him, but he's no different. Maybe he's even worse. I guess I did a horrible job parenting him." Gene is turning his head from side to side. "And he keeps asking me when he's going to meet the owners of the Fed."

Peter remains silent.

"He'd be better off at another bank or some other line of work," Gene concludes. "Away from here, away from me. He needs to cut his path." Thirty seconds pass before he asks, "What about Jack?"

"It's difficult to read him," Peter begins. "There are times when I think he's not following, but then he surprises you. Rather than not keeping up, it feels as if he's been ahead of you all along and he's been waiting for you to catch up."

"I understand," Gene answers with a knowing smile.

"Do you remember when you asked me to check references from Harvard and MIT on your sons?" Peter asks. "Jack's counsellor at MIT said Jack is one of the most intelligent people he's ever met. He can read a book on a new topic with one hundred percent comprehension. He puts concepts together that others can't. It's effortless. He's a lot smarter than me and you, Gene."

"Hell, I know that Pete."

Peter continues, "I'm not sure how much more we can teach him. He's progressing at his own pace and reading more than we asked him to. Seems to know what's coming before we teach it. He's no longer studying business or banking. He's more interested in government or the intersection of business and government. Your challenge is simple. He doesn't want to be here."

Gene stands and looks out over the skyline. "Isn't that parenting? One son could be great and doesn't want it. The other one wants it and isn't capable."

73

East Hampton, New York

Gene bought a vacation home in the Hamptons shortly after reaching the position of partner. He sold that home after the bank's initial public offering and upgraded to his present home. He became aware of the property through a client. It was held in a trust created over two hundred years ago. There were two structures on the property, a farmhouse style home and a barn. Both were in horrible condition. The trust's beneficiaries could no longer afford the property taxes and repairs. Real estate developers had been trying to buy the property for years, but couldn't get around the terms of the trust. Ownership of the property had to remain in the family in perpetuity.

Gene became aware of the property and the trust. He drove out to see it and immediately fell in love with it. The property consists of forty acres. On one side of the property is the Atlantic Ocean with its own private beach. On the other side is conservation land and a bay.

Gene immediately had the property appraised. The appraisal was absurdly low due to the constraints of the trust. It was valued at just seven million dollars.

He considered all options, including adopting a family member if that's what adherence to the trust required. Instead, he chose to lease the property from the trust. There was nothing in the trust prohibiting a lease. Lawyers drafted a letter saying the lease was consistent with the spirit of the trust. It suggested historical precedent. Leasing parcels of land for farming was common in the 1700s when the trust was created.

Gene paid seven million dollars to the trust. In return, he received a lease for the property "for as long as the lessee and his beneficiaries choose." As lessee, Gene is responsible for all taxes, insurance, and maintenance.

As one of his lawyers put it, "Gene stole the property fair and square."

#

Gene took Grace for a drive one Sunday along the main road that runs east to west in the area. There's a bend in the road at this property where people stop and look around at the unspoiled beauty. Gene pulled the car over and suggested they take a short walk. He brought a picnic basket and a bottle of wine. They sat on a blanket, enjoyed their meal, and he told her about buying the property.

She was thrilled. They made plans to build their dream home as a project that they'd work on together. Not surprisingly, Grace took control. She built an eight-bedroom home and a two-bedroom guesthouse. A pool and tennis court were added. Gene wanted a large lawn and flower garden.

The property is split by the road. On the southern side of the road, the property consists of six acres with its own private beach. In the 1930s a concrete sea wall was built to protect this stretch of land from possible erosion. The wall sits between the road and the water. There's a seating area on top of the wall with stairs on either side.

Grace had a stone wall constructed on both sides of the road. It was tastefully done, but wasn't built for aesthetic reasons. Its purpose was to prevent cars from stopping at the bend in the road to enjoy the view.

Grace spends most of the summer here. There's an active social scene between Memorial Day and Labor Day. She enjoys riding and owns a dozen horses.

The entire family enjoys vacations here every year during the July 4th holiday and two full weeks in August. Gene's family from Scituate, Massachusetts joins them for the first of the weeks in August. The Rossi family will spend the second week due to Gene's invitation at the Harvard Club.

#

The Fourth of July holiday arrives. Grace is at the house. Gene, Teresa, and Jack will ride by helicopter to their home. They depart from the roof of the bank. Using the helicopter shortens the commute considerably. The drive out on the Long Island Expressway can take hours.

Two displays of fireworks are scheduled. The town manages an event on the evening of the Fourth. The family will enjoy a private show on July third. The location for their show is just off their own private beach. A barge will park and shoot off the fireworks. Gene and a couple of neighbours pay for the show.

Their display gets larger every year. The family will enjoy a clambake on the beach, light a bonfire, and watch the fireworks. It is Gene's favourite day of the year.

#

Shortly after they get into the helicopter, Gene asks, "Teresa, tell me, how are you enjoying New York?"

"I like it," she answers. She's not comfortable calling him Gene, so she doesn't address him by name. "It's weird because it's so big and there are so many people, but sometimes you feel all alone." She pauses and jokes, "The hard part is that my boyfriend's job keeps him busy all the time. His boss is brutal."

"Have you ever been to the Hamptons?" Gene asks.

"Nope. I really haven't been many places and never been out there," she answers. She's been looking at the crystal decanters in a cocktail bar inside the helicopter. She picks one up, takes the top off and smells it. Her head recoils.

"It's Irish whiskey, twenty-three years old," Gene says.

"Wow," Teresa responds as she puts it back.

"And what does your family do on this holiday?" he asks.

"Well," she begins, "there's a fireworks display in Boston along the Charles River. My dad gets one of the Transportation Authority's boats and we all go out to watch the show. That or Molly and me go on one of the fire department's boats with Mr. McCann."

"The Transportation Authority has boats?" Jack asks.

"Yeah. Everyone has boats. Police, fire, the T, State House. You'd never know it because they aren't painted like that. They look like any other boats. The Fourth of July is one big party up there. You could almost walk across the river by stepping from one boat to another."

"Jack, what about you? How does it feel to be back in the city? Have you looked up old friends?" Gene asks.

"It's ok, Dad," Jack answers.

It occurs to him that his response wasn't very enthusiastic. Intending to improve on it, he adds, "I mean, yes, it's really ok, but I haven't looked up anyone. Too busy. I keep in touch with Cheese, from school, you know. Mostly on video calls."

"I think you talk with Cheese more than you talk to me," Teresa adds with a smile.

They're all in a good mood and looking forward to the weekend.

#

Gene starts, "At the conclusion of the bond auction I told you we'd spend time together and I'd explain how we got to that point." Gene is always working, always making the best use of his time. "Let me tell you a story. It's a great story, and it's a great story because it's all true and very few people know it. In fact, it's the greatest story in the history of business."

Teresa's interest is piqued.

Gene continues, "Back in 1913, our country passed two bills. The first was the United States Revenue Act and it imposed income taxes for the first time on individuals in the United States. The second law was the Federal Reserve Act and it created our Federal Reserve Bank. Do you know about these laws and do you know why they passed the laws in that order?"

"Yes, Dad, I get it," Jack answers. "You need taxes for the government to show income. If you have income, you can take out loans. Individuals, companies, and governments take out loans. The more income and collateral then the more you can borrow. First, the country needed to pass a law to show taxes will be coming in as income. Then you pass a law to create an entity to lend money to the government, control money supply, interest rates, everything. It allows a small number of men to gain control over our money, economy, and almost everything. The plan was hatched in secret at a place called

Jekyll Island, off the coast of Georgia. It included rich foreigners who did it in Europe."

"Not all that was in your course material," Gene says.

"Yeah, well," Jack begins, "I've read a little more than the course material. You're with the Federal Reserve somehow and that's why you wanted me and JR here now. You think our government has too much debt. You rigged the bond auction as a show of force."

"Very good," Gene says, nodding in obvious approval. "Very good. Do you have questions?"

Jack looks at Teresa.

Jack answers, "I suppose I have a hundred questions, but maybe just a few for now. First, is it true the owners of the Federal Reserve created the stock market run up during the 1920s and then sold their stocks right before the crash in 1929?"

Teresa is floored. Does Jack think the stock market crash was an intentional act?

Gene adjusts in his seat. "Well, I don't know all of the details. I'd say they understood that the Roaring Twenties was a time when the economy was overstimulated. It couldn't last. Sometimes you start something that's hard to manage or slow down. All of the owners of the Federal Reserve sold their stock months before the crash."

"They knew the crash was coming? That a depression was coming?" Jack asks.

"They knew some downward correction was coming," Gene answers. "They couldn't have foreseen how bad it was going to get."

Jack nods before continuing. "Second question is about Ian Fleming's claim. Is that true? You know, the author of the James Bond 007 spy novels?"

"I don't know what you mean," Gene answers.

"He said," Jack explains, "that the United States government conspired with the Federal Reserve to buy all of America's gold from its citizens in the 1930s for pennies. Forty years later in the 1970s, our government took us off the gold standard. The price of gold skyrocketed to two thousand dollars per ounce. He estimated the profits to be over a trillion dollars. Is that true?"

"Very good," Gene answers. His smile shows that he's pleased. "Our president in the 1930s, Franklin Delano Roosevelt counted on the patriotism of good Americans to turn in their gold. They did, and at cheap prices. The

Fed figured they needed the gold because we were in the midst of a depression. Tax revenues would go down and America needed to borrow a lot of money to spend their way out of the Depression. The Fed needed the gold as collateral for all that borrowing. They couldn't count on tax revenue because the economy was too weak. Getting our hands on the gold was necessary, as was FDR's deception."

Jack noticed his father say, 'our hands.' He included himself in that group. "Third question," Jack continues, "why get involved with them, Dad?"

Gene's confused, "I'm sorry?"

"I'm not sure what they're doing is right, the Fed I mean," Jack begins. "I'm not sure anyone should have that kind of power. Why get mixed up with them?"

You could knock Gene over with a feather. He sits back in his chair. *Why get involved?* he thinks. Gene was a young man with nothing in life. He was simply trying to get ahead and make a career for himself. He never had the luxury of asking that question.

"We'll have time this weekend and during the August vacation," Gene answers. "We'll get into all of it. We can talk about where this is all heading and your role."

#

As they approach the O'Neil home, Teresa is awestruck by the view. The helicopter circles the area. The homes resemble the mansions she's seen in Newport, Rhode Island.

The property has room to land the helicopter. They land on the backyard lawn, grab their bags, and walk to the front door.

The home has a long driveway with a circle at the front door. There's a flower garden in the middle of the circle with a flagpole. A wide porch wraps around the entire home.

"Where's the statue?" Jack asks his father as they reach the front door.

Gene smiles, "Charleston, backyard, hopefully hidden away under some of that Spanish moss."

Teresa shoots Jack an inquisitive look. He explains, "A couple years ago, one of Dad's friends, Bruce Savosik, had a statue installed in the flower garden. It was a life-sized statue of King Midas. It was bright gold and just hideous. Mr. Savosik thought it was the funniest thing ever. He used to say Dad had the Midas touch because he always knew the direction of the markets. They love to play stupid jokes on each other. You'll meet him. He's the one that plays in the golf match tomorrow that I told you about."

Teresa nods her head and has heard stories of the golf match. "What's in Charleston?" Teresa asks.

"Mom bought a house there and restored it. Her family has roots down there. We should go see it sometime," Jack explains.

"Another house?" Teresa inquires. "How many houses do you own anyway?"

"That's it, or one in Florida too," he answers. "As far as I know."

"Jack, you understand this isn't normal right? I mean these houses, helicopter rides, talking about gold and crashing markets? This isn't normal." Teresa's concerned.

"I know," Jack answers with a large smile. "I know it's not normal, and Dad's wealth doesn't really mean all that much, but it is pretty cool, huh?"

74

East Hampton, New York

Friday morning. Gene and his sons leave the house to meet up with Bruce Savosik at the golf club. Gene belongs to several private golf clubs even though he only plays golf a few times a year.

The golf match has become an annual tradition played during this holiday. It's been played the past six years. They play by their own rules. "Whiffs," meaning you swing and miss the ball, don't count towards your score. Everything that happens during the match is negotiable.

The golf club is less than a mile from the O'Neil home.

The teams are Gene and JR against Bruce and Jack. The game can take over five hours because the quality of golf is so poor and they rarely concede putts.

The bet starts at one thousand dollars on the first tee and can be doubled with each shot. JR and Jack agree in advance that they're not going to pay each other regardless of who wins. The match is about bragging rights between Gene and Bruce for the next year.

Gene and JR have won the match all six years. Bruce has a strategy for today's match. He wants to get as much alcohol into his opponents as possible. He's arranged to have a golf cart accompany them that's equipped as a mobile bar. He instructs the bartender to over serve his opponents; her gratuity depends on the outcome of the match.

The weather is perfect. It's a beautiful sunny day with temperatures in the low 80s. There's a constant wind off the ocean. The wind feels good, but adds a challenge to the golf.

Their custom is to break for lunch after nine holes.

JR drove out to the Hamptons late last night. He purchased a large sailboat a few years ago and prefers to stay there. He brought Lynn along for the weekend. The two of them drove to the O'Neil house this morning. JR left her there with Grace and Teresa.

#

Tracey Savosik, Bruce's wife, arranges to have lunch with Grace, Teresa, and Lynn at the club. They sit on a terrace overlooking the course. Beyond the golf course and tall, native grass is a view of the ocean.

The ninth hole putting green sits directly below the terrace. The ladies watch the men play the hole. It's an odd-looking sight. In addition to the four contestants, there are two caddies, two golf carts in case anyone wants a ride, another cart with a bartender and waitress. It makes for ten people and three golf carts.

As the men get closer, women can hear the trash-talking going on. It appears there's a disagreement.

"Boys will be boys," Grace says as she sips a mimosa.

Tracey thinks it's wonderful. She can hear Bruce's laugh a hundred yards away. "What a wonderful way to enjoy the holiday," she says. "You know he looks forward to this all year. He's been taking lessons and practicing. He even bought a thing for the house where he hits golf balls into this movie screen and he plays different courses. He's gotten crazy about the game."

After completing the hole, the men join them.

"How's the match going honey?" Tracey asks.

"We have a problem, a disagreement," Bruce begins. "We won the front nine, but Gene and JR think that it's all square. You can't trust bankers, sweetheart."

Gene carries a glass up the stairs. It looks like lemonade. Grace asks, "Are you having fun, honey?"

"Absolutely," Gene answers, but his speech is slurred. She realizes it's not lemonade. She's happy for her husband, glad he's got a day to relax with friends and family.

The disagreement with the score is resolved by calling it even, but doubling the bet again going forward.

"How much is the bet?" Lynn asks.

"Substantial," Bruce answers.

JR suggests to Lynn that she and Teresa come out and watch them play.

"We'd rather play than watch," she answers.

JR arranges a lesson for Lynn and Teresa. The men resume their match. Grace and Tracey go into the village to shop.

75

East Hampton, New York

Their clambake will begin at 7:00 p.m. A caterer begins setting things up around 4:00 p.m. She knows how Grace likes things done. The meal is cooked in large kettles with a mix of freshwater and seawater. Wooden Adirondack chairs are positioned in a large half-circle surrounding the fire and facing the ocean. The dinner consists of New England style clam chowder, lobster, clams, sausages, potatoes, and corn on the cob. Key lime pie, Grace's favourite, is the dessert.

The fireworks are great fun and bring out the child in everyone. A grand finale lights up the sky. The group toasts their neighbours to the left and right who are also out enjoying the show.

JR invited friends Mocha and T-Bone to join them for the fireworks. They brought along dates as well. They're going out to meet up with a larger group of friends after the show. Teresa and Jack decline an invitation to join them.

#

The day has taken a toll on Gene. He's not used to spending the day outside in the hot sun. The combination of the golf, sun, alcohol, and the excitement of the fireworks catch up with him. He feels lightheaded. He considers sleeping in the Adirondack chair on the beach. Grace notices his condition and helps him walk to the house.

Jack has been drinking but he's feeling good, excited. Teresa and Jack walk behind Grace and Gene. As they enter their home, Jack asks his father, "So Dad, how did you ever get involved with these guys, the owners of the Federal Reserve, I mean?"

"Well, I'll tell you," Gene answers, "but it'll take a few minutes. I'll need a beer."

Grace decides to stay and listen. She'll help him upstairs when he's finished.

Gene sits down on the nearest couch. Teresa gets a beer for Gene and Jack from the kitchen.

"Back in the 1980s," Gene begins, "my bank was asked to help with a presidential commission set up by Ronald Reagan. My mentor at the bank was a fellow named Ed Pendergast. He was a wonderful man. Ed gets me involved. The objective of the commission was to consider putting the United States back on the gold standard. Reagan wanted us to return to gold, to back up the United States dollar with gold again."

Jack nods his head and opens his beer.

Gene continues. "So we go to Fort Knox and take an inventory of the gold there. I had to go count the gold bars and report to the president and Congress on how much gold our government owned." Gene takes a large drink from his bottle of beer. "I go to Fort Knox, which is a little south of Louisville, Kentucky. It's actually an army base. I meet up with a fellow who is there to help me, a colonel. There were television reporters filming us as we entered the main depository building. We figured that it was going to take about five hours to count all the gold. We had to weigh some bars, random test counts, we had a system all mapped out."

Gene finishes his beer and asks for another. Grace hands him a bottle of water. "I remember seeing you on television," she says.

Gene looks at the bottle of water with disappointment.

Teresa thinks the two are cute together.

"I go in the first room and there's a giant pile of gold bars stacked in a criss-crossed manner. This colonel and me look at the inventory sheet. We count the number of bars per row and the number of rows in each pile and it all checks out. Our count agrees to the inventory. We move on." Gene shrugs his shoulders.

"We walk into a second room. There are three folding chairs in the middle of an enormous room. Ed Pendergast is sitting in one of the chairs waiting for us. Ed says to me 'let's take a walk.' We walk through Fort Knox. There's nothing there. The one room, that first one, was the only one with any gold in it. Ed opens these giant doors as we walk around. The place is massive and it has all this security. One room had gold. The rest of the place is completely empty."

Gene's audience is getting more interested.

"Ed tells me that first room is the only gold our government owns," Gene says. "The Federal Reserve Bank owns what used to be stored in Fort Knox. They took it as collateral for the debt the federal government has run up. The Fed owns the gold, not the United States Treasury and not the people of the United States."

Grace, Teresa, and Jack are hearing information that only a small number of people know.

"Ed told me what he wanted me to do. He wanted me to go out and tell the world that the gold was all here. It was all safe and secure and we'd report that formally to the president. Privately, we met with the president and told him the truth; there is no gold and we can't return to the gold standard. There are other reasons, but you can't support the United States dollar with gold when you haven't got any."

"There's no gold in Fort Knox?" Grace asks.

Gene shakes his head. "Nope. It's all for show, Gracey." After a pause, Gene adds, "Wonderful day today, huh guys? Gosh I love those fireworks."

"You lied for them? That's how you started working together. Is that what you're saying?" Jack asks.

Gene looks surprised by the question. He adjusts his position from sitting to lying down on the couch. He begins talking again and in a slightly weaker voice. "Well, remember, Ed liked me. He handpicked me for the job. About a month goes by before he asks me to join him on a trip. It was my introduction to the owners of the Federal Reserve. I was Ed's choice to replace him. He was going to retire. They accepted me into their circle. Maybe that lie was a way of testing me."

"Teresa, would you be a dear and fetch me another one of those beers?" Gene asks. His head is flopping from shoulder to shoulder.

Teresa looks at Grace, who shakes her head no. Gene then fluffs a pillow on the couch to get more comfortable. He kicks off his flip-flops onto the floor.

"That's how I met them. They've been good to me and I've done a good job for them. The world economy has done well over the past thirty years. We've avoided armed conflicts for the most part. I've made them a lot of money. Now, we're going to be rewarded with shares in the bank. The O'Neil family will join five other families as part of the new ownership group. That's the plan. That's why I did it."

There's a silence when all you can hear are waves crashing on the beach. Jack breaks the silence, "And another reason why you wanted JR and me to join the bank now."

"We're having a problem with the president," Gene explains. "That's why I wanted you to be here. I don't know where it will all lead, but I've taken precautions. The food you eat? That comes from one of four communities we've built around the world that are large and self-sustaining. We may need to relocate our family to one of those communities for a period of time. Might be safer for us."

"You want us to leave the country?" Grace asks.

Gene explains, "Maybe, but these communities are beautiful. You've been to one of them. Back in 2013 when we went to New Zealand. Remember? It was the one-hundred-year anniversary of the Federal Reserve Bank. We lived in luxury for five days and celebrated each evening. I didn't tell you, but we bought the island and constructed everything there. We own it, or the shareholders own it and three others just like it."

Grace is visibly upset. "You lied. I remember when you were on television. You lied about the gold. Now you tell me we may need to leave our country? I don't like any of this, Eugene."

"I'm sorry," he replies. His tone says he's not at all sorry. "We're going to pass on ownership in the bank to our sons. Ownership that's worth hundreds of billions of dollars."

Grace is having difficulty processing all this. When her father died, his estate was valued at over five million dollars. She considered that quite an achievement. Gene lied, but now he's talking about an enormous sum of money.

"Are you saying the lie was worth it?" Jack asks.

"No one understands," Gene answers. His eyes are closed. His head is buried in a pillow. "No one understands banking even though great men have written in detail all about it. No one even bothers to read them. The average citizen is getting screwed and they refuse to learn about it. Instead, they want everything for free from their government all the way up to the point where their government is bankrupt. You need to learn it, Jack. All of it. I may not be around." Gene's speech is now barely audible as he's sinking off to sleep. "I lied about the gold. I did it for us. I'd do it again."

Grace grabs a blanket from another couch and covers her husband. "Well, that was some finale to the fireworks. Couples shouldn't have secrets. Maybe from the rest of the world, but not from each other."

Jack jokingly defends his father. "But, Mom, he's the invisible hand."

"Yeah, well, he's going to need it."

76

East Hampton, New York

Saturday is another beautiful day.

Grace got up early and left for the equestrian center. She wanted to begin her day with a ride before it got hot and stressed the horses.

Gene is sitting in one of the Adirondack chairs on the beach under a large umbrella. He's reading a book.

Lynn arrives. She lays out a beach towel next to him. "Gene, I want to thank you for your hospitality. You have a beautiful home." She is wearing a very small, red bikini.

"Of course, dear. I hope you're having a good time," he replies.

"Do you mind if I join you?" she asks.

"No, not at all. Please."

Lynn settles in close to him. "Do you know that I host a nightly television show broadcast in New York? We discuss all sorts of business issues."

"I'm familiar with it," Gene answers without looking up from his book.

"Is there any way I could get you to come on air with me?" she asks. "I have a co-host every night, leaders from the business community. You could come on and share your thoughts."

"Thank you," Gene answers, "but I don't think that's for me."

Jack and Teresa appear and say, "good morning." They've been walking the beach collecting shells. Jack helps Teresa settle into a chair on the other side of Gene. Jack offers to get her an umbrella but she declines. She loves the sun and tans easily.

"It could be great for the bank if you came on the show, great exposure I mean," Lynn continues.

Gene smiles, "Thank you again, but I think the bank has all the exposure it wants."

"Well, Jack, maybe you'd be willing to come on my show?" Lynn inquires. "Perhaps an evening's show featuring today's young stars from leading banks? Leaders of tomorrow kind of thing."

Jack smiles. "I'm no star and I wouldn't be any good on television. JR should do it. He'd be great."

Lynn reaches into her bag for her business card. She hands one to Gene and one to Jack. "Take my business card. It's got my contact information in case you change your mind or want to talk about it. My cell phone number is on the back."

Gene accepts it and places her card in his book for use as a bookmark.

#

"What are you reading?" Lynn asks Gene.

"One of my favourite authors, Ralph Waldo Emerson. I like to read fiction out here, but I reread Emerson every now and then."

"Democrat or Republican?" she asks.

Gene puts his book down in his lap. "Off the record, Miss LaRoyo? I mean everything I say and for as long as we know each other is off the record. Agreed?"

Lynn answers, "Yes, off the record unless you tell me otherwise."

Satisfied, Gene answers, "I'm neither Democrat nor Republican. Both parties conspire to monopolize power. Their objective is to share power and deceive the American people. You can't have good without bad, and both parties understand they need the other to blame for the country's problems. Americans vote one party into office. When things don't go well, they throw them out and vote in the other party. They take turns, but share power. It's an illusion. Behind the scenes, it's the same people paying politicians for what they want done. Politicians get rich off a system that's not working for the American people."

"Do you really believe that?" Lynn asks.

"I do. It's my business to know that."

"Well, if that's true, then why don't you fix it?"

"It's not my job to fix it," Gene answers. "I'm a banker. I should ask you that question. The press is one of the biggest problems in our country. Every news organization has chosen a party to favour. Their version of the news is slanted and what they report is more propaganda than news. You can't get the news reported honestly today and that's a tragedy. The press was supposed to keep our politicians honest. Now, they're part of the problem. No, it's not my job Miss LaRoyo, it's yours."

JR arrives. He's wearing running shorts and sneakers. He's dripping in sweat. "Good morning everyone," he says.

"How was your run?" Lynn asks.

"It was good, tough you know. I'm going to jump in the water. You wanna come?" he asks Lynn.

She shakes her head, "No, not yet. I'm going to wait until I get hot."

JR takes off his T-shirt and sneakers and walks down to the water.

#

"Ok, so not Democrat or Republic and anti-press." Lynn doesn't slow down with her questions. "What do you think of America today?"

"Maybe this will help," Gene begins. "I heard a joke a while back. I forget the punch line, but you'll understand the point." Gene is speaking slowly, as if he's got all the time in the world. It's fitting for a lazy day on the beach.

"There are five college friends who graduate together," Gene says. "They make a pact to get together one night a month for dinner to keep in touch. Let's just call them numbers one through five. Now, friend number one is going into social work, admirable, and accepts that he won't make much money. Friend number five goes out, works hard, is fortunate, and makes a lot of money. Friends two, three, and four fall between the other two in terms of their jobs and earnings. You follow me, right?" Gene asks.

Lynn nods her head and answers, "Yes."

"Jack, Teresa, are you listening?" Gene asks.

"Yeah, Dad," Jack answers.

"The young men go to dinner once a month and remain close. It's all good. Years go by and friend number one announces that he can't afford to do dinner anymore. His wages as a social worker are too low. Friend number five won't hear it. Number five is making a lot of money and he agrees to pay for both his meal and friend number one's. All goes well for a period of time again." Gene pauses. "Everyone still with me?"

Lynn, Jack, and Teresa all answer yes.

"Friend number two," Gene continues, "shows up one night and says he has lost his job and can't afford to do dinner either. He has two kids now. His marriage is in trouble and his wife doesn't want him spending money on this dinner. Friend number five again offers to help by paying for his dinner too but a problem arises. Want to guess why?" Gene asks.

Lynn shakes her head no.

"Well, friend number three gets annoyed," Gene explains. "See, he wants his meal paid for also. An argument breaks out. Friends number two, three, and four debate how to split the bill. They decide that friend number five will now pay for the meals of numbers one, two, three, and half of four's. Want to guess what happens?" Gene asks.

"I suppose," Lynn answers, "you're going to say that friend number five pays for the entire meal."

"No," Gene answers. "Friend number five says 'no thank you.' To him it's simple. They all went to school together and had the same opportunities. He worked hard and succeeded. He's annoyed that they're telling him what he should pay even though he feels he's been generous. He says he won't be coming to any more dinners. They stop getting together."

"Ok," Lynn says, "but that's not America."

"Of course it is," Gene replies. "Everyone complains about the top one percent or top ten percent in our country, but they're paying the expenses for everyone else. Over half our country doesn't pay a penny in taxes and that doesn't count the illegal aliens. We're a country of two groups; producers and parasites. Unfortunately, our government rewards parasites and penalizes producers. An increasingly smaller percentage of the population are the producers, and it's not sustainable. At some point very soon, they're going to say, 'No thank you.' American billionaires are already taking steps, talking about leaving the country."

#

Grace and Tracey Savosik appear. They're wearing swimsuits. Grace drops off a large beach bag. They say good morning to everyone and continue walking towards the water. Grace overhears the conversation, but isn't at all interested.

Gene replies, "Good morning." Grace doesn't turn around or acknowledge him.

"But," Lynn protests, "don't you think wealthy people have a moral obligation to take care of others? I read that you're a religious man. Isn't that what the Bible tells us?"

"The Bible doesn't say that. Read it," Gene instructs. "St. Paul's letter to the Thessalonians; 'If any man would not work, neither should he eat.' The Bible is clear; if you're not willing to work that's fine, but you can't take from others. No man is entitled to the fruits of another man's labour."

"So you wouldn't help others?" Lynn asks.

"I wouldn't say that," Gene replies. "We have an obligation to take care of those that can't help themselves. I have a brother with intellectual disabilities that falls into that category. I don't know what percentage of the population needs that kind of help. Ten, fifteen percent? Let's say there are three hundred and twenty million Americans. We should support the disabled and the elderly, so let's say fifty million people need to be cared for. Do you know how many Americans count on the government for support?"

"No, I don't know that number," Lynn answers.

"Our government provides supports to over two hundred million people. We support illegal aliens and people overseas through foreign aid. It's simply gone so far that it doesn't make sense anymore. We're supporting people that have no right to the amounts they're receiving. Do you know who gets hurt the most from our policies? The ones that need it the most, like the disabled, veterans, and the elderly. They don't get what they should and that's the worst part of it."

There's a break in the conversation before Gene asks Lynn, "Out of questions?"

"No," Lynn answers, "just thinking."

"The twentieth century in America will go down as the beginning and end of the progressive movement. Progressives can take credit for a lot of good, but they went way too far and crippled America. Our official national debt is over twenty-four trillion dollars because several decades ago we ramped up social programs and spent that same twenty-four trillion. Do you know what we have to show for it? The poverty rate has gotten worse. Education is worse. Our infrastructure is worse. Our government can't solve these issues. They've spent all this money, put this huge burden of debt on us and have nothing to show for it."

"I didn't expect all that," Lynn says. "Maybe I could come by your office and talk about some of your ideas. It would be great if you'd say all that on television."

Boy, she is aggressive, Teresa thinks. *She never stops.*

#

"Your turn," Gene says. "I'll ask you the same open-ended question. What do you think of America today?"

Lynn smiles, "I don't know if I'm prepared to answer that."

"Come on now, fair's fair," Gene says and jokes, "and don't worry, it's off the record."

Lynn takes a deep breath. "I think Republicans favour the rich and the big corporations. They give them tax breaks. Democrats stand up for the little guys, the working man. Republicans want a strong military and the Democrats would rather put money into social programs, foreign aid, those that need it most, including newly arriving immigrants. Our government is huge and can fix our problems. We're a generous people and we should take care of everyone. If that means more taxes on rich people and corporations, then so be it. They can afford it."

Gene nods his head. "You're a Democrat."

"Yes," Lynn answers.

"You know," Gene says, "I hear Democratic congressmen promise free healthcare for all, they'll rebuild our infrastructure, allow illegal aliens to walk right into our country. We'll provide free education and healthcare for everyone. I've never heard them explain how they're going to pay for it. We simply can't pay for it. All we've done for several decades is borrow money. It's immoral. You won't like your Democratic politician when that bill comes due. Heck, you won't even be able to find them when we hit that point."

"So, you are a Republican," Lynn concludes.

"No party, remember?" Gene reminds her. "I have the same problem with Republicans. They have their own priorities of spending and tax reform, but an equally irresponsible approach to the budget or working together. They're no better or worse. There's no getting around the laws of physics or finance." Gene holds up his book "Like Emerson, I believe in the old truths of self-reliance: a strong character and paying your debts."

#

There's a ringing sound in the distance.

"Hear that?" Gene asks.

"Yup," Jack answers.

"What is it?" Lynn asks.

"Ice cream truck," Gene answers. "Anyone want ice cream? Jack, do you need to stretch or need a head start?"

Teresa asks Jack, "What's he talking about?"

"It's stupid," he answers. "When you hear the bell, you know the truck is going to be at the bend in the road in a minute. We used to race to it."

"Anyone want ice cream?" Gene repeats. "Buck, buck."

"And what's that?" Teresa asks with a laugh.

"It's a horrible imitation of a chicken," Jack answers. He turns to his father. "You're just sore that you lost in golf yesterday.

"Buck, buck," Gene replies, clearly getting a kick out of himself.

"I'd like ice cream," Teresa says.

"Me too," adds Lynn.

"Go," Jack announces, and he and Gene get up and take off in a full sprint up the steps and over the sea wall.

#

While the group sits and enjoys their ice cream, Gene turns, "Teresa and Jack. I'm sorry, we left you out of our discussion. What do you think?"

"I don't know," Jack answers.

Teresa tells Jack, "They asked. Tell them what you think."

"Should I be worried about what's coming?" Gene asks.

"Oh, I don't know about that."

"Then maybe I should be worried," Lynn asks.

"No. I haven't been thinking of this stuff for as long as you two," Jack begins. "I'm just starting." He looks out at the ocean and sees Grace, Tracey, and JR sitting in the surf. "I'm reading what our founding fathers thought about all this. They studied great men before them. What's the role of government? What responsibilities do individuals have as members of a society? We made a contract with one another when we came together to form our country. We made promises. Our founding fathers put them in our Constitution and Bill of Rights."

"Interesting," Lynn says.

"My thoughts thus far," Jack pauses. "Dad, your point is the debt. We're spending more than we can afford. Paying it down will take decades and require sacrifice. Thomas Jefferson wrote: '*it is incumbent on every generation to pay its own debts as it goes.*' It's ok to incur debt for an existential threat, like a war, and you pay it off. It's clear our founders believed every generation had the responsibility to pay off its debt, so I agree with you on that."

"Good," Gene states.

"But the progressive movement isn't dead. It may have gone too far, but that's the very nature of progressives, and progressives can be both liberal and conservative. Maybe this has led to too much spending on social programs whose benefits aren't clear. Lynn might argue that too much was spent on the military or lost as tax breaks."

Lynn picks up on what she wanted to hear, "Right, the military, tax breaks. We can pay off the debt by raising taxes on corporations and the rich."

"I'm not sure," Jack answers. "Two challenges; the first is a practical one. You can't get enough tax revenue from the rich and corporations to pay off this much debt. Going too far creates negative impacts on tax revenue and actually increases the debt. Tax increases can't solve the problem. The second challenge has to do with what's fair and consistent with our country's founding principles, our social contract. How high could you raise taxes on the rich?"

"One hundred percent," Lynn answers.

Jack wasn't expecting an answer. He posed the question rhetorically. "Maybe taxing the rich makes people feel better, but it's not going to raise enough money to address the debt. Do you think that would be fair, Lynn?"

"Yes, the rich can afford it."

"But it doesn't solve the problem, and is it fair or just?" he asks again.

"It's not fair that rich people live in luxury while poor people have so much less." She is passionate about this subject.

"How much do you pay in taxes a year?" Jack asks Lynn. "Not the dollar amount, but what percentage of your income do you pay in taxes?"

She stops to think. "It's probably sixty percent of my earnings if you include federal, state, city, sales taxes, and everything else."

"You spend sixty percent of the year or over seven months working for the government, working for others. Do you feel like that's fair?"

Lynn considers it before answering, "Yeah, I guess so."

"Consider," Jack continues, "that over half of the American people don't pay a penny in taxes, but they get benefits. You work seven months for others and half of America doesn't work one day a year for others. Do you think that's fair?"

"Probably not," she acknowledges.

"You said one hundred percent. Would it make sense to tax our highest income earners one hundred percent? First, it means they'd work all year for the government, which isn't fair to them. Second, it means they wouldn't work. I mean, why work when you can't keep any of your earnings?"

"I know one hundred percent doesn't make sense," Lynn answers. "It feels like we have this big income disparity, that the playing field in America isn't fair, so we should ask the rich to pay more."

"But taxing the rich doesn't solve the problem and maybe it's not fair to them?" Jack asks.

"Why do you keep asking about what's fair to them?"

Jack slows down his speech because Lynn is getting more emotional. "Remember in history, the stories about our Revolutionary War, the Boston Tea Party, taxation without representation?"

"Yes, of course," Lynn answers

"Do you know what the tax rate was when the colonists rose up to fight England? The tax rate when we decided to fight the largest military force on the planet?"

Lynn shakes her head, no.

"Eight percent."

There's silence.

"Eight percent," Jack repeats. "When it got that high, we decided to go to war. That's when our founding fathers thought it was unfair enough to risk their own lives. That was our social contract. They never envisioned a government so large, or powerful, or needing tax rates like we have today. Honestly, Lynn, I don't know what the limit on taxes should be. I'm thinking of this for the first time, but it strikes me odd at how far we've come. I don't think we're utilitarian where the majority can take from a minority just because it wants to."

After a period of silence, Gene starts again, "For years, only property owners could vote in our country. Our challenge is that over half the voting public pays no taxes and takes money from the government. That means they can just keep voting themselves more giveaways. Maybe we shouldn't let government employees vote, or anyone getting handouts. Politicians have rigged the system with financial incentives."

"Lynn," Jack says, "maybe I'll agree with you more as I keep processing all this. I guess for now I'm glad that people in our government have a plan for how this is all going to work out."

"They don't," Gene replies. "There's no plan. I like your idea of starting at the beginning, but you need to get some real world experience."

Jack turns and smiles towards Teresa.

"I keep telling him that," she says.

"The government doesn't have a plan," Gene repeats.

"They must have one, Dad."

"I want you to spend some time with Slugger Bingham," Gene replies. "He's a lobbyist and a good one. He works for the bank and gets things done for us. You need to see the real world. Spend a week or two with him."

#

"Your turn," Gene tells Teresa. "You've been quiet. What do you think?"

It makes her feel good that Gene wants to hear her opinion. "I've never heard our country broken into producers and parasites," she begins.

"Maybe that's right. I guess I've mostly seen the parasites. My job, I mean. If we get to the end of the year and we haven't spent everything in our budget, then we look for ways to spend it. Everyone in government does it. If you don't spend it all, then your budget gets cut. We spend it like crazy, justify new ways to spend, like buying boats." She looks at Gene and smiles.

"But," Lynn interrupts, "don't you think that money is doing good for a lot of people."

"Sure. I'm sure it does good for some, but so many employees do absolutely nothing. We have so many consultants that are supposed to study stuff, but come up with the dumbest ideas. They're all friends or donators to our politicians. I know people need help, and some get it, but the waste on bureaucracy, consultants, undeserving recipients, and political kickbacks makes you sick. Help wasn't supposed to mean giving away so much that there's no incentive to work. I don't want to pay higher taxes because I see where it goes."

"The government does good," Lynn states, "but needs to be improved. Is that what you're saying?"

"Yeah, improved or blown up and completely reorganized might be a better description. It's just far too corrupt." Teresa pauses and looks to Gene and Jack. "I've got a question for you guys. I keep coming back to the lesson on bonds."

Gene nods.

"We learned that bonds are debt, like mortgages. You use long term debt to pay for long term assets. A government might sell thirty-year bonds to build an airport. They rent terminal space to airlines and use that rent money to pay off the bonds. The public good is the airport. That makes sense, right?" She looks at Gene for confirmation.

"That's correct," he confirms.

"You wouldn't take out a thirty-year mortgage for a car because at the end of eight years your car might be worthless and you've got another twenty-two years of payments. The useful life of the asset and corresponding debt periods have to match up."

Gene nods.

"But," she concludes, "we've got it backwards now here in the U.S. We've borrowing long term money, twenty- and thirty-year bonds to pay the operating costs of our government bureaucracy. We're using long term debt to pay the salaries of government employees. We're not investing in long term assets like roads, bridges, power plants, and education. We've spending on short term things and borrowing for the long term. It doesn't make sense. At some point soon, we're screwed."

"Bravo," Gene congratulates her. "Well done, Teresa. More long-term debt every year to pay annual operating expenses while ignoring long term reinvestment."

#

Grace and JR approach the group from the water. Grace begins, "I hope you've had enough talk of business and politics for one weekend. My father would talk with men for hours about hunting and fishing. Why can't you talk about hunting or sports or cars? I swear, I need to buy you men shotguns. I don't want to hear anything more about business and politics this weekend."

The group turns quiet.

Grace announces, "Tracey suggested we join them for dinner at the new French restaurant in town. We need a headcount. Who's interested in joining us?"

JR looks at Lynn, who nods. "We'd like to join you," JR answers.

Jack asks Teresa, "Want to?"

Teresa answers, "Yes."

"Ok then," Grace says. "If anyone wants to drive with us, we'll be leaving the house around 7 o'clock. I'm going up to the house now. Anyone care to walk with me?" she asks.

"I'll come," Gene answers. He gets up from his chair and collects his things. "And Jack, I'm going to put you in touch with Slugger. I want to talk with you after you get time with him."

"Me too," Lynn adds.

#

Grace and Gene walk up the wooden steps over the sea wall. They stop at the road to let traffic pass.

A black suburban with tinted windows is parked on the side of the road about fifty yards to their left. It's causing traffic problems. There's no room on the two-lane street. Cars are forced to stop and go around them.

"What's the matter with him?" Grace asks.

Gene knows that it's likely someone watching him. He'd prefer not to alarm her. "It's probably just someone from the city out for a drive."

They cross the road and walk across the lawn. He asks, "Are you mad at me? I mean, our talk last night, for not telling you the truth all those years ago?"

"Not mad exactly, honey," she begins. "Not disappointed either really. You did what you thought was right, and I suppose it's all turned out for the best. It would be hard to complain about what we have. I don't know how I feel. Melancholy? I really don't want to leave our country, especially if it feels like we're running away."

Grace has been walking a step ahead of Gene. She adjusts and walks beside him. She puts her arm under his and her head on Gene's shoulder as they continue walking.

"You got too much sun again," she says.

#

"How are you feeling?" Jack asks Teresa. "Are you sure you want to do dinner?"

"Good. Yes. Dinner should be fun." After a pause, she adds, "I'm glad you spoke up, glad I did too. The world is kind of scary right now. I think about your father and the success he's had. It's good to know that whatever happens, however crazy things might get, he can see the future. He knows what's going to happen in the markets so everything will work out. It's comforting to know everything will be ok for us and our baby."

"He can't predict the future any more than you can," Jack answers. "He knows where the market is going because he's moving the markets. He knows or directs Federal Reserve policy. There's no trick to that, but it does explain his exalted position at the bank. The bank needs him more than he needs the bank. Still, everyone has limits. I think he's worried right now."

#

JR and Lynn walk down to the water. She wants to get in and cool down.

"Let me guess," JR says. "You asked my father to come on your show. He said no and then you peppered him with a million questions. Is that about right?"

"He did say no, but you have to go through a lot of no's to get to a yes. You know Jack is a lot more than a computer geek, and Teresa is smarter than I gave her credit for."

77

Sag Harbor, New York

The group enjoys a quiet dinner with Tracey and Bruce Savosik. The restaurant is small with limited seating. The theme is farm to table, with organic food served with unique sauces and delicious wines.

Towards the end of dinner, Grace asks JR to accompany her outside. They walk into a patio area overlooking the ocean. Grace lights a cigarette.

"JR, dear," she begins. "Why aren't you seeing Jenny Furash? You two are perfect together. We've known her family for years. She's beautiful and intelligent. She's the kind of young woman you can build a future with."

"Mom," JR would prefer his mother abstain from matchmaking. "You know when you're driving down the road and you hear a great song come on the radio?"

Grace nods her head yes.

"You know what I do, Mom? I change the station, hoping to find something even better." He smiles. "I don't know how to explain it, but that's kind of been my dating life too."

She shakes her head from side to side. "At some point, you need to consider your future, and you need a strong partner to accomplish things."

"Lynn is great Mom. She's got a lot going for her."

"I saw what she's got going for her on the beach," Grace answers.

"No, really," JR explains. "I'm happy with her. I hope you'll take the time to get to know her. Give her a chance. I think you'll see she's great. She's intelligent, ambitious, and maybe a great partner. I think she wants the same things I want."

"You know how close I am with Jenny's mom?" Grace asks.

"I know Mom; just give Lynn a chance ok?"

#

At the conclusion of dinner, JR announces that he and Lynn are going to go out to meet up with some friends. Gene reminds him that an important guest is joining them for breakfast in the morning. His and Jack's presence are required. Gene tells him, "Be on time and on your best behaviour. No hangover. Clear-eyed and clear-minded. Do you understand?" Gene is firm.

"Yes, Dad, I understand," JR responds. He asks, "Is it ok to bring Lynn?" He looks at his father, who doesn't say anything. JR turns to his mother. It's awkward because Lynn is standing next to JR.

"Of course," Grace replies based on JR's just asking her to give Grace a chance. Grace turns to Lynn, "We'll see you both in the morning."

78

East Hampton, New York

Teresa and Jack are in bed together that night. She snuggles close and puts her head on his chest. "I'd like to raise our child Catholic. Is that ok with you?"

"Well," Jack pauses long enough to make Teresa nervous. "I suppose so."

"Why the pause then?"

"I don't care," Jack answers. "if our child chooses to be a Christian, Jew, Muslim. or whatever. I'd like our child to be thoughtful and consider things with an open mind. He or she may not believe in a God. There's value in learning different religions, their histories and beliefs. We should start them early. I need to learn more."

"So that means you're ok with starting Catholic?"

"Yeah, I guess, but let's not set limits or define one course of action as the only one or the right one. You know what I mean?"

She pats his chest and says, "I know. We'll start Catholic."

79

East Hampton, New York

A car arrives at the O'Neil home around 9 a.m. Sunday morning. Grace and Gene greet their guest, Madeline Rothschild, as she walks from the car to the front steps. They escort her through the front door and introduce her to Lynn, JR, Teresa, and Jack.

"Call me Maddy," she instructs.

She's carrying a thick, legal sized envelope.

They move to the dining room and sit down to enjoy breakfast. Lynn quickly moves to sit next to Maddy and begins asking questions. "How do you know Gene? Are you a part of the famous Rothschild banking family? What's the family doing these days?"

Gene is stunned. Grace is appalled. She attempts to intercede but her subtlety is lost on Lynn.

"What kind of accent is that, Maddy? I mean where are you from?" Lynn continues.

Madeline doesn't seem upset, but doesn't answer her questions.

Gene suggests that Maddy might be more comfortable eating breakfast outside by the pool. He instructs Maddy, JR, and Jack to come with him outside. "JR, Jack, carry Maddy's plate and place setting for her." There's tension in the room as Grace, Lynn, and Teresa remain at the dining table.

Once seated outside, Gene says, "I'm very sorry about that, Maddy. That was unexpected and terribly unfortunate. She's a journalist, a television person."

"Quite alright," Maddy replies. "No harm done. I assume you've asked your sons to join us because you'd like them to be a part of our conversation?"

"I'd like them to stay if that's ok with you," Gene replies. "As you know, they've recently come to work with me at Morgan Sachs. I'd like to create a possible succession plan if that can be worked out."

Maddy nods her head, "I understand. It makes sense if they're up to it. They'll need to be vetted."

"Of course," Gene acknowledges.

"We're working hard these days," JR offers, "in a training program created by my father specifically for us." He's very excited to be meeting Maddy and to hear his father say, 'succession plan.'

She hands Gene the legal sized envelope. "Here are the executed contracts granting you five percent ownership interest in the Federal Reserve Bank of the United States of America. The contracts are contingent on your completion of both the Winthrop and Kuhn transactions. It's not the ten percent you asked for, but we both know the value of these shares."

Gene is ecstatic that the shareholders have accepted him into their circle. Having his sons witness the event feels overwhelming. He's speechless. He doesn't respond.

"Gene," Maddy inquires. "Are you ok? I mean is there a problem with the five percent?"

"Yes, Maddy, and thank you. Thank you very much. There's not a problem. It's been my honour and privilege working for you. I'll get those transactions done." Gene turns and looks towards the house to see if Grace is watching. He doesn't see her in the kitchen window.

"As for the matter of the president, do you have any updates?" Maddy asks.

"I've been speaking with the treasury secretary regularly," Gene answers. "He's provided a plan that will work for everyone. He tells me the president will support it. It's a good plan. I'm just having trouble believing it."

"That's good news. Why are you having trouble with it?" she asks.

"Just a hunch; maybe it's your warnings. The president has given in easier than expected after such a long, arduous delay. It feels like it's too easy all of a sudden."

She turns to JR and Jack. "Throughout our history, we've encountered unscrupulous types that lie without pause. They change course whenever it suits their needs. You must remain ever vigilant when dealing with politicians. They cannot be trusted."

"Gene," she turns, "we'll prevail when it comes to this president or any president, but you must be careful. They can move quickly and irrationally when put in a difficult situation."

#

At the conclusion of their meeting, Grace and Gene escort Maddy to her car.

"Grace, it was a pleasure to see you," Maddy says. "It's been too long since I saw you last. Thank you for breakfast and I'm sorry I don't have more time this morning."

"It was great to see you Maddy. Thank you for coming. It always feels like a special occasion when you share your time with us. I hope I'll see again soon. Also, I apologize if our guest caused you any discomfort. That was terribly rude."

"No, no discomfort," Maddy responds. "Gene, thank you again and congratulations. Grace, your husband is the most talented banker I've ever known."

Maddy gets in the car's back seat and is driven away.

Grace noticed that Gene is holding the envelope that Maddy brought. As she's waving good bye to Maddy, she asks, "What's in the envelope, Eugene?"

"Forty years of hard work and a whole lot of good fortune. I guess you could say that anything you want for the rest of your life is in this envelope."

They turn, look into each other's eyes and smile.

"I imagine we won't be seeing any more of Lynn," Gene asks.

"No. We won't. Are you going to miss her red bikini?"

80

Boston, Massachusetts

Jack calls Mary Rossi for help. He'd like to come to Boston and meet with Joe. He explains to Mary that when he tells Teresa he's leaving town, she'll immediately travel home to Watertown. He asks Mary to come to New York to visit Teresa.

Mary understands, arranges the trip, and doesn't ask questions.

#

While in Boston, Jack schedules time to hang out with Cheese. He lets himself into the apartment and says, "Hey" to announce his arrival.

Cheese is sitting on the couch working on his computer. He stands and welcomes Jack by saying, "Look at you. What the fuck did they do to you?"

Jack is dressed well for a meeting he had with Joe Rossi. He's wearing a dark suit and expensive watch. Cheese is unaccustomed to seeing Jack this way.

"You're not an alien that's taken over Jack, are you? Maybe we should to do an MRI."

Jack smiles. They shake hands and that turns into a mini-hug. "How are you doing?"

"I'm good. Come in, sit down, ah, I guess not all good. My sister just got turned down on her admission here to M.I.T. She just found out an hour ago. That kind of sucks."

"I'm sorry about that," Jacks says. "I remember you always said great things about her."

"Yeah, she's brilliant. Only reason she didn't get in is because she's Chinese, and that's bullshit." Cheese complains. "It's this affirmative action thing, basically discrimination, racism, you know? The school has quotas."

"Oh, wow," Jack answers.

"Yeah, wow."

"What's she going to do?" Jack asks.

"She got full scholarship offers at Stanford and Cal Poly." Cheese sits back down. "She wanted M.I.T. and this is bullshit. Fuck affirmative action. It's racism and in any form it's wrong."

Jack is silent.

"You don't think so?" Cheese questions.

"No. Racism is wrong. I get it. I agree. I guess I'm thinking, thinking a little differently is all," Jack answers.

"What does that mean?"

"She'll get a great education wherever she goes. We both know she'll do great. It's not like any school has a monopoly on education. Affirmative action probably started with noble goals, but these government programs get bigger and more screwed up over time. It feels like changes are needed. Big changes in everything, and our government doesn't do well with change."

Jack looks at Cheese, who is just sitting blank-faced.

"I'm against discrimination and racism in any form," Jack says.

"Well, that's good to hear," Cheese answers. "I've never heard you talk about that stuff. What changes are you talking about?"

"Education. Affirmative action. Look at the statistics of young, unemployed minorities, mostly from our cities. They get a horrible education or no education at all. It leaves them with little or no upward mobility. It would be so easy to give them a world-class education using computers and the internet at a fraction of today's cost. Know why we don't do it?" Jack asks.

Cheese shakes his head no.

"We put teachers ahead of students. We pay too many teachers, school administrators, and bureaucrats all this money. Money gets recycled through their unions back to politicians. Bad teachers get tenure, pensions, and healthcare for life. There's no accountability and great teachers are so important. The students get screwed. We could fix it. Give kids a great education, a future, and a more fulfilling life. We could be part of that."

"I've never heard you say word one about any of this," Cheese responds. "Where is this coming from? You work in a bank for Christ's sake. Maybe you are an alien."

"The unfairness part of it bothers me," Jack answers. "Everyone deserves opportunity and it starts with a great education."

"I'm glad to hear you say it. By the way, are you hungry?"

"A little," Jack answers.

"Wanna order delivery and play video games?"

"No, let's go out. Are you still using my credit card for food delivery?" Jack asks.

"Maybe," Cheese answers. "You know, we could get involved. At best, affirmative action can only help a small number of people. We could help millions if you're talking about education online. We always talked about teaching here. This might be better, reach more people and change lives."

#

During dinner, Jack begins, "About this summer—"

Cheese interrupts, "Don't tell me I'm not invited to the Hamptons."

"No, you're invited, and you can stay in the pool house again if you want. Stay as long as you want. You just gotta let me know when you're coming. My mom's planning."

Cheese takes out his phone and looks at his calendar. "I know you guys are having a baby, but that shouldn't interfere with my trip to the Hamptons. It wouldn't be fair to the ladies out there."

"Yeah, I'm sure the girls are wondering when you're coming."

"I'll be there from Wednesday to Wednesday during your two weeks. Is that ok?"

"Yeah, sure."

81

New York, New York

Teresa walks to the bank one evening to visit Jack. It's a little after 10:00 p.m. when she enters the conference room. He's sitting alone, reading. She loves seeing him in a suit, starched shirt and tie.

Jack's face opens into a broad smile when he sees her. His reaction makes her feel good. "How are you feeling?" he asks, "It's good to see you."

"I'm good. I just needed to get out of the apartment and see you." Teresa walks behind him and wraps her arms around him.

"How's it going?" she asks.

"I don't know. The deeper I get into some of this, the worse it makes me feel."

"Yeah."

Jack shares his feelings, "There's got to be a better system than our Federal Reserve with their powers. All our country's greatest leaders have opposed it. It's the antithesis of what our country stands for. Read this." Jack puts a book in front of Teresa and points to a passage.

"I believe that banking institutions are more dangerous to our liberties than standing armies... The issuing power should be taken from the banks and restored to the people, to whom it properly belongs."

Thomas Jefferson

"Banks can't be more dangerous than standing armies. That must be wrong," she says.

"Banking isn't necessarily bad or evil, but central banking and the power over a country's money supply is different. Read this," Jack instructs again, and points to a passage in another book.

"History records that the money changers (bankers) have used every form of abuse, intrigue, deceit, and violent means possible to maintain their control over governments by controlling money and its issuance."

James Madison

Jack explains. "You remember when my dad said that this is all written down and no one bothers to even read it?"

"Yes."

"I'm reading it," Jack says. "Men like Thomas Jefferson and James Madison didn't want our country to have a central bank. When they wrote our Constitution, they made sure that neither the president nor Congress had the power to create the bank."

Teresa begins rubbing Jack's shoulder to ease his tension.

"I'm sorry," Jack says. "It's just wrong. There has to be a better way."

"If there is, you'll find it." She turns Jack's chair sideways and sits in his lap. "You're working too hard and I'm hungry. Can we get some Chinese food?"

"Sure, one more quote, because maybe the answer is in what we first had in this country," Jack explains.

"I'm hungry," Teresa objects.

"Ok, I'll read it to you. I'll be quick. It's interesting. It's from Benjamin Franklin. See, the reason we fought the American Revolution was over money. We had our own money, but England wanted us to use theirs."

"In the Colonies, we issue our own paper money. It is called 'Colonial Scrip.' We issue it in proper proportion to make the goods and pass easily from the producers to the consumers. In this manner, creating ourselves our own paper

money, we control its purchasing power and we have no interest to pay to no one.
When bankers in England place money in circulation, there is always a debt of principal to be returned and interest or usury to be paid. People must bear the endless burden of unpayable debt and usurious interest."

Benjamin Franklin

"Let's get some food," Teresa says.

Jack collects his things and they leave the conference room. Teresa says she needs to use the bathroom.

Jack continues, "There's more with leaders like Andrew Jackson and Abraham Lincoln." He follows Teresa into the ladies room. He uses the stall next to Teresa to urinate. Upon exiting the stall, he sees a middle-aged woman wearing a sharp business suit standing in front of the mirror. She's applying lipstick.

"Can I help you?" she asks Jack.

"No ma'am," Jack answers. He heads to the door and a quick exit. "Sorry ma'am," he adds.

"Stop," she instructs. "I imagine you could have used the men's room and waited patiently for your friend."

"Yes, ma'am," Jack replies, and moves again to exit.

"Wash your hands." She points to the sink. "No one wants to do business with a slob." She turns, shakes her head, mutters "interns," and walks out.

Jack's heart is pounding. He washes his hands. A moment later Teresa exits her stall. She has her hands over her mouth to hold back laughter. "No, ma'am. Yes, ma'am," she repeats with a big smile.

#

While eating Chinese food, Teresa asks, "So this stuff is all true. Capitalism is taking over the world, the central bank, our government being so fucked up? I guess I knew that one."

Jack answers, "Yeah, hard to believe some of it, you know." Jack feels dirty. He was never interested in banking. He had looked up to his father and older brother. As they talk, he's working on an origami puzzle with a paper napkin.

Teresa watches. "Still playing with paper puzzles. I bet you're still hacking into computer networks too."

He flashes a small, guilty smile.

"Incorrigible," Teresa says.

"You know," Jack says. "My mom told me once that I'm naïve and I'd be better off not to think the best in people. Better off to think the worst and focus on their motives. She said I'd be right far more often and could even predict behaviours."

"That's kind of sad, but true," Teresa replies. "I guess most people do what's in their best interest and then figure out a way to justify it to themselves."

"What if I told you I don't want this life? The money and all. It feels like stealing, on a bigger scale and with a professional aura about it, but wrong. What if I were just a poor graduate student?"

Teresa answers, "Ok with me. We'll be ok whatever we do. My folks always said to do what you love in life. Choose what you love because you're going to be working hard for a long time. We'll be fine as long as we have each other. I'd be happy with you wherever we are, even living under a bridge. Your Uncle Dave told me it's more important who you're with than where you are."

#

A black van is parked across the street from the Chinese restaurant. Two men inside the van are wearing headsets and listening in on their conversation. Another man stands outside the van. They work for the government.

One man says, "Sounds like the kid has a conscience. We're not going to dig up any dirt here."

The second man responds, "Our profiler says it's not in him to do things wrong. He wouldn't turn on his father even if we pressure him. It's ok. If we can't find dirt then Duffy will just make shit up again."

82

Washington, DC

Jack's been shadowing Slugger White for two weeks, following him all day long and sitting in on meetings and calls with clients. It's providing him with a first-hand view of how our government and lobbying works.

It's a Tuesday evening at 6:50 p.m. when Teresa reaches him by phone in his hotel room.

He sees her name show up on his cell phone. "Hi, how are you?" he asks.

"I'm good," Teresa replies, "but I miss you."

"I know. I miss you too, but I'll be home Friday night. How are you feeling? Have you been to the doctor again?"

"I'm feeling good and yes, she says everything is fine. I'm horny. Maybe it's the pregnancy, but I can't wait to see you."

"Lucky me I guess," Jack replies with a smile.

"You know," she considers, "I could fly to Washington and see you. First class or maybe by private jet. We could have some alone time in your hotel room."

"I see you're learning how to spend money."

"Yeah. It's pretty easy," she answers. "How's your time with Slugger going? Are you learning anything?"

"Yup, good and bad. I'm learning. He's a really nice guy when he's not working. He's got a great family and all, but he has this way of compartmentalizing his life. He sees government as a business. He uses money to buy congressmen, you know, buy votes. He sees nothing wrong with it."

"Really," Teresa answers.

"It's worse than I ever could have imagined. Did you know that a car company once released a new model knowing that it had problems with its gas tanks? They knew the cars would catch fire and kill people. They did some financial projections and figured the cost of the lawsuits and payouts to families would be less than fixing the problem? People died, burned to death in their own cars and the car company knew it was going to happen. How messed up is that?"

"That's awful," Teresa responds.

"Another car company just recently lied about their fuel emissions to get around government regulations. The top guy instructed people to create software that lied. They made a ton of money all based on a lie."

"Are you enjoying your education?" Teresa asks.

"I'm glad to learn stuff, but I get really upset to see how everything works. Money is everything for these scumbags. It's not just car companies, it's every industry. You know about the country's opioid epidemic?"

"Of course," Teresa answers.

"It wasn't some Columbian drug cartel or the Taliban in Afghanistan. It was created by Congress changing the law and allowing drug wholesalers and distributors to market differently. Lobbyists paid our politicians to change the regulations that protected us. It put all these drugs on the streets. Our own government created this mess that's killing Americans and destroying communities."

"Are you sure of that?" Teresa asks.

"Yes. They were actually bragging about the money they made," Jack explains. "And it goes deeper. Insiders invest in the companies that are going to profit from the change in law. A senator literally called his stockbroker from the floor of the Senate when the healthcare bill passed. Buying shares of stock at that very moment. No one would believe it unless they could see for themselves how bad it is here. I'm going out to dinner again tonight with another client and congressman."

"I guess I'm not surprised," Teresa admits.

"I'm surprised and shocked," Jack explains. "It touches everything and no one here wants to stop it. Cars, drugs, raw materials, appliances, and food. You've taken an interest in food. Did you know today's food companies are the same companies that used to produce cigarettes? Years ago, their CEOs knew that cigarettes cause cancer and they lied about it. They sat in front of Congress and lied to them. They said they didn't know it was bad for people when their own research proved cigarettes caused cancer and death."

"I remember something about that," Teresa replies.

"They used to produce cigarettes and now they produce food. The CEOs are doing the same thing and lying about the food they're selling. They know it's causing health problems and death. Our government's solution isn't to fix the food supply or expose their lies, it's to manage the healthcare system. That way food companies, healthcare companies, insurance companies all pay more to congressmen. Their answer to everything is more government and more for themselves. It never occurred to me that this was possible in America."

"There are a lot of bad people in this world," Teresa answers. "Things get messed up when corrupt people get in positions of power."

"You and Dad were right about learning about the real world. I can't wait to get home. I feel dirty here in Washington."

83

New York, New York

At the conclusion of Jack's time with Slugger, he asks Steve and Billy to join him and Teresa in the conference room for a meeting. It's been several weeks since the group has met.

Jack asks, "Do you remember our first day together in this room?"

"Of course," Steve answers. Billy adds, "Yes."

"You guys said that you were unsure of your next career steps. Do you remember that?"

Both men answer in the affirmative.

"How's that possible?" Jack asks. There's a pause before Jack adds, "I mean, two young guys that are highly regarded at the biggest bank in the world. In order to get here and succeed you needed a plan. You've always had intelligence, a strong work ethic, and a clear plan on how to achieve your objectives."

Steve and Billy look at Jack and seem to understand where he's going with this.

"Somehow you no longer have a plan or you're not sure where you're going in life?" Jack shakes his head. "That doesn't fit. What have you not been saying? There were questions on subjects where you didn't answer."

Steve looks to Billy to ask who wants to answer first.

Billy begins. "We didn't like what we learned. At first, it was kind of a rush to learn about the owners of the Federal Reserve; their wealth, power, lifestyles. I think it's easy to get caught up into thinking that we could work here and make a ton of money. Maybe we'd end up being in a role like Peter's and handle all sorts of big stuff. We could run in some exclusive company, buy whatever we want." He pauses. "It just didn't feel right, especially all the payoffs and the abuse of power in our government. Don't misunderstand, you should go for it. You're in line for your dad's spot, so you should definitely do it."

Jack looks to Steve.

"Didn't feel right," he answers concisely in his Texas accent.

"Are you guys going to go to business school?" Teresa asks.

"No," Billy replies. "I was going to go, but it was really about getting the network of contacts and getting 'Harvard' on my resume. I'm going into private equity. Gene got me into the firm I really wanted to work with. I'm going to focus on small, healthcare technology companies, super interesting stuff. I want to learn how to build great companies that have a purpose."

They turn to Steve.

"I'm going to law school at Harvard, and then I'm going back to Texas. Your dad helped. I want to get into government and politics. Maybe start at the local level and see if I can make a difference."

"We don't have any more lessons planned or stuff we're supposed to cover, do we?" Jack asks.

"No," Billy says.

"How much time before you go off in different directions?" Jack asks.

"Three weeks," Billy answers.

"I'd like your help," Jack begins. "Stuff doesn't feel right to me either. Is it ok if we go in a different direction in our remaining time together? I want to talk about how we might create change."

"Sure, great," Steve answers.

"It's going to be a lot of work," Jack warns.

"Even better," Billy says.

84

New York, New York

Teresa and Jack have their first appointment at a lamaze class that evening. They walk the four blocks together.

"That was really great today," Teresa tells Jack. "I really like them both and I'm glad they opened up like that. We covered a lot of ground."

"Yeah, they're good people," Jack replies. "Maybe a lot of us share the same concerns about our government."

"We should do something nice for them, maybe get them a present," she suggests. "You guys should keep in touch."

"My dad is paying them to train us. It doesn't feel like the way a friendship starts."

"Don't be silly. Friendships can start anywhere and anytime. You just need to be open to them. And the answer is education."

"What's that mean?" Jack asks.

"You asked the highest priorities for our government. You asked them. You didn't ask me. It's education."

Jack smiles. "I'm sorry. I just figured I needed to get their thoughts while we're together."

"I know. It's ok. You know it's education too," she says.

"Give a man a fish and he eats for a day," Jack replies. "Teach a man to fish and he eats for a lifetime. Our government's focused on feeding people day to day. In that way, people feel the need to keep voting them into office. They feel reliant on their politicians."

#

Later that evening, as the couple prepares for bed, Teresa asks, "Do you think your parents are happy?"

"What?" Jack asks.

"Your folks," she answers. "I mean, look, I never knew this kind of money even existed, do you think they're happy or happier than normal people?"

"I think they are normal people."

"You know what I mean. Do you think they're happier than my parents?"

"Um. I don't know. I guess I never thought of it. What do you think?"

"I like your parents," Teresa begins. "I think they both have gotten what they wanted in their lives. They probably feel a sense of accomplishment. I don't get the sense their money makes them any happier than other people. In some ways it isolates them. Maybe they're happy, but they have a different way of showing it."

"Maybe," Jack replies. "I think they're as happy as anyone else I guess."

"I want us to be happy," she responds, "at every age, and I want it to show. I want us to have friends, good friends, close friends, and keep our family close. That would make me happy."

She looks at Jack. He agrees. "What would you make you happy? Time to do research?" she asks. "Tell me. I'll be on board. Let's promise that we always tell each other so we can help each other be happy. We don't need much money for that."

85

East Hampton, New York

The family's August vacation arrives. Time to relax and spend time together. The daytime temperatures average in the 80s, and the ocean is warm and comfortable. The evenings feel like heaven.

Gene loves the two week break and spending time with family. He used to run into the city during this break. He stopped doing that a few years ago to be more present and focused on what's important.

JR's plan is to spend the time enjoying the active social life in the Hamptons. He doesn't want to miss a thing.

Jack and Teresa will spend the two weeks connecting with family from both sides. Teresa is well into her pregnancy and prefers to take things slowly.

Gene's family from Scituate, Massachusetts will be spending the first week at the house. Uncle Dave O'Neil, brother Steve and Connie and Tom Murray are expected.

Mary and Joe Rossi will come for the second week. Saturday will be the crossover day where one family leaves and the other arrives.

#

The group from Scituate arrive a little after noon on Saturday.

Gene, Tom, and Stevie carry the luggage upstairs.

Gene receives a call on his way up the stairs. It's Treasury Secretary Martin. "Gene," the secretary begins, "the president has agreed to our plan. Almost all of it anyway. He plans to announce it next Friday. He's asked that you and I come to the White House next Thursday to work on the final details."

"Next week?" Gene answers. Gene would prefer not to travel during these two weeks. "Yes, I can come, but can we make it a day trip? Is it ok if I fly down and back on the same day?"

"The president suggested a midday meeting so yes, that should work fine. I'll meet you at the airport in Washington. We can ride together to the White House. This is good news, Gene."

Gene puts Connie's suitcases next to a bed. Tom puts his suitcases down on the other side. He asks, "How come you got such a big lawn, Gene? I mean, it's enormous. Do you use it for anything?"

Gene was lost in his own thoughts. Tom's candour is refreshing and welcome. Many people are afraid to ask Gene anything.

"I don't know really," Gene answers. "I just wanted it. It's the only lawn I've ever had. Our family lot was small growing up. I've lived in the city without a lawn. I always just dreamed of a big, green lawn. I used to look at houses with big lawns and figured rich people lived there." He shrugs his shoulders, "Pretty silly, I suppose. No, we don't use it for anything, a helicopter pad."

#

One of the things Gene likes best about the August vacation is that very little is scheduled. It's a welcome change in his life. He'll spend most of the first week sitting and talking with his brother, sister, and brother-in-law. They'll reminisce about their childhoods, old friends, and relatives.

Gene enjoys walks with Stevie. They'll talk about whatever Stevie wants to talk about. Some days they say very little. *There by the grace of God go I,* Gene thinks.

Family members gather on the front porch in the late afternoons. They enjoy cocktails, playing games, and watching the sunset. Gene and Tom Murray enjoy cigars and whiskey.

#

Families are predictable. Behaviour patterns emerge each year like clockwork. Gene, Stevie, Connie, and Tom enjoy time together. Connie does most of the talking.

Grace and JR come and go. They enjoy running around the Hamptons.

Jack enjoys time with Uncle Dave and pushing his wheelchair along the bicycle paths. On one such walk with Teresa along, he confides, "You know, Uncle Dave, I know you were only kidding about something years ago, but you were right. Right about something big."

"Oh, yeah," Dave responds. "What's that?"

Jack stops and stands beside the wheelchair. He hunches over close to Dave. Teresa is on the other side of the wheelchair and curious about what Jack's up to.

"You were right about the printing press," Jack says. "Turns out my dad does own a printing press, or is part-owner now of the real printing press."

"Ah," Dave says, dismissing the remark. "I thought it was going to be something good."

#

The vacation is proceeding wonderfully.

The group gathers for dinner Tuesday evening on the front porch. It's a beautiful evening with a light breeze off the water. Everyone is present, including Cheese who showed up a day early.

Gene tells the group that he has to leave on Thursday for a day trip. He'll be gone for the day and back home that evening. He apologizes.

Jack has an announcement too. "Teresa and I want to get married here on Saturday. Just a small ceremony. You guys will be here, and Teresa's family will be coming. We know it's short notice, but we'll get married before our baby is born. Mr. Rossi is ok with it. I went to Boston a few weeks ago and asked him for permission."

Cheese thinks, *That's why he came to Boston.*

Gene is pleased with the news. He stands, hugs them both, and offers sincere congratulations.

Grace is unsure how she feels. It's a shock. There's too much to get done. It's impossible to pull together a guest list, get a caterer, band, florist, everything. Her mind is racing. It's just not possible.

86

Washington, D.C.

Gene gets an early start to his day Thursday. Doug Martin greets him at the airport in Washington, DC. He's standing beside a limousine when Gene arrives by private jet. They drive to the White House together.

On arrival, they're escorted to the Oval Office. The president is waiting. Bobby Ferguson, Will Duffy, and the attorney general are with the president. An armed marine guard stands by the door.

After handshakes and greetings, the president gets down to business.

"Gene, I want to thank you for coming," the president begins. "As I'm sure Doug has told you we've been working hard on a plan to satisfy you and others. We've been working hard on the draft that Doug prepared but…." The president hesitates. "But we just can't seem to move forward with it."

"What?" Doug exclaims.

"You see, Gene, while I appreciate these suggestions, they go too far. Treason might be a better word for your plan." The president looks to the AG.

"Mr. President, you told me that we had a deal," Doug complains.

The president answers, "That's right, Doug, but upon further examination, we had to change course." The president then turns to Will Duffy and says, "Will."

Will hands Gene a piece of paper. "Mr. O'Neil, this is a list of charges that the United States government is prepared to bring against you in the event you don't discontinue your efforts. We believe that we've found sufficient evidence to think you were behind the latest financial crash. It looks to us that you've broken laws trading in public securities and sharing insider information. We're prepared to begin prosecution immediately. You'll lose your license to work in the banking and securities industries while this is prosecuted. It could take years. It means you'll have to give up your position at Morgan Sachs. We have a press release ready to go this afternoon should you not agree."

Bill attempts to hand Gene the piece of paper and copy of the press release. Gene doesn't reach out a hand or accept them.

"Mr. President, this is complete bullshit," Doug is beside himself with anger.

"Am I free to leave Mr. President?" Gene asks calmly.

"Gene, didn't you hear what Will just said?" Bobby asks.

The president is sitting and watching Gene.

"Am I free to leave?" Gene asks the president a second time.

The room is silent, tense, before the president answers, "No. Guard, place Mr. O'Neil under arrest."

"Am I being charged with anything?" Gene asks.

"No, Mr. O'Neil, there are no charges," the AG answers. "Mr. President, we didn't talk about holding him."

"No, we didn't," the president, answers. "But this is now an issue of national security, and I have broad powers at my sole discretion under the Constitution."

Bobby turns to the marine, "Take him to Situation Room A in the basement and take away his phone."

The guard escorts Gene out of the room.

Doug is fuming in anger. He grits his teeth to keep from screaming at the president. "Mr. President, this is outrageous. You made promises to me. You know Gene is innocent and the thought of any press release to damage his good name is unconscionable."

The president walks behind his desk and sits down.

Bobby turns to Doug. "Allow me to walk you out, Mr. Secretary."

Doug doesn't budge.

Bobby suggests, "Go talk to your friend. Tell him to accept our offer or we'll drag him and his family through the mud for years. Even if we can't make any charges stick, he'll be done, done on Wall Street, disgraced and a pariah anywhere he goes. Yeah he's innocent, but we can drag this on for so long that everyone will believe he must have done something wrong."

"You're a piece of shit," Doug replies.

Bobby's heard that many times. He's unfazed. "Go talk to him. Get him to change his mind or he's finished. And if he's finished then what do you think that means for you?"

#

A Secret Service agent accompanies Doug to Situation Room A. There are eighteen chairs surrounding an oval table. Seven flat screen televisions cover the walls.

"I'm sorry, Gene," Doug begins. "I can't believe this shit. I had no idea they would sink to this level. Please forgive me. I had no idea this is what they had in mind."

"I understand. You couldn't have known," Gene answers. "I had a feeling."

"What can we do?" Doug asks. "Do you think that maybe we should postpone the changes you're looking for? Maybe back off for a year or two?"

"No," Gene replies and shakes his head.

"But they're going to destroy you. You'll be labelled a villain to everyone. By the time you're exonerated, all the damage will have been done to your name and reputation. Maybe you give in now in order to come back to fight another day."

"Please do me a favour."

"Of course, name it."

"Please call Peter Hollingsworth," Gene instructs. "Let him know what has happened and call Grace. Let her know what's happened and reassure her that everything will be fine. Tell her not to worry about anything."

87

East Hampton, New York

Doug calls Peter once he's outside the White House. The conversation is brief. He tells him what happened and asks for Grace's phone number.

He then calls Grace. "Grace, this is Doug Martin. We've met on several occasions," he begins.

"Of course, Doug, it's good to hear from you," Grace answers. She's in her kitchen preparing a fruit salad. She's looking out the back window and watching a tent erected for the wedding. She can see Jack and Cheese sitting by the pool. Caterers and florists are all over the place. "Are you looking for Eugene?" she asks.

"No, I was with him this morning." Doug is struggling with how to break the news. "I was with Gene and the president. Grace, the president isn't allowing Gene to leave the White House. He's being held in the basement of the White House for questioning. They're considering bringing charges against Gene for causing the financial crisis, for treason against the country, insider trading. It's all bullshit. Please understand that I had no idea today's meeting was just a setup to get Gene to the White House."

"What?" Grace immediately thinks of Gene's warnings and his suggestion to leave the country. She should have understood. She should have heeded his warning and been ready to leave. "What do you mean being held? What happens now?" she asks.

"I don't know. He asked me to call you and Peter. We'll need to think of something. He wanted me to assure you that everything will be fine. I'll call back as soon as I have any news or ideas."

"Yeah," Grace replies and hangs up. She feels like she's been punched in the gut. She knocks hard at the kitchen window and waves to Jack to come inside. She calls JR's phone, but it immediately goes to voicemail. When Jack comes through the back door, she tells him what happened. She asks, "Where's your brother?"

"I don't know," Jack answers.

Jack walks out the back door and tells Cheese, "Grab your computer, grab everything. We gotta go. Fast, Cheese. I'll meet you at the car," Jack points to the garage.

88

Washington, DC

Fifteen minutes pass after Doug leaves Gene before there's a knock on the door. Will Duffy enters the room.

"You left this paperwork upstairs," he says to Gene. Will puts a manila folder on the table. "We figured you'd want to look at the press release and the list of charges that we're bringing against you."

Gene doesn't react.

"The plan is to take you out of here," Will tells him. "Offsite. The CIA has a spot where we'll hold you. Treason is a very serious charge. It carries the death penalty. Maybe you'll get lucky and just get life in prison. I wonder what prison they'll send you to. I don't think there's any in the Hamptons."

Gene sits quietly.

"Suit yourself," Will says, and exits the room. He's clearly enjoying himself.

89

East Hampton, New York

Grace calls Gene's phone. There's no answer. She calls Peter.

"What the hell is going on Peter? Is this true? Eugene is being held captive by the president?"

"Yes, Grace. That's my understanding," Peter answers. "We're working on things."

"What do you mean you're 'working on things'? That doesn't tell me anything. What can we do against the president?"

"Calm down, please," Peter responds. "I'm working on things so please trust me and I'll get back to you as soon as I have some information."

"Fucking useless," Grace complains so that Peter can hear her and she hangs up.

She calls JR and again it goes directly to voicemail.

#

Jack races upstairs as fast as he can.

Teresa was sitting on the front porch with the family. Jack's pace surprises her and she follows him to their bedroom. He's putting computer equipment in two backpacks.

"What's going on?" she asks.

"My dad's been taken into custody by the president. He's being held at the White House. All this shit is coming to a head now. I gotta do something. I gotta help him."

"What? What are you talking about? What could you do?" Teresa asks. "The family needs to stay together whenever there's trouble. You can't leave."

Jack's focused on a plan. He picks up the two bags and looks at Teresa. "Trust me."

"Jack, stop, you can't leave me now," she cries out.

"I'll be back as soon as I can," he says, and dashes downstairs and out the back door.

#

Jack and Cheese get into one of the family cars and leave. Jack tells him the news.

"That's messed up," Cheese says. "But what are we going to do about it?"

"We're going to get him out of there."

"Ah," Cheese answers. "Nice, but where are we going and how are we going to do that?"

"I know we're good at keeping our location secret while we're online," Jack explains, "but I need to be extra careful. If we give up our location, then I don't want to do it from home. We'd put family in jeopardy. Hell, some of the president's men might be coming here right now."

"Ok, but what do you suggest out here?" Cheese asks.

Jack has driven a short distance. He pulls into a driveway and up to a security gate. The logo of a whale hangs on the gate in front of them. He tells the guard his name and he's allowed in.

"The golf club?" Cheese asks.

"Think about it," Jack explains. "It's got high speed internet, private rooms to work in, and its members include senators, judges, and a bunch of very rich people. No one is going to come barging in here."

"Makes sense I guess," Cheese answers. He follows that with, "Jesus, will you look at this fucking place?" Now on the other side of the security gate and fence, Cheese sees the beautiful clubhouse and perfectly manicured grounds.

Jack finds the general manager and requests a private room. A few minutes later, the two are unloading their bags and getting online.

90

Washington, D.C.

Bobby Ferguson visits Gene in Situation Room A. Gene is sitting in the same spot and in the same position as when Will Duffy left.

"Are you comfortable?" Bobby asks. "Is there anything I can get you?"

"No," Gene answers.

"Look, I'm really sorry that it had to come to this," Bobby begins. "But you really gave us no other option. I mean, what did you think was going to happen?"

Gene sits quietly with his legs crossed, hands in his lap.

"Have you thought about making this whole thing go away?" Bobby asks. "I mean you're in some serious shit here. That press release is ready to go out. We're going to drag your name through the mud. The public will hate you. You may or may not go to prison, but your name is going to be shit for the rest of your life. For a guy that hates any press, you're about to get a lot of it."

Gene sits quietly, stoically.

"Ok," Bobby says. "Look, the president is in the middle of an important meeting. We'll hold you here until he's finished. That means you have a little more time to change your mind. Then he'll come here. That's your deadline. After that, we move you out of here and issue the press release. It could get messy holding you here so we need to move you. You should reconsider before this thing gets out of hand."

"You don't think it's not out of hand already?" Gene asks. "I've got a wedding to go to."

"We know all about your wedding," Bobby answers. "Hell, we know everything when it comes to you and your family. I don't think you fully grasp what's happening here. The president and the attorney general have deemed you a national security threat. What else could they do? They needed to defend our country." Bobby has a big smile on his face. "You know how this goes. I'm the guy that makes up the news. I create stories and feed them to the press. They'll publish anything I feed them. This one is easy to follow; a good guy, the president, versus the rich, law-breaking, greedy banker. The president saved the day. We'll get a bump in his favourability ratings."

Gene says nothing.

"The president will visit you. He'll need an answer. After that, everything gets put in motion. We'll get a picture of you in handcuffs surrounded by uniformed marines. That will go out to every newspaper in the country. Or you change your mind and go to your son's wedding. It's your choice."

91

East Hampton, New York

"So, what's the plan?" Cheese asks.

"We're going to put pressure on the president in order to get my dad released. I have access to the Federal Reserve's computers. My dad made sure I had the password so we don't even need to break in," Jack explains.

"What do you want me to do?" Cheese asks.

"While I'm working," Jack replies, "I need you to break into the White House's security system. Find my father. Secretary Martin told my mother he was being held in the basement."

"Jack, slow down and think," Cheese replies. "I don't know if we can break in, and even if we can, it's going to take some time. It could take a long time. They must have a strong security system. I'm sorry to point that out."

"I forgot to tell you," Jack explains. "I've got access to MIT's supercomputer. It's a long story, but that's how we're going to speed things up. I can log you in."

Cheese looks up and with excitement asks, "Really? The supercomputer? This could be fun."

"Remember, we need to keep you invisible," Jack instructs. "I'll go rogue, create enough traffic for a disturbance. I'll look like the real threat and draw their attention and resources. You find an exposed channel. Find my dad. Make sense?"

The two begin typing away on their keyboards.

92

East Hampton, New York

Grace goes upstairs to the master bedroom to be alone. The house is in panic mode. Teresa is upset and has told the others.

Grace calls Peter again. Her southern charm and slowness of speech have vanished. As soon as Peter picks up the phone, she begins. "Peter, what do you have for me?"

"Grace, hello," Peter responds. "I don't have any news. I've passed word along and—" Peter is unable to complete his sentence.

"What do you mean?" Grace interrupts him. "What's your CEO doing? Get him on the phone with the president," Grace instructs.

"Well, it's not that easy," Peter explains.

"What the fuck is going on, Peter?"

"The president has been speaking with David," Peter explains. "You have to understand that David is in a very difficult position."

"Transfer me to David now," Grace instructs.

"I'd be glad to transfer you, but I don't think he'll take your call. I'm working on this from a different angle if you'll let me explain."

"Transfer me now and tell him to take this call," Grace commands.

#

Peter transfers the call. A woman answers, “Hello, Mrs. O’Neil. Mr. Sandler is in a meeting right now. Can I take a message?”

“Get him out of his fucking meeting and on the phone right now,” Grace instructs.

“Yes, ma’am,” the woman responds. “I understand, but Mr. Sandler cannot be interrupted. I will pass along your message as soon as I’m able.”

“Don’t you know who I am?” Grace asks.

“Yes, Mrs. O’Neil, I understand who you are.”

“Don’t you understand that my husband has devoted his life to that bank? He’s made David and a bunch of other assholes very rich.”

“Yes, Mrs. O’Neil. I understand. I’ll get the message to Mr. Sandler as soon as I’m able.” The woman is only going to repeat what she’s been told to say.

“And tell him he’s a fucking coward for not taking my call.”

Grace hangs up the phone. She walks to the window and stares out at the ocean. She doesn’t know where to turn next.

Grace is standing on Gene’s side of their bed. His book with Emerson’s essays is sitting on the bedside table. Grace sees Lynn’s business card sticking out. The press? She considers calling the *New York Times,* but if the CEO at Morgan Sachs is under the president’s influence, then others are also likely compromised. Lynn’s cell phone number is written on the back of her business card. Grace calls Lynn.

Lynn answers and is shocked to hear the words, “Lynn, this is Grace O’Neil.” The two haven’t spoken since breakfast with Madeline Rothschild.

“Grace, yes, hi, it’s nice to hear your voice,” Lynn says.

“I have a story for you, dear,” Grace explains. “I imagine you’re eager for stories. I’m giving this to you exclusively but I have one condition in return.”

“Yes,” Lynn answers.

“You must broadcast this story loudly and quickly. I mean as far and wide as you possibly can,” Grace instructs. She then tells Lynn that the president is holding Eugene at the White House. She tells Lynn that the disagreement between the men has to do with the president’s refusal to address the nation’s debt.

Every time Grace tells her something, Lynn repeats it slowly. Grace is frustrated. She’s anxious for the conversation to be done and the story to get out. Maybe this is protocol for news people—make sure they're hearing the story accurately. Then something occurs to her. "Lynn, where are you right now?"

Lynn pauses. "Ah."

"Put JR on the phone," Grace instructs.

Lynn was repeating things so JR could hear the news.

"Hi, Mom, what's going on?" JR asks.

"Where are you?" Grace asks.

"We're at the Yacht Club, on the boat," he answers. "What's going on? Dad's being held by the president?"

"Get your ass over here now," she instructs. "No. First, make sure Lynn gets this story out to everyone she can reach and then get your ass over here."

93

Washington, D.C.

The president is meeting with a group of people working on his presidential library. They're in the Roosevelt Room of the White House. Sitting on the conference table is a model of the proposed library. The group is going through the plans and various options. They compare the library to others of past presidents. They talk of how this will be better than all the others. It will be larger, more expensive, and include more technology and interactive exhibits. The goal is to make the president's time in office look as good as possible. The estimated cost is two billion dollars.

Bobby enters the room and walks up next to the president. "Mr. President, may I have a word with you?"

"Of course. Excuse us," the president instructs, and the group leaves the room. As soon as they're out of earshot, Bobby begins. "Mr. President, we've been listening to the O'Neils' phone calls. Grace O'Neil called a newsperson, Lynn LaRoyo. She's going to release the story that Gene has been taken prisoner at the White House and this is about your disagreement over the nation's debt. It seems we have two options. First, we could take Miss LaRoyo into custody. Stop her. I've got people in position for that. Second, we could release our story before she can. We just move our timetable up a little bit."

"That's ok. Let her run her story. We've got all the major news outlets on our side. They'll believe us over whoever she is."

"Yes sir, Mr. President. We're ready when you say so."

"I suppose we should get Gene transferred out of here before her story breaks. Has he changed his mind yet?"

"I don't know, Mr. President."

"Let's find out." The president and Bobby proceed downstairs to Situation Room A.

94

Washington, D.C.

The president and Bobby enter the room. Gene is sitting in the same place as when Bobby last saw him.

"Gene," the president says, "I hope you've been comfortable. This is terribly unfortunate."

Gene doesn't stand or move when the president enters.

The president sits down next to Gene and unbuttons his suit coat. "Have you reconsidered your situation? Do you think you'd be willing to help, um, work together? Can we hold off on things for a while?"

Gene doesn't move or say a word. Fifteen seconds of silence pass.

"I don't want to drag your name through the mud." The president appears sincere. "You've done a lot for me, for my career, and I appreciate it," the president shakes his head from side to side, "but this time you've forced my hand, left me with no other options. It appears your wife has called a reporter, Lynn something-or-other. She's going to broadcast a story that you're being held captive. Things are going to happen faster than we planned. We're going to move you now. In about thirty minutes the White House press secretary will begin a public relations campaign from which you'll never recover. It will be all over for you. I'm deeply sorry, but our time is up. What's it going to be?"

Gene remains silent.

There is a loud knock on the door. The president's executive assistant, Samantha, enters the room followed by the secretary of state. Samantha says, "Mr. President, I'm sorry to interrupt you."

"What is it?" the president asks.

"You have a call from the Chinese president," she answers. "He says it's urgent. He's waiting for you. He's on hold."

"President Zhi is on hold?" Bobby asks with surprise.

"Yes," Samantha confirms.

People like the Chinese president are never put on hold. Calls are prearranged so that neither president waits or holds for the other. The president is confused. "I'll take it next door," he instructs.

#

The president, secretary of state, Bobby, and Samantha walk across the hall to an identical room. Samantha is wearing a headset with a microphone. She instructs an operator to forward the call here.

The president answers the call on speakerphone so that all can hear and possibly assist. "Mr. President," he answers. "Good afternoon, or should I say good evening to you?"

"Good morning to you, Mr. President," Chinese president Zhi begins. "I understand you are holding someone against his will, holding a prisoner."

"A prisoner?" the American president answers, sounding surprised.

"Gene O'Neil. I understand that you're holding him against his will. Mr. O'Neil is a citizen of the People's Republic of China. He has full diplomatic immunity. I'm sure I don't need to remind you that holding him prisoner constitutes an act of war."

The American president is stunned. "Hold on, I'm sorry, what do you mean Mr. O'Neil is a citizen of the People's Republic of China?" The president presses the phone's mute button. He looks at Bobby, "What the fuck is he talking about?"

Bobby shrugs his shoulder to say, "I don't know." The anxiety level in the room immediately elevates to a fever pitch. Everyone understands that you can't touch anyone with diplomatic immunity.

President Zhi explains, "Don't you recall the banking regulations you signed? I'm sure you remember your speech where you took credit for the bill. It granted Gene O'Neil and others dual citizenship and diplomatic immunity with several countries for life. You cannot hold him. You cannot touch him."

The American president feels out manoeuvred. "Can you hold for another moment please, Mr. President?" he asks. He presses mute again.

"Is this right, Bobby? Was that part of the bill?"

"I don't know, Mr. President, maybe I can ask the treasury sec—" Bobby stops in mid-sentence.

President Zhi offers, "Mr. President, if you are having difficulty with Mr. O'Neil, then I will gladly welcome him to our country. I can arrange to have him transported immediately."

The secretary of state gets a look of panic. The mute button is still on. "You can't allow that under any circumstances," he says firmly. "The Chinese want to replace the United States dollar with the Chinese yuan as the world's reserve currency. That would be catastrophic for our country."

The American president doesn't say anything, but his expression shows that he doesn't understand.

The secretary of state is embarrassed for the president and that he has to explain. "It would make the Chinese the world's dominant superpower immediately. Our military and diplomatic strength are all based on our economic strength. You can't give that away under any circumstances. You cannot turn him over to the Chinese."

The American president unmutes the phone, "Mr. President, thank you for the call. I was not aware of any of this. Let me dig into the matter immediately and get back to you. Does that sound reasonable?"

"Yes, Mr. President," comes the response. "It is reasonable, but I'd like an answer shortly. I mean very shortly."

#

"Jesus," Bobby says when the call ends. "It's like Gene was planning this shit all along."

The president gives Bobby a look of disbelief. "Ya think?" he asks sarcastically.

The secretary of state then offers, "Mr. President, I don't know why you're holding this man, but we don't have any options here. We must release him immediately and communicate that to the Chinese president."

The president takes a deep breath and appears to be contemplating options. He's sitting with his right index finger tapping the table.

Bobby turns to the secretary of state, "Do you think you could buy us some time? Could you hold him off for a few days or a week maybe?"

The secretary is disturbed by the question. He answers emphatically, "Absolutely not."

Samantha has been standing beside the door. She's wearing the headset and says, "Mr. President, you have a call from Secretary Martin. He wants you to turn on the television to a business channel. He says to tell you it's important."

Bobby grabs the television remote control, turns it on and says, "What could he want?"

There is a view of Wall Street's trading floor. "All Trading Halted" in red letters is scrolling across the screen. People appear to be in a panic. The television changes to another scene. People lining up to automatic teller machines and fighting for position in line.

Samantha puts Doug's call on the speakerphone.

"What's going on, Doug?" the president asks.

"The banks have seized up, Mr. President. The check clearing system is frozen. No transactions are clearing, not even credit cards. ATMs are working and everyone is running to them to get all the cash they can."

"You're behind this," Bobby declares. "You've done something. You're responsible for this and you're going to pay for it."

"What, no," Doug denies the accusation. "I had nothing to do with this. I wouldn't even know how to do this. You have to understand this is a catastrophe. It's the biggest disaster I could even imagine. We could be on the verge of an economic collapse. We need to consider emergency measures to keep the peace."

"The Chinese," Bobby says. "This is a cyber-attack. We're at war. President Zhi has already acted. We need to call an emergency Cabinet Level Meeting and include the joint chiefs, immediately."

"I agree, sir," the secretary of state adds. "Our battle groups need to be put on alert, highest state of readiness with counterattacks ready to go on your order. We have protocols which must be followed. There's no time to waste."

Seconds pass as they look to the president for orders.

He stands, buttons his suit coat calmly, and walks across the hall.

95

Washington, D.C.

The president returns to Gene. The others follow.

Gene is still in the same position as when they left the room. The president sits down. He's moving slowly, deliberately. "A whole lotta shit going on now, Gene. I guess you heard Samantha say the Chinese president called. I suppose you knew that was coming. Now the financial markets have seized up because the banks won't clear any transactions. Did you leave some kind of doomsday device behind? A poison pill or computer virus in the event you were ever in danger?"

"No," Gene answers calmly. When news of the call from the Chinese president came, Gene knew Peter called Madeline and she called the Chinese. Adding diplomatic immunity to the banking regulations was her idea as an added safety measure for Gene's protection.

The president is curious. "How did you know people weren't going to pick up on your diplomatic immunity in the banking bill?"

Gene smiles. "Do you remember when the House Speaker said we have to pass a law to know what's in it? They don't read anything. They're all told how to vote."

The president nods his head. "We're going to a heightened state of readiness as possible war preparations. Someone is fucking with all commerce in the country and we can't let that happen." The president points to Bobby and his secretary of state. "They think it's the Chinese. We have a cyber-strategy we can implement immediately. It's short of launching a thousand missiles, but it's an aggressive counter measure to their attack on our banks. I've got—"

Another interruption, the president stops, the flat screen televisions come on. Jack's face is on all the screens. He's sitting in a conference room at the golf club in East Hampton.

"Hello," Jack says.

The president looks bewildered. He points to the screen and looks at others for an answer.

"Mr. President, I'm Jack O'Neil. I understand you've taken my father prisoner."

"Jesus," the president says.

"Mr. President," Jack continues, "the banking system is shut down. It will remain that way until my father is released and gets home safely."

There's no reaction from anyone in the room. It's not the Chinese. It's not an act of war. Gene's son is responsible for stopping every transaction in the country. He's also hacked into the White House's security system.

Everyone is dumbfounded. No one moves or responds.

"Mr. President did you hear me?" Jack asks.

The president looks at Gene and asks, "Is the Federal Reserve responsible for clearing transactions between banks?"

"Yes," Gene answers.

"You're really not going to like what I do next," Jack warns.

"Hold on, Jackson," Gene instructs. "I was just about to leave the White House. Isn't that right, Mr. President?"

The president sits quietly and weighs his options.

"Isn't that right, Mr. President?" Gene repeats.

"Yes, that's right," he answers.

"Don't do anything, Jack," Gene instructs. "Go back and undo whatever you've done. It's important not to inflict any further damage and get this fixed. I'll call you from my plane." Gene leaves the room.

The president remains seated. Bobby is standing by the president's side. He doesn't say a word.

Jack's unsure what to do or say next. He's surprised the conversation didn't last longer. "Ok," he says. He looks at Cheese.

Cheese turns Jack's laptop towards him so that his face is now projected on the television screens. "Hi, Mr. President," he says. "I voted for you. I mean, I would have voted for you if I voted." He cocks his head to the side and adds, "You or that other guy."

Jack disconnects the call.

96

East Hampton, New York

Jack wakes on Saturday morning to see Teresa sitting in a rocking chair. She's slowly rocking back and forth and looking out the window. It's a cloudy morning with a chance of rain in the forecast. The week feels like a blur.

"You okay?" he asks from bed.

Teresa nods yes. She's looking out over the backyard, which now includes an enormous tent. There are over two dozen people working on wedding preparations.

"So much for our small wedding," she says.

Jack gets out of bed and walks to the bathroom. "I'm sorry. I guess Mom got a little carried away. She means well."

"I know," Teresa answers. "She doesn't have a daughter. You're her baby. I may not have been her first choice to be Mrs. John James O'Neil but…" After a pause, she asks, "I've got the *New York Times* if you want to see the news."

"News about Dad?"

"No, well, maybe but there's an article about the wedding. It's got a picture of us and a list of some of the guests. The mayor is coming, a list of senators, and even the archbishop."

Jack isn't interested.

He walks to Teresa and kisses her. He looks into her eyes and says, "I'm sorry if the wedding got bigger than we wanted, but we're getting married. Our family is here. That's all the matters. It's going to be a great day. I love you." He gives her a big hug.

As he hugs her, he can now see out the window at what Teresa was watching. "Holy shit!" he says.

#

The wedding ceremony begins. Teresa is wearing a beautiful white dress.

Guests are seated. The band plays "Here Comes the Bride." Teresa's father escorts her down the aisle. Jack is standing on the right side of the altar waiting for her. He watches her approach with a large, loving smile.

Standing to Jack's left and steadied by his walker is the best man, Uncle Dave. Next to Dave are JR and Cheese.

#

While the Hamptons group is relatively small, the neighbours include titans from Wall Street and entertainment celebrities. They're a lot of fun to be around. Members of the board of the New York Metropolitan are present. So too are David Sandler, Peter Hollingsworth, Jarrett Washburn, Steve, Billy, and their wives and girlfriends. Molly McCann and friends from Watertown drove down for the event. Molly serves as the maid of honour. Everyone has a wonderful time.

#

Mary approaches her daughter during the reception. She's holding a card and looks confused. "What is this honey? We give you presents on your wedding day, not the other way around."

"What do you mean, Mom?"

"This," Mary answers, and holds out a card for Teresa to view.

She reads it. It explains that the Mary and Joe will be getting food deliveries. They can select their choices each week from a wide variety of healthy, all-natural foods. The cost has been taken care of. *Grace,* she thinks. This is her wedding present. Teresa couldn't have hoped for anything better.

"We're just glad to do it, Mom. I love you."

#

Gene is happy that Madeline Rothschild came for the ceremony. He approaches her during the reception, "Maddy, thank you very much for coming. It means a lot to me."

"Thank you for having me. This was quite a week."

"What did I tell you about Jack? I think he could serve the shareholders well for a long time."

"Perhaps," Maddy replies, "in time, but he's very young. While brilliant and decisive, he may be too impulsive. We have power, but he needs to understand restraint and using that power wisely. Perhaps a woman should be considered."

"You can blame me for what might be interpreted as impulsive. I told him that if a family member was ever in danger, act immediately and go right for the jugular."

"Do you like Teresa?" Maddy asks.

"I do, very much."

"We'll talk again soon," Maddy says. "Go enjoy your party."

97

East Hampton, New York

Sunday morning and the home is quiet. Many guests will have difficulty getting started as the reception ran well into the night.

A chef prepares omelettes on the porch. A large buffet is in place with everything you could ask for.

Guests are either dressed casually or wearing the same clothes as the day before. Molly and others are sleeping in chaise lounges around the pool.

Jack and Teresa are waiting for their omelettes when Gene appears. Jack asks his father if he has time to talk.

Gene smiles and answers, "Of course, and congratulations again Mr. and Mrs. O'Neil."

Gene fills a large cup of coffee and tells Grace. She chooses to join them. Thursday's events were unnerving and she prefers to remain close to him.

Grace, Gene, Teresa, and Jack walk across the front lawn towards the beach. After crossing the road, they sit down on the benches on top of the sea wall.

"Dad, I love you," Jack begins. "I want to thank you for everything. It feels like I've taken everything for granted my whole life. You've provided everything. School, money, apartment, job, wedding. Everything. I really want to thank you and Mom."

"No need to thank us," Gene replies. "That's what family's for. I should be thanking you for your actions the other day. You acted brilliantly and decisively. You can see why I want you to take my place."

Jack pauses before responding. "Yeah. I love you, and I appreciate everything, but I can't do that. I can't work at the bank. I'm sorry."

"Do you remember," Gene begins, "when I told you to keep an open mind? Take a vacation. Enjoy a honeymoon and the birth of your child. Take a month or two. You'll see things my way."

"I agree with you on a lot of things, but not everything," Jack states. "The ownership of the Federal Reserve Bank is wrong. It's the people's money."

"No, our government is broken," Gene explains. "There needs to be a control over our politicians and the people. The Federal Reserve is that control."

"Why do you think the Fed is the answer?" Jack asks.

"Money is always the answer. Money and wise men overseeing things," Gene answers confidently.

"Do you have a different thought?" Grace asks.

"The people, Mom. The American people. They're the answer. They're the control and it's their country after all. It's our destiny as Americans to govern ourselves."

"No, God no," Gene answers with a strong tone of disapproval. "There's an old saying in business that you'll never go broke underestimating the American people. Don't put your faith in the people."

There's a pause in the conversation.

#

Jack looks at his father. "I know what you have in mind. You're going to create a long and painful recession that will hurt all but the wealthiest Americans. We're talking about lost jobs, lost savings, a loss of self-worth. Something short of the Great Depression but lasting years and causing suffering. Isn't that right?"

"Not quite that devastating," Gene answers, "but yes. Unfortunately, it seems to be the only way for our politicians to get in line."

"Our best hope is the American people. Everyone knows that Washington is broken and corrupt even if they don't understand the details or just how bad it really is. We need to fix our problems by enlisting the help of the American people."

Gene replies, "It can't be done. Americans are lazy or just not interested. They're not involved and don't care to be. They want others to do everything for them."

"I suppose that's been true, but it can change. We can get them energized and involved. We can get them to want to take responsibility for governance."

Gene shakes his head. "And why do you think Americans are going to care enough to get involved now?"

"Two things," Jack begins. "First, we've got enormous challenges now. We've run up this massive debt and addressing it is going to cause pain for a lot of Americans. Our standard of living is going to decline. We'll have to live with less. Government workers counting on their pensions are going to find out they might get half of what they were expecting. Social Security will be cut along with Medicare, Medicaid, and food stamps. Military spending cuts, so loss of government jobs and lost jobs for suppliers and defence contractors. Many millions will be out of work. The stock market will drop and people's savings will be cut. All this pain is coming and the people will turn to the government for help. That's coming, right?"

"Yes. We've gotten used to this spending and it's going to stop. The government has made promises to people that it can't keep. There's no money for it."

Grace asks Jack, "What's the second reason that you think will get people involved?"

"People are going to find out that their leaders knew this was coming all along. The politicians promising free healthcare, pensions, jobs, and everything else created this mess. Those in office got rich and made promises they knew were lies. The anger that people are going to feel towards their politicians will motivate them to take control of the government and their own economic futures. They'll realize that counting on our politicians and our press to tell us the truth was a mistake. We need change. We need honesty and transparency."

#

Teresa interrupts them, “Wait a second. I know we’ve got challenges and I know our government is messed up but is it really that bad?”

Jack asks, “Dad, you probably know the numbers. What’s the real debt? Not the $24 trillion dollar number that politicians use, but the total debt. I mean the total dollar amount of promises our politicians have made as pensions, Social Security, entitlement programs, everything?”

“$320 trillion,” Gene answers. “And our politicians want even more to cover it up. It’s insanity.”

Jack shakes his head before answering Teresa, “Jesus. It’s worse than I thought. Our overspending has been colossal. We’ll need a correspondingly massive cut. People are going to get hurt. If the cuts aren’t done in an orderly and transparent way, then it’s going to tear away at what holds the country together.” Jack faces Teresa, “Think about it. Say your father loses his pension. First, he’s going to be pissed off, angry. He’ll become even more upset when he realizes the politicians who made those promises lied to him. They knew it all along. Next, he’ll look around to see if everyone else is making sacrifices. If the process of spending reductions isn’t fair, then we’ll have social unrest on a scale America has never seen. We need spending cuts and Americans can’t trust our current politicians to do that fairly.”

Teresa warns the group as she thinks she knows the average person better than they do. “If that’s true, then I don’t think you understand how ugly people can get. And our politicians are still talking about more spending? Pay off student debt, reparations, Medicare for all? What the fuck?”

“We need to leave the country,” Grace tells them. “I should have listened to you, Eugene. We should relocate and get away from this.”

The group sits quietly for several moments, each processing for themselves what’s been said.

#

Jack turns back towards Gene. “You told me to look for an opportunity in everything. “Do you remember that dinner?”

“I remember,” Gene replies. “Your thought is to use their anger as motivation to get them involved in their own self-governance?”

"Yes."

"Assume you're right for a moment," Gene considers. "How would you get millions of people to listen to you or help on such a scale?"

Jack answers, "Technology."

Gene's disappointed with the answer. "You can't fix everything with a computer, Jack, despite what you accomplished this week."

"Today's technology allows us to reach people directly, quickly, and more broadly than ever before. We'll start with a website and recruit millions of Americans. Get their input, best thoughts, and unleash their creativity. 'We the people' after all, remember those words? Our politicians have corrupted our institutions and betrayed our trust. Everyone will understand that we can't rely on them to lead us out of this problem. We need to do it ourselves."

"Are you talking about social media?" Grace asks.

"Some of those tools, yes, and I have some new thoughts," Jack answers. "I don't want to use them because they're only interested in making money on the data they collect from people. I'm thinking this is a not for profit kind of thing. No one can profit from what I'm envisioning."

"I think we should leave the country," Grace repeats.

"Politicians will be against you," Gene warns. "The bureaucracy too. These are powerful forces that will work against you and shouldn't be underestimated. You saw how far the president was willing to go."

Jack nods. "You know what President Kennedy said about this, he said; '*Those who make peaceful revolution impossible will make violent revolution inevitable.*' I know you're right. It will be those that are most corrupt that work hardest against us."

"You can't do this, Jack," Grace objects strenuously, "if we're talking about taking risks or your personal jeopardy."

"It's worth it, Mom. Our country needs this."

"I've never seen you so passionate about anything but school," Grace continues.

"I know, Mom, isn't it great?" he answers.

Gene is sceptical. "You think enough Americans will unite behind it and get involved?"

"I think one political party moved hard left and the other moved hard right. Neither party is interested in compromise or solutions. They want us divided. Along with the press they've worked hard to keep us divided. They don't solve issues; they keep issues alive that we're passionate about to keep us divided. That's our opportunity. Most Americans are reasonable, live in the center of the political spectrum, and want solutions. I didn't appreciate that until my time with Slugger. Most of our country's differences can be solved fairly easily. The opportunity could be for a third political party, one in the center of American politics and against the extremes from both existing parties. Maybe we force one party back to the center."

"A third party?" Teresa asks.

Jack continues, "We can represent the majority of Americans, solve problems, provide transparency, and get to compromises that people will support. You know, Dad, when you first talked about a clash coming, I thought you were referring to you against the president. Then I thought it might be liberals against conservatives or rich against poor. It's not any of those. The clash is about the people against our own government. We've got a ruling class in Washington and that has to change."

"We should relocate to another country at least for a little while," Grace suggests for a third time.

"I'm not going anywhere, Mom. This is my country. I'm an American and I'm going to do my part."

"But," Gene continues, "this is just a massive undertaking. I like the idea, but I'm not sure it can be done."

"Here's a comparison I like. It demonstrates the power of people working together. Years ago, the largest software company decided to put an encyclopaedia online. They employed a lot of smart people and invested tens of millions of dollars. At the same time, another site was created. No one was paid, it was volunteers only, a not for profit. People contributed their time and knowledge. A huge, well-capitalized company vs. an idea. The volunteers won and it wasn't even close. That's what I'm talking about. Tap into the power and imagination of concerned Americans. Pull Americans together and there's nothing they can't do. That's what I'm excited about."

"Are you going to need money for this?" Gene asks.

"No. The time and money need to come from the community that comes together to make this work. It's when people give of themselves that they become vested in its success."

"It's a website?" Gene asks, "That's the start?"

"Yeah," Jack answers. "A website to define the vision and build a community of concerned Americans. I can think of a lot of priorities, but the community will decide on where this goes. Start a new political party. Create an unbiased media outlet, maybe a thirty-minute news show online where we tell Americans the truth behind news stories and political votes. We could write the laws that Congress won't write. Address where the money comes and goes in Washington. We need accounting rules to force politicians to fund their promises or drop them. It starts as a website, but there's no end to where the community can take it."

"If bringing people together in this way works," Gene asks, "could it be used to bring people together from different countries?" He contemplates his dream of helping allocate resources more equitably without causing resentment from those giving. He dreams of trying to help the world's poorest.

"Yeah, Dad, of course."

#

The group sits quietly for several moments.

Teresa spots JR's car and says, "JR and Lynn are here. They must have spent the night on the boat."

"Is Lynn in any kind of trouble," Jack inquires, "for releasing that news story? I mean she ran it right after you called her, Mom. No one else did. People must question her reporting."

"Well," Grace answers with a smile. She puts her arms around Gene's neck. "Eugene took care of that. The bank's public relations department said it started as an online hoax by an unidentified party. It was leaked to Lynn as factual. And Eugene is going to be on Lynn's show. Isn't that right sweetheart?"

Gene is shaking his head, smiling. "Yup, that's right." He then turns back to Jack. "You promised me a year at the bank. That was our agreement. Maybe you'd feel differently if you waited until next spring."

Gene looks at Grace for support. She shakes her head slightly from side to side, no.

He asks Jack, "Is this going to be a full-time commitment for you?"

"No," Jack answers. "I'm going back to school. I'm going to teach part time over the internet and I'm going to start this part time. I'll get it started. Hopefully Americans embrace it. It's up to them where it goes. They need to get involved. They need to understand why the country is going to struggle, why their benefits are getting cut and where we go from here."

"If you start a new political party," Gene warns, "then the two parties will use everything they have to discredit you. They have a lot of power and money."

"Right," Jack nods. "It's weird that we only have two parties. It's a third party or we change the existing ones. You know other countries have three or four parties. The two parties haven't served us well. We need someone to speak for the majority of Americans. Here's an opportunity."

"You'll do it part time?" Grace asks.

"Yes. That's how it has to work. It's what our founding fathers envisioned, a government of the people. I can't ask others to donate their time if I'm not willing to do it. Everyone needs to give a little of their time or money. I'm not asking people to pick up a rifle and risk their lives. I'm encouraging them to get involved because it's in their own best interests. It's too important to leave it to others. That didn't work."

#

There's another pause before Teresa shares her thoughts. "I get that we'll make big spending cuts and I know they're needed. People will be pissed off at what it means to them personally and they'll turn on their politicians. I agree. Everyone will need to get involved because it's going to touch everyone. If we leave cost cutting to our politicians or today's government then the corruption would continue—they'd make cuts to everyone but themselves. You're missing the best reason why people will get involved."

Jack's head recoils slightly and faces her with an inquisitive look.

"People want meaning in their lives. They get it from God, family, their work, whatever. Americans love their country and can get meaning or purpose here. We don't care about rich or poor, black or white, gay or straight, or any other differences. We want our country to be great and stand for something. Being an American is more important than being a liberal or conservative. We need to rise above our politicians and work together. Americans will get involved because they're patriots; they love their country, they want to fix this, and they're the only ones that can."

Gene looks out over the ocean. “Is your mind made up? Is there any talking you out of this?”

“Probably not. I’m sorry if you’re disappointed in me.”

“Disappointed?” Gene says, raising his eyebrows. He looks at Jack and shakes his head, “No, that’s not the word I’d use. So, you’re gonna change the world, huh?” Gene asks.

“Something like that, Dad. Yes. I hope so.”

Gene nods acceptance. “Well, you best get on with it.”

THE END

About the Author

The author is an American who's concerned about his country.

He has spent the majority of his career working in business and in the area of mergers and acquisitions. In that role, he has travelled extensively throughout the United States.

He has lived in the North and South, in a "blue" state and a "red" state.

He is a father and a grandfather.

CPSIA information can be obtained
at www.ICGtesting.com
Printed in the USA
LVHW081330011119
636075LV00026B/264/P

9 781950 339341